Tyler Anne Snell genuinely loves all genres of the written word. However, she's realised that she loves books filled with sexual tension and mysteries a little more than the rest. Her stories have a good dose of both. Tyler lives in Alabama with her same-named husband and their mini 'lions.' When she isn't reading or writing, she's playing video games and working on her blog, *Almost There*. To follow her shenanigans, visit tylerannesnell.com

Regan Black, a *USA TODAY* bestselling author, writes award-winning action-packed novels featuring kick-butt heroines and the sexy heroes who fall in love with them. Raised in the Midwest and California, she and her family, along with their adopted greyhound, two arrogant cats and a quirky finch, reside in the South Carolina Lowcountry, where the rich blend of legend, romance and history fuels her imagination.

LAST STAND SHERIFF

TYLER ANNE SNELL

COLTON 911: DETECTIVE ON CALL

REGAN BLACK

MILLS & BOON

First Published in Great Britain 2020
by Mills & Boon, an imprint of HarperCollins*Publishers*
1 London Bridge Street, London, SE1 9GF

Last Stand Sheriff © 2020 Tyler Anne Snell
Colton 911: Detective on Call © 2020 Harlequin Books S.A.

Special thanks and acknowledgement are given to Regan Black for her contribution to the Colton 911: Grand Rapids series.

ISBN: 978-0-263-28047-0

0920

MIX
Paper from
responsible sources
FSC™ C007454

This book is produced from independently certified FSC™ paper to ensure responsible forest management.

For more information visit: www.harpercollins.co.uk/green

Printed and bound in Spain
by CPI, Barcelona

LAST STAND SHERIFF

TYLER ANNE SNELL

This book is for Tyler, my husband.
Thank you for always being my smart, hilarious
and cat-loving rock. If you're reading this,
then let's go make some brownies.

Chapter One

Declan Nash wasn't having the greatest of days.

Not only was it raining cats and dogs and elephants, his trusty old pickup had decided not to be so trusty.

"Come on, Fiona." He rubbed the dash trying to coo the truck into stopping her lurching and ominous rattling sound. Fiona the Ford wasn't impressed. Declan admitted defeat by taking the upcoming exit. There was a gas station at the corner of the short road. He pulled in, sighing. "After everything we've been through, you decide to pitch a fit now and here of all places?"

The city of Kilwin, Tennessee, was an hour out from where he had been on the highway. Which meant his hometown of Overlook was an hour and twenty minutes out of reach.

Not that he was reaching for it.

He might have been the sheriff of Wildman County but, as of that morning, he was just a man on vacation.

Or, at least, he was trying to be.

Declan sighed into the empty cab again. His dark blue Stetson, one he only wore on his off days—which meant he hardly ever wore it—sat on the passenger seat mocking him.

"You're about to become an umbrella," he told it.

The rain was having a great old time drenching Declan to the bone after he got out and propped up his hood. He hadn't parked under the gas station awning, worried about his truck catching fire and making a bad situation way worse. That decision got him wet but was reassuring as steam billowed up, angry, at him from next to the engine. There was also an overpowering oil smell.

Declan jogged back to the cab and grabbed his phone.

Just in time for the interior lights to blink out.

His battery had died.

So, Fiona was finally going to pitch a fit. After fifteen years of not making a peep, she was doing it during the first vacation he'd taken in at least five.

Declan hung his head and swore. The motion dumped water from his hat into his seat.

Declan swore some more, spied the diner next to the gas station and decided that he was at least going to get some coffee out of all of this. He could deal with the truck once the rain let up.

Still, he grabbed his duffel bag knowing there wasn't an inch in this world to give when it came to the accordion file he had tucked in with his boxers and toothbrush.

"We'll get you figured out, Fiona," he told his truck with a pat after locking her up. He dashed across the gas station parking lot and right into the diner. When he pushed through the front door, heralded in by a chime, an older woman with a nice smile met him.

"When it rains it pours, huh?" she greeted, motioning to one of the large-pane windows that ran along the front of the building. He could see his truck through the one next to the last booth. "We have some fresh hand towels in the kitchen. I can get you some to dry off a little if you'd like."

Declan took his hat off and pressed it against his chest. He gave the woman—Agnes, according to her name tag—a smile that he meant.

"That would be much appreciated, thank you."

Agnes went off to the kitchen while Declan took the booth in the corner so he could keep an eye on his truck. He set his duffel on the floor next to the seat.

Then he had a moment of internal crisis.

His hands itched to open his bag and pull the folder out, to riffle through the pages he'd already read and reread countless times. To look at every piece of evidence that had been collected for over twenty-five years. To see his own notes and compare them to the ones his father had made when he had been a detective.

Then Declan heard an inner voice warning of doing just that.

It wasn't his conscience; it was a collective featuring Madi, Caleb and Desmond. They'd all made it clear that they were concerned Declan was blurring the line between dedication and obsession. That finding justice, finding the truth, wasn't worth the toll of the quality of his life.

Not after the same obsession had taken their father's life.

Since Declan was their big brother, a part of him prickled at being directed at what to do or, more aptly, what not to do. Just as quickly, though, as his gruffness reared its head, he'd remind himself that in the small town of Overlook, they weren't just bystanders.

Madi, Caleb and Desmond had told him that from experience they knew what it was like to be slowly consumed by a mystery. He had to learn to let go and live a little.

Considering the case was about their abduction, Declan figured they might have a point.

Now, though, with his truck broken down and the rain trapping him inside a diner that had only two other patrons, Declan couldn't help deciding his vacation hadn't *re-*

ally started yet. This was more of a pit stop. Which meant if he looked at the files now, it didn't count against him.

Agnes returned with a few hand towels, cutting off the physical action of taking the folder out. He ordered a coffee and some bacon and eggs and returned the towels. Then he retrieved the folder and put it down on the table-top with minimal guilt and maximum focus.

He hadn't been there at the park that day.

He hadn't been attacked and taken and held in a basement.

He hadn't had to trick a man and fight to get out as the three scared and hurt eight-year-olds had done.

He hadn't had to make the terrifying trek through the woods to find help.

No, Declan hadn't been there at all.

He'd been too consumed with his own little world to notice the triplets had disappeared until an hour after the fact.

And then he'd had to wait with the rest of Overlook for three days, hoping and praying they would find nothing but good news.

Declan could still feel the helplessness that had nearly crushed him during the wait.

And now?

Now Declan was older, smarter.

Now Declan had focus and patience and a lot more experience.

Now Declan was the sheriff.

He couldn't save the triplets from what had happened, but he could damn sure finally give them the peace they deserved.

The rain continued to fall. Music from the kitchen floated to the front. Declan didn't wrestle with his choice anymore. The diner would actually be the perfect place to look over the newer evidence. No one from his family at his shoulder. No one from the sheriff's department by his side.

He opened the folder.

No one was going to distract him here.

The time for questions was over. Now it was time for answers.

REMI WAS, AS her cousin Claudette said, a "Hot Mess Susan."

Not the worst thing she'd been called in her thirty-three years of life but definitely not the most flattering, either.

What was worse than being called a Hot Mess Susan?

When the nickname actually applied to her.

And now, pulling into the diner off Exit 41B, it definitely applied.

Remi cut the engine in a parking spot and let out a sigh that had apparently been trapped in her chest for the last hundred miles. It dragged down her shoulders, slouched her back and put pressure on the stress headache that had been brewing all morning.

"'Go see your father,'" she muttered to no one, adopting her mother's pushy voice. "'It'll be fun. Stop stalling, Remi. It'll be *fine*.'"

Her mother wasn't right about much...and she was wrong about that, too. It hadn't been fine. In fact, it had been awful and exactly what she had expected.

Josh and Jonah had met her with hugs and sibling love, and then all of that mush had soured when their father had sat them down at the dinner table. The questions had started and they'd all daggered her. Remi had felt like she was interviewing for her job at Towne & Associates all over again. However, instead of sitting across from a group of public accountants she was looking at three cowboys who didn't understand a lick of why she'd left the ranch all those years ago in the first place.

Which was why she hadn't told them of her current problem. One that she'd been wrestling with before she ever decided to heed her mother's advice and go see the Hudson men in Overlook.

How she ever thought they'd take a second to think outside of the ranch and help her, she didn't know.

But now with the rain hitting the roof of her car, reminding her that she didn't have a rain jacket or an umbrella, Remi felt her troubles being pulled back to her. That, and the weather, had been one of the reasons she'd taken the exit and parked herself outside of a diner. It's neon open sign was a distraction she was ready to fully embrace.

She grabbed her purse, tucked her phone in the waist of her exercise leggings and tried to think about how see-through her shirt was going to become just from her short jaunt between the car and the front doors.

Then she ran.

And immediately became drenched.

A chime sounded over the door as Remi danced inside. She was met with cool air that made her now-wet clothes cold. A song was playing somewhere in the small space, and through the cook's window behind the counter a man gave her a look. An older woman in uniform also looked through the window and called out.

"Be with you in a sec, hon!"

Remi gave a polite smile and decided not to check her shirt to see if her bra was showing through the beige. Instead, she ran a hand through her dirty-blond hair that was probably dark now and took a quick look at the few patrons already seated.

To her right was a couple immersed in their own conversation, and a gray-haired man in a booth two down from her spot in the middle of the space. Straight ahead was a woman and her small son at the counter, making quick work of what looked like apple pie. To her left sat one man in the last booth.

He was facing her but looking down at the table. Remi noted first that he had wide, muscled shoulders; second, that he had dark brown hair as messy as hers must be; and, third, that he was, even with his face angled down, attractive. Then, with a little start, Remi realized the fourth and most intriguing detail.

She dripped water across the linoleum and walked right up to a face she hadn't seen in ages.

"Declan Nash?"

The cowboy hat resting on the table was all the confirmation she needed, but the man still raised his eyes to hers and nodded. Remi couldn't help feeling a bit of heat as he looked at her directly.

She saw both the boy her father had warned her about when they were kids and the man who had grown up quite nicely.

When he cut a grin and recognition flared behind his green eyes, Remi felt more heat rising in her.

"Well, if it isn't Remi Hudson."

Declan surprised her by standing and extending his hand. She felt her eyebrow quirk up as she shook his hand.

The young Declan hadn't been so formal, especially when it came to her. Why shake the hand of the person you're competing with or fighting against?

He didn't make a thing about her questioning look as he motioned to the seat opposite him. Before he officially asked her to sit, he looked behind her.

"Are you here alone?"

She didn't miss his glance down at her left hand.

So she held that hand up and thumped her ring finger.

"Alone in the diner and single outside of it."

Declan chuckled as Remi slid across the plastic seat. Her wet leggings made it squeak.

"I don't think I've seen you this close to Overlook since we were, what, nineteen?" He closed the folder on the tabletop and leaned back against his seat. The new position highlighted how the years had been more than kind to the man. His face was all angles and strong. The bump in his nose from the time he broke it after getting into a fight with Cody Callers at a house party when they were sixteen was still visible but, instead of looking awkward as it had then, now it added to the intrigue that was him.

Because, while Remi had known the wild child that was Declan Nash, she hadn't seen him since graduation day.

"I haven't seen *you* since I was eighteen, but I've been home quite a few times between then and now. I'm a bit hurt you haven't noticed. It's not like Hudson Heartland isn't the Nash Family Ranch's next-door neighbor or anything."

"There's a good hundred acres or so between the ranches, so forgive me for not having superhero-grade vision," he teased.

"You're forgiven, I suppose. Besides, I hear you've been busy since you became *the sheriff*."

Saying it out loud created the same shock she'd felt the first time her father had told her about the eldest Nash sibling running for sheriff. When he'd won, well, that had been a much stronger shock.

The boy wilder than the horses her father used to tame had become the man put in charge of policing the entire county.

"Don't worry, you're not the only one surprised by the news," he said. "Though I am impressed at your reaction. Last time we saw each other you were more on the reserved side."

Remi couldn't help but laugh at that.

"I was a mouse," she exclaimed. "It took college for me to open up and see the virtue of speaking my mind. Something I assume you can relate to."

It was Declan's turn to laugh.

"Being the sheriff has shown me the value of holding your cards close to your chest."

Remi leaned back to mirror his stance.

"Well, it looks like we might have switched personalities since we last saw each other."

Even though she said it, Remi didn't believe it. People couldn't change their stripes. Not when it came to someone as wild and bold as Declan.

The waitress appeared at their table, took Remi's order and was kind enough to give her a hand towel to dab off the excess water. Declan was polite enough to keep his eyes north of her potentially see-through shirt. Sure, he'd been wild when they were younger, but his mama had still raised him right when it came to respecting women.

"So what brings you to this diner?" Remi got around to asking. She looked at the folder beneath his hand. "Is it work related?"

Declan took the folder and slid it beneath his cowboy hat.

"I was actually on my way to one of my deputy's rental cabins for a long weekend." He pointed out the window. The rain had, of course, lessened a minute or two after she'd entered the diner. "You see that—"

"You mean Fiona?" she finished. Like the cowboy hat, Declan had had that truck for years and years. She'd recognize it anywhere and probably would have earlier had it not been raining so hard when she'd pulled up.

Declan smirked.

"Yeah. Fiona." He sighed. "She finally decided to have a fit. I was going to call my roadside assistance when the rain died down since, well, I don't know much about cars."

"Except stealing them from Rodney Becker's garage to prove you were smarter than him," she added.

Declan lowered his voice but there was humor in it.

"Listen here, Huds, you promised you'd take that one to the grave."

The way Declan said the nickname he'd used for her when they were in high school, all rumbling baritone, made some of the heat at seeing him swirl around again. She held up her hands in surrender.

"I keep my promises. But, may I point out, you're not in Overlook right now. In fact, you're not even in Wildman County."

He shrugged.

"You can't be too careful about these things. You know how powerful talk in town can be. One slipup and that's all we'll hear about for years."

He said it in a joking way, but she heard the resentment deep in his words.

Remi was an Overlook native. Her parents had been born and raised in town, and she and her brothers had been born and raised there, too. It was impossible to keep people from talking in a small town, but when it came to the Nashes it was an entirely different ball game.

After what had happened to the triplets, the family had been become famous. A horrible fame that, as far as she knew, hadn't gone away despite the years that had passed.

Remi's coffee showed up at just the right time, and the two of them spent the next half hour talking about the people they'd gone to school with, old friends and annoyances, and what had been going on with their respective families. They hit all the social cues that were expected of a conversation between old acquaintances.

He was sorry to hear about her parents' divorce, and she was happy to hear about his siblings' marriages and kids.

He could barely talk around his laughter about Clay Reynolds being arrested for public intoxication after his girlfriend bought him a fake lottery ticket, and she admitted, with much shame, that she'd dated Matthew Shaker for a year after running into him on campus.

He seemed interested in what her stepfather, Dave, did for a living, and she genuinely was excited that Claire's Café was expanding into the shop next door due to its popularity.

It wasn't until he excused himself to call about Fiona that Remi realized she didn't want the conversation to end just yet.

So when he said that a local mechanic couldn't look at his truck for a few days and would tow it back to Overlook instead, she decided she could take an hour detour back to town.

As long as he'd be with her.

"I don't want to inconvenience you," he said at her offer of driving him back. She waved off his concern.

"You're the one who's going to listen to me talk about my work dilemma all the way there," she said. "May I remind you that I'm an accountant so, honestly, you might just want to ride with the tow truck driver."

Declan smirked.

Hot dog, what a sight.

"I'm always being asked about my job, I'd love to listen to someone else's for a change."

They paid their bill, made arrangements for the tow truck and then headed back to the town they'd both had a mind to leave that morning.

Then the rain went from crummy to bad to worse. It was only when they were between Kilwin and Overlook that they admitted defeat and pulled into another parking lot.

This time it was for a surprisingly nice motel.

"Fun fact," Declan said, pointing in the direction of the vacancy sign. "My sister-in-law is good friends with the woman who owns this place."

"Then I bet you could get us a good deal on a room, huh?"

Remi had meant it as a joke.

Yet, when she looked at Declan, his cowboy hat on his head and a smirk on his lips, she wasn't quite sure of her own intentions.

She'd always wondered how a kiss between them would feel.

When Declan's eyes moved down to her lips, she had a suspicion he was just as curious.

Chapter Two

A month later and Declan's patience was spread so thin it was damn near transparent.

"Cooper, you called *me* out here, not the other way around," he reminded the always-a-little-left-of-the-law young man. "I have a press conference in a few hours that I need to prep for. I don't have time to just be shooting the breeze."

They were outside the local hardware store, standing in the parking lot between Declan's truck and Cooper's little sports car. Declan was wearing his uniform and had his sheriff's badge hanging on his belt. The black Stetson on his head had just been cleaned. Cooper had on a well-worn Nirvana graphic tee, hole-ridden jeans and an expression that said he needed some prodding to get to talking.

"Come on, Coop," he added. "I'm not a mind reader over here."

The man, twenty-two, cut his eyes to the lot around them and sucked on his teeth a second. Then he got to the point.

"Okay, well, don't get your panties all in a twist, but I've heard a rumor that I don't think you've heard yet." He shrugged. "Since you helped me out of that dumb warrant last year I figured telling you about it would be a good way to say we're even."

Declan cocked his head to the side, instantly curious. There weren't many rumors that didn't make it to every pair of ears in Overlook. Considering Cooper lived in town, Declan couldn't imagine he hadn't already heard it, too.

A day without talk about the Nash family, especially over everything that had happened in the last few years, was rare.

"I'm listening."

Cooper stood up straight, no longer leaning against his car, and dropped his voice a little. Declan couldn't help but angle forward.

"You know the Waypoint, right?"

Declan nodded. It was a bar in the city of Kilwin, twenty minutes from Overlook. The clientele had been mostly law enforcement back in the day. Now it catered to the crowd in the newly erected business plaza across the block from it. A family friend who was a detective with the Kilwin Police Department had said the new vibe was too modern and trendy for him. Declan hadn't been there in months.

"Well, for the last month or so there's been a lot of talk about what happened to your family. You know, with the, well you know." Declan nodded again. There was always some kind of talk, even in Kilwin, about the triplets' abduction, despite it having taken place decades ago. That wasn't anything new.

What Cooper said next was.

"Some guy keeps talking about a note in the wall at the cabin and everyone who knows the story keeps telling him he doesn't know what he's talking about. But he just keeps talking about that darn note in the wall, preaching it like it's gospel. It's probably nothing but I thought I'd let you know."

"A note in the wall," Declan repeated, still not sold.

Cooper shrugged.

"He said it's in the hallway and hidden real good. Said it took the law a while to find it, but I didn't remember hearing that."

There had never been a note found in a wall or otherwise at the cabin where the triplets had been held in the basement apartment. Considering it had been swarmed with law enforcement for months, and revisited by his father for years, Declan was sure he would have known about any note that had been found.

"It sounds like you were listening to a drunk guy wanting attention," Declan said.

Cooper shrugged again.

"Listen, if it had been Piper or that Grant guy who are always trying to rope you into their pyramid schemes, I wouldn't have said anything," he said in defense. "But this guy only ever had one beer in front of him, and it was mostly full. And his suit was so high-end he just kind of seemed to have his crap more together, you know?"

Declan had spent his career in law enforcement learning how to perfect his facial expressions and body language. How to control it so it didn't betray how he was really feeling. In that moment it took all his training to keep his face impassive and his body from visibly tensing.

"That bar has a lot of men in suits, though," Declan said, playing the devil's advocate, careful not to get ahead of himself. "I'm sure more than one of them has their crap together."

"Not like this guy. This dude looked like he belonged on a magazine cover. He looked way out of place there."

Declan's phone started to vibrate. He pulled it out to see a text from his chief deputy, Mayne Cussler. They needed to prep for the press conference.

He sighed.

"I have to get going," he said. Then, with a little more politeness he addressed the young man directly. "Thanks for the info. I do appreciate the effort."

Cooper nodded with a smile.

"Just trying to stay in the sheriff's good graces!"

"I thought you were trying to repay a debt?"

"Can't I do both?"

He laughed and got into his car. Declan, despite the text, hung back as Cooper disappeared down the road.

A note in the wall.

A man in a bar.

A man in a fancy suit.

The last two Declan had run into over the past few years. In fact, a man in a bar had been a detail in the chaos that all three of his siblings had gone through in their personal lives recently.

There had always been a man in a bar who had given bad ideas to bad people.

A man in a fancy suit? They'd run into a few of them, too. Most recently, a man in a high-end suit had gotten tangled up in a dangerous situation with Desmond and his then girlfriend, now wife, Riley. One who actually bore the same scar that the triplets' abductor had had. Though he wasn't the man who had done it, that had been the last new lead they'd had in years.

But a note in the wall of the cabin where they were held?

That was a new one.

And coupled with a man in a suit at a bar?

That was too enticing not to investigate.

Declan put his truck into Drive and moved out onto the road, pointing in the direction that would lead him to that cabin. His phone started to vibrate and he was ready to stall, when he saw the caller ID wasn't one he recognized.

"Nash, here," he answered.

"Hey, Declan, it's me."

That voice gave him a split reaction.

Confusion and primal excitement.

Remi Hudson.

He hadn't seen her since she'd dropped him off at the ranch.

The day *after* they'd stopped at the motel.

"Well, hey there, Huds. How's it going?"

Hesitation, silent and as loud as could be, was his answer. Declan moved the phone away from his face to make sure the call hadn't dropped.

It hadn't.

Remi finally responded.

"I'm, uh, actually in town and was wondering if we could get together?"

She sounded different. Distracted.

It made his gut go on high alert.

"Yeah, sure. I have a press conference in two hours. Can it wait until after then?"

"Oh, yeah, that's fine. Can you just call me back when you're ready? I'll be at my dad's but would prefer to meet up somewhere else."

That didn't surprise Declan. During their last meeting he'd gotten the impression that she was having some issues with her father, Gale, and her brothers. He hadn't pried and he still wouldn't when they met up.

"How about I call you when I'm done and we can meet at my house?"

"Okay, great. Yeah, okay. Well, I guess I'll talk to you later."

Remi ended the call before Declan could say another word.

For the next few minutes he wondered why she sounded

so off, but when he turned onto *the* road that eventually led to *the* cabin, all thoughts flew back to the past.

Declan tightened his grip on the steering wheel.

Being haunted by the past was never a good feeling.

REMI FELT LIKE she was about to vibrate out of her skin with nerves. Which wasn't like her at all. Not anymore. Not since she'd grown up.

Yet, there she was, driving up Winding Road toward the Nash Family Ranch that sat at its end while the butterflies in her stomach hitched a ride for free.

It was only December 10, but it felt like a lifetime had passed since she'd last been here dropping Declan off at his house. She'd been lucky then to avoid his family all while she and the sheriff had been able to avoid talking about what they'd done, *several* times, at the motel. That had been fine by Remi.

She'd always wondered what it was like to kiss Declan outside of a teenage dare and she had found out. Along with a few other exciting things.

Declan hadn't seemed put out in the slightest at their time together, or that it had to end.

They had separate, nonintersecting lives. The only reason they'd run into each other in the first place at the diner had been a fluke. Nothing more, nothing less.

Sure, the entire ride back to her home in Nashville had been filled with thoughts of the man. She'd compared the quiet, reflective Declan to the wild child she'd grown up with. She had tried to recall every piece of gossip about his life since she'd moved away after graduation, and she'd kept thinking about the *move* that had made her see fireworks. Remi would also be lying if she didn't admit thinking about Declan had become a routine thing. Maybe not every second of every day, but occasionally she'd found that her mind had wandered right to a cowboy with a gruff exterior and the softest lips she ever did kiss.

Then *it* had happened.

The heat. And not the good kind of heat. The kind that made her feel sick and worried that she was somehow dying from some rare disease. One second she was *fine* with a capital *F*. The next she was opening her windows and sticking her head out into the cold night air.

When it happened two more times over a few days, Remi had done the only sensible thing.

She'd googled.

Her anxiety had gone through the roof as sicknesses she was *sure* she suffered from filled her computer screen. It just about soared when one answer in particular kept recurring.

That's when she became a mathematician. One who tore through the house looking for her phone and its calendar app. When the numbers didn't match up, she ran them again.

Then she'd given herself a pep talk about the stress of the huge life-changing decision she'd just made.

It was *stress*.

That was it.

That was all.

"Stress my butt," Remi told the inside of her car now as she passed under the ranch's entrance sign with a snort. Remi might have become a woman ready to say what was on her mind, but that didn't mean she was always eloquent about it.

The Nash Family Ranch had several things in common with the Hudson Heartland, and Remi never got tired of admiring both.

The Nashes owned several hundred acres of the most beautiful fields, stretches of forest, natural bodies of water, as well as picturesque farmhouses, barns and a stable. In the distance the rise and fall of mountains could be admired. From Hudson Heartland those mountains were closer. Remi and her brothers had spent many a hiking trip out on them.

The main difference between the ranches was the number of homes on the properties. On their property there were only two. The biggest, a four-thousand-square-foot house was where she'd grown up and where her father and brothers lived now. On the other side of the ranch stood the second home, which belonged to Jerri and Margot Heath. In a role reversal that had been quite the talk of Overlook when it had first happened, Margot was the stable master while her husband kept the main house clean and the useless-with-cooking Hudson brood fed. Their son, around Remi's age, hadn't felt comfortable with the arrangement as he'd gotten older. The moment he'd turned eighteen he'd moved out west.

Not that Remi could fault him for doing almost the same thing she had done.

The Nash family, on the other hand, had several homes across their acreage. According to Declan, not only did he have his own house on the property, but so did Caleb and his wife, Nina, Desmond and his wife, Riley, and his mother, Dorothy, who still lived in the main house. There was even a new set of structures she'd never seen. The Wild Iris Retreat was a nice walk from the stable and run by Dorothy, Nina and Molly, a family friend who also happened to be one of the only friends Remi had kept in touch with once she'd left Overlook.

Remi had been particularly curious about the retreat, considering Madi and her husband, Julian, ran a bed-and-breakfast on the other side of town but she hadn't pried too much for any more details. Being around Declan had been bad for her focus, especially after they'd done what they had.

It was like eating a slice of the best cake you'd ever tasted and then having to sit next to the rest of it and pretend your mouth wasn't still watering.

A different kind of heat engulfed Remi at the memory. Even hearing Declan's voice over the phone had had an effect on her. She wondered if the feeling was mutual. He'd seemed so surprised by her call that Remi couldn't help but feel a little sting.

As she pulled up to his house, Remi couldn't begin to guess how the news she was about to deliver to the cowboy would be received.

Not only had she taken his advice on her career troubles and decided to accept the job she'd been offered in Colorado, she'd found out two weeks later while packing up her house that she was pregnant.

With Declan's child.

Remi cut her engine in his driveway and jumped out into the cold air. The sound of tires against gravel forced her attention to the truck pulling up behind her from the main road.

Declan gave her a polite smile through the windshield as he parked.

Boy, was she about to blow his mind.

Chapter Three

"Do you mind if we ride out somewhere? I could really use a second set of eyes."

The moment Declan saw Remi outside of her car, he'd had the idea that she could be exactly what he needed. The cabin in the woods was empty, just as it had been for years and years. Declan had swept the hallway before looking through every other part of the space, trying to find a clue he'd somehow missed.

Then he'd left for the press conference.

But his mind was still in that cabin, suspicious of the man in the suit.

When he saw Remi, he realized what he needed was peace of mind. He needed a second pair of eyes, ones that weren't as close to the case as he was.

He needed her to confirm there was nothing there.

Then he could let it go.

For now.

Remi's eyebrow rose in question. She tilted her head to the side a fraction. Her hair shifted at the movement in a sheet across her shoulders. She'd cut it since he'd seen her last.

It looked good.

Then again, Remi always looked good.

"Do I need to wear my good dress?"

Declan didn't understand until she pointed to his suit blazer, pressed button-up, and slacks. He chuckled.

"No. I have to get spiffy for the press conferences," he said. "Something about jeans and flannel not being appropriate."

Remi looked him up and down openly. Declan tried not to do the same.

While he'd in no way expected to do what they had done the day *and night* his truck had broken down outside of town, the truth was they had. And they'd been good at it, too. Just as they'd both been clear about it being a one-time thing.

Two ships passing in the night.

Catching up, and dressing down, with a friend.

Remi had a promotion in wait, he had a county to protect.

She'd left town for one reason; he had stayed for many.

They'd been adults about parting ways. Coolheaded and relaxed.

That didn't mean Declan hadn't occasionally thought he smelled her perfume or snorted at a joke she'd told during their time together.

Remi had been fun to hang out with when they were kids, even when she was quiet. Adult Remi had been a change that he had still enjoyed, as the woman said exactly what was on her mind.

But now, standing opposite her, there was a hesitation that seemed to be moving across her expression. Declan realized he might have done it again. He'd focused on the case more than he had the present. Remi was in front of him, in Overlook, and there he was already trying to rope her into playing junior detective. Why was she here?

Still, it was hard to forget about the note in the wall. It clawed at his mind, despite the company.

"We don't have to go if this can't wait or can't ride along with us?" he ventured.

"Location won't change the conversation," she said with a shrug. "But I am worried you don't remember that I'm an accountant and *not* a detective."

"I need a second opinion, is all."

"And you picked me because you know I have a lot of those?"

She started to walk around him toward the truck. Declan opened the door for her before answering.

"I know you're about the details," he said. Then, moving to the driver's side and sliding in, he gave her an even look. "And I'd like a civilian and non-Nash to help look for those details."

Remi's eyebrow rose again. Declan noted the freckles he'd remembered from her teenage years were still peppered around her eyes and across her cheeks.

"Where exactly are we going?"

Declan put the truck in Reverse. He didn't answer until they were back on the main road that ran through the ranch, heading toward Winding Road.

"The Well Water Cabin."

He could detect her confusion without her voicing it right away. She shifted, her hair moving across the seat's fabric as she must have turned to look at him. He sighed and explained.

"I heard about a man in a bar who keeps talking about a note in the wall that law enforcement missed. Sounds like a weird riddle or bad nursery rhyme, I know, but I went there earlier and looked around anyways. Like I thought, it was empty. But there are so many coincidences that have popped up lately that I'm inclined to think it might be worth looking into." He gave her a quick look and half shrug. "I also know how close I am to this case and how many times I've been over every single detail. I could be missing something I haven't seen *because* I've seen it too much. You know?"

"Like having someone else proofread an email before you send it off because you've read it too many times already."

Declan snorted.

"Exactly. There could be nothing there and I just can't let go, which I know is a concern. Or, there could be something." He gave her a sidelong glance as they slowed going through the main gate. "I need another set of eyes to proofread."

Remi nodded and stared out the windshield. Her brows were knotted together in thought.

"And asking Caleb, the actual detective, would be worse than going by yourself," she surmised. "Not to mention, he probably doesn't want to go back there in the first place."

"None of them do. Ma won't even drive on the road that leads up to the place. Not that I blame any of them. They've had their fill for more than a lifetime."

Out of his periphery he saw Remi nod again.

One thing he had valued in his friendship with her when they were younger was her ability to not enjoy the drama surrounding the triplets' abduction. Some people thrived on it, still bringing the case up in casual conversation with throwaway theories about the man behind it. Ones they thought up on their lunch break and brought up like it was some party game. Declan's father had entertained any and all of them, but Declan had had the benefit of seeing his father run himself into the ground and had changed tactics. He and Caleb had heard many theories and kept their expectations at zero.

Still, Declan knew his family wished people would stay quiet about it. He did, too. He and his siblings had spent middle and high school dealing with children and teens with no tact. He'd hoped that as they aged their need to reach into the past and stir up gossip would ebb away.

It hadn't for a majority of Overlook residents.

Yet, Remi had never been one of those people. Whether they were kids or teens, she only spoke on the subject when he brought it up. Even then she stayed thoughtful, not at all interested in fanning the fire.

Now, sitting next to her, Declan was reminded of that thoughtful girl who had been his friend even though she'd adopted a new outgoing personality since college. A part of him wished he'd kept in touch when she left. The other part reminded him that she'd left to get away from Overlook and start a new, different life.

It was for the better.

"What do you mean coincidences?" Remi asked. "People *talking* about the case? Surely that can't be out of the ordinary for around here."

It was Declan's turn to hesitate. The man in the suit. The man in the bar. The man with the scar on his hand. All of that information had been kept within the family and only between the detectives at the sheriff's department and his chief deputy, Cussler. Everyone knew what it meant for any potential new information on the case to get out. What was already a long shot of an investigation would become impossible.

Declan had dropped his guard for one night with Remi, it was true, but they weren't in that room anymore. They weren't in her car, heading home before heading in opposite directions.

What he knew held a weight that he didn't want to put on her even though Declan was taking her back to the scene.

She didn't have to know everything to be helpful, and

he decided then and there that he could keep some things from her without being a grade A jackass.

"A few cases have had a similarity that could be connected," he went with. "Again, it might just be someone doing it on purpose to throw us off or pull our legs, but I can't let it go just yet unless I know for sure."

"So, we need to find a note in the wall or nothing at all."

"That's the goal."

Remi smiled. Declan knew because he heard it clearly in her voice. He was surprised at how much he was reminded again of the girl he'd known. Even when she had been quiet, he'd always been able to tell when she was smiling without looking at her.

"Well, I'm sure not about to say no to the sheriff, now am I?"

THE ROAD THAT led to the Well Water Cabin looked like many roads to older houses in Overlook. Dirt mixed with gravel, tree-lined, worn by weather, age and use. Narrow, too. If you met another vehicle you just had to pray you had the good luck that at least one of the two wasn't a truck and that there was enough room to crunch onto the nearly nonexistent shoulder so the other could pass by.

Isolated but not without purpose.

Yet, the road that led to Well Water was different.

It felt almost forgotten. Or maybe lost. Not because of its location and beautiful scenery, nestled within one of the thickest parts of the forest that stretched across Overlook, but because people had tried to lose it.

There was an eeriness that crept into every visitor's bones when driving up to the cabin. Whether they admitted it out loud or not. Remi was sure of that just as the odd feeling moved across her like she'd walked into a cold spot during the summer heat.

While she'd had every intention of telling the man about her pregnancy as soon as she could, he'd said just about the only thing that had made her wait. Or, really, if she was being honest it was the way he'd looked when he talked about going to the cabin. His eyes had somehow softened and remained hard at the same time. Like someone trying their damnedest to appear the picture of strength while trying to hide the vulnerability tearing at them.

It was such an intriguing and surprising juxtaposition that Remi had decided to tell Declan after they had examined the cabin. Maybe the news would cheer him up.

Maybe it wouldn't.

Either way Remi didn't believe there was a note in the cabin, hidden in the wall or not.

Someone would have found it by now.

At least she thought so.

"How did you get in?" she asked as he followed the last curve before the cabin. "Did the Fairhopes give the department a copy of the key?"

The Fairhopes had owned Well Water for years before the abduction. They had lived in Chicago and used the cabin as a vacation home when it struck their fancy. Remi had heard through the grapevine that, after being interviewed and investigated extensively, the family hadn't been back to Overlook. Remi realized she didn't know if anyone else had rented the place from them.

Declan's voice went hard.

"I own it."

Remi's hair slapped her cheeks, she turned her head so fast.

"You own it?"

Declan's jaw was set. He nodded.

"Dad bought it from the Fairhopes. When he passed, it passed on to me."

"That gives me some mixed feelings, I'll be honest."

"You're not the only one."

You'd never guess such a cute, quaint cabin could breed such heartache, confusion and fear.

Well Water came into view like the beautiful terror it was.

Remi had never been inside but, like most of Overlook, had found her way to the outside to look.

A true log cabin exterior with a storybook chimney and wraparound porch. The green on the window trim and front door had aged well over the years, but the front gardens had not. They were equally overgrown and barren.

Declan parked next to the mailbox. Remi watched as he pulled a key out of the middle console. The hardness in his voice had transferred to his body.

She had no doubt he was becoming the sheriff.

There was no banter-heavy lead-up to going inside. No flourish or outpouring of emotion. Declan got out, Remi followed. He unlocked the front door, she moved past him. He hung back by the door, she started to explore. It was a silent dance between them. One that completely consumed her.

As long as they were in *the* cabin, all thoughts of being pregnant with Declan's child, moving to Colorado and how insanely different her life was about to become quieted.

Then it was just the two of them in an empty cabin.

Chapter Four

Well Water wasn't a spacious place by any means. The layout was simple. The front door opened into a narrow hallway that went back to the kitchen but opened up to the living space on the right and two small bedrooms and one bathroom on the left. The stairs to the basement were pushed against the only stretch of wall between the living room and the doorway to the kitchen. Down there, however, things took a turn for the creepy. That was where the Nash triplets had been locked up. A basement apartment was how it had been described in the news. A bedroom, kitchenette and bathroom.

A door that had once had four sets of locks on the outside.

Remi didn't want to go down there yet. Instead, she walked through every room upstairs with fresh attention.

First of all, she was surprised that the cabin was fully furnished. She'd expected to walk into an empty, stale space. Instead, it looked very much like a vacation home, albeit from the eighties. Some furniture was covered with drop cloths, other pieces had a thin layer of dust. Again, she never would have picked this place to be the site of a town-wide legend whose story continued to terrorize.

Remi was careful as she picked her way through each room until eventually she made it back to the hallway.

Declan looked like a statue leaning against the wall opposite the bedroom and bathroom doors. Cast in stone, the man was rigid. Jaw set sharp and intimidating, shoulders broad and unrivaled, muscles a testament to his discipline and focus, and bright green eyes narrowed and seeing only the past. Remi felt a tug at her heartstrings for him. The greatest upset in her family life throughout her existence was her parents' divorce and, honestly, it had been a blessing for everyone. She hadn't had to deal with fear and then death like he had.

And she certainly hadn't taken those experiences and been elected into a job that dealt in both on more than one occasion.

"If there's something here, I'm not seeing it," she said with sympathy. He nodded and tried to smile. It fell short, but Remi wasn't going to fault him for it.

"It's okay. I guess I didn't expect there to be something."

Remi glanced at the stairs across from him.

"So do we go down there next?"

Declan sighed. He took off his Stetson and thumped it against his thigh.

"This place has gotten a lot of attention but downstairs is another story altogether. I'm confident that not even a speck of dirt has gone undocumented from that apartment." His attempt at a smile dissolved completely. It looked so odd in comparison to the faded but still bright blue paint that covered the hallway's walls. The rest of the rooms were painted in similar, bright shades. Remi had somewhat expected wallpaper given the date of the cabin, but all the other rooms had a texture to them like they'd been sponged instead.

She guessed the Fairhopes hadn't liked the effort since the hall didn't have the same effect. It looked like they'd simply painted over wallpaper. Remi could see the seam right above the wooden chair rail that ran around the hall.

"We can go," Declan continued. "You've already done enough by just coming out here."

He pushed away from the wall, but Remi didn't move. She felt her eyebrows furrow in together as she continued to stare at the wall.

"What is it?" Declan asked. He turned around after Remi pointed.

"That seam that's been painted over."

"You mean the wallpaper? Yeah, they painted over it."

Remi shook her head, finger still poised in midair, and looked around the small hallway.

"Where are the other seams?" she asked. "If you paint over wallpaper you're going to see more than one, or bubbles from the paint over the paper. Something over the chair rail or at the corners. Not just *one* seam. No one is that good at painting over wallpaper, especially not in the eighties or nineties."

Declan touched the seam beneath the paint.

"Unless it's not a seam from wallpaper."

Green eyes met hers. Remi saw the excitement. The potential. The possibility that they were close to something new. She felt it, too.

What she didn't expect was what happened next.

Declan touched the wall next to the seam and then reared his arm back and punched that same spot. Remi gasped as his fist went right through the drywall.

"Declan!"

"I'm okay," he said. Then he did it again, beneath the hole he'd just made. It expanded the open space. Remi was prepared to grab his arm to keep him from doing it again when he slowly put his hand into the hole and pulled more of the drywall out. It came off with ease. He tossed the blue-painted chunks to the left of her. There was no trace of wallpaper on any of the pieces.

Then he kicked the wall, opening a new hole.

Remi took a step back.

It was oddly intriguing to watch the man pull, punch and kick away an entire panel of drywall with such ease. And in a blazer and slacks, no less.

Soon there was a Declan-sized hole in the wall. Remi moved closer again as the sheriff stepped just enough inside of the hole to peer straight at the spot where the seam was. Without looking anywhere else, he pulled two things from two separate pockets of his blazer.

One was a pair of plastic gloves, which he put on with lightning speed and precision. The other was a pocket-knife.

He opened it, wordlessly.

Then he slid the blade beneath the seam like an expert surgeon.

Remi held her breath.

The chill from outside had found its way into the cabin. Goose bumps moved across her skin.

A long, agonizing minute crept by.

When it was over Declan had cut out what had made the seam.

"My God," he breathed out after holding it up. He met Remi's gaze with a look of total bewilderment. "Huds, it's a piece of paper."

THE PAPER WAS small but thick. One side was covered in paint, but the blue hadn't bled all the way through. The ink that was scrawled across the other side, the one that had been against the original cream-colored wall, was still legible.

In fact, it was nearly pristine.

"What does it say?"

Remi followed him into the kitchen, careful to keep her distance as he gently laid the paper down on one of the counters. The power was off, but the natural light kept the first floor bright. Still, Declan set the paper beneath the window that ran across the kitchen wall, not wanting to miss a thing.

"It's a name." The handwriting was tight, neat. Declan didn't recognize it, though he did the name. "Justin Redman."

"Who? Is that all it says?" Remi went from a careful distance to right up against his side. She smelled like the beach. Sunscreen and sunshine. It might have knocked him off his game had they been in a different setting.

But not now.

Not here with the note from the wall.

"That's all it says," he confirmed, tilting the paper up so she could see it better. "Justin Redman."

"Does that name mean something to you?"

Declan nodded.

"He was a part of one of the cases my dad was working when the triplets were taken. Aggravated assault. Redman was attacked outside of the old gas station at the turnoff to County Road 11. The one that shut down when we were around fifteen, sixteen. He couldn't give a good description and there were no witnesses. Then Redman died in a car accident. The department never found out who attacked him but suspected it was drug related." Declan pulled out his phone to take pictures. "I don't know why his name would be here. Or, for that matter, why it was painted against the wall."

"Or how that man in the bar knew about it," Remi added.

A shot of adrenaline went through Declan.

"Or how he knew about it," he repeated, chewing the words over.

Remi shifted and walked away. Declan took several pictures before laying the paper gently back down on the cabinet.

"What are you doing?" he called.

"What do you think I'm doing? I'm looking at the walls again! Check for any seams or bubbles or discoloration. If there's one hidden piece of paper, who knows how many more there might be!"

Declan followed his rising excitement and Remi's instructions. Together they inspected the first-floor walls in silence. Sometimes Remi would be the one running her hands over different spots, other times Declan would rub certain stretches of faded paint.

When they ended their search at the top of the stairs again, Declan took pictures of the wall he'd partially demolished.

It had been easy to punch through the drywall but had left his hand stinging. A glance down showed blood. He tried to keep that hand out of Remi's view.

"What now? Do we go downstairs and look?" Declan was surprised at how eager Remi was to help. Surprised and pleased. It helped remind him how easy it had been to hang out with her as kids and teens. Being in her company was nice now, even if they were looking for hidden clues in walls.

It also reminded him how bizarre their current situation was compared to them hanging out in the loft space of his family's barn or out behind the high school complaining about Mrs. Darlene's too-hard geometry homework and Coach Kelly's ridiculous rules about dressing for PE.

Declan was surprised at himself for what he said next.

"We got way more than I bargained for already. I need

to take that paper back to the department and do some digging. I can come back out here later and look downstairs, though I stand by there being not a speck of dirt or dust down there that hasn't been cataloged already." He motioned to the walls around him. "This, though… This was a surprise."

"Are you sure you don't want to keep looking? I don't mind."

Declan shook his head.

"You've done more than enough already, Huds. Thank you, I mean it."

Remi's cheeks darkened slightly. From rosy to rosier. She was blushing. It was an endearing sight.

"It was no problem."

Declan went out to his truck, grabbed one of the plastic sandwich bags he always carried in the cab, and bagged the note. Remi waited outside, leaning against the truck and looking off into the woods. It was a nice sight when he came back out, ready to leave.

It wasn't until they were both back in the cab of the truck that Declan realized the weight of what they'd just done.

What they'd found.

A new clue to the abduction case.

The case that had torn his family apart.

The case that changed all of their lives.

Justin Redman. Declan had already reviewed the cases his father had worked on through his career. Michael Nash had been a great detective. Which had been the leading point of fact that had contributed to his obsession with the case and then led to his downfall. He was the great detective who couldn't for the life of him solve an inch of what had happened to his own family, in his own hometown.

It wore him down until there was nothing left.

And now Declan had a piece of something his father had never seen.

Could this be the missing part of the puzzle that finally led to some answers?

Could he finally help his family find the peace they'd been searching for?

A hand touched his arm. Declan was startled by it. Remi's eyebrow was arched, her expression soft.

"Did you say something?"

She smiled. It was soft, too.

"I asked if you were okay."

Declan took off his hat and set it down on the center console. A restlessness was starting to settle on him. An itch he needed to scratch. But that was how it had started with his dad—focusing to the point of isolating himself.

Declan didn't want to do that.

Not to the woman who had seen what he couldn't.

"Sorry," he said, starting the truck. "I get caught in my own head sometimes. Yeah, I'm good."

"And that blood on your hands?"

Declan smirked.

"Hazard of the job."

That earned a snort from Remi, and soon they were back on the dirt road.

The farther away they got away from Well Water, the more he tried to relax and be in the moment.

It wasn't until they were on the main road pointed back to Winding Road that Declan realized how much of a grade A jackass he'd still managed to be.

"What are you doing?" Remi asked the moment he slowed and started to pull onto the grassy shoulder.

Declan switched on his flashers, put the truck in Park, and turned in his seat to face her.

"You called me because you said you wanted to talk,

and I pulled you out to a crime scene without even asking what it was that you wanted to talk about. I swear my mama taught me manners. Now what's on your mind?"

A peculiar look changed Remi's expression from confusion to somewhere between amusement and hesitation. He thought she might not tell him for a moment, but then she angled in her seat to face him better and began.

"Well, you know how stressed I was trying to decide if I should take the job in Colorado and you said you thought I should?"

He nodded.

"Yeah! You said it would be a huge step in your career, right?"

It was Remi's turn to nod.

"It would be and, the Monday after I left here last, I accepted the position."

Declan smiled.

"That's great, Huds! You busted your tail to get it!"

Remi's cheeks tinted a darker shade of rosy again.

"It *is* great. I've actually already started packing up the house. What's *not* great is how slow that's been going since the morning sickness kicked in last week."

For a second, Declan thought he heard her wrong. Then Remi raised her eyebrows as if to say, *Yeah, you heard me right, big man.* When she didn't speak for another moment, Declan realized he must have heard her right.

Then he finally added up some things he should have probably already been questioning.

Declan might not have been as good a detective as his father or his brother but, by God, he'd be a damn near a fool to not understand the real reason Remi Hudson had come back to town again.

Chapter Five

"You're pregnant."

It was more a statement than a question, one that didn't seem to match Declan's increasingly inquisitive expression. Remi didn't know what she had hoped to see from the man at the news but was glad, at least, he hadn't tried to rebuff her immediately.

And that she hadn't had to spell it out for him, either.

"According to the lab tech who took my blood and the nurse who called me with the results," she said with a nod. "Not to mention more than a few tests." Remi pulled her phone out and went to the Gallery app. When she got to the cluster of pregnancy test photos she'd taken originally in disbelief, she passed him the phone.

Declan was quiet as he swiped through them. There was another odd contrast between the muscled sheriff and her pink-and-blue-floral phone case. He stopped on the last picture and zoomed in with his fingers, expanding the part of the digital test that clearly read "pregnant."

"You're pregnant," he repeated when he was done. Remi took her phone back. Their fingers touched. Declan was warm. Just as he had been the night that had led them to this moment.

"I didn't notice at first that my period didn't come, and then when I did I assumed it was because of stress, but then I was *just so hot* and Googled my symptoms. I started to do the math. I grabbed a test and made an appointment the next day for the blood draw. Though they took a urine test, too, and it was also positive."

Declan's expression was passing from curious to shocked. His green eyes, tall grass in a breeze, were the size of quarters. A man trying to process as much information as he could while seeking out more.

"But we used protection," he pointed out.

"And yet, here we are at almost six weeks. I guess the Nash swimmers are Olympians."

"Six weeks?" Declan's voice jumped at that.

"Five weeks, five days. Based on conception since, well, that was easy to pin down." Remi held her phone up again. "I have an app that I can show you. It explains *a lot*, which is good because I grew up with three men and—" Before she could finish the thought Declan's cell phone shifted their focus. A rhythmic set of beeps filled the space of the cab around them. Remi could see the caller ID read Detective Santiago. Declan didn't reach for it.

"My news isn't going anywhere," she said with a light laugh. "You can answer the phone. I won't be offended."

Declan still wavered, but by the fourth ring he hit Answer.

"What's up, Jazz?"

A woman's voice floated from the receiver, though Remi couldn't hear what she was saying. A slight panic took over as Remi realized she didn't know if Declan had started seeing someone in the time after they'd been together. She *had* told him several times he needed to lighten up and live a little as they'd been trapped between the sheets together. Had he taken her advice as she'd taken his about her promotion?

And, if so, did it really matter?

Remi did want children. Eventually. Now was unexpected, but she was taking the surprise with a cautious, slightly terrified smile of acceptance. Telling Declan had never been a question in her mind.

However, her expectations of a future together had never been set.

Declan Nash might have been wild when they were younger, but his love for his family had never been in question. He adored his mother, looked up to his father, and he'd die to protect each and every one of his siblings. The man he was now? Remi was seeing the sheriff, a respected man filled with responsibility and the need to protect. Even now, years and years later, he was still trying to protect that same family he'd fiercely loved when they were younger.

No, there was no doubt in Remi's mind that Declan would absolutely step up to his role as father.

What she *didn't* know was what that meant for the two of them in the future.

And where that future might take place.

Because, as much as she liked and respected the man next to her, Remi hadn't for a moment wavered in her desire to move to Colorado. As she'd told Declan when they last spoke, her new job wasn't just a career maker. It paid extremely well.

Financial stability hadn't always been something the Hudson family could claim, and Remi would be damned if she didn't change that for her kid.

She didn't have to hear the conversation going on next to her to read the changes in Declan's demeanor. The shift to sheriff was quick. His brow furrowed, his forehead crinkled, and a frown ate away whatever emotions he was feeling about the news she'd given him.

He nodded even though Detective Santiago couldn't see it.

"Yeah, you were right," he said, gruff. "Thanks for the heads-up. I appreciate it." A sigh pulled his chest down. "Yeah. I'll head that way after I change. Give me twenty."

He ended the call. Then he was staring again.

"I have a *situation* I need to take care of at work."

"Everything okay?"

That sigh came back. She didn't like how it brought the man down.

"Everything is up in the air," he answered. "I'll know more when I get there. Is that okay?"

Remi held her hands up to show no offense was being taken again.

"Listen, I promise you that me being pregnant hopefully isn't going anywhere. We can talk about it more later on. If you want."

Declan's expression was hard.

"I want to."

He put them back on the main road and soon they were on Winding Road, leading up to the ranch. In the time between their stop and the arch that read Nash Family Ranch, Declan had called two people and hurriedly given them information she didn't understand. Remi wasn't trying to snoop, though. Instead, she watched out the window as trees whipped by. Winter had stripped some of them bare. Others were shades of dark green and dark brown. Remi wondered if it would snow for Christmas.

How would the holidays look now?

She started her new job two days into the New Year. This was the last time she'd be in Tennessee for the foreseeable future.

How would her family take the news that she was moving so far away? Not well, she imagined. The last time she'd come to town she'd almost told them about the decision she had to make. To accept the new position or not. Yet, she'd found herself back in their old fights of leaving the ranch for school and after. Moving to Colorado? She doubted that conversation would end in anything but a fight. Especially once she added in the news of a baby on the way.

"Sorry," Declan grumbled as he ended his last call. He cut the engine in the driveway at his house. "If it's not one thing, it's another."

"Well, I'm sure that note and, well, *this*—" Remi motioned to her stomach, which was bloated if she was being honest "—isn't helping your sheriff to-do list."

She meant the comment in humor; Declan didn't smile.

"How long are you in town for?"

"Until Christmas, though I might head back if I need a break from the boys at the ranch."

"Have you told them yet? About, you know?"

Remi let out a sigh that mimicked Declan's earlier stress-infused ones.

"No. Other than the nurse and lab tech, you're the only one I've told so far." She gave him a look she hoped was severe. "And I'd like to keep it on the down low for now. Not only is it too early to tell anyone, I also feel like *we* need to talk it out first."

"Agreed. What about tonight?" He nodded out the windshield. "I can make us dinner. If you don't mind subpar cooking."

Remi couldn't help laughing.

"Considering the microwave was my most-used appliance at my rental in Nashville, anything you make I bet would be ten times better than what I would cobble together at Heartland."

After they got out of the truck, Declan paused next to

her car door. He looked like he wanted to say something and couldn't seem to find the right words. Remi felt a wave of sympathy wash over her. In its wake was a surprising and vicious pull of the fear of the unknown.

She could have misjudged the man opposite her. Children and teens *did* grow up, and there was no denying he had. He could still love his family. That didn't mean he would want to be a part of their child's life.

Either way, Remi wasn't about to find the answer right now. She put her hand out and patted Declan on the shoulder.

"Let me know when you want me to come over and I'll be here," she said, trying to sound happier than her thoughts had just become. "And try not to stress too much about everything. I can already see some wrinkles trying to break through."

He smiled. It was tight.

"I guess you're too short to see some of the gray hairs I've been sprouting already."

"Just remember, that's when cowboy hats serve a dual purpose. Slap that puppy on and aim that stress somewhere else. Okay?"

He nodded, but she knew her words were just words. They didn't have the power to wring the stress from his life. Just as his didn't have the power to smooth over hers.

He opened her car door and shut it gently when Remi was inside. By the time she was pulling out of the driveway, she couldn't help but look in her rearview.

Declan was already gone.

Cooper Mann looked two shades of panicked when Declan walked into the viewing room at the sheriff's department. The young rebel was handcuffed to the metal table in the room opposite, visibly freaking out even though there was a thick, soundproofed two-way mirror between them.

Detective Jazz Santiago, Caleb's partner and best friend, shook her head in greeting.

"I couldn't believe the call when it came in," she started. "I almost asked if there was another Cooper Mann who drove a white Corvette with a piece of duct tape along the bumper."

"But there's not," he finished.

She shook her head.

"Still hard to believe, though."

Declan had to agree with her there.

"Where's the woman he tried to grab? You said her name was Lydia?"

Jazz pulled a slip of paper out of her pants pocket. She handed it over. "Lydia Cartwright" was written in sloppy handwriting. It was a far cry from the neatness of the note he'd found less than two hours ago.

If the current situation hadn't been what it was, Declan would have considered telling Jazz what he had found. Even though she and her husband had lived in Overlook for years, they weren't locals. Her fascination with the triplet abduction stopped and started only when it was relevant to the conversation and only if that conversation was started by a Nash. Her loyalty, friendship and top-notch detective skills would be an asset to figuring out whatever it was that Declan and Remi had found.

Yet, he held his tongue and forced himself to focus on the present and the woman who had almost been kidnapped herself.

"She's at the hospital getting seen about still," Jazz answered. Her shoulders tensed. "He cut up her face pretty good with the keys on his key ring. You can still see some of her blood on his hands."

Declan cursed beneath his breath. Sure enough he could make out smears across parts of Cooper's hands and fingers.

"Is Caleb out there with her already?"

Caleb had been one of his calls as Declan tried to assess the situation before knowing all of the facts. He'd needed to deploy one of his best to figure out those facts. Pronto. But then he'd spent the majority of the ride over talking to his chief deputy. Mayne Cussler was, and had been, Declan's right-hand man for a while now. When Declan had nearly died a few years ago, Cussler had stepped up in a big way while making it known he liked where he was.

"Being sheriff one day could be nice," he'd said once Declan had been cleared for work again. "But I like where I am right now."

Cussler was a reserved man, quiet. He hadn't been as much when Declan had told him that Cooper Mann had tried to abduct a woman. In fact, Declan had heard the man cuss more during their conversation on the drive over than Declan had heard in the ten years of knowing him.

"Yeah. He and Nina were downtown with Parker when you called so he was able to get there pretty quick," Jazz answered. "He said he'd update us the second he finds something out."

Declan nodded. He tried to untangle the knots of facts threaded together in his head. One line of thought was begging to be pulled out, but Jazz angled her body toward him and dropped her voice before he could inspect it.

"Cooper isn't asking for a lawyer. He's asking for you. He said you two met up today?"

The question of "why" was clear in her expression, yet he was glad there was no suspicion there. She might not have been Declan's partner but she trusted him.

Which made his omission of the entire truth even harder to tell her.

"He heard a rumor about the triplets' abduction case and wanted to pass it on to me, to pay me back for helping clear his warrant."

Jazz's eyes widened considerably.

"What was the rumor?"

That one thread of thought, begging to be pulled out, became the only one left in his head.

"It doesn't matter," he said, anger rising. "I have a feeling it was all just a distraction."

The paper in the plastic bag in Declan's pocket felt heavier. The hope Declan had been harboring since Remi had pointed out the seam in the hallway was now souring into him feeling like an idiot.

Cooper Mann had, for whatever reason, set him up.

He should have known better.

And that just made Declan angrier.

"It's time for me to have a little talk with our friend."

Chapter Six

Cooper was sweating bullets. His face had paled considerably from earlier that morning. There was a slight shake to him. He wasn't exactly the picture of a man who had brazenly attacked and then tried to kidnap a woman. But Declan was no stranger to the adage that looks could be deceiving.

He settled into the metal chair opposite Cooper in the interrogation room and laced his fingers over the top of the table, leaning in. Declan was outraged and trying his best not to let it show.

Cooper, again, wasn't faring well when it came to keeping his own emotions in check. Declan didn't get a word in before the young man was nearly talking over himself to get his side of the story out.

"I didn't do this, man, you gotta know that, right? She came after *me*!"

"Don't call me 'man,'" Declan responded, voice even. "It's Sheriff Nash."

Cooper's eyes widened, a deer caught in headlights. He shook his head.

"*She* came at *me*, Sheriff Nash," he tried again. "Honest to God, I was just stopping to get something to eat, and she got my attention and then *bam*!" He tried to bring his hands up to his face. The handcuffs kept the movement from extending past his chest, so he jerked his head down to meet his hands. He didn't touch his face but made stabbing motions. "She grabbed my keys out of my hand and started shredding her own face!"

If Caleb had been sitting next to him, Declan imagined he would have snorted and said something along the lines of *Well, that's a new one.*

However, Declan wasn't in the mood in the slightest. He wasn't about to encourage Cooper's story.

"The man who called 911 said he came out of the shop because he heard her screaming and saw *you* trying to push *her* into your car."

Cooper made a strangled sound between frustration and fear. He hit his hands against the top of the table.

"I was trying to get her *out* of my car! After she did that crazy thing to her face, she opened my door and tried to get in! I thought she was trying to carjack me! Then someone was grabbing me and you guys showed up acting like I was the bad guy!"

Declan didn't roll his eyes.

He wanted to, though.

"Why would she want to do all of that?" he asked.

"The hell if I know! She's crazy!"

Cooper was nearly panting. Declan believed something traumatic had happened. What he was having a hard time believing was that Cooper had been the victim.

"You have to understand how this looks from my point of view, Cooper," Declan said, easy on the tone. "First you come to me today about new information on the abduction case and then you're seen with an injured woman who swears you tried to abduct *her*. Were you trying to use the triplets' abduction to distract me from you trying the same? Or were you just trying to double your chances at making headline news?"

Cooper opened and closed his mouth a few times. Objectively, Declan thought the boy looked terrified and surprised at the accusation. Then again, trying to abduct someone on his watch wasn't just an affront to Declan's job, it was a hard prod into his family's past.

He wasn't going to give Cooper an inch.

Not until he had proof otherwise.

"After we finish talking to Ms. Cartwright, I'll be back in here," Declan said, standing to his full height and drawing in his chest with authority and sincerity. He adjusted his Stetson and made sure his sheriff's badge was showing. "Then we're going to get to the bottom of this. And, Cooper? If you lie to me, you're going pay for that lie. It's as simple as that. Got it?"

This time Cooper found his words. They jumbled together as he again tried to tell Declan he was innocent, that Lydia had been the one lying, and he'd just been in the wrong place at the wrong time.

Declan shut the door behind him with Cooper still talking.

Jazz met him in the hallway.

"This is going to be a nightmare in the press," she said. "Cussler can only sweet-talk Delores and the media away for so long."

"I know." Declan sighed. "Which is why we have to move fast and get this thing settled before it takes over the town."

DECLAN DIDN'T CALL.

Remi shrugged deeper into her jacket and kept her leisurely pace along the dirt path across Hudson Heartland. It went from the front door of the house all the way to the front gate, and she was on her way back for the second pass. The distance wasn't anything she couldn't handle, yet she felt a soreness already creeping into her legs. She was also somewhat out of breath.

Was that a pregnancy thing?

Or was she just looking for pregnancy symptoms and finding her own when there were none?

Remi shook her head. She needed to calm down. Her next appointment was at eight weeks, a little too far away if she was being honest, and she'd given herself that deadline to figure out what the heck going to happen next for her, her child and Declan.

She knew the sheriff was out there being the sheriff, yet, when seven o'clock turned into eight and then nine, Remi had felt a sting of rejection at his absence. Rescheduling their talk was okay—she'd understand that—but Declan hadn't even texted her.

The reasons he hadn't gotten in touch with her all stemmed from issues Remi had been afraid of when she found out about the pregnancy.

Declan being so busy with work that he'd forgotten about their chat was the leading suspect in her mind. Which opened up a Pandora's box of potential issues for her. One, Declan's job was chaotic and dangerous. Not a point against him but definitely not a point of stability for Remi's comfort or liking. Two, he was a sheriff who didn't just do his job, he *was* his job.

She took in a deep, cooling breath. She'd recognized the look in Declan's eyes after finding the note. It was one of purpose. It was one of excitement. It was a solid stubbornness.

Stubbornness to do whatever it took to see through what he meant to see through.

She'd encountered it before in her father. A dogged approach to life: the job came first because it had to, the rest of them be damned.

Remi knew the balance between family and obligation to protect that family was a difficult dance. One her father had lost when she was younger, resulting in her parents' divorce. And that had revolved around taming horses for clients and then boarding horses, not solving kidnapping cases and trying to protect an entire county of people.

She also knew that she and Declan were friends who had *momentarily* become more.

Could she really expect him to keep her within his orbit? Especially with his job?

And if Declan *hadn't* forgotten about her?

Well, then, that was another set of issues she'd have to deal with.

Remi saw movement ahead of her. The outline of a man was illuminated by the exterior lights set up around the house. For a moment her stomach turned into an excited mess of static, then she realized the proportions of the man didn't fit the wide stature of the sheriff.

He came close enough that the light shifted. Jonah had his eyebrow raised in question.

"You know it's cold out here, right?" he greeted, zipping up the plaid monstrosity their mother had given him a few Christmases ago. Of all the Hudson clan, Jonah and Remi resembled each other the most. Lean, on the shorter side, dark blond hair, and freckles that had faded since they were children. Along with their mother, they both had almond-brown eyes. Remi had liked to think hers resembled more of a burning ember in the right light, but she seriously doubted Jonah would ever want such a frilly descriptor of his features.

Jonah Hudson might have looked like her, but he was all their father in personality. No-nonsense, no-frills, just hard work and a stifling need to guilt others about family obligation while rising to equally intense and set-way-too-high family expectations. Jonah might have been a year younger than her but Remi had always felt he was light-years older.

Even now his gaze felt belittling.

It did nothing for her current mood.

"You know that's what jackets are made for, right?" She motioned to hers and returned his eyebrow raise.

Jonah rolled his eyes but turned so he was at her shoulder. He matched her steps as she followed the curve of the path that went around the house and to the back porch.

"I don't know why you're out here right now anyways," Jonah kept on. "Last I heard you weren't a fan of the ranch. Now you show up two weeks early for the holidays and you're out walking it?"

Remi groaned.

"Just because I don't want to run the ranch doesn't mean I can't love it, you know," she shot back, neck getting hot as her anger spiked.

Jonah raised his hands in surrender.

"I didn't come out here to fight," he backtracked. "I saw you and thought I'd join you. Dad and Josh are in a mood together."

Remi heard the annoyance she often felt for the three Hudson men coming out of one of those men now. Her anger took a turn for the curious.

"Really? I didn't pick up on that at supper."

Jonah's breath misted out in front of him for the smallest of seconds. It wasn't cold enough to sustain a more noticeable cloud. It *did* show Remi a frustrated side of her brother that wasn't, for once, aimed at her.

"You haven't exactly been around the last few years so that doesn't surprise me. Dad and Josh butt heads more and more every day, but ever since Josh started dating this new woman he's been more *vocal* than normal. One moment he's talking about turning the ranch back into *the* place to tame and train horses, the next he's talking about running off into the sunset with this new fling."

Remi was absolutely stunned at that news. A common theme she'd encountered since leaving for college had been how living a life outside of the ranch was akin to familial treason. Josh hadn't pulled any punches as Remi had decided to commit that treason with every new choice that wasn't coming back to Overlook and taking an interest in Hudson Heartland.

"A fling is making him rethink his gospel?" Remi mocked, unable to keep the bad feelings of her brother's disappointment from slinking into her words. "Does that mean I finally get a pass if he decides to run off into the sunset?"

"This is serious, Remi," Jonah tried. "He barely knows this woman and yet he's ready to throw everything he's worked for away? For what? A few rounds in the sack?"

Remi made a disgusted noise.

"I don't need to hear that," she said. "Please and thank you."

They made it to the back porch. The light in their father's bedroom room was off. Josh's room was at the other corner of the house along the back. His light was on. Jonah looked up at it with concern clear on his face.

Despite their differences and the chasm that had opened up between them since becoming adults, Remi softened and took pity on her little brother.

"Josh will be fine. He's been the dutiful son, brother and horse trainer since he could walk and talk. Let him have his moment. If you don't, you'll only be pushing him to do the exact thing you don't want him to in the first place." Remi placed her hand on Jonah's shoulder. He gave her a look that also clearly said he wasn't used to the sibling closeness. Still, he didn't pull away. "It wouldn't hurt for you to relax a little, too. Maybe spend less time worrying about those two—" she motioned to her father's room and then Josh's "—and a little more about yourself. When's the last time *you* had a fling?"

Jonah snorted. Remi was glad he hadn't taken offense to what she'd said.

"I'll have you know that I actually went out on a blind date last week, thank you very much."

Remi couldn't stop the wide grin that moved across her face.

"Oh, yeah? And how did that go?"

Jonah shrugged. It was a cocky movement.

"Must have been okay since we're supposed to meet up tomorrow."

Remi laughed and bumped her shoulder against his.

"Way to go there, Jonah boy! What's her name? Do I know her?"

He was already walking to the back door, shaking his head.

"She's new in town but, even if she wasn't, I'm not going to give you any ammo to dog me…or stalk her online."

"Oh, come on! That's not fair!" Remi followed him inside, mood lifting. It was nice to laugh with her brother. It made her forget for a moment about the insecurities swarming in her head. "How old is she? What does she do? When did she move to Overlook?"

Jonah kept shaking his head. He hurried to the stairs but paused when she threw out a last teasing insult.

"Did you know that you're a wet blanket? Has anyone ever told you that?" Remi said.

Jonah rolled his eyes.

"Her name is Lydia," he said. "And that's all you're getting."

He dashed up the stairs. Remi didn't follow. Her eyes

caught on an old picture framed on the wall next to the stairs. It was of her and her father. She was sitting on a horse, her father standing next to them.

He was beaming, no doubt sure about the future.

One with his wife, his ranch, and his eldest child on a path that would certainly lead to taking over that same ranch.

But the thing about certainty was that it didn't exist.

At least, not for Remi.

She ran a hand over her stomach. Then she pulled out her cell phone.

There were no missed calls or texts.

Remi looked back at the picture for a few more moments. Then she went to bed.

Chapter Seven

Remi fell asleep next to an empty fruit-snack wrapper and woke up to Jonah looking a far cry from the humor-filled man he had been when they parted ways at the stairs the night before.

"What's wrong?" she asked, sitting bolt upright. She couldn't remember the last time Jonah had even been in her childhood room.

"You have a visitor out on the front porch," he said, his voice weirdly low. "I thought I'd give you a warning since Dad doesn't seem to much care for the Nashes and he's the one who's out there talking to him."

Remi tossed the blanket off her, threw her legs over the side of the bed and rushed to the window. Unlike her brothers' and father's rooms, hers was the only front-facing bedroom. Which meant from her window she couldn't see the covered front porch, but she *could* see the truck parked in the drive.

Declan.

It wasn't ladylike but Remi cussed under her breath. Jonah snorted and headed back for the door.

"Probably way friendlier than Dad is being to the sheriff," he said over his shoulder.

Remi didn't doubt that one bit.

She hurried to the bathroom and got presentable like

it was the big triathlon she'd been practicing all year to win. Teeth brushed, face washed, mascara applied, hair detangled, and a blue flannel button-up with jeans and boots put on. She knew she could stand to be slower if she wanted. On his own Declan was already a grumpy spot for Gale Hudson. Him coming to the ranch to ask to see his daughter?

Remi bet every paycheck she'd ever made at Towne & Associates that the only way the sheriff was coming inside was if he had a warrant. And even then he might have to bust out the handcuffs to keep her father from making a scene.

December stuck to its guns on mimicking a real winter. Remi ripped her jacket off the hook by the front door and walked into the cold without properly bracing herself for it. She sucked in a breath as she tried to zip up the jacket, all while trying to gauge the situation on the porch.

Declan was standing on the bottom step, her father on the top. The latter was leaning against the railing, all casual. Declan, however, was tense. His badge had been pinned to the outside of his jacket. He greeted Remi with a smile.

It was also tense.

"Hey," Remi said, sliding into whatever conversation they'd been having. She caught Declan's gaze. "I saw your truck and thought you might be here for me?"

"And why would you think that?" her father asked so fast she got whiplash looking back at him. A heat pulsed up her neck and into her cheeks. It was born from embarrassment and quick anger.

It could have been pregnancy hormones; it could have been the fact that her father had barely said two words to her since she'd come back for the holidays.

"Because why would anyone want to visit a bunch of

grumpy men holed up in one house?" she shot back, deciding it didn't matter what was fueling her sudden fire.

Her father turned, surprised but obviously ready for rebuttal. Remi was, too.

Declan went to the next step. When he spoke, his tone was so harsh that both Hudsons redirected their attention.

"I'm actually here for Jonah."

Neither Hudson said a word for a moment. Remi was too busy nursing the stab of disappointment that had pierced her. Declan hadn't called the night before and now he wasn't even there for her.

His expression softened.

"But I would like to talk to you after."

"Why do you need Jonah?" Her father had lost all illusions of being casual.

Declan's jaw was hard. He seemed to choose his words carefully.

"An incident happened yesterday involving an acquaintance of his and I'd like to ask him a few questions."

Remi shared a confused look with her father. Well, *her* expression expressed *confusion*. Her father's read *defiance*.

Declan must have recognized it.

He took one more step up the stairs. When he spoke he kept her father's eye contact.

"This isn't a request, Gale."

Whether it was intentional or not, Declan shifted in his jacket, which made his sheriff's badge catch the sun's glare. It was enough to get her father moving, though he grumbled as he did so.

When Gale was back in the house, Remi descended to the step Declan was on.

"What's going on? Is Jonah in trouble? I mean he's a pain in the backside, but you know he's harmless, right?"

Declan didn't give away anything with his expression.

"He's not in trouble, but I still need to talk to him."

"You? Why not one of your detectives?" Remi lowered her voice. "Is this about the note from Well Water?"

Declan was quick to shake his head.

"It's about that call I got yesterday. I'll explain after I talk with him."

Remi's emotions fluctuated again. She couldn't help what she said next. "Will you call me like you did last night? Or should I just wait around again and hope you'll show up tomorrow instead?"

Declan's entire demeanor shifted, but she didn't have a chance to see what emotion it was shifting into.

"Remi, I—" he said but the front door opened again. Jonah came out, followed by their dad. "I want to talk to you after this," Declan finished instead. Then he met Jonah's stare with another impassive expression.

"Jonah can we talk in private for a minute?" Unlike their father, Jonah agreed without fuss. They walked out to Declan's truck and stopped by its hood.

Remi couldn't hear what they were saying as, alongside her father, she watched their body language. It changed quickly. Jonah clearly was surprised and then angry.

But not at Declan. In fact, Declan put his hand on Jonah's shoulder for a moment.

Then Jonah turned on his heel, yanked his keys from his pocket and was rushing to his car. That put Remi and her father into action. While he went to Jonah, Remi went to Declan.

"What's going on? What's wrong?"

Declan didn't seem offended or angry that Jonah was obviously leaving the conversation. He watched as Jonah quickly spoke to her dad.

"A woman was attacked in an attempted kidnapping yesterday," he explained, not mincing words. "She said she knew Jonah so I thought I'd ask him a few questions to help clarify some things for me."

Remi gasped.

"Lydia?"

"Wait. You know her?"

"I heard about her last night. Jonah went on a blind date with her. Is she okay?"

"Yeah. Shaken up and has some superficial wounds, but she's okay. Considering."

Stressed wasn't the word that described Declan in that moment. It wasn't strong enough. The crinkles at the edge of his eyes that showed a life that had had many a laugh were woefully absent when he met her stare.

"Have you had breakfast yet? I need to eat if I have any hope of continuing to think straight."

Remi didn't have to think about it long. She hurried back to the house for her purse and phone and was sliding into the cab of his truck soon after. It wasn't until they were off Heartland that she realized they were headed toward town and not the Nash Family Ranch.

Which meant they weren't going to be alone after all.

Remi wondered if Declan had made that decision on purpose.

DOWNTOWN OVERLOOK WAS SIMPLE. A main strip with shops, eateries and slow but even foot traffic no matter the day. From the aptly named Main Street there were a few branching streets that led to a park, businesses and one that even went all the way to Second Wind, Desmond's foundation.

When Declan suggested getting something to eat, though, his mind only went to Claire's Café. It was a local favorite and run by a friend. One who, unlike most of the town, knew not to pester Declan for information when it came to a current case. Claire smiled from behind the counter after they walked in and motioned quickly to a table in the corner of the room. Partially hidden behind the pastry cabinet, it gave its patrons a slight privacy advantage while still keeping the front door in sight. Considering it was a seat-yourself establishment, that meant Claire was trying to help him out.

Which meant the town had picked up on the story of Lydia and Cooper way faster than he'd hoped.

Which *also* meant that the press conference he would be attending in two hours might not be soon enough.

"Ahh. I haven't been here in way too long," Remi said with obvious fondness. "Please tell me her homemade pecan squares are still a thing."

Declan pulled out her chair and eyed the glass cabinet near them.

"They are and it looks like she just made a new batch. You got lucky."

Remi grinned and only stood again when Claire bustled over. They hugged, said all the pleasant, polite things exchanged between old friends and then Claire dropped any guise that that was the real reason she'd come over.

"Declan, I thought you should know that all anyone was talking about this morning was Cooper and what he did to that poor woman," she said, lowering her voice so the handful of patrons already in the restaurant couldn't hear. "And, if it were me, I'd avoid talking to the new news editor of the paper. Delores doesn't say it out loud but I can tell she's having a hard time keeping Kellyn from doing the whole tabloid thing instead of using the facts."

Declan took off his hat and decided if he sighed every time he felt like it, then he might never get the chance to talk. Or breathe.

"Thanks, Claire," he said. "I'll make sure to keep a wide berth until the press conference today."

She tapped the tabletop in confirmation and went to get them two pecan squares and two coffees. Remi changed her order to decaf before Claire could get too far away.

"I've been away a lot longer than I realized," she said. "Who are Delores and Kellyn?"

"Delores Dearborn is the editor in chief of the *Overlook Explorer* and Kellyn is the latest news editor. While we—that being me and the department—are personal fans of Delores, we're definitely on the fence about Kellyn. She likes to…*sensationalize* every story she gets her hands on. Sometimes at the expense of the facts. Delores has had her hands full keeping her on track since there aren't a lot of people at the moment who could or would want to take her place. Overlook might be a magnet for some pretty dramatic stories on occasion but it's not the most exciting place in between them."

Remi glanced at the people settled in at a few of the tables across the room.

"Like a kidnapping attempt. The same day we found a note in the wall at Well Water," she whispered.

"I'm not so sure the note even is legit anymore," he admitted. "The man who told me where the note was just so happens to be the same one who tried to take Lydia."

Remi's eyes widened in surprise.

"You think he put it there recently to—what—distract you? That seems pretty darn elaborate for something he surely could have done easier."

Declan shrugged.

"That's the only thing that makes sense right now for me. It wasn't a secret that Dad had been working on Justin Redman's case back in the day. Picking his name to write down would definitely link back to the right time frame."

"That's all so wild." Her expression softened. "Considering I'm stressed out about this, I have to believe you're just swamped with it. How do you cope?"

Declan wanted to say he didn't. His version of coping with the stresses of the job was throwing himself deeper into that job to try to put whatever case was going on to bed. Instead, he smiled at Claire's reappearance with pecan squares and coffee. He pointed to both when she walked away.

"Sweets and coffee help."

Remi laughed. It was a light sound and it helped his mood.

It also made him feel another wave of guilt.

"Listen, Huds, I'm sorry about last night. This case just got really involved and by the time I realized what time it was I didn't want to wake you." He held up one hand in a Stop motion. "I know that's no excuse, but not calling you had nothing to do *with* you. I'm sorry."

A small smile passed over Remi's lips. It was fleeting.

"It's okay. I get it. Really, I do." She took a steady breath. Her lips, glossy and pink, parted. Declan read her body language before she spoke a word. She was about to tell him something.

Something important.

Declan didn't have a chance to find out what that something was.

Suddenly all hell broke loose outside the café. Without thought he threw himself between the rest of the café and Remi and their unborn child.

DECLAN HAD HIS gun up and out. Every patron in the room backed away from the front door. Claire, who was behind the counter with wide, searching eyes, moved behind the baked goods case. She shared a worried look with Remi.

The screeching tires and screaming had happened in

an instant. Just as quickly as the appearance of Declan in front of her as a human shield. She'd barely had time to register that anything was wrong before the wall of a man was between her and the door.

Remi reached out to touch that same man, drawn to his protection like her other hand had been drawn to her stomach, linking the three of them in one fight if needed. It was a bizarre reaction Remi didn't have the time to address. When the screaming outside didn't result in an attack inside, Declan finally moved.

"Stay here," he barked over his shoulder, gun still raised.

Remi watched the door bang shut behind him but couldn't see what the commotion was through the front windows. Whatever had happened must have been just out of view.

Remi's heart hammered in her chest.

She still had her hand raised from touching Declan.

The screaming outside stopped.

But the fear rooting her feet to the ground and snaking up to her heart did not.

Chapter Eight

Declan almost mistook the bystander helping the woman as the person who had hurt her.

"Hands where I can see them," Declan ordered on reflex.

Then the details filtered in.

There were three people outside. One was an older man, gray hair haloed around a bald spot that shone in the patch of sunlight not covered by Claire's awning. He stood in the street, his full attention on the other two people outside. Which brought Declan to the younger man kneeling on the sidewalk.

He had dreads pulled back against a plaid button-up and a nice tie. They matched his pants and dress shoes. They did *not* match the blood that was on the arm of his shirt or the woman leaning against him.

Declan realized it was her scream he'd heard.

Blood, bright and angry, was smeared across her cheek. She held it with one hand and the man held her with both of his. He didn't let go as he addressed Declan.

"That man just jumped out of a car and hit her, then took off!" He motioned his head to the side.

Declan lowered his gun and followed the man's sight line, already mentally calling in backup to search the area for the man in question.

Yet, Declan couldn't believe his eyes.

A few yards away there was a man with red hair standing in the middle of the street. When he saw Declan, he smiled.

"Stop right—" Declan started to yell.

The man turned on his heel and ran like a bat out of hell.

"Call 911," he said to the man on the sidewalk.

Then he lowered his gun and dug his heels into the concrete.

Boots and dress shoes slapping the ground echoed across Main Street as the man of the hour hauled over the span of two blocks. Unlike Caleb, Declan was more muscle than speed. Unlike the man he was chasing, however, Declan was the sheriff and damned determined.

His legs burned as he pushed every muscle to eat up the distance between them. Shouts behind him filled the street as shop owners and patrons came outside to see what all the fuss was about. Declan sidestepped two bystanders with shouts to get back inside. That effort, plus yelling out for the man in question to stop, cost him a bit of endurance. But when the man hung a right around the hardware store at the intersection of Main and Juniper streets, Declan could have laughed.

Whoever the man was, he wasn't a local. Or, at least, hadn't been downtown in a while.

Tilting forward into the run, Declan curved around the corner of the building and immediately had to swerve around an orange caution cone. And then another. The intersection, sidewalk and part of the hardware store were in a construction zone thanks to a nasty spring storm that had used the trees across the street as battering rams. This week they'd started repaving the sidewalk. The road was still sectioned off.

The man didn't know that.

He cursed something awful, already halfway through a stretch of wet cement. Two cones with tape between them were knocked over. A string of workers were littered around the street and watched as Declan let out his booming voice once more.

"Sheriff's department, *stop now!*"

One man, a long-haired younger worker, sprang into action and tried to grab the culprit. Instead, he became a human shield. One that was erected so fast all Declan could do was stop and huff. The man he had been chasing grabbed the younger one and put a gun Declan hadn't yet seen against his temple, stopping them both in the wet cement.

"You stop or he dies," he panted out. He pressed the gun against the man's head again. It made him wince.

Declan didn't move his aim, but he did freeze.

"Whoa there, buddy," he tried, dropping some of the command in his voice and picking up some, as Caleb's wife said, goodwill honey. Some people responded the way Declan wanted to the commanding voice. He had a gut feeling the man with the gun across from him wasn't one of those people. "Take it easy."

He glanced between Declan and the men in neon vests along the road.

"No one do anything stupid," Declan called to them. When the man's gaze was back to him, he addressed him directly. "Drop the gun, let him go, and let's just talk. There's no need for this to go any further."

The man in question did something Declan wasn't expecting. And certainly didn't like.

He laughed.

"And what would we talk about, Sheriff?" he called. "The weather? Christmas plans? How you may be a good shot, but there's no way this would end in a good light if *you* don't put down *your* gun?"

He laughed again and then settled into a smirk.

"I'll make you a deal, though," he continued before Declan could say a word. "Throw your gun into the wet cement and I'll throw you this." He shook the young man he was holding enough to put emphasis on his control of his well-being.

A worker near Declan cussed loudly. He was older and, even with just a glance, undeniably favored the man caught between Declan and his target. It was probably his son.

Which made Declan even more uneasy at the balance of power between him and the smirking man.

"Who are you?" Declan stalled. "What do you want?"

"I'm someone who wants you to *throw your gun* into the cement."

The man didn't lose his smirk but Declan could see his patience was going as he pressed the gun harder against his hostage's head. The man winced.

Declan relented.

There were too many variables, and he didn't have the upper hand with any of them.

"Fine," he said, lowering his gun. "Just let's stay calm."

Declan's service weapon could be replaced, yet he couldn't deny he didn't like seeing it hit the light gray muck and sink in an inch or so.

He also didn't like how it felt to be that vulnerable.

There wasn't anything stopping the man from using them all as target practice.

They were at a severe disadvantage.

That is, until the younger man he held against him decided to even the playing field. He brought his elbow back so fast that Declan almost missed it.

What he didn't miss was the other man groaning out

in pain as that elbow bit into his stomach. It was enough to make him lose his stance. Which also made him lose his target.

"Son of a—" The man cried out, trying to regain his composure. His captive wasn't having it. The younger man ducked and spun as much as the wet cement would allow and grabbed for the wrist of the hand holding the gun.

Declan wasn't about to wait around to see the outcome. He jumped into the cement and slogged over. He wasn't alone. Every man wearing a construction vest converged, even though the gun was still in hand.

Pride swelled in Declan's chest despite the fact that he'd much prefer there be no civilians in danger. Yet, the man who had grown up in Overlook couldn't help but be proud.

It was a feeling he carried with him as he closed the space between them with speed. Declan heard the gun hit the muck beneath them just before his shoulder connected with the attacker's chest. They sank into the cement, and Declan knew he'd won.

The man didn't fight back as Declan got to his knees and kept his hand pressed down on the man's chest.

"Don't you dare move unless I tell you," Declan ordered. The construction workers flanked him. He looked back at the discarded gun and scooped it up.

The man's head was just above the cement while his body had sunk in a bit. He smiled.

Declan didn't like when a losing man smiled.

It usually meant he didn't care enough to notice he'd lost or he hadn't actually lost at all.

A twisting thought pushed those worries aside. Declan got to his feet and the man merely pushed up on his elbows as best he could. He met Declan's gaze. In the chase and struggle, part of his shirt had drooped down around the collar.

That was when Declan saw the tattoo.

A scorpion.

The brand of the Fixers, the men and women in suits who had a reputation for being the organization other criminals called when a job was too hard to do. Or too messy to carry out.

Declan swore.

The man kept on smiling.

That twisting thought turned into a question. Declan heard the low thrum of ascending rage in his own voice as he asked it.

"Why didn't you just get back into your car after you hit that woman? Why run away if you could have driven away?"

The man was absolutely enjoying himself when he answered. It made Declan's blood run cold.

"Because, *Sheriff*, I knew the only way to get you to leave that café was if I ran."

THE WOMAN CLUTCHING at her face said her name was Rose Ledbetter. She, like Remi, the pedestrian named Sam who was holding her, and the patrons of Claire's Café, had no idea why the man had jumped out of the car to attack her and then run off. One second she had been on her way down the sidewalk and the next she'd been pistol-whipped by a stranger.

"Pistol-whipped?" Remi asked, fear flowing out of her words before her body could feel it. "He had a gun?"

Rose nodded, whimpering along with the movement. She sat at the table Remi and Declan had been sharing while the rest of the patrons crowded around. Claire was behind the counter, on the phone with the sheriff's department.

"I only saw it after he'd already hit me with it," Rose said. "I—I thought he would shoot me, but he ran instead."

"And Declan chased him."

Chased the man with the gun, she wanted to add but didn't.

Declan was the sheriff. Dealing with bad guys who had guns wasn't new to him. However, the fear uncoiling in Remi's chest was.

Declan wasn't just a boy she'd had a crush on as a girl or kissed once as a teenager. He wasn't just a man she'd shared a bed with after getting reacquainted. He also wasn't just a man who made her question if she wanted to be more than the friends they used to be.

No.

Now, and forever, he'd be the father of her kid.

No matter if they became enemies, lovers or any variation in between.

Declan Nash had cemented his place in her life the moment she'd seen the first positive pregnancy test.

And now?

Now he'd chased a man with a gun.

Normal or not, that made Remi afraid.

A feeling that must have translated into an expression she didn't have time to hide.

Sam, standing between them, looked her in the eye and was fierce with his words.

"The sheriff will be all right."

Remi gave him a small smile.

That smile died right after.

The door to the café opened with a bang. Remi already knew it wouldn't be Declan standing in the doorway, if only for the almost-violent movement, but she hoped all the same.

When she saw a man in a suit wearing a grin, a gun at his side, Remi couldn't help but suck in a breath. She wasn't alone. Everyone around her tensed.

No one spoke until the man walked farther inside. A woman in a matching pantsuit came in behind him and stopped just inside the doorway. She held her gun, aiming it at Claire.

"End the call, show me the screen, and then put it down on the counter," she ordered. Her accent was weirdly devoid of anything Remi could place. Not that it mattered. Claire was staring at a gun. She did as she was told and soon was standing with the rest of them.

The man stopped a few feet from their makeshift line next to the table. There were seven of them in total. Remi stood between Sam and Claire, Rose stayed sitting behind them.

"Don't worry, everyone," the man started. "We're not going to kill anyone as long as no one here does anything stupid."

Remi's adrenaline spiked. He didn't say anything about not *hurting* them.

"Now, let us get down to business and then we'll leave." He scanned their faces quickly, moving his head to the side to see Rose behind them. She whimpered at the eye contact.

Then he was staring at Remi.

He looked her up and down.

"Looks like you might be perfect for the job," he said conversationally.

Remi's heart was hammering in her chest.

The job? she wanted to ask. Instead, all she could do was remember to breathe as he moved directly in front of her and started to pull his gun from its holster.

"Wait a second," Sam jumped in. The man in the suit held the gun but didn't aim it. He addressed Sam but raised his voice for the crowd.

"Anyone moves and you'll make me a liar," he interrupted. "I'll end up killing you all. We good?"

Sam was tense but didn't say a word. No one did. Not even Rose's whimpers could be heard. That went double for moving.

Remi didn't want to break the only rule they'd been given, but the moment he took a step away from them and moved the gun so it was aimed at her, she had no choice.

"I'm pregnant."

The words left her mouth on a trembling plea.

Surprisingly, it seemed to have an impact. The man in the suit glanced back at his partner then to Remi.

"You're not the first person to try and lie about that."

"I have pictures on my phone," she hurried. "Of the tests. It's on the table."

There was a moment where Remi was sure trying to save herself had done the opposite. That she'd been pregnant for such a short amount of time and had already made a wrong choice as a parent. That Declan was about to suffer from another senseless act.

Yet the man sighed.

"Well, that's more trouble than it's worth," he said. He started to lower the gun. Remi felt a part of her unclench. Then the man in the suit turned to Sam. "Which I suppose means bad luck for you."

When he raised his gun and shot, Remi didn't even have time to scream.

THE SOUND OF the gunshot carried down Main Street, around the corner and right into Declan's bones. He was running before the construction workers could utter a word after him. Declan didn't care that he was leaving the man in the suit with civilians.

He had the man's gun.

What he didn't have was eyes on Remi.

Declan cursed into the wind he was creating as he ran full tilt back to the café. The gun in his hand was partially covered in cement, but he could wield it like a club if he had to. Or he'd use his bare hands.

Anything to protect the patrons he'd left behind.

Anything to protect Remi.

The ferocity of that desire should have surprised him, but he didn't have the time to dwell. Sirens started to go off in the distance, and right outside the café a car screeched to a stop. A woman ran out of the café, a man behind her.

"Stop," Declan yelled, still too far away. Pedestrians and bystanders were dotting the openings of stores and buildings along the thoroughfare, or else Declan would have tried out his new gun.

As it was, he watched as the woman ducked into the passenger side of the car and a man in a suit jumped into the back. Neither one paid attention to him; neither did the driver. Declan couldn't make out who it was as they sped off and hung a left up toward the street that ran in front of the community parking lot.

Declan looked at their license plate.

Then his focus shifted to the café.

For the first time in his career, he hesitated. With his hand on the handle of the door, he imagined the worst.

In that moment Remi was both safe and not safe. All at the same time. Just as their unborn child was unharmed and *not*. Going inside would confirm one truth. Staying outside gave him the option of keeping hope even if there was none inside.

So, for the briefest of moments, Declan hesitated.

Just as quickly he remembered that a person couldn't live in a moment. They could treasure it. They could fear it, hate it, wish to never remember it, but *staying* in a moment wasn't realistic.

It wasn't fair.

It wasn't possible.

Declan pushed open the door and saw the blood first. Then he saw her.

Chapter Nine

The last time Remi had been in the hospital she was sixteen and, oddly enough, Declan Nash had been within earshot. At the time he'd been with his brothers, Caleb and Desmond, while she had been with their friend Molly.

They'd been placed in a room outside of the ER unit because, as Remi's father said, Declan was a wild, dangerous boy. That same wild, dangerous boy had saved the day from the stupid yet fun game of Keep Away with a bag of chocolate-covered peanuts during their hike along the mountain. A hike they had gone on after skipping school.

Remi remembered it fondly, at least the part before they'd taken the game too seriously. Caleb had thrown the package of candy to Molly, and Molly and Remi had taken it too close to a sloped edge that had more tilt than either of them realized. Remi had lost her footing first, but Molly had let out a scream before either girl started their slide down the leaf-covered incline.

In hindsight Remi realized that scream was probably why Caleb had run the way he did after them, spurred on by memories of what had happened to him, Desmond and Madi when they were younger. At the time Remi had barely hit the even ground with a groan before Caleb had lost his footing, too, and was tumbling down to meet them.

Remi remembered being terrified that she'd hurt herself

enough to go to the hospital. That her father would add another notch to the post of reasons he disliked the Nash children. Yet, she'd been fine. A little bruised but no visibly broken bones or radiating pain. Though when Declan had made his way to her, he'd made her question herself. The concern in his eyes, the searching touch as his hands had seemingly been trying to find and fix whatever was hurt, and the warmth in his voice as he'd kept calm, had caused sixteen-year-old Remi to hope there was something that would keep Declan's careful attention on her.

That want had disappeared, however, when Molly and Caleb hadn't stopped their cries and grunts of pain after they were back on even ground. The walk to their vehicles had been spent trying to lay out all of their options, though they'd ultimately chosen to go with the only one that made sense.

Molly had broken her arm, Caleb had twisted his ankle, and Remi had caught lava-hot heat from her father for skipping school with her friend and a bunch of boys, Declan the Wild King among them.

Now Remi was in another room, Sam's, just off the ER in Overlook, this time older. Maybe not wiser, but with enough years between then and now to feel the full terror of a situation that could have been much worse.

When the door opened behind her, Remi didn't have time to hide the swirl of emotions starting to make her feel sick.

It was another moment of déjà vu. Declan came in, sheriff's badge on his belt and cowboy hat firmly on his head, and stopped at her side. He looked at the hospital bed and spoke to her with a lowered voice.

"I'm going to cut to the chase and tell you it's not your fault," he said. "You watching him sleep off his pain meds isn't going to do anything other than feed that guilt fire I know you've been stoking for the last two hours."

"And me pretending he didn't take a bullet that was probably meant for me isn't going to make me walk around this hospital with any pep in my step." Her words were more harsh than she'd meant them. Still, she didn't take them back.

Declan's face went a bit stony.

"All you did was tell that man you were pregnant. *He's* the one who shot Sam. Not you. I'd like to see anyone else in your shoes do anything differently." Declan motioned to Sam on the bed. He was asleep, his biceps bandaged. The damage hadn't been that bad, but Sam was a local and his friend had been the attending nurse. Remi imagined that had played into the swiftness of the pain meds he'd been given, despite his injury not being severe. It was more of a graze than anything, they'd been told. "Sam didn't blame you for what happened. No reason to blame yourself. Okay?"

Remi sighed and nodded. She followed him back out into the hallway.

Since Declan had come through the café's doors they hadn't been alone. Now, though, Remi didn't know what to say or how to act.

Seeing Declan, after he'd chased Rose's attacker, come back into the café unhurt had been a relief unlike any other. That relief seemed to be reflected in him, though Remi couldn't know how much. Chaos had erupted around them. Only now was it calming down.

Remi didn't know how to handle it so she stuck with the questions that had been piling up since the man and woman in the suits had left.

"I heard the man you chased got away?" she started

in, following along with Declan as he led them down the hallway.

His body tensed. He nodded.

"After the two at the café left they hightailed it around the block and made the men holding him let go." He swore and made no looks of apology for it. "My guess was he was only meant to get me away from Claire's so the other two could go in without meeting me and my gun."

"But why? What was the point of all of that? It seems a lot of trouble to go through for not trying to steal from us or kidnap anyone."

If it was possible, Declan tensed more.

"They were making a statement."

Remi felt her eyebrow rise in question. Declan seemed to catch himself. He shook his head slightly and stopped.

"I'll tell you more later when I know more. For now I need to talk to Rose and then go back to the scene. I can get a deputy to take you home, but I thought you might like some company." He rapped his knuckles against the closed door next to them. "Since this town talks so much I figured you might want to get on top of the news." Now he looked apologetic. "And if not, I'm sorry."

Remi had a sudden fear of whoever was on the other side of the door, but it vanished as soon as it opened. Jonah gave a nod to Declan and then surprised her with a tight embrace.

"I ran into Declan in the lobby when I was at the vending machine," he said into her hair. "He told me to wait here since it was so hectic with everyone trying to get what happened straight."

Jonah pulled back and looked her up and down.

"Rusty called me and said he saw you coming out of the café with a woman who was all bloody. Are you okay?"

Remi nodded.

This was why Declan had already apologized. He must have known she wouldn't have told her family about what had happened if she could avoid it. Instead, apparently, the news was already traveling. It was best she get on top of it, starting with the closest relation to her.

She met Declan's eye. His expression was pinched. He was already getting lost in his own thoughts.

"I'll stay here, if that's okay," she said to him. Then she said to her brother, "If that's okay with you."

"I wasn't going to let you leave without telling me what's going on."

"Then this is where I'll leave you," Declan decided. He seemed to want to say more but stopped himself.

"Call me later?"

He nodded. It was a rigid movement.

Then he was gone.

Remi sighed and faced her brother. Then she realized why Jonah was there in the first place. Peeking around his shoulder she saw the covered legs of someone lying down in the bed in the center of the room.

"Is that Lydia?" she whispered.

"Yeah, she's asleep now, though. They just gave her something for the pain. She asked me not to leave her since she doesn't have anyone else in town." He smiled a little. Lydia must have left quite the impression on him.

Jonah motioned her farther inside the room and over to a couch next to the bed. Remi cringed as she saw the bandages over most of Lydia's face.

"It looks a lot worse than it is, I think," he said at her side. "But we can talk in here. I've been watching TV and it didn't bother her."

Remi settled into the seat next to him. Like being alone with Declan for the first time since everything had happened at Claire's, Remi was at a loss of what exactly to say to her brother. She loved him, she knew that, but there was more of a disconnect between them than there ever was one of understanding.

The Hudsons weren't the Nashes.

Tragedy hadn't tightly fused an already tightly fused family.

There was no triplet connection that created a unique bond between them.

There wasn't a sense of protectiveness that was forged from being in the public eye and at the center of rumors for years.

There was just a family of people who didn't understand the others' choices in life.

Which was why she became a coward when recounting what had happened at the café. Remi hesitated without an ounce of grace when she got to the reason the man in the suit had shot Sam instead of her.

She could have lied.

She could have omitted that part altogether.

She'd been caught between loving her brother and worrying at his reaction to the news that he'd be an uncle.

He wasn't an idiot. He knew something was off.

"What aren't you saying, Remi? Tell me."

She felt like sighing and then realized how much she'd been doing that lately. Acting defeated or frustrated when, given everything that had happened, she had made it out unscathed. Lucky.

Plus, she figured she'd have to tell her family at some point. Why not now?

"The reason the man in the suit shot Sam and not me was because I told him something that changed his mind." Jonah gave her a questioning look. Remi put her hand on her stomach as she finished. "I told him I was pregnant."

Jonah's eyes widened. They trailed to her stomach and then back up to her gaze.

"And was that true or were you lying?"

"It's true."

Suspicion was quick to line his expression.

"Why didn't you tell us then?"

This time Remi did sigh.

"I wanted the father to be the first to know. I told him yesterday. We were supposed to talk about it today at the café when everything happened."

Jonah had never been considered book smart—he'd rather be outside than studying—but he was well versed in common sense. Remi watched as he connected the dots from the little information he had.

When he spoke his voice rose an octave.

"Declan Nash is the father." It wasn't a question. "When you gave him a ride back to Overlook…" He shook his head. "*That's* why he came to the house personally today instead of sending his brother or a deputy. He wanted to talk to you."

Remi nodded.

"No one else knows. Well, no one else *knew*. I was going to tell you and Josh and Dad after Christmas."

"After?" A look akin to hurt passed over his face. It pushed guilt and anger to the surface for Remi.

"I figured if I told you all right before I left I wouldn't have to hear everyone complaining that long." Jonah opened his mouth to, she guessed, protest. She cut him off. "Dad hasn't liked the Nashes for a long time. He's disliked Declan, specifically, for longer. Throw in the fact that the three of you love to tell me with every other breath that I'm dishonoring my family by 'abandoning' Heartland, I thought that hiding an unexpected, out-of-matrimony pregnancy until I had an escape was a smart, sane move to make. Don't you think?"

Jonah again looked like he wanted to object but then stopped himself. He let out a long breath and nodded.

"We're not the easiest people to talk with, huh?" He gave her a small smile. Remi snorted.

"Not unless we're talking horses."

Jonah gave an identical snort. Then his expression softened.

"And how do *you* feel about being pregnant with Declan's kid?"

Remi was honest.

"Nervous, terrified and weirdly excited."

"So… I'm allowed to be excited, too, right?" he asked.

"Right."

Jonah smiled.

"You know, I've always wanted to be an uncle."

Remi couldn't deny hearing him say that was a relief. It was a feeling that relaxed the part of her that had been tense since finding out she was pregnant.

However, with one glance at Lydia, bandaged and still in the nearby bed, Remi slid fully back into her worries.

Why had the man and woman in the suits attacked Sam?

Why had the other man attacked Rose?

And when was the next attack going to happen?

THE ONLY REASON Declan went back to the hospital that night was because he knew Remi was there.

He'd spent the last several hours putting out fires their suited attackers had created. There was no keeping their brazen attacks against Rose and Sam under wraps as they'd somewhat been able to do with Cooper Mann's attack on Lydia.

And even that news hadn't been out of the spotlight for

long. Declan had gone to the press conference set up for what had happened with Lydia as planned and then had to add a vague recount of that morning's chase and attacks. The news editor Claire had warned him about, Kellyn, stood on the front lines with a recorder in her hand and hungry excitement in her eyes.

For once, Declan couldn't blame her or any of the others in attendance.

If Declan hadn't been used to chaos, he would have been overwhelmed.

The note in the wall.

An attempted kidnapping.

The reappearance of a man in a suit.

Three culprits getting away.

Remi Hudson pregnant with his child.

Declan didn't count the last point as a bad one, though he couldn't deny it was heavier than the rest.

Almost as heavy as the exhaustion weighing him down as he made his way to the hospital from the department. He'd called Remi when there was nothing more he could do for the night. When she said she'd brought dinner for her brother and Lydia, Declan had changed course without a second thought.

And when she came out to the lobby to meet him, Declan did something else without a second thought.

He relaxed. If only a little.

"You okay?" he said in greeting. She didn't look tired, but she did look annoyed.

"Well, I thought I was hungry, and then I smelled the chicken I brought Jonah and it made me gag," she said in one hurried breath. "And *now* all I can think about is Pop-Tarts." Her eyes swept over him. Her pink lips turned into a line of concern. "But I shouldn't complain. How are you?"

Declan opened his mouth, fully intending to lie, and then found that the idea didn't sit well with him. Not to Remi.

So he didn't.

"I'm dog-tired." It was a simple answer and a simple truth. "I haven't gotten much sleep lately."

The corner of Remi's lips turned up into a grin. She reached her hand out, palm facing upward. Declan felt his eyebrow rise in question.

"Then you're in luck. It sounds like you need a trusted friend and confidante to take the lead for a little bit. Give me your keys and I'll drive Fiona and you back to the ranch. All the while I can regale you with some of my most harrowing accounting stories, guaranteed to help you fall into a deep, relaxing sleep." When Declan didn't immediately agree, Remi pressed on. There was an edge to her voice. "You might not be the same boy I remember on some fronts, but your stubbornness seems to be intact. Then again, so is mine. You *look* exhausted and need some sleep. I'm fine and know how to get you home. Let me."

"What about your car?" he tried.

She rolled her eyes.

"I trust it'll be just fine in the parking lot, but I'll let Jonah know so he can check on it when he leaves. Okay?"

Declan relented. He dug out his keys and dropped them onto her palm.

"Good sheriff," she said with a smile. "Now, let's go home."

She took his elbow and turned him toward the door. Through the weight of exhaustion, the best Declan could tell, Remi didn't realize what she'd said.

Her gaze remained ahead, and there was no blush in her cheeks, no hesitation in her steps.

An off-the-cuff comment that didn't mean anything past a friend taking another home.

Yet those three words had packed quite the blow.

Let's go home.

It was right then that Declan realized something. Something big. Something life changing.

But something he wasn't going to think about just yet. Not when the men in the suits were out there.

Chapter Ten

Declan Nash lived in a simple house furnished with simple things. Remi walked into the entry and slowly turned in a circle to take in the open floor plan. The living room was to the left, the kitchen was straight ahead, and an open archway to the right showed a small office. The door off the living room must have led to the bedroom. Declan moved to it while waving her toward the kitchen.

She'd spent most of the car ride to the Nash Family Ranch complaining about being hungry, complaining about not being able to drink more than a cup of coffee and then complaining about how cold it was getting.

Remi didn't know if it was pregnancy hormones making her grumpy or if she was looking for safe topics to talk about. Nothing that brought their future with a child into account. Nothing about the uptick in Overlook's bad-guy population. Nothing about any notes in the wall.

Just the two of them going down a dark road, her complaining about nothing in particular and him nodding along.

It was nice in a way.

Comfortable.

But now they weren't on the road.

Remi accepted his hospitality by raiding his pantry with a squeal.

"You okay?" Declan called out from the open bedroom door.

"You have Pop-Tarts," she yelled back, mouth already watering.

Declan didn't respond, and Remi settled at the small four-chair dining table set up between the kitchen and the living room couch. She was already through half of her pastry when Declan reemerged.

It was a struggle to keep her jaw from hitting the tabletop.

Remi had seen Declan naked. That was how she came to be sitting at his table, scarfing down Pop-Tarts and knowing in less than ten minutes she'd have to go pee. Again. She knew that the boy she'd grown up around had developed a firm chest and stomach and all the lines that muscles had carved in between. He even had the V that some actors and models sported in the movies and magazines. The one that led the eyes from the stomach and right down into the imagination.

She'd run her fingers along one of those very same lines, marveling that she had found herself in the situation where that touch was wanted.

After that Remi hadn't had to imagine where those lines led.

So when her lust for the sheriff went from a passive five out of ten to a red-hot, volcanic two thousand in the span of him walking through the doorway to dropping down onto the couch cushion, Remi had to double-check the scene.

Declan wasn't naked, first of all.

In fact, he'd merely swapped out his button-down and pants for a plain tee and sleep pants.

But, boy oh boy, was he wearing them.

The shirt hugged his muscled frame while the pants

hung lower and a bit baggier than his jeans. It was such a casual outfit, and yet somehow sexier.

It was a glimpse into Declan behind the scenes.

A place where he could just be.

It spoke of vulnerability and it spoke right to Remi's hormones, apparently.

"I couldn't remember if I had them or not," Declan said from his spot on the couch. He leaned back, put his feet up on the coffee table and met her eyes with a smile. If she looked like an idiot, he didn't say it. Even when she scrambled to look normal while finishing her bite of Pop-Tart. "I babysat Riley's nephew the other week and that boy was all about some frosted strawberry. I didn't really think about it until we were in the car."

Remi held up the uneaten portion in a salute.

"Well, I thank you for it."

Declan seemed satisfied that she was satisfied and leaned his head back, put his arms over his chest and closed his eyes.

"I'm sorry I'm so tired," he said after a yawn. "Sometimes I forget that I need to recharge, even though I tell Caleb and my deputies to do it all the time." His eyes opened again, but there was a lag to the movement. He didn't move his head as two grass-green eyes found hers.

Remi put her food down. She felt a tug at her heart-strings. Declan Nash might not be a great talker, but when he did speak he managed to put a whole lot into what he said. Simple statements, yet with so much depth they were nearly overwhelming for Remi to hear, especially when she thought of the always-smiling and mischievous boy she'd once kissed on a dare beneath the moon and stars when she was nothing more than a quiet girl.

The time after they'd parted ways had been kind to him

in some respects, but Remi believed it had also run him down in others.

And then he said as much to her utter surprise.

"My dad always used to say that even though there's never enough time to do everything you want to do, there's always time to do at least one thing. Just make that one thing count." He let out a small breath and domed his fingers over his lap. Remi realized she was hanging on his every word. "I didn't think I had a *one thing* for years until I met Bobby Teague."

The name rang a bell.

"The mayor when we were teens?"

Declan shook his head.

"His son," he replied. "Not the nicest man, not the most patient, either. I didn't like him, just like his dad hadn't liked mine back in the day. They were men who wanted attention and became annoyed when they actually got it. A son who became an even grumpier version of his father. And then a pain in my backside. Then one day Bobby Teague came into the department with nothing but fear in him. His sister had gone on a date and hadn't returned to her house." Declan sat up a little. The frown of remembering settled into his lips as he took a moment. "It hadn't been twenty-four hours yet so we couldn't count it as a missing person but, well, after what happened to the triplets, the rules for missing persons in Wildman County are a bit different. I wasn't waiting around hoping that his sister was fine and was just lost in a new love bubble. And Bobby refused to be sidelined. So, he rode with me as we went all over town looking for her."

Remi saw the subtle shift in the man, though she couldn't place the emotion behind it.

"It took us a bit to track down where her date lived, but when we did everything changed between me and Bobby.

His digs at me and my family, his sarcasm and ego getting into every word he said, it just all went away the moment we got to the end of that driveway. One second we were two people who didn't much like each other. Nothing in common. No love lost at all between us. And in the next, we were two people who wanted nothing more than for Lori Teague to be okay and would do anything to see that happen."

His words were tired and the rest of what he wanted to say seemed to stall out. Remi hated to prod the man, but she wanted to know what had happened.

"Was she there? At the date's house?"

"She was and she was fine, too," he said with a small smile. "Her phone had died so she hadn't gotten any of the calls and then she lost track of time…doing what happens with some dates, if you catch my drift."

"I do."

"It was a good call. One that could have turned out much worse. Weirdly enough, *that* was when I realized what it was that I wanted to be my *one* thing." Remi leaned in as Declan's expression hardened, resolute. "Making sure people like Bobby Teague didn't have to spend their lives worrying. Instead, they could sigh in relief or, ideally, never have the need." Declan shrugged. "So I threw everything I had into my career, to Overlook, to the county. I woke up worrying about everyone and went to bed wondering how I could make their lives better."

A vulnerability that Remi hadn't been prepared for took over the sheriff. Not only did it pull at her heartstrings, it made something else within her stir.

"When you told me you were pregnant, I didn't act the way I should have. Running off to work, losing track of time and not calling, and then pulling you back into trouble… I should have said, and done, more. It's just… Well,

I think I've been so focused on what everyone else wants and needs for so long that, along the way, I forgot to wonder what it is I want."

Every part of Remi went on alert. She could have sworn if a pin had dropped in between his earlier words, she could have heard it as easily as if a bowling ball had been dropped onto the hardwood.

"And what do you want?" she chanced.

The father of her unborn child smiled.

"I know I want to be a part of my kid's life, from now until I'm old, gray, and then in the grave. Everything else? Well, I'm just too tired to think about any of that right now." His mood darkened. He didn't need to say it but Remi knew his thoughts had found their way back to Cooper Mann and then the attack and chase at Claire's.

It was the only reason she didn't push him for more.

And the only reason she didn't give any of what she wanted to say back.

Instead, Remi tried to be reassuring.

"No one has their entire life planned out. You'll have plenty of time to figure out what's next for you. Until then, why don't you go get some sleep."

Declan snorted. He kicked his feet up and swung his legs over onto the couch. Then he slid down against the cushions with a sigh. It reminded Remi of when she slid into a much-needed warm bubble bath.

"I'm good right here," he said, his eyes closing. "Feel free to eat whatever else you want. There's a spare toothbrush in the cabinet over the sink and some more pj's in the dresser."

That surprised Remi.

"You want me to stay?"

He nodded, eyes still closed. Then he yawned.

"I can't make you but I'd feel better if you were close.

Last time I—" He yawned again. This one was deeper, longer, too. The man was dancing near the edge of sleep, there was no denying it. "Last time I left you all hell broke loose. Not gonna happen again. Bed's yours."

Remi smiled into her Pop-Tart. Then she remembered something she needed to tell the man before sleep claimed him.

"Hey, Declan. I told Jonah about the baby in the hospital today."

Declan opened his eyes.

"Did you tell him I'm the father?"

"I did."

Declan surprised her with a nod and a simple response. "Good."

Remi smiled. Declan returned it. Then his eyes closed and, just like that, Declan quieted. By the time Remi had finished her Pop-Tarts the man was sound asleep.

THE HOUSE WAS different in winter.

The heater made it smell like something was burning sometimes. Not like an all-out fire or anything but more of a lingering firepit smell that always reminded Declan of the day after a bonfire had burned out. That smell, rare since Declan hardly ever turned the heater on in the house, combined with the lack of noise he was used to surrounding the ranch, sometimes disoriented him when he first woke up. It didn't matter that he'd had just as many years knowing winter in Overlook as he'd known summer. There was just something about the cold outside that threw off his internal navigation and understandings.

Like when he opened his eyes to the darkness, smelled something burning and heard something he wasn't used to hearing.

Declan sat up so quickly he nearly pulled a muscle.

It was dark in his immediate area, but on the other side of the room there was a soft glow. That light was enough to show him a space he knew. It clicked in place with the smell of the heater and the feel of the couch beneath him.

And the old wool blanket he was particularly fond of that he'd thrown to the ground in half-asleep earnestness.

He rubbed at his eyes and then worked at blinking away the haze of sleep. Wondering what had wakened him, he turned toward a window. Through the open slats of the blinds he could just make out another glow, though this one wasn't as focused.

It was dawn, and Declan bet that routine had been the thing that had wakened him. He'd never quite shaken waking up early on the ranch as a kid, especially when school was out. As the oldest child he'd had the most to do. Now he normally used the time to go on a run or drink coffee and worry.

He snorted in the dark.

I sure am exciting, he thought ruefully.

His gaze returned to the soft glow nearest him. The one that he knew came from his bedside lamp in the bedroom. Moving slowly, careful to be quiet, Declan got up, went to the open doorway and looked inside.

Dark blond hair was splayed across a navy pillowcase while the covers he hadn't gotten beneath in days housed a woman wearing his clothes.

Remi.

She'd stayed.

Her face, slack with sleep, was turned toward Declan, as beautiful as when she was awake.

And what do you want?

Declan hadn't meant to come clean with what he was feeling the night before. He hadn't meant to admit he'd had tunnel vision with his job the last several years. Just as he hadn't meant to say that her news had finally made him confront the fact that he'd forgotten about himself in the grand scheme of things.

He'd honestly just been tired as hell and ready to fall asleep so he could start fresh in the morning. Yet, when he'd seen Remi sitting at the dining table eating a pack of Pop-Tarts of all things, Declan hadn't been able to stop himself. He'd seen the woman just as he'd seen the girl who had once been his friend.

He'd felt comfortable. So, he'd opened up.

What he *had* meant to say was his realization that, no matter what his future held, he knew without a doubt he wanted it to include their child. It was just a declaration he'd hoped to make in better circumstances, not in his sleep pants after a majorly crappy day.

Also, not immediately before he'd fallen asleep.

But there she'd been and there he'd told her.

And now there she was, asleep in his bed.

It wasn't a new sight for Declan to see her asleep. One time he'd seen her drift off at a school assembly, bored out of her mind. Lon McKinnley had tried to pull her hair to wake her then, so Declan had thumped the boy on the head and dared him in silence to do it again.

What *was* new was how it felt to watch her do so.

The urge to join her was almost as strong as the urge to run a hand across her cheek and tuck behind her ear the strands of hair that had escaped. To feel the warmth of her skin. To feel the smoothness. To—

Adrenaline shot through Declan's bloodstream. It zipped his spine straight and had him retreating into the living room to look for his phone.

Shame, deep and biting, mingled with the new sense of urgency.

How had he not put together the pieces before?

How had he been so blind to not understand what was going on?

Declan cussed, low and with vehemence.

How had he not seen the pattern until now?

Rose hadn't been targeted, per se, but her face had.

Sam wasn't the plan, getting shot in the arm was.

Just like Madi and Caleb.

The day they had been abducted.

Chapter Eleven

"He's not going to figure it out," the woman whined. Her name was Candy and, unlike it, she was not at all sweet. She'd spent the entire car ride back complaining that she hadn't been the one to shoot the man or hit the woman or even put a gun to the other man's head.

Candy was what some professionals might call a sociopath. For him, he thought of her as nothing more than a nuisance.

"He'll put it together," he assured her. "He's smart."

She snorted.

"He sure didn't seem like a man who had put it together at the hospital. He just stood there and made puppy dog eyes at the pregnant chick from the café."

"Remi Hudson," he interjected.

Candy cocked her head to the side at that.

"Hudson? As in—"

He nodded, not needing her to finish the thought.

"The very same."

Candy, for once, looked slightly satiated. It never lasted. Her need to always be doing *something* was a big part of why she'd been chosen to join him.

She rarely shied away from what they needed to do.

"Well, while this has some potential to finally be interesting, it won't matter at all if our dear sheriff doesn't put any of the pieces together. Why leave bread crumbs if the idiot won't ever follow them?"

He sighed.

"He's dealing with a lot. Give the man a few beats. He'll get to where we need him."

Candy's eyebrow rose in thinly disguised disgust.

"You sound like you're fond of the eldest Nash. Then again, I've heard you have a soft spot for all of the Nash kids. Had several chances to take them out over the last few years and now look where we are. Here, waiting for a man to find breadcrumbs."

Unlike some of the men and women he surrounded himself with, *he* kept his cool, even if he would have liked nothing more than to tell the woman off. Point out her brazen attitude would only ever get her, and maybe him, killed. That she might have joined them two years ago, but she was nowhere near his level.

"It wasn't my job to kill them, just like it's not my job to kill Declan now," he said, keeping his voice as crisp as the chill outside of the building above them. "I come up with plans and I follow plans. *That's* how I serve this organization and *that's* how I stay off the radar and alive."

"Whisperer."

He snorted at the moniker he'd been given by the men and women within their group. One that hadn't yet made it to any law enforcement ears.

"There's something to be said about the power of suggestion." He lost all humor. "Just like there's something to be said about the Nash family." He leaned across the table enough to focus her attention. Candy lost her humor, too. She might have been insolent nine times out of ten, but for that one time she knew when to bite her tongue and listen. "In the last few years people, for whatever reasons, have taken their cracks at them. Threatened them, attacked them, tried to hurt them and the people they loved. Now, answer me this…" He ran a thumb across the raised skin on his hand, a scar he'd had for years. "Who's still standing? The people who went after the Nashes or the Nashes themselves?"

Candy didn't answer.

She didn't have to because they knew exactly who had come out on top in those encounters.

"Respecting the enemy means you don't underestimate them," he added. "A lesson you might want to learn."

Candy opened her mouth, but approaching footsteps kept the words back. The man who filled the doorway next demanded quick respect with his silence.

Even more with the pointed stare. He addressed Candy, who tried her best to look as if she wasn't afraid of him.

"Go tell Hawthorne to shut up about today. You two keep bragging like you've done something a child couldn't easily do. Go."

Candy didn't sneer or back talk him or try to be clever. She fled the room like her life depended on it.

And maybe it did.

Depending on his mood, their boss could be a very *difficult* person to be around.

Still, when it came to the boss he wasn't like Candy. His fear of the boss was surrounded by a thin protective layer that had been built over time.

They had something in common.

Something none of the others had.

That didn't stop him from being worried that the boss was standing in front of him.

"I heard about yesterday. You did a good job." He came closer but didn't sit down. "I also heard that you didn't use Miss Hudson because she said she was pregnant."

"It was a complication I wanted to avoid. Once she said

it out loud, it didn't matter if she was pregnant or not, that kind of news might have inspired someone else in the café to be a hero. I didn't have the time for it."

The boss nodded.

"I would have made the same call. No sense in muddling the message with unnecessary drama. But, as it turns out, she *is* pregnant." His expression transformed into something he hadn't seen in a long, long time. Glee. "With Declan Nash's child."

"You've got to be kidding me."

He shook his head with a little laugh.

"She told her brother in the hospital after yesterday's events."

For a moment the two marveled at the news. Then the boss slowly hardened back into the determination that had been driving him for over two decades.

"Using Declan was always a risk. Miss Hudson has taken that risk out entirely. We get her, we get him. The other Nashes will follow, trying to save the day." He moved back to the doorway, his mind no doubt already spinning a revision to his plan. Even though they'd gone over every variation there had been to it, every possible outcome, every contingency they could think of, the hair on the back of his neck stood on end when the boss got to the bottom line. The endgame. The only reason they were all there.

"Then we'll kill them all."

Chapter Twelve

Madi Nash had a thin scar across her cheekbone.

Caleb Nash had a scar across his upper arm from a bullet graze.

Desmond had a limp that would never fully heal.

Cooper Mann had none of the above. The only affliction he seemed to have was that he tended to be more nerves than anything else. Like right now, through the bars of a Wildman County cell. His eyes were wide and tired. He'd seen better days and it showed.

Instead of pleading his case, repeating over and over that he hadn't tried to take Lydia Cartwright, he simply watched Declan stop just outside of the bars. Even as Declan studied him, the young man remained quiet.

"Cooper, do you know what I did this morning before I got here?" Declan started. He didn't wait for Cooper to try to guess. "I went out to the impound lot and took a look at your car because something just isn't sitting right with me. You know what I found? An oddly clean car, leather seats that were well taken care of, and a CD player. I can appreciate you having one because I know that isn't the standard with newer cars, but I just have to question the CD that I found *in* it." Declan recalled the name from memory with a slight head tilt in question. "*How to Learn Spanish in Three Easy Steps*. It was on the third track of five and in the middle of a lesson. Were you listening to it before you got out of the car and saw Lydia?"

Cooper's eyes flitted from one side of the room to the other. He didn't move off the cot he'd been sitting on as he answered.

"Yeah, I was."

"Can I ask why?"

"Because I'm trying to learn Spanish," Cooper deadpanned. Declan almost laughed. He'd sure walked into that one.

"No. I mean, *why* are you trying to learn Spanish? Is it something you've been wanting to do for a while now or something you tried on a whim?" Cooper straightened. He crossed his arms over his chest, defensive. Declan sighed. "Cooper, I left a beautiful woman at my house and in my bed to go to the lot before hours to check your car and now I'm here. The case against you is already as damning as damning can be. Lydia Cartwright swears up and down that you are the man who attacked her. Answering me now, about a CD in your car, isn't going to do any more harm. Not answering will only make me grouchier than I already am."

Cooper seemed to weigh his options.

"A beautiful woman," he said. Declan thought he was repeating him and then realized it was an answer.

"A beautiful woman is why you're trying to learn Spanish?"

Cooper nodded.

"Her name is Inez. She works at Waypoint as one of the bartenders." He sighed deeply. It deflated him. "It was love at first sight for me. Dark hair, dark eyes, and this laugh thing she does when she's brushing drunk guys off. Most beautiful woman I ever saw."

"Have you asked her out?" Declan prodded when the man trailed off.

"Yeah," Cooper exclaimed with sudden vigor. "I sure did! And do you know what she said? 'Ask me in Spanish and then we'll talk.' Can you believe that?" Even though his voice was raised in frustration, it was clear he wasn't angry at the bartender. In fact, when he spoke again it was akin to being impressed. "Nothing worth having is ever easy, though, is it? I ordered the CD since I like driving around a lot. Was hoping to go back this coming weekend and show off but…" Cooper's face fell. Any and all feeling he'd had went with it. He didn't bother finishing his thought.

Sympathy started to sprout in Declan's chest. A seed that had always been there, watered by Cooper's story.

One that was growing now.

"Cooper Mann, come over here and look me in the eye," he barked, a little more forcefully than he meant.

But it did the trick.

Cooper hopped up and came to the bars. Through them he met Declan's stare.

"Why would you try to kidnap Lydia Cartwright if you were so worried about learning Spanish to ask out the most beautiful woman in the world this weekend?"

Cooper might have been nervous and he might have been scared, but he answered with a steady voice.

"I wouldn't."

And, by God, if Declan didn't believe him.

THERE WAS A package of Pop-Tarts on the kitchen counter with a sticky note stuck to it. Declan said he was sorry for leaving, but he'd gotten her car to his house and he'd call her later.

Remi was both let down and touched.

She changed back into her clothes, pocketed the pastries and decided it was time to go to Heartland.

While Jonah had promised to keep the pregnancy under wraps until she told Josh and their father, she remembered how bad Jonah had been at keeping secrets when they were younger. He had too much honor when it came to their father. He snitched quicker than Josh could gallop between the stables and Heartland's outer fence.

Which was pretty damn quick.

Remi still hadn't completely forgiven him for blabbing about the belly button piercing she'd gotten with her friend Molly in high school.

That fallout had lasted a good while.

At least now she couldn't be grounded.

There were clouds in the sky and the air was cold. Remi pulled up beside Josh's truck and could see her father's and Jonah's off to the side of the house. She decided dawdling wasn't going to make anything easier.

She took a deep breath, pushed out into the cold, and didn't make it two steps into the house before Jonah appeared.

"I told him you stayed at Molly's," he hurried in greeting. "I didn't know how you wanted to handle everything with the, you know, so I kind of panicked."

Despite her earlier annoyance, Remi laughed.

"Afraid he'll find out I was bunking with Declan?" she asked, lowering her voice. "Do you think he'd be worried I'd, I don't know, gotten pregnant?"

She gave him a look that showed she was teasing.

Jonah rolled his eyes but smiled.

"Listen, I'm just trying to keep the peace before you break it. Can't blame a guy for trying."

Remi started up the stairs.

"I blame whoever I want for whatever I want," she said, grinning. "Don't you forget that, Jonah Bruce."

Remi bounded up the stairs to the sound of Jonah being annoyed and locked herself in her room. One thing that had been a surprise for her about pregnancy so far was how energetic she was during some parts of the day. Like now she felt as if she'd already had an entire cup of coffee on top of eight hours of sound sleep. She knew these moments didn't always stick. Exhaustion and fatigue were always waiting around the corner, ready to strike. That had been her mother's only major symptom when she'd been pregnant. Remi hoped it would be the same for her going forward.

Then again, she wasn't holding her breath for that.

Remi took her prenatal vitamins, ate the Pop-Tarts on her bed and then went to take a nice, long shower. Her mind wandered to days when she was younger and her biggest concern was trying to keep her grades up and then right over to seeing the man in the suit shoot Sam.

She left the shower in a less good mood than when she'd gotten in.

Jonah and Josh were in the living room. One was reading, the other on his laptop.

"It's a rare sight to see you two inside," she noted. Jonah snorted. Josh was more direct. He always was, despite being the youngest. He had more of their mother in him than the rest of them.

"Until we get the ranch back to how it was, there will be a lot more downtime than what you remembered from when you last called this place home," he said, close to sneering. It made Remi's adrenaline spike in a flash of anger.

"This is my home as much as it is yours. Just because I left doesn't mean I didn't grow up here, same as you."

Josh pushed his laptop onto the couch cushion next to him.

"And just because you're visiting for the holidays doesn't mean we've forgotten how happy you were to leave in the first place. And how often you *don't* visit when it's not the holidays."

Guilt stabbed Remi quickly in the chest. Her anger overcompensated. She dropped her voice low, seething.

"And how often will you visit after you've skipped town with your one true love?"

Josh looked like a deer in the headlights. When he recovered, his expression matched her mood. He turned it on Jonah.

"You told *her*?"

Jonah abandoned his book.

"That *her* is our sister," Jonah defended. "Wouldn't you rather me tell *her* than Dad?"

Josh didn't have to chew on that question long. But that didn't mean he was ready to roll over. He whipped his head around to her so fast Remi was surprised it didn't pop right off.

"If you tell Dad so help me—"

"So help you what?" Remi interrupted. "Are you threatening me, baby brother? What you and the other two Hudson men keep seeming to forget is that before *'my betrayal of house and home'* I got to see you grow up, too." She laughed. It was unkind. "I saw you try to fight Marlin Crosby. Operative word, *try*."

Josh's face changed to the color of her cherry bomb lipstick.

"Marlin Crosby cheated," he said, frustration at the humiliating fight ringing clear through every word. "He rushed me when I was talking to *you two*!"

Remi took several steps forward, putting her into the

same orbit as her brothers. Men might have been sitting a few feet from her, but all she saw were the little boys who used to annoy her to no end. Little boys playing at being adults while she had already graduated.

"He hit you from behind because you were too busy telling us, and everyone else watching, how you were going to beat him up. He didn't win because he cheated. He won because your mouth is bigger than your brain!"

That did it. That activated her younger brother like flipping a switch. He jumped up, face as red as ever, and she reacted by squaring her shoulders, ready to wrestle like they had done when they were kids.

"Whoa there!" Jonah was faster than either one of them. He put his body between them and hands out on Josh's chest.

Remi was ready to knock both of them silly, absolutely done with their talk of her abandoning her family because she had had the *audacity* to live her own life, but the sound of boots against hardwood silenced them all.

Gale Hudson filled the doorway between the living room and the kitchen. He must have come in through the back door and they hadn't heard him because, in hindsight, Remi realized they'd been yelling awfully loud.

"I can't ground you like I used to," their father started, voice always booming. "But I can sure enough make life harder for the lot of you if you don't stop your bellyaching. You hear me?"

All three Hudson children took a breath and relaxed their tensed muscles.

"Yes sir," they sang in a chorus.

Their father nodded, satisfied.

"Good. No one should be fighting this close to Christmas, if nothing else. What is it that your mom used to say about it?"

"Fighting on Christmas will only get you the present of shame," Jonah recalled. However, there was still some kick in Josh.

"She meant that about Christmas Day, not the rest of them."

"Well, then, I'm making an amendment," their father said. "No fighting during December."

This time it was Remi who decided to try her luck.

"Can I add 'no guilting your children for their life choices' to the list?"

"Remi," Jonah whispered in warning.

Their father, however, surprised them. He chuckled.

"Your mom used to say you reminded her of herself, but there's a lot of times I hear my stubbornness come out of your mouth." His expression softened. "Instead of you all yelling, why don't we make an early lunch and eat together? It's been a while."

And just like that all the tension left the room.

"Brunch," Remi said, following him into the kitchen.

"What?"

"It's called brunch. A meal between breakfast and lunch."

"Sounds like nonsense to me."

Remi laughed and soon the four of them were moving around the kitchen, preparing whatever food was in the fridge. It was nice. Their father started to complain about a horse they were boarding whose owner wouldn't stop calling him, while Josh pointed out that that was probably because she had a crush on him. Remi and Jonah were paired up to the side of the refrigerator and cringed at the news that someone had a crush on *their* dad when Josh slid a plated sandwich to her. It was and had been her favorite since she was a kid. A peace offering in the form of turkey, jalapeños, cheese and wheat bread.

Remi hesitated. Not because of the surprising offer but because she couldn't accept it. She didn't know a lot about pregnancy yet, but she did know she couldn't eat sandwich meat.

Jonah bumped her shoulder, a questioning look on his face.

She pointed to her stomach and shook her head.

He pointed to his plate. Leftover chicken potpie. *His* favorite.

Remi nodded.

If Jonah had accepted her pregnancy this fast, what was stopping her from giving the other two Hudson men the same chance to do the same?

Because old wounds don't heal just like that.

Remi might have gotten lucky with Jonah but that didn't guarantee it would be as easy with the others. So, she decided to keep stalling a little while longer. At least she could wait until she had a full stomach.

Her and Johan were in the middle of switching meals when an odd sound filled the house.

The doorbell.

For a moment they all looked at one another as if to say, *We're all here so who is using the bell?* Everyone who frequented the ranch knew to knock because their dad hated the bell.

Except for Declan. He had no idea.

"I'll get it," Remi said, hurrying past the boys before they could answer it. Remi's phone was in her back pocket. She brought it out to check to see if she had a missed call or text from the man.

She hadn't.

And it wasn't him at the door, either.

Remi opened the door wide as soon as she saw the angry tears and stitches across the woman's face.

"Lydia?"

The last time Remi had seen the woman was right before she and Declan had left the hospital. The doctors had said she was being discharged but probably not until that afternoon. Jonah had told her he'd pick her up from the hospital himself when that happened.

Now there she was on their doorstep, wearing a blouse with blood on it and jeans that had a tear. It must have been the same outfit she'd been wearing when she was attacked by Cooper Mann.

It was a jarring sight. Made even more so by the fact that the woman didn't seem bothered by any of it.

"Hi there, Remi," she greeted in return. "Do you think I could come inside?"

"Oh, yeah, of course." Remi might have been thrown off her game, but she hadn't lost her manners. She stepped aside, waving Lydia into their home.

"Jonah is in the kitchen," she said, already moving that way. Lydia shook her head.

"I'm not here for Jonah," she said.

"Oh?"

Lydia smiled.

It should have been a red flag.

It should have been a lot of things.

What it wasn't was enough to make Remi use the phone in her hand to call for help.

Instead she listened, intently, for the reason.

"I'm here for you."

Chapter Thirteen

Lydia struck out before Remi could move a muscle.

The hit landed against her chest, just below the collarbone. It hurt. Remi staggered backward from the force and surprise. She didn't have a chance to catch herself. Her backside hit the hardwood just as her periphery was filled with the bulk of her father and Jonah.

They hadn't seen the hit.

Remi heard her father say her name just as Jonah called out to Lydia. Neither had a chance to finish their thoughts or get answers in return.

Lydia pulled out a gun and aimed it at the men.

Remi reacted on reflex.

From her angle on the floor she couldn't do much, but she was close enough to do something. She brought her fist up and paid the woman in kind for the hit she'd been given. But Remi could only get as high as her stomach from where she was on the ground.

It did the job well enough.

A gunshot exploded inside the house, pushing pain through Remi's ears at the sound just as fear rang through her heart, but Lydia gasped for different reasons.

She hadn't counted on the hit to the stomach, just as Remi hadn't counted on the hit to the chest.

Lydia stumbled but didn't fall. She kept the gun but lost her aim.

Remi took advantage of the distraction. She pushed up off the ground and right into the woman. Lydia completely lost her footing this time. Like a rag doll, the woman fell back and out onto the front porch.

Then Remi did the only thing her adrenaline and slightly good sense would let her do.

She slammed the door shut and threw the dead bolt.

The sound of Lydia cursing became the soundtrack behind the next important, life-altering thing in Remi's world. She turned, heart in her throat, and hoped to every god there ever was that none of her family had been shot.

Her father was rushing over to her. Josh and Jonah watched wide-eyed from the doorway.

No one was bleeding, no one was on the ground.

It was a relief that didn't last long.

"Get away from there," her father grunted out, grabbing her wrist. Another explosion went off as Lydia shot through the door. It barely missed them as her father slung Remi around and pushed her to the stairs. Remi didn't hesitate in running up them, out of line of the door.

"Stay low, boys," he yelled over his shoulder.

Remi hit the landing as another gunshot went off. It was followed by two more. She spun on her heel, but her father pushed her farther onto the second floor.

"There's a gun in my room," he said. Remi would have marveled at how calm he was being if not for the directive he gave her as he pulled her along with him to the bedroom at the end of the hall. "Call for help, Remi. Do it now."

Remi went for her phone only to have her stomach drop. Just as she had done with her phone after being hit by Lydia.

"I—I don't have it." She heard it then. In her voice. A waver of terror, strengthened by adrenaline and confusion.

They ran into the master bedroom and made a U-turn to the closet.

"That's okay." He was using his soothing voice. The one she'd once heard when she'd accidentally cut her hand with a knife and needed stitches. He'd brought her nerves down simply by the cadence of his voice.

Whether or not he agreed with her leaving town, there was a comfort in knowing that, with just the sound of his voice, her father could make her feel better.

"What about the landline?" she asked, hopeful. It didn't last long.

"I took the cordless to the kitchen yesterday. Haven't put it back."

Remi doubled back to the bedroom door as her father opened his safe in the closet. He'd always been diligent about keeping all weapons locked up, even when his children had grown, but what he had in there Remi had no idea.

She watched the hallway and the top of the stairs with a twist in her gut. Her brothers hadn't attempted to go for the second floor. She hoped they had fled through the back door as soon as the shots kept coming and that one of them had called for help.

"The front door open yet?" her father asked, rushing back to her side.

They both paused.

The house around them was eerily silent.

Remi opened her mouth, ready to call for her brothers, but her father grabbed her wrist.

"Shh, keep quiet," he whispered. "We don't know if she's alone or not, and we don't want to let her know exactly where we are."

He had shut the bedroom door and locked it when two things happened at once.

First, she heard glass shatter downstairs. The living room windows maybe.

Then she felt a peculiar wetness against her arm.

"I need you to listen to me," her father said, but Remi stopped him when she realized what that wetness was.

"You're bleeding."

The last few shots hadn't missed them.

At least, not her father.

"I'm okay," he tried, pulling her again. The wetness grew against her arm. He stopped when they were in the en suite, and turned to shut and lock the door.

Remi turned her attention to his bullet wound.

"Dad."

There was no denying he'd been hit. His button-up was turning dark at the side of his stomach. He was trying— and failing—to keep his left forearm pressed against it.

"I'm okay," he repeated.

Remi was devastated to hear the waver in his voice this time.

Instead of fear, she heard pain.

He swung around and showed her something else she hadn't had the mind to notice yet. It was a revolver. He held it out to her. Remi took it with a sob stuck in her throat.

"Do you remember how to use that? No safety and no cocking it between shots. Just shoot. Understood?"

"I don't want to use it. I want *you* to use it."

He shook his head and moved to the window.

"If there's more than one of them and they come up here, I want you to use the lattice next to Josh's room to get down to the ground. Then, only if it's clear, make it to the stable. That's where you're all supposed to go if bad stuff happens in the house. Josh and Jonah will be there."

Remi watched, her heart nearly crushed with helplessness as the strongest man she knew fell against the wall and slid to the floor.

"Dad." It was all Remi could do not to yell. She knelt down in front of him, the hand not holding the revolver, trying helplessly to grab onto a part of him as if her touch alone could help heal him.

It did no such thing.

Dark eyes searched her face. His expression softened, but his words were stern. Harsh.

"That was a good move you made with that woman downstairs, but bullets count for more than courage. You can take on one person—don't try to take more if there are more. Promise me, Remi. You run if there's more than one person out there and use that thing to protect your brothers. Don't be afraid to shoot."

Then he gave her that look.

That look of unconditional love. The same one her mother gave them. The same one her grandmother had given her mother before she'd passed away.

The love of a parent for a child.

The same love Remi already felt for hers.

She nodded.

And then, in the simplest of terms, she told her father the news she should have already told him.

"I'm pregnant."

Gale Hudson took all of two seconds to respond.

"Shoot to kill, baby girl."

Remi wanted to say more, to *do* more, but an awful sound cut off any conversation.

Wood splintered. A thud sounded.

Then a man spoke. Followed by another.

"We know you're in there," he yelled.

It wasn't her brothers.

Which meant Lydia wasn't alone.

Which meant Remi was supposed to abandon her father.

The doorknob shook.

Her father touched her stomach. Blood transferred to her shirt, but he got his point across with it.

He was trying to protect her.

And it was her turn to do the same for her child.

Remi looked at her father one last time and then slid the window up. She was up and out of it within a breath. Her shoes hit the roof that hung over the wraparound porch. The backyard was, at a glance, empty. No one shot at her. No one yelled.

She ran.

Josh's room was at the corner of the house. Attached to the overhang outside of his window was a thick lattice their mother had built herself. She'd wanted it for decoration. Her children had used it to sneak out of the house.

Now her daughter was using it to escape.

Why was Lydia there for her?

Who were the men?

Were there more?

Remi didn't have any answers. She knew only that she didn't want to find them by letting Lydia get ahold of her or her brothers. Sibling protectiveness combined with maternal protectiveness drove Remi's hands and feet as she got to the edge of the roof outside of Josh's room and onto the top of the lattice.

She slipped twice as she tried to find footholds not completely covered in vines, then dropped the last two feet to the ground. Pain radiated up her shins but she didn't stop.

Hudson Heartland had several stables. Some were at the front of the acreage, others were tucked toward the back. The stable they had been taught to go to if there was ever a fire, break-in or other disaster in the main house was a

faded red barn a hundred yards or so from the back porch.
It had housed Heartland's personal horses and had never
been used by clients.

It also had a landline.

Remi ran full tilt toward it, knowing if anyone was on
the roof or in the bathroom looking out, they'd see her. If
anyone came after them they could just keep running until
they made it to the woods.

The Hudson children knew the ranch.

She doubted Lydia and whoever was with her could
claim the same.

At least, that was her hope as she struggled to breathe
while running away from the house.

From her father.

Remi ignored the ache in her heart.

She had to protect her brothers.

She had to protect her baby.

"LYDIA CARTWRIGHT DIDN'T exist until five years ago."

Declan should have felt something at hearing the words
out loud, but a part of him was going on autopilot. A routine created out of necessity for being sheriff. A detached
acceptance of what he was learning. A bridge between
throwing his hands in the air with anger and confusion
and complete silence. An in-between where he could stay
for a while until he figured out how he needed to, as sheriff, react to whatever news he received.

Caleb ran a hand through his dark hair and then hung
his hand on the detective's badge on a chain around his
neck. Jazz was sitting in the chair he was hovering over
while both looked at the computer screen.

"Why do you say that?"

Caleb touched the computer screen, but Declan couldn't
see what they were looking at.

"First of all, that's when all of her social media accounts popped up," he answered. "Secondly, that's also when her car was registered and she moved into an apartment in Kilwin…" He slid his finger across the screen. Jazz pulled it off the glass as if she'd done it countless times in their partnership. It didn't stop Declan's brother from continuing his explanation. "All within the span of a week. Before that there seems to be no trace of her. At least not on the internet or through the databases we have access to."

"But just because she isn't showing up on either doesn't mean Lydia didn't exist before then." Declan had to be the devil's advocate. Caleb looked up. His eyes were just as blue as Madi's and Des's.

"And yet you still think something's off with her," Caleb guessed.

Declan eyed the desks around them. A few deputies were in, their heads bent over paperwork. There wasn't any use in lying to his brother. Or Jazz, for that matter. They both were sharp as tacks when it came to reading someone. Even sharper when it came to their family and friends.

"I think Cooper Mann is telling the truth," he admitted. "I think Lydia either initiated the attack or carried it out against herself."

Caleb cringed. Jazz's sour expression wasn't too far off.

"Victim blaming is an absolute nonstarter, you know that, right?" Caleb pointed out. Declan didn't need the no-brainer statement. But, in this instance, his gut was starting to kick up a fuss.

Declan lowered his voice, leaning in so only they could hear him for sure.

"Which is why I want to be certain we check her out. If I'm wrong, then we've helped her case by shutting down any opposing argument Cooper's lawyer could put up in court. And if I'm right?" He shook his head. "Then we might start getting some answers around here. Some answers we desperately need."

Caleb kept his stare for a moment before sharing a look with Jazz. Declan remembered the first case they'd worked together as partners. Oil and water. Now? They could communicate in looks alone if they had to.

The look they shared must have been an agreement.

Both nodded.

"So what do you want to do?" Caleb asked. "Want us to go talk to her?"

"What's her last known address? She said she lived in Overlook when we spoke in the hospital."

Jazz went back into the computer. It wasn't long before she had an answer. All three recognized the location. They'd passed that house countless times in the last year or so since Desmond's wife, Riley, used to live in the neighborhood with her twin and her son. Jenna and Hartley still resided in the house but Lydia's address, if memory served, was more toward the front of Willows Way.

Declan had to remind himself that just because he'd grown up in Overlook didn't mean he knew everyone who lived there, especially those who weren't longtime locals.

"Okay, let's divide and conquer on this." Declan looked at Jazz. "Keep digging here and see if you can find her employer. If you do, give them a call and feel them out about her. Caleb, I want you to go to Cooper's house." Declan pulled a key out of his pocket. That earned a questioning look from both detectives. "Cooper gave me permission. He lives alone and in an apartment over where Delores stays. The number is on the key." He tossed him the key. Caleb caught it with ease. "See if you can't find something that helps us see if he's innocent or if he's playing us."

"And you?"

"I'll head over to Lydia's house to see if anything jumps out at me."

"I'm assuming you don't have a key to that one?"

"I don't."

Caleb and Jazz shared another look with each other and didn't comment out loud on whatever conclusion they'd reached. Instead, they all went about their tasks immediately.

Declan looked at his phone before jumping into Fiona.

No missed calls or texts from his chief deputy, Cussler. Which meant no news or leads on the two men and woman who had been a scourge against Main Street.

That should have concerned him more than the other nagging thought prickling at the back of his mind.

There were also no missed calls or texts from Remi.

He'd gone years without any contact whatsoever.

Yet, there he was. Thinking about her. Wondering what she was doing now. Craving more contact.

He knew her car was gone from his house and she was probably back at Heartland. Usually knowing that much would have been enough. Now he found his thoughts circling the woman.

Declan pulled her number up on his phone. He nearly called it right then and there. Then he tossed the cell onto the seat next to him and started toward the neighborhood of Willows Way.

The best thing he could do was rein in the chaos and sift through it until he could make his home, his county and the people within it safe.

If he couldn't do that?

Then what good could he ever be for his child?

Chapter Fourteen

The house was nice. One story. Brick. A ranch-style. There was a small front porch and a welcome mat on the concrete. The gardens on either side of it were well-kept, as were the yard and exterior of the house.

The neighbors were more than a stone's throw away, and no one appeared to be home in at least three of the houses.

It looked like a normal scene. A single woman who lived alone in a nice house in a nice neighborhood in a nice town.

Yet, after Declan knocked on the front door several times, he couldn't stop his gut from being loud again.

He'd met liars. He'd met scum.

He'd dealt with con artists, thieves, killers and men and women who wanted to watch the world burn.

He knew clever people who had lit the metaphorical or—on occasion—real match and the hapless idiots who believed they needed to be the ones to put that flame right where it needed to go.

Declan had met a lot of people, and only after a career of meeting those people did he think he was a good enough judge of character. Still, he knew he could be wrong. No man, woman or child could escape that human flaw.

Being wrong was what made being right feel so good.

It gave you a goal.

It gave you a purpose.

It made Declan know, logically, that he might be wrong about Cooper Mann.

The only thing that stopped that thought from really taking root was another fact he knew to be true.

Cooper Mann wasn't that smart.

As his mother would say, bless his heart, but Cooper wasn't burdened with an abundance of common sense.

There was no way that that boy could try to fool someone into believing he hadn't done what he had.

No, what had Declan believing him had to do with something he'd seen. Or, really, hadn't.

Cooper wasn't trying to hide a single thing.

He was just trying to get someone to believe him.

He wasn't clever enough to do anything else.

Declan didn't get back into his truck when no one answered the door. He moved to the living room windows and peered inside. The wooden slats of the blinds were open and through them he could see a standard living room setup. Couches, a TV, art on the wall, and a pair of tennis shoes next to the coffee table.

Declan kept moving. He left the front porch and rounded the side of the house next to the driveway. The house was flush with the ground and gave him easy access to look into each of the rooms along the exterior wall.

Easy access to *try* to look into each of the rooms.

Blinds were closed tightly over each window. The other side of the house was the same. Declan doubled back to the back porch. There were no blinds over the only window. He looked through it to a small, tidy kitchen.

Then he did something he shouldn't have.

He tried the back door.

When the knob turned without resistance, he expanded on what he shouldn't have been doing.

There were no beeps of an alarm or gasps of surprised

houseguests. There was also no heat or air-conditioning. The smell of disuse was as prevalent as the chill. Although Declan didn't believe anyone was in the house, still his hand went to the butt of the service weapon at his hip. He moved past the kitchen and took the first right he could, gut as quiet as the silence around him. He opened the first door he came to.

Then he moved to the next closed door and opened it. He went across the house to the last bedroom. And, just to be thorough, he checked the bathroom and moved to the kitchen and peeked at cupboards and drawers.

Declan cussed. Loud and true.

Empty.

The bedrooms, the bathroom, the kitchen.

He didn't know what was going on, but Declan would bet his badge that no one lived in the house.

Which meant Lydia had lied.

THE BARN WASN'T COLD. Remi assumed they'd had the heaters running early that morning and the closed doors had kept in the warmth for the horses. There were two of them in the stables. Diamond Duke, a bay-and-white tobiano-patterned Tennessee walker who belonged to Josh, and Raphael, a chestnut Tennessee walker who belonged to Jonah.

Remi didn't know them like she had her horse, Jackson, growing up, but seeing the beautiful horses in their stalls made her feel better. For a moment it was just like any other normal day on Heartland.

Just as the thought took root, it was torn away from her.

A hand slapped around Remi's mouth as someone grabbed her arm.

Her grip had tightened around the revolver, ready to listen to her father's directive, when Jonah's voice floated next to her ear.

"One of them is around here somewhere," he whispered. "Keep quiet."

He moved his hand and, once again, Remi was led from out in the open to somewhere more hidden. This time instead of a bedroom, Jonah led her into Diamond Duke's stall. The horse watched with little interest as they came inside and closed the door behind them. Then again, his favorite human was leaning against him, hand running over his pristine coat.

Relief at seeing that Josh and Jonah were unhurt was, once again, short-lived.

"Are you okay?" Jonah asked, turning her enough to look her up and down. His eyes widened at the blood. Their father's blood.

She nodded. Josh met her eye.

Jonah touched the blood on her shirt, looking for a wound. When he didn't find it he came to the same conclusion their brother already had. She could see it in both of their faces. Still, Josh voiced the question.

"Where's Dad?"

Remi knew this was the moment that could change everything. This was the moment she could do one of two things. She could let the unknown and the sorrow and the blood soaking through her father's shirt consume her. She could break down right then and there and let her brothers take over. Give them the gun, let them show her how they were both capable adults now and could handle themselves.

Or, she could woman up. Keep her father's promise and, instead of leaving Jonah and Josh to figure out how to get them all to safety, she could help. Show them that leaving the ranch didn't mean she'd retired the cowgirl.

"He made me leave him," she answered, no waver in her voice. It hardened like water being thrown into the freezing wind.

"He made you—" Josh started to repeat.

Remi didn't have time for it.

"He made me promise that we'd stay safe and that's what we're going to do," she steamrollered ahead. Remi looked to Jonah. Pain pinched his expression, though she knew it had nothing to do with anything physical. "Did you use the landline and call for help?"

He nodded, but then a different emotion momentarily took over his face.

"It didn't work. Not even a dial tone."

"And I'm assuming neither one of you have your cell phones."

It wasn't a question. Whereas most people around their ages were glued to their smartphones, Josh and Jonah were much like their father. There was no reason to have a phone out with the horses or while doing chores. Their father had preached that until it became second nature to *not* take their phones out of the house unless they were going to town. Even then Remi knew the chance of leaving the phones at the house was still great. The only reason she had bucked the anti-phone sentiment was because she'd stopped living on the ranch. Worrying about dropping her phone in horse droppings or having it crushed by a tractor hadn't been an issue in college or Nashville. Definitely not at her job as an accountant.

Which made the fact that the one time she actually *needed* it and didn't have it that much more frustrating.

"They're in the living room," Jonah answered. "Once the shooting started we had to bolt back into the kitchen and then out the back door."

"You said there's someone around here?" she asked, her mind building up a new plan.

"Right after we got in here we saw two men walking

the backyard." Josh eyed the revolver in her hand. "They had guns."

"Two men were upstairs. Dad told me not to shoot if there was more than one. So five against three, including Lydia."

Jonah flinched at the name.

"Why is this even happening? Why is *she* here? Did I do this somehow? Is she here because of me? I don't understand!"

"Me." Her brothers' eyebrows rose in tandem. "Before Lydia attacked she said she was here for me."

"But why?" The question was barely out of Josh's mouth before Jonah's eyes widened even more. He looked at Remi, and she knew he'd stumbled onto the same theory she'd already been working on in the back of her mind.

One that made her stomach drop and blood boil at the same time.

"Is it because you're pregnant with the sheriff's baby?" Jonah asked. "She could have heard you tell me in the hospital."

"It's a long-shot guess but that's all I can figure. He's the only one of us who does anything that might catch this kind of heat."

"Wait, you're pregnant?"

Remi turned to Josh and nodded. She felt bad he was finding out like this but, as was the current story of her life, she just didn't have the time to address the topic with loving care.

The best she could do was give him a brief, apologetic smile.

Then it was down to business.

"Which is another reason we're about to get the hell out of here." Remi motioned to the gun, careful to keep its aim away from the three of them and Diamond Duke.

"From what I remember this has eight rounds. I'm going to go ahead and assume our five bad guys all have guns, all have more bullets, and all know how to use them better than us." She waited a beat for her brothers to interject. They didn't. "So, since we haven't been able to call for help, standing our ground in here with eight bullets that aren't even guaranteed to hit their target sounds like an awful plan."

Remi looked to the stall across the aisle from them.

Raphael, ever content, let out a little neigh.

"Which is why we're going to focus on being the best cowboys we can be."

"You want us to ride out," Jonah said.

Remi nodded.

"Our best option is to put distance between us and them. Ride to the Nash Ranch and hope somebody's home."

"That's a long ride out in the open," Jonah pointed out. "Once we clear the last barn on Heartland that's easy pickings in the fields between us and them. What…maybe ten minutes or so."

Josh motioned around them.

"I'd rather be the fish in the pool than fish in the barrel." He put his hand on Remi's shoulder and nodded. His support rallied her even more.

"I'll unlatch the back doors. Y'all tack up your horses like our lives depend on it." Which they did.

"There's no doubles saddle in here. Going to be a bumpy ride for you," Josh said.

"Better than being those fish."

They got to work quickly. Remi went back to the door she'd come through and barred it, checked the main double doors to make sure they were still locked, and then hurried to the back two. They were usually only opened to take advantage of cool air and breezes for the horses.

Now they were all that stood between her relative calm and all-out fear.

Remi checked that the doors were still locked. She undid the latch slowly, careful not to make a sound, but didn't open them.

Not yet.

She didn't know where any of the men or Lydia were. They could be in the house still or the area around the barn, or they could simply have left. The fact that she had no idea was terrifying.

How long ago had she run from her father's side? Five minutes ago? Ten? Maybe more?

If they were still on the ranch, Remi had to believe they'd check the closest building to the house. Sooner rather than later.

It put her nerves closer to the edge and sent pricks of adrenaline across her body. Her muscles tightened in anticipation. Her palms grew sweaty. Remi strained to listen past her brothers tacking up their horses in record time.

Then she heard something she'd prayed she wouldn't.

A feeling of dread rolled over in her stomach. The hairs on the back of her neck stood on end.

The door they'd all come in through might have been locked but someone jiggling the handle was like a gunshot in the silence. Remi hurried to the space between the horse stalls her brothers were in. Both had paused what they were doing.

"Keep going," she whispered.

Someone coming to the barn didn't change their plan. There was nowhere to hide, and their odds of five against one gun was still not something she wanted to test.

She stood there and listened.

The door was at the head of the barn, off to the left. Stalls blocked her view of it. If someone broke through she'd have a few seconds to react. Whether that was jumping on a horse or shooting.

"Done."

Remi could have sung in relief as her brothers whispered in unison. Josh opened his stall's door. Remi went to Jonah's.

Whoever was on the other side of the barn door decided they were done trying things the normal way. The *bang* of someone ramming the door made Diamond Duke do a little jump as Josh led him into the aisle. He waved Raphael through but didn't follow as he and Jonah went to the door. Remi held back, too, and together they heard another loud bang followed by the splintering of wood.

They'd run out of time.

There was no way all three of them could mount up and ride out now. Not without being targets.

What would Declan do?

The question popped into Remi's head so quickly she answered it before she thought of why she'd asked it in the first place.

She took a small step forward so that she was in front of her little brother and raised the revolver.

She wasn't going to let anyone hurt any more of her family.

Not today.

Not ever.

Chapter Fifteen

The moment he saw her, Declan thought he was dreaming.

Honest to God, he thought he'd somehow fallen asleep somewhere between Lydia's house, Winding Road and his mother's house.

He wasn't even supposed to *be* on his way to the main house on the Nash Family Ranch. After he'd discovered Lydia's place was empty, he'd called Caleb to tell him the news. Caleb thought that was wildly peculiar but hadn't been able to make it to Cooper's place yet to see if there were any more wildly peculiar finds. Instead, he'd said he was almost to their ranch.

"Cooper Mann's family must have some crazy Spidey senses," he'd said. "Ma just called and said his grandma June is sitting at her dining table, wanting to talk to us."

"Why didn't she go to the department or call us?"

Caleb had snorted.

"Southern women are most powerful when they have a glass of sweet tea in front of them and some kind of wicker chair beneath them. But seriously, if you had to talk to the law, wouldn't you rather do it while basking in Mom's hospitality?"

Declan had seen the logic in that. Plus, there was probably some way their mother knew June Mann through everything she did in the community. Which meant telling the older woman to go to the department was a no-no. Not unless they wanted to catch their mother's wrath.

So Declan had decided to meet his brother and Grandma June at the ranch. On the drive there he'd percolated the information he did and didn't have and had almost tuned so wholly into his own thoughts that he didn't clock the movement streaking across the field he was driving alongside.

If seeing Remi galloping through an open field, hair blowing in the wind behind her wasn't a dream then maybe it was fate.

Because Declan didn't have to know the circumstances around why she was booking it for him to know exactly where she was going.

The same place he was.

Declan might have spent a bit more time speculating dreams and fate and Lydia's empty home and Grandma June's unannounced arrival if the other shocking details hadn't filtered through.

Remi wasn't alone.

Her brother, Jonah judging by his height, was trailing behind her on another horse. While someone was pressed against Remi's chest. The man was slumped, head bent.

Something was wrong.

Something was horribly wrong.

Declan honked the horn, unlocked his phone and dialed the last number on his recent calls list. The second it rang he put it on speaker and then cut his wheel.

The Nash Family Ranch and Hudson Heartland both had fenced in most of their acreage. However, after a dispute that came before any of the children of either family were born, there was a stretch of land between them that neither believed the other should claim. A no-man's-land, his father had called it. Owned and not owned by two families. Their only agreement concerning the expanse was that neither could erect a fence or let livestock or horses roam there.

Declan had never cared about the space.

Until now.

Caleb answered the phone just as Declan navigated the slight dip of the road's shoulder and began driving out into the field. He honked the horn again. This time Remi turned her head to look.

She must have yelled something to Jonah. Both slowed.

"What's going on?" Caleb asked.

"Remi and Jonah are booking it on horses to the ranch through no-man's-land. Remi's carrying someone who looks hurt."

Rustling carried through the airwaves. Caleb was moving.

"How hurt we talking?"

Declan was eating up the distance between them and came to a stop a few yards off, not wanting to spook the horses.

He swore as Remi and Jonah trotted over.

"She's holding Josh and there's blood all over both of them."

Declan threw open the door, adrenaline shooting through him so fast that he thought it might make him explode. Josh was pressed against Remi's front, and he could see blood across her arm and the hand holding the reins.

And the gun she had clutched in the hand pressing Josh against her.

"Lydia Cartwright and at least four men are on the ranch," Remi dived in, panting. "Dad's upstairs in the house with a bullet in the stomach. Josh just got hit in the chest. They need a hospital. *Now*."

Declan put his phone between his shoulder and his ear.

"You get that?"

"Yeah," Caleb answered. "Calling for EMS and backup."

Jonah swung off his horse and Declan motioned to Josh. He was unconscious. Remi's expression was blank.

"Let's get Josh in the truck," he said. "Hold on, Caleb."

He dropped his phone into his front breast pocket and, together with Jonah, pulled Josh down from the horse. Remi stayed astride while the two of them slid Josh into the passenger seat.

Then Declan only had eyes for Remi.

If the blood on her arm and hand had been alarming, the blood on front of her shirt was downright heart-stopping. She caught his eye.

"It's my dad's, not mine."

Declan knew that shouldn't have made him feel better. It did.

He pulled his phone back out.

"Caleb, call ahead to the ER and say we have Josh Hudson with a gunshot wound to the chest coming in hot with Jonah and Remi in my truck."

Jonah didn't need any prodding. He looped around the truck to the open driver's side door. Declan held his hand up to Remi to help her down.

She wasn't having it. Her grip on the reins tightened.

Declan was reminded of the girl whose father used to tame wild horses. The one who could outride him and his siblings even if they'd never admit it. The girl who had grown up more cowgirl than he had cowboy, if he was being honest.

"You're going back to the house. So am I."

Remi straightened her shoulders.

Declan, Jonah and even Caleb spoke at once.

She didn't listen.

"I left Dad for my kid's sake. I'm going back for him for the same reason." She pulled the reins to the side, turning her horse around and effectively ending the discussion. She turned to Jonah. "Go. Now." Then she gave Declan a long, low look. "I can outride you and you know it. Telling me I can't go only wastes time we don't have."

What Declan felt at her statements of fact was jarring. On the one hand he wanted to cuff her and throw her into the truck, sending her off to safety, kicking and screaming if need be. On the other hand, he'd never been more proud.

Remi Hudson was a fighter.

So was he.

And they'd both be damned if their kid didn't get the chance to be, too.

Declan nodded to Jonah and then went to his horse.

"Caleb," he said, "Remi and I will be approaching from no-man's-land."

"Des is here so I'm bringing him with me. Be safe, keep your phone on and in your pocket."

"Roger that."

Remi and her family might have been near-professionals when it came to horseback riding, but that didn't mean Declan was an amateur. The second he was upright in the saddle and fingers laced around the reins, he felt something like what he thought a professional swimmer might feel when first diving into the lap pool. Adrenaline, natural and exciting, flooded his veins, tensing his muscles and making his heart gallop. Being on a horse was being at home.

He knew Remi felt the same.

In tandem they struck out back toward Heartland. Thundering across the field like a battle cry. Hooves against the earth. Cold air biting at their faces. Furious justice at their heels.

Two horses and their riders in sync.

It felt right, even if the reason they were riding was so wrong.

Declan glanced over at the woman next to him and knew without a doubt that he'd never find another person like her ever again.

Remi Hudson was one of a kind.

And he loved her for it.

Declan slowed as the barn nearest the house came into view. Thankfully, so did Remi. Although her bravado was still displayed fiercely across her face, he saw caution there, too. She'd come back for her father but wasn't about to put their child at unnecessary risk. At least, no more than coming back had.

"For us to get out on the horses I had to shoot one of them," she said with effort. Her cheeks were red with windburn and exertion. Being pregnant probably wasn't helping. He remembered how tired Madi and Nina had been during the beginnings of their pregnancies.

"Did you kill him?" he had to ask.

The question didn't even make her flinch.

"I thought I did but he shot Josh before I could make sure. We barely got him on the horse before another one of them ran into the barn. We took off, but no one shot at us again."

Declan nodded, hoping that one man was out of commission by now.

"Stay behind me," he said. "If anyone shoots at us, use me and the horses as cover if you have to."

Declan took the lead, trotting ahead with eyes peeled and gun in one hand.

No one moved.

He led them to the side of the barn facing away from the house and jumped off his horse. Remi followed suit. She hung back as he moved around the corner to look inside the barn.

Blood was in the aisle between the stalls. Two spots of them on opposite ends. There was no one inside to match them.

"The barn nearest the house is empty," he said down to his pocket so Caleb could hear through the speakerphone that was still on. Caleb said he understood.

"Des and I are coming up the drive now."

Declan could feel Remi's anxiety mounting as he peered around what used to be a door, splintered off the hinges and facing the house.

"No movement."

Caleb repeated the sentiment when they made it to the end of the driveway opposite them.

"Let's clear the house," Declan ordered. "Be careful."

Remi stuck to Declan's back as they moved to the house in a hurry. For the next few minutes the four of them went from room to room, only to clarify it was empty.

The men and Lydia were gone.

And the only things they'd left behind were blood and Gale Hudson.

Sirens blared up the driveway when they finally made it to the upstairs bathroom the Hudson patriarch was in.

It wasn't a pretty sight.

Remi cried out, pure anguish breaking down every part of the woman. She reached out for her father before she'd even cleared the doorway. Declan grabbed her, trying to shield her from a terrifying reality if only for a few seconds longer.

Even if he didn't know what had happened in the bathroom, it was clear that Gale had fought. Blood was smeared everywhere, the man himself in the middle of it all and as still as still could be.

Remi fought against Declan's chest.

Desmond ran past them and knelt beside Gale. He checked his pulse.

He didn't shake his head, but he didn't look relieved, either.

UNLIKE THE LAST time chaos had reigned within their orbit, Declan didn't leave Remi's side once.

From Heartland to the hospital to roaming the halls of the hospital to even standing outside of the bathroom door, the sheriff kept his cowboy hat on but metaphorically seemed to take his badge off.

"Go do what you need to," Remi had said after Josh had first gone into surgery. Declan had shaken his head. She'd noticed for the first time that day that dark stubble was lining his chin.

"I'm with you now," was all he'd said in response.

These were words that were comforting in an increasingly uncertain world, and words he stayed true to.

He made and answered phone calls, spoke to his brothers, deputies and chief deputy in person, and when it was time for her to relay everything that had happened at Heartland, he was the one who took her statement personally.

Remi had been ready to ride solo back to the ranch to try to save her dad but now she was grateful for the close proximity. Especially when, hours later, Jonah met them next to a vending machine in the lobby.

He ran a hand through his hair. He was exhausted.

"I just talked to the doctor about Dad."

Remi perked up at that. She'd been hovering around the hallways in the hopes of talking to a doctor sometime soon. Her father was still alive, a miracle by all accounts, and had gone through a series of touch-and-go surgeries. He'd only been sent to a room an hour ago. Josh, who had undergone his own surgery, had been out for four. He'd regained consciousness only to ask about them and then the "new fling" Jonah had told Remi about.

After a deputy had found and brought their phones to the hospital, Remi had made sure to call the woman after she realized how important she was to her brother. They had all been surprised when a brightly dressed, extremely expressive woman named Lilianna had rushed into the hospital and immediately to his bedside. Talking to the woman, seeing how worried she was, had eased Remi's guilt at leaving Josh's side.

It had given her more time to worry about their father.

"How is he?" Remi asked, heart jumping back into her throat. "Does he have to have another surgery?"

Jonah shook his head. Then he did something she'd truly not seen coming. He smiled.

"His rehab is going to be extensive and he'll have to take it easy for a long while to come, *but* the doc said he should be out of the woods now. He's stable and both surgeries did exactly what they wanted them to do." Remi threw her arms around her brother in an embrace. He spoke into her hair. "If you hadn't gotten him help as fast as you did, it would be a different story."

Remi squeezed and then pulled away. She looked him in the eye with certainty.

"And if you hadn't gotten Josh here as fast as you did, *he* would have been in worse trouble, too."

Jonah took the truth with a smile that waned.

"But if I'd never gone out with Lydia—" he started.

"They would have still probably come," Declan finished.

They'd already had this conversation while waiting for Josh and their dad's surgeries to finish. Jonah told Declan and Caleb everything he knew about Lydia, which hadn't been much. She'd been nice and funny and had done a good job at pulling Jonah in with limited interaction.

The truth was, no one blamed him one bit, yet Remi could see he'd be blaming himself for a long while despite that fact.

Jonah shook himself a little.

"Did you talk to Mom?"

"Yeah. Her flight got grounded because of the weather and it took all I had to convince her and Dave not to drive through it instead. She only relented after hearing that Josh and Dad would be okay. She'll call one of us tomorrow with an update but said *you* better call her soon."

Jonah glanced at Declan. He lowered his voice.

"Does she know? About the…you know?"

Remi felt Declan's gaze switch to her. She shook her head.

"I want to tell her in person."

"She'd like that." Jonah let out a loud, long sigh. "What she *wouldn't* like is you running yourself into the ground while pregnant with her only claim to a grandkid." He fixed her with a mock stern expression. "Get out of here and get some rest."

Remi opened her mouth to complain, but he cut her off.

"I called Rick, Dad's friend, and he said he wants to come up here and stay the night with Dad while I stay with Josh. There's no reason you need to stay here, too." He looked to Declan. "I'm assuming Remi has a place to stay with you, though?"

"She does."

"But what if—" Remi tried.

Jonah still wasn't having it.

"But what if nothing. I'll let you know if *anything* happens. Plus, it's not like the ranch is that far from here anyways." He put his hands on her shoulders to focus her attention so that it stayed solely on him and his next words. "You shot a man to get us off the ranch and then went right back to it to get Dad. Let me do this very simple task of watching over everyone here." His expression softened. "Give me this, Remi. I need it."

So, she did.

Then, before she knew it, Remi was standing in Declan's bathroom back on the Nash Family Ranch and staring at a mirror that was starting to steam over from the shower heating up behind her. She'd already stripped naked but couldn't get her feet to move from the tile floor.

All because of the stain on her skin.

Blood from her father or her brother that had seeped through her shirt.

Remi knew they were okay now, but that crimson smear held too much power still.

Way too much.

It wasn't until two beautiful green eyes met her gaze head-on that Remi realized she was sobbing.

And it wasn't until Declan's arms wrapped around her naked body that she realized how much she needed the man.

Chapter Sixteen

Sometime in the dark of late night or early morning, Remi woke up in bed alone. It wasn't her bed, and she sussed that out pretty quickly through the haze of sleep thanks to the way the pillow smelled beneath her still-wet hair.

It smelled like spice and the woods and Declan Nash.

Remi rolled over and felt the empty space next to her.

After her breakdown in the bathroom, Declan had gone above and beyond the call of supportive. Not only had he taken her into the shower with his jeans still on, he'd scrubbed the blood off her skin and held her while she cried some more. Only after she'd regained her composure, or enough of it to stop crying, did the man dry her off, put a too-big shirt over her head and deposit her like a child in bed.

Remi had been so exhausted from her outburst to the adrenaline-filled day she'd had that sleep had overtaken her within the space of two blinks.

Now she guessed that the man who had saved her from herself hadn't gotten beneath those same sheets next to her.

Remi rolled back over and found her phone on the nightstand. No new calls or texts from Jonah. She took that as good news and slowly got out of bed. She flushed when she realized she was wearing a pair of boxers. She didn't remember putting those on.

Declan surely was a caring and sly man.

If he hadn't already seen her as naked as naked could be, she might have been so embarrassed that she'd try to escape. Instead, she opened the door between the bedroom and living room with all the hope in the world of seeing the sheriff.

She wasn't disappointed.

Declan looked up from his laptop on the coffee table with alarm. That alarm softened after a moment. He smiled.

"Hey, Huds."

It was such a simple greeting, yet it shifted something inside of her that had already been moving.

"Hey, Sheriff."

Remi settled in the chair kitty-corner to the couch so she could face him the best she could.

"Thank you for earlier, by the way. I kind of *lost it*, lost it."

Declan waved off the apology.

"I only did what I could do to help." He sighed and glanced at the computer. "I just wish I could do more."

"I take that to mean no one has found Lydia and the men?"

He ran a hand over the stubble along his jaw. Whatever had softened his expression was now gone. Stress and frustration took its place.

"No. We've checked all the hospitals in the county, and even reached out past it, to see if we can't locate the guy you got. We have so many APBs out on them *and* the three who pulled what they pulled on Main Street that the gossip mill is about to shatter. Mom said that Cooper Mann's grandmother let her know in no uncertain terms that Overlook is losing faith in the department. In me. And, honestly, I can't blame them." He dragged his gaze to hers. "We have so many weird little pieces to this chaotic puzzle, and I just can't seem to find a way to force them to fit. For a moment I'll think I have something and then it gets lost in the chaos. It's driving me crazy."

Remi didn't say anything right away. She knew the man well enough that telling him everything was going to be okay, telling him that he *would* get all of the bad guys in the end, wasn't actually going to help him.

So, instead, she told him a story.

"One time when I was younger Dad and I went to a ranch out in Texas to visit a friend of his named Barry. The boys were too young and Mom had to stay to watch them and, to be honest, I wasn't that excited to be the one who had to go. Dad knew it and tried to talk the place up before we even got there. He told me it was three times bigger than Heartland and had all kinds of animals everywhere you looked. I didn't believe him—to me Heartland was massive—but then we drove the road to the main house and it felt like it took a lifetime to get there. All along the way I watched herds of cows grazing, people horseback riding, and even saw some goats running around. I was mesmerized." Remi couldn't help the smile that she knew passed over her face. The little-kid awe she'd felt then was hard to forget even as an adult. "So when Barry invited us to move the herd of cows to a field at the opposite end of his property, I was actually excited. We got our own horses, our own tents, and some stuff to make s'mores, and rode all day until we got them to where they needed to be. That night I passed out with chocolate on my mouth and a sore butt from riding. It was magic."

Declan smiled in turn at that.

"Later that night, though, I woke up to the sound of two hundred scared cattle. I'd barely gotten on my horse before they took off in all different directions," she continued. "I couldn't figure out what was going on, and neither could

Dad or the ranch hands who had come with us. There was too much noise, too much movement, and not enough light. And do you know what Barry did?"

Declan raised his eyebrow in question. Remi leaned forward in her seat.

"He took a breath, tuned the world out and reminded himself that he'd been a rancher for years and was damn good at it. *That's* when he spotted the wolf."

Remi moved from her seat to the spot next to Declan and put her hand on his knee. She wanted to encourage him and comfort him all at the same time. She hoped that she'd at least hit one of her targets.

Declan angled his body so he could meet her gaze more easily.

Once again Remi marveled at how different this scene would have been if they were younger. *He* would have been the one talking while *she* listened in silence.

"With what I know from growing up in Overlook and from what I've heard since I've been gone, chaos seems to be more frequent than not. You've lived in it and still live in it. You're *good* at navigating it. Now you just need to take a breath, tune the world out, and trust that you're—"

Calling him *fast* was an injustice to the move he actually pulled off. In one fluid movement Declan went from a statue beneath her hand to heat against her lips.

He cupped the side of her face and Remi leaned in to the surprise.

She kissed the man back.

Hard.

Their lips parted and the taste of him was all she wanted in the world.

When he broke the kiss, Remi was left blinking and confused.

"You," he rasped out.

"Me?"

"You," he repeated. "That's what I want."

He was back to her lips within the space of a breath. The wild boy from her childhood and teen years. The reunited friend. The good—and not mention to last—fling. The accidental father of her child. The sheriff savior.

Declan Nash had a list of ever-evolving meanings to her.

But what was he now? Between a night of passion that wasn't supposed to last through the next day to always being connected through their unborn child.

What would happen next?

Coparenting across state lines due to her promotion?

Getting married in no-man's-land while her belly grew?

Or some form of in-between?

Remi had no idea about their future.

But she did know something about the present.

She looped her arms around Declan's neck and pulled him against her until they were lying across the couch. He followed her down while never breaking their kiss. In fact, he deepened it with his tongue, trapping a moan of pleasure between them.

Declan's hand tangled in her hair while the other gripped her hip. She moved up and against him as he tried to maneuver himself so his body weight wasn't solely on her. In the process Remi felt how much Declan Nash truly wanted her.

It put fire straight through her. She dropped her hands down and went for the hem of his shirt. Remi had never wanted something gone as badly as she wanted that shirt off.

Declan felt her frustration. He broke their kiss and nearly ripped it in two. The shirt went flying and then he was focused on hers. Which was *also* his. A fact that must have encouraged him. He grabbed its hem and then tore it right up the middle.

Cold air hit Remi's bare chest as the two sides of the fabric fell away, but there were only flames in her blood. When he dropped his mouth down to the skin of her neck and then followed a tantalizing path to her nipple, Remi almost cussed him.

When his hardness pushed against the boxers she was somehow still wearing and through the shorts *he* was somehow still wearing, Remi nearly lost it.

The second he came up for air, she decided to end the torture.

She pulled him back down on top of her and moaned.

It seemed to do the trick.

Remi moved against him as, one-handed, he took off his shorts. Then he focused on her. She moaned again as his hand, strong and warm, skimmed down the boxers on loan and then came back up her leg. Trailing heat and lust right to the spot where she wanted his attention next.

There was no trapping her moans now.

She yelled out in absolute bliss as he pushed inside of her and filled her with hard passion. She moved against him with uncontainable desire.

A man and a woman desperate to be closer.

Lips to lips.

Skin to skin.

Galloping heartbeats.

Remi didn't know what their future held but she did know one thing.

She wanted Declan, too.

THE PHONE CALL didn't wake Declan, Remi did.

Tangled together between the sheets of his bed, she couldn't help thrashing around to escape to the bathroom.

Declan immediately went on high alert, fighting through the haze of the good sleep he'd fallen into with the naked woman wrapped in his arms. He followed her up and out of the bed, fists balled and eyes wild. It didn't matter that he was as naked as the day he was born, he was going to fight tooth and nail to combat whatever had woken Remi so violently.

Then he heard her in the bathroom heaving.

There wasn't anything he could punch or shoot to cure morning sickness.

So after Remi shooed him away, Declan went to the kitchen and poured her a glass of water and took stock of what he had to eat. Nina, Caleb's wife, had claimed that sour candy had been a lifesaver when she'd first been pregnant with their son. Madi hadn't really felt sick with Addison but with her second pregnancy she'd always had crackers, some kind of Popsicle, and a lot of snacks. Declan hadn't been grocery shopping in a hot minute. All he had that met the criteria was a bag of pretzels Desmond had left the week before.

They would have to do.

He plated some, set the water next to it, and brought his phone back out to him.

That was when he saw the missed call. It was from Cussler and time-stamped at just after three in the morning. It was now almost five.

There were no texts or emails as a follow-up. No voice mail, either.

Declan wondered if it had been an accident. His chief deputy was a married man and a father to four. Declan only liked to call him when it was absolutely necessary. He decided to send a text, instead. He put the phone down and the ringer up, surprised he'd missed the call in the first place. Normally he was a light sleeper. Then again, normally, he didn't have a naked Remi Hudson in his bed.

No sooner had he set the phone down than the woman of the hour made her entrance. She was wearing another one of his old T-shirts. It was too big for her and somehow still she made it an attractive piece. The urge to rip it off her like he'd done earlier was nearly overpowering. She frowned at him, picking up on his thoughts.

"Don't go getting any ideas, buddy. I feel like death incarnate. I know it's cliché to blame you for how I feel right now, but—" she took a seat at the dining table next to him "—this is all your fault."

Declan chuckled.

"The words every man wants to hear after a night of rolling around naked in bed with a beautiful woman."

That pulled a smile from her. It was small but there. She motioned to the plate of pretzels. He nodded.

"I didn't know if you would want to eat but read that if you eat a little every few hours that it might help with morning sickness, especially when you first wake up."

Remi's eyebrow arched high.

He unlocked his phone and found the app he was looking for. He tapped it and slid the phone over.

The surprise was clear on her face.

"You downloaded a pregnancy app?"

Declan shrugged.

"I figure I'm already behind on the game, might as well try to catch up best I can."

Remi gave him a look he couldn't quite place and grabbed a handful of pretzels.

"If I didn't feel like I was about to be sick, starve, and cry all at the same time right now I'd kiss you."

Declan smirked.

"And if you kissed me right now I might just destroy another one of my shirts."

Remi's cheeks flushed pink and she laughed.

"Smooth one, Sheriff."

"I try."

The phone between them buzzed.

Remi tensed.

"I missed a call from my chief deputy. I texted him I was up," he explained, spinning the phone around to face him. "If something was wrong he would have called more than once or probably just come here to wake me up himself."

He trailed off when the phone started to ring. He stopped whatever he was going to say and took the call right there. Cussler was quick and precise. He'd called Declan, then decided to let the sheriff get some sleep when he hadn't answered. It was no secret Declan hadn't gotten enough of it lately. Cussler recounted what had happened and had handled the situation.

Declan thanked him and ordered him to seek the same sleep he'd let Declan get.

As they ended their call, Declan was already slipping deep into his thoughts.

Finally Remi said, "What's wrong? What happened?"

He didn't answer right away. If it had been yesterday afternoon the new information would have been another piece in the bizarre puzzle. Another stroke of chaos. Another reminder that he had no idea what *exactly* was going on.

But Declan had since had some sleep, some comfort, and a woman who'd told a story about a rancher and a wolf.

Now he finally saw some sense in the chaos.

Declan met Remi's gaze. She had a pretzel at her lips and was undoubtedly the most stunning woman he'd ever seen. "I think it's time I called a family meeting."

Chapter Seventeen

The last time Remi had been in the same room as all of the Nash siblings, they had been in the loft of their stable and hoping they wouldn't get caught by the adults they'd snuck away from. There had been others there, friends and crushes and hangers-on, because being a Nash in Overlook earned a certain amount of fame. Unwanted by them, given by most.

When the triplets were together, even more so.

Remi had never liked the attention thrust upon them. They clearly didn't want it. However, talking to each as they showed up at Declan's house, she was glad to see it hadn't beaten them down.

Like their older brother, the triplets were and were not the same as she remembered.

Outside of the sheriff's department, Caleb was smiles and humor. He had a coffee cup in one hand and a baby teething ring in the other. He declared to everyone that he'd found it in his truck and wasn't going to let it out of his sight until he could pass it to his wife, Nina, since it was one of their son's favorite things to play with. Love had drenched every word.

Madi, who been closed off to everyone who wasn't her family when they were younger, embraced Remi with a warm hug. The scar along her cheek was just as noticeable as it had always been, but it did nothing to dampen her lighthearted spirit. She plopped down on the couch next to Caleb and started to tell him about her two children's current favorite toys. One was the remote control to their TV. The other was a gardening bucket with a painted smiley face on it. Both laughed at that.

Desmond came in last. The limp he walked with hadn't changed from when they were younger but there was definitely something different about it and him. A lightness? A carefree air around him? Remi couldn't place her finger on it but accepted a hug from him with pleasure. He was a businessman who had spent his career helping others. He hadn't had to come with Caleb to Heartland the day before, but he had, no hesitation. Remi thanked him for it and he accepted the kind words with a charming Nash smile before moving into the living room to sit.

Then there they were.

The Nash triplets.

Once they had been three eight-year-olds forced to live through trauma no kid should have to experience.

Taken from a park during a game of hide-and-seek. Hurt, scared and terrified.

Now three adults, happy and healthy—and no idea they were about to revisit a past they'd all seemed to move on from.

Remi knew this same thought was moving through Declan's mind the moment he came in from the bedroom and saw them. He shared a look with her.

She tried on an encouraging smile.

It wasn't missed.

Madi stopped whatever Caleb was saying to Desmond by putting her hands on both of their arms. They followed her gaze to Declan. The three of them looked up at their big brother as he pulled a chair from next to the dining table opposite them. He waited until Remi was sitting in the armchair before he started.

"I'm going to dive in because I've already held off telling any of you this for too long as it is." Still, Declan took a breath before continuing. The triplets lost their earlier humor. Three sets of baby blues were focused solely on him. "The morning before Cooper Mann allegedly attacked Lydia Cartwright he asked to meet me because he thought he had information on a cold case. *Your* cold case." The shift was subtle but there. The triplets tensed in unison. "He said a man in a fancy suit at the Waypoint Bar kept rattling on about a note in the wall at Well Water Cabin that law enforcement had missed. I thought it was a bunch of nonsense but, well, I had to check. Remi was in town and nice enough to indulge me with a fresh pair of eyes. Which made the difference because she found it."

"A note *in* the wall?" Caleb repeated.

Declan nodded.

"It looked like a painted-over wallpaper seam," Remi explained. "Basically it was glued against the wall in the paint. I almost didn't see it."

"What did it say?" Madi scooted to the edge of the couch cushion. Her darkened expression reminded Remi of how she'd often looked as a teen.

Declan pulled out his phone, selected one of the pictures he'd taken of the note and passed it to her. They took turns looking at it even though Declan answered.

"Justin Redman was the only thing written on it."

"Why does that name sound familiar?" Desmond asked.

Caleb was quick to answer.

"Dad was on a case trying to find his attacker just before the abduction, right?"

Declan nodded.

"I took another look at the file last night to see if anything stuck out to me, but it was pretty cut-and-dried. Dad was about to go after his attacker hard and then had to let someone else handle the case after the abduction. Justin was killed in a car accident before another detective could take the case so it was ultimately dropped."

Madi scrolled through Declan's phone.

"I guess he got really lucky, then," she muttered. Then she amended, "The attacker. Not Justin, obviously. You know how good Dad was at cases like that."

They all nodded in agreement. Declan continued.

"Before I could really get a grasp of what we'd found, Cooper was arrested. I assumed he was pulling my leg with the note, painted it in there a while back and used it to distract me. Or it was a twisted way to drum up *more* publicity for himself after he tried to kidnap Lydia. You know how some of these bad guys love the spotlight."

Desmond snorted.

"It would have been a doozy of a news bulletin, too. 'A new lead following Overlook's most infamous kidnapping case found at the same time local idiot kidnaps, or tries to, an innocent woman.' If he did it for attention he'd surely get it."

"But you didn't go public with the note." Caleb's voice held an edge. He was angry he hadn't been told. Not only was he Declan's brother, he was one of his detectives.

"We had to handle the situation as delicately and quickly as we could, given the town's history," Declan defended. "I had to put the *maybe* of the abduction case on the back burner while I dealt with the very real and present attempted abduction. And all before the press tore into us to make that job harder."

Madi continued looking at Declan's phone. Desmond nodded. Caleb was satisfied enough not to argue.

"Cooper denied he attacked Lydia and said *she* attacked

him, mutilated her face with his keys, and then jumped into his car. A witness saw him and assumed he was pushing her inside. He said he was trying to get her out while Lydia swore up and down that he attacked and was trying to take her when we interviewed her. I was going to dig deeper into Justin Redman, still, but the next day I got distracted again."

"Claire's Café?" Madi guessed.

What had happened across Main Street had already circulated twice over throughout the county.

"Yeah," Declan answered gruffly. "A man jumps out of a car outside, attacks a woman, and I give chase. Once he's standing still he tells me, in so many words, that he wanted me to chase him away from Claire's. I run back to find out a man and woman, both wearing suits, had come inside and shot a man in the arm before escaping back to their car. They then go and pick up the man I'd been chasing."

None of the triplets commented. Again, they knew this part.

Well, most of it.

They didn't know why Remi hadn't been shot and, somehow, the news hadn't made its way to them.

"And then we have yesterday," he continued. "I talked to Cooper on a hunch and became convinced he's not lying."

"Then Jazz and I figure out that Lydia Cartwright didn't exist, at least not online, until five years ago," Caleb supplied. "And you go to her house and find out it's empty, meaning she lied."

Remi hadn't known that part. She gave Declan a questioning look. He returned it with an apologetic one.

"I was heading to Heartland to talk to Jonah again. See if he knew anything about the house and why she'd lied. But changed course here when Cooper's grandma showed up to plead his case. I saw you in the field before I ever made it off Winding Road." He redirected his attention to his siblings to, she guessed, tell them about what had happened on Heartland before they'd met in the field. However, the words stuck in his mouth.

Declan became angry. A muscle in his jaw twitched. His hands fisted.

Remi spoke for him.

"My brothers, Dad and I were making some food when Lydia showed up. She said she had come for me, not Jonah, and immediately attacked. I was able to get her out of the house, but she opened fire." Remi felt her own bad memories tensing her body. She took a breath and skipped the heart-wrenching parts. "It wasn't until I made it out to the barn behind our house to where Jonah and Josh were that I found out there were four men with her, all armed. I shot one in the stomach before Josh was shot. After that we managed to ride off. My brothers said no one spoke to them or around them when they were trying to hide. If— if my dad heard anything, it might be a while before we can find out what that was."

Each Nash gave her a sympathetic look. She was thankful they didn't say anything. There wasn't much reassurance they could give her at the moment. Sometimes a look of understanding or a pat on the back helped more than words. A sentiment the family was, no doubt, well versed in by now.

"Which brings us to early this morning," Declan continued. "Cussler called this morning to tell me that a man named Joe Langley was taken to the ER early. He was attacked during a jog through his neighborhood after he couldn't sleep. He said a man in a suit came out of nowhere, did the deed, and left him with his phone to call for help."

"It seems like the Fixers are our common link between everything that's happened," Caleb jumped in. "We might not be able to see their scorpion tattoos but their suits *and* frustrating-as-hell ability to stay a few steps ahead of law enforcement? It can't be a coincidence."

Declan shared another look with Remi. After his call with Cussler they'd spent the next few hours talking out his theory and going over what they knew.

Once again, Madi didn't let the exchange lie.

"There's more," she stated.

Declan nodded.

"For the last few years the Fixers organization has been popping up in our lives. From talk about men in suits to men in suits actually showing up as hired guns, they've been around. I have no doubt that the man at Waypoint Bar was a Fixer, the two men and woman on Main Street were Fixers, and even Lydia and the men at Heartland were Fixers. But, what is the *only* thing we know about them?"

"They do what they're paid to do," Desmond offered.

"Which means that *someone* out there is pulling the strings."

"But why?" Madi asked. "And to what end?"

Declan sat up straighter and then domed his hands over his lap.

Remi knew what he was about to say and yet goose bumps erupted across her skin when he said it.

"The woman outside of Claire's Café wasn't just attacked. She was pistol-whipped in the face. The man inside the café, Sam, was shot in the arm. The *side* of the arm. And Joe Langley had his leg broken. Badly." Silence filled the room so quickly Remi felt suffocated by it. Declan caused that silence with his deafening theory.

She looked at Madi and the scar that had been created by being pistol-whipped.

She looked at Caleb, remembering the scar across his arm from a bullet grazing it.

She looked at Desmond, the man who had grown up with a limp after having his leg broken from the sheer force of a man twice his size.

No one moved.

Declan had to bring the conversation home.

"I think everything that has happened in the last week is because someone is sending us, the Nash family, a very personal message."

MADI TOUCHED HER SCAR. Caleb rolled his shoulder back. Desmond put his hand on his knee. Then the three did something that only they seemed to be able to do on occasion.

They said the same thing at the same time.

"Why?"

Remi's brown eyes found his. Sometimes he believed they were a dark amber, beautiful and dangerous depending. Her brow was pinched, expression thoughtful. This was a question they'd already tried to tackle in the early hours of the morning. In fact, the case had become the only thing they'd talked about since Cussler had called.

Yet, here they were with no clear answers.

"One theory is someone is trying to rattle us. Maybe someone from an old case is ticked off at Caleb or me. Maybe someone is angry with Des because of the work he's been doing with the foundation. Maybe it's a blast from the past who's angry with Madi."

"But we know who it is," Caleb said. "It's the Fixers. We find them, we find answers."

Even though he said it, they both knew that was a tall order. As much as it pained Declan to admit, finding the Fixers was a damn near impossible feat. Over the years they'd managed to catch a few, but once behind bars, the Fixers died by their own hands or another Fixer.

That was how their reputation had grown so much and so quickly.

They rarely got caught and, even if they did, they took their job, client and any other nefarious details with them to the grave.

Des had had a run-in with who they believed to be the leader of the Fixers in the last dealings with the group before now. He adopted a look of deep concentration and equal skepticism.

"The only time I was offered an answer from them, the cost would have been Riley and her sister's lives." He shook his head. "And that option was given to me by the man with the scar on his hand."

Declan sighed. The man they thought was the Fixer's head honcho had a scar in the shape of an X on his hand. It was identical to the scar the triplets' captor had had on his own hand when he'd taken them. This discovery was one of the main reasons Declan had been unable to completely walk away from trying to solve the case again.

"Which gives weight to the theory that someone has been playing with us for a while now." He ran a hand through his hair and then curved it down to run the top of his knuckles against the stubble beneath his chin. Frustration coursed through him. How he wished to be back in bed with Remi at his side.

"It could be him." Madi's voice was soft as she said it, and Declan heard the pain. "It could be the man who took us."

That had been another theory. The triplets' abductor was toying with them. Declan didn't put too much stock in that possibility, and Caleb voiced the reason for that.

"Getting away with taking and scarring three little kids, who also happen to have a father in law enforcement, once, was a miracle on its own. For him to come back to mess with us would be an idiotic thing to do. He might as well throw self-preservation out the window."

Declan agreed. What would be the reasoning behind doing that? Especially all these years later?

"But no one knows why you were taken in the first place."

Everyone turned to Remi. Her cheeks tinted at the sudden attention, but she remained focused.

"When you were kids. No one ever figured out *why* you were taken." She straightened in her seat. "Because you're right. It was a miracle the guy never got caught. Everyone in town was looking for you, including your dad, the county's best detective at the time. *Everyone* was looking for you." She turned to Declan. "Which meant no one was looking for Justin Redman's attacker, someone who also was never found. How sure are you that Justin's death was an accident?"

Declan opened his mouth to answer. Nothing came out. Caleb also seemed to be at a loss. In the shadow of the abduction they'd never focused on the case that their father had abandoned.

"You think we were taken as a distraction," Madi spelled out. "So Dad wouldn't look into Justin's attack?"

Remi shrugged.

"If Cooper Mann didn't try to take Lydia, then he probably didn't put that note in the wall at the cabin, either. He was telling the truth and probably heard about it from a Fixer at the bar, knowing it would eventually get back to one of you. Whether they are toying with you all or not, Justin Redman has to have *some* kind of significance to all of this. Right? Why else go through the trouble of painting a note in a wall?"

Declan's heart rate sped up. The wheels in his head began to turn. For a moment no one spoke.

Had Remi just found one of their missing pieces?

Chapter Eighteen

"This is a bad plan."

"You've already said that. Three times now."

"Because it *is* a bad plan."

"For the record, I never said it was a good plan."

Declan snorted.

"Well, that doesn't help me feel better."

Remi ran her fingers through her hair and then tried to flatten the parts of it she'd pinned back. They'd had an eventful day. Some of it had included going back to Heartland. Remi had stayed stone silent as she'd led him to her childhood room. She'd kept that silence while finding the clothes she needed and changed. Declan had gone behind her, packing her bag with things he thought she might need for the foreseeable future. When she eyed him with a question seconds from her lips, he'd told her the simple truth.

"Sorry, Huds, you're stuck with me until this whole thing gets sorted out."

Remi hadn't fought him then, but he was back to fighting her hours later.

They were sitting in the parking lot of Waypoint Bar in Kilwin. He was in his best pair of dark jeans, a black button-up at her request and had on his vacation-only dark blue Stetson. His sheriff's badge was in his back pocket. The blazer in the back seat would hide his shoulder holster.

Remi wasn't armed, which didn't mean she couldn't do some damage. She was decked out in a sheer white blouse that dipped low and tucked into a pair of navy pants—which he noted matched his hat—with legs so wide Declan had thought it was a long skirt at first. She'd chosen black flats that wrapped around her ankles and lipstick that reminded him of a bull's-eye. One he very much wanted to hit.

"I wore this to a party one of my clients threw for Towne & Associates after I cleaned up the absolute mess that was their finances," she'd said after debuting the look. "I packed it on the off chance I could convince Molly to go out while I was in town."

Now, looking at her in the glow from Waypoint's lone light at the back of the parking lot, Declan found the outfit to be too much. Just like the plan.

Remi sighed and slapped him lightly on the shoulder.

"Stop it. Stop that broodiness right now. We need to do this and do it right." She motioned to her outfit and his. Her brows drew in together. She rolled her shoulders back. Then she reminded him why he'd agreed to the bad plan in the first place. "Justin Redman said he was supposed to meet Dean Lawson the day he was attacked. No one ever got around to asking Mr. Lawson what for. Now we can, thanks to your brothers pulling some hefty favors to find this Lawson guy and get us a meeting *twenty-five years* after the fact." She motioned to their outfits again. At the movement his attention redirected to the curve of her breast. Remi was nice enough not to call him out for it. "If Lawson can't give us any information we can use about Justin Redman, then we can leave him be and mingle with the rest of the crowd and see if we can't at least find something about the man who told Cooper about the note in the wall. If you go in with a sheriff's badge on your chest, guns blazing, I don't think we'll get the response we want. Right now we just look like two people on a date. It's not like everyone in the city knows you're the Wildman county sheriff."

Declan saw the logic in it, but he didn't have to like it.

Remi let out a frustrated huff.

"You told Julian to keep watch on Madi. You have Desmond with your mom. Caleb is with his wife and son. Jazz is working with your chief deputy to find Lydia and the people who have been attacking strangers and my family home." She reached out and took his chin in her hand. It was soft and warm. "You told me earlier that you're not leaving me. I'm telling you right now that *I'm* not leaving *you*."

She kept his gaze for a moment before letting go.

Then she was smiling.

"So, now that that's out of the way, can we please go in already? I have to pee. Again."

Despite every reservation he had, which numbered many, Declan chuckled.

"Yes, ma'am."

Declan had already been told that Waypoint had lost its law enforcement hangout roots, but it was still odd to see in person. What had once been walls covered in framed pictures of fallen heroes, graduating classes, candid stills from on the job and an assortment of police memorabilia had now been swapped for a moodier aesthetic. Posters from old movies, handmade wall art and pictures of people relaxing after, he assumed, a long day on the job surrounded a clientele who were in varying stages of after-work comfort. Declan led Remi past two dartboards mounted against the interior faded brick, a dimly lit pool table, a wall lined with flat screens, clusters of tables, and up to the massive bar that lined the back wall. No one paid them any mind as they walked through. Not even a way-ward glace as Remi stopped just shy of the counter and turned to him.

"That's him," she whispered, trying and failing to be covert about her head nod. The man in question was sitting hunched over in the middle of the bar, a few feet from them. Declan would have questioned her ability to pick him out so easily from the angle if it hadn't been for his hair. Stark white and falling past his shoulders. Just as it had been in the picture from his online profile and the several magazine pieces written about him.

Dean Lawson was a businessman, like Desmond. However, unlike Declan's brother, Lawson was in real estate and was more known for throwing extravagant parties for wealthy clients and driving sports cars with bikini models than charitable giving. His idea of helping the community, as far as Declan could tell from a general Google search, was putting attractive people in expensive houses. The latest article about him had been his announcement that he was passing his business on to his son. They'd been lucky he was visiting Kilwin before heading back to his current home of Miami.

Declan was hoping they'd be even luckier before the night ended.

"How do we play this?" Remi asked. "Good cop, bad cop?"

Declan raised his eyebrow at that.

"We're just going to see if he knows anything about Justin that can help us. We don't really need a good cop or a bad cop."

Remi snorted.

"That's what they always say."

"They?" he asked with a laugh. She nodded. Her eyes darted back to Lawson. She was excited. Declan couldn't much blame her. Just the *chance* of a lead could get his adrenaline going.

"Okay, there, hotshot, why don't we sit next to him and just talk first?"

"All right, but if you want me to turn up the heat or to help you, just say 'coconut.' That can be our safe word."

"Coconut? How am I supposed to work that into a conversation?"

Remi shrugged.

"If anything goes wrong, then you'll find a way."

She threw him a teasing grin and nodded toward Lawson.

The seats on either side of him were unoccupied. Declan touched the small of Remi's back before passing her and sliding onto the bar stool to the man's left while she took the right.

Declan noticed two things about Mr. Lawson from the get-go. One, he was working on at least his third drink. Two empty shot glasses hadn't been cleared yet from in front of him. The current glass his hand was wrapped around looked to contain whiskey. Two, the man matched the mood of three drinks. His shoulders were drooped over, his elbow propped up on the countertop, and his gaze was on the liquid of his drink. The word *dejected* popped into Declan's head at the sight of him.

When he dragged his eyes up to meet Declan's, his expression was blank.

"Mr. Lawson," he greeted, offering his hand to shake. "I'm Declan Nash and this is Remi. Thank you for meeting us."

Dean Lawson's handshake was a half-hearted affair. One he didn't extend to Remi, who gave Declan a disapproving look over the man's shoulder.

"You know, I hadn't been back to Kilwin in ten years

and then I'm in town for less than a week and everyone wants a piece." He took a sip of his drink. "What a wild ride."

Again Remi gave Declan a look.

"Well, thank you for coming out to meet us, then," he said, using his cordial voice reserved for press conferences. "We won't keep you long."

Lawson waved his hand dismissively.

"Don't worry, son, tonight is the last time I worry about managing my time. But whatever you're going to ask, better go ahead and ask it."

Declan didn't like Dean Lawson, he decided. Then again, he didn't need to like him to ask a question.

"Do you remember a man named Justin Redman?" he started, easing into it.

Lawson nodded.

"I do."

He didn't make any attempt to elaborate. Declan kept on.

"Twenty-five years ago he was attacked at a gas station by an unidentified man. Justin was killed in a car accident before the case could be investigated. The only information we had about the incident was the day it happened Justin said in a statement he was on the way to meet you. Do you remember why?"

Lawson ran his index finger up and down the side of his glass. He didn't look to Declan as he answered.

"Funnily enough, I don't remember why exactly he wanted to meet then. I remember the man, though." His face became pinched. "A child in men's clothes. That's what he reminded me of. A man who, for whatever reason, thought he was more than he was. An annoying little twerp." He laughed. It was unkind.

Remi's look of concern rivaled Declan's own confusion.

Dean Lawson was showing signs of disgust and hostility for a man who had died over two decades ago.

Lawson took the last long drink of his whiskey and shook the glass at the passing bartender. He was an older man who paid no attention to Declan or Remi. Not that either had planned on drinking, but the oversight added to the list of reasons Declan liked the old Waypoint Bar over the new version of it.

The bartender refilled his glass.

Lawson smiled down at the new drink.

"Did you know that I grew up in Kilwin?" he asked. "Not too far from this bar, actually. My dad was in sales and my mom inherited all of her father's money in lieu of an actual job. I grew up watching my dad, a proud and honest man, continue to work himself to the bone to provide for a family already provided for while my mother couldn't understand why he resented her. *Then* he died and Mom finally understood that all he'd been trying to do was show her the best things in life are earned, not bought." Lawson gave Declan a look of such loathing he nearly felt it as a physical thing. "So, in a drastic one-eighty to honor my father she decided I wouldn't see an ounce of her or his money ever. Not a dime, not a penny." Declan didn't miss his grip tighten around his glass. "Now, that might seem like an okay and even normal thing for most families but, you have to understand, I'd already spent my life relying on that money. My father was always away on business trips and my mother had already made the choice to make my life as easy as possible. When she decided that was a mistake and one she wouldn't continue to make? I was *days* away from striking out on my own."

He took a drink.

Declan's body was tensing on reflex, readying for something. He just wasn't sure what yet. Remi's body language had changed, too. She sat taller, more rigid. Neither had any idea what was going on.

Lawson finished his most recent drink and shook his head.

"Boy, was I stubborn about still sticking to the plan I'd made when I'd had the money and, boy, was I bad at it. It wasn't long at all before I was going to bed hungry in a crappy little apartment, filled with worry over what I'd do next. Then one night everything changed. One night I decided something that has been the guiding motivation of everything I've ever done since." Lawson shook his glass with one decisive shake. "There is no honor in starving, so why be honorable if that's what you'll get?"

Declan couldn't stay quiet any longer.

"Why are you telling us this?"

Lawson went back to staring at his drink. When he spoke next he sounded almost wistful.

"Because I wanted someone to know that, while I don't regret the things I've done over the last few decades to build the life I've lived, I did want someone to understand why I did them."

"And what are the things you've done?" Remi asked.

He didn't look up from his drink as he answered her.

"I made money and I protected that money. No matter the cost."

"Justin Redman didn't die in an accident, did he?" Declan formed it as a question, but his gut was already telling him it was true. "You killed him."

Lawson didn't deny it.

"The man was an idiot. He gets into a fight with one of my suppliers and then has the nerve to give a statement saying he was supposed to be meeting up with me after?" Lawson's anger was as potent as his loathing had been earlier. Declan readied for anything, including body slamming the man against the ground behind them if he even so much as blinked at Remi now or dropped his hands off the countertop. "Our standing arrangement was supposed to be confidential and only one of the many other confidential things he knew. Once your father was tasked with finding his attacker, I knew it was only a matter of time before Justin slipped up and damned me and everything I'd been working for. Deciding to kill him was easy. It was the other parts that were hard."

He laughed. It held no humor and sounded weaker than the one before.

"I thought I'd made it out. I really did. I went twenty-five years without ever hearing Justin's name and, yet, one week back in town and he's one of several names I've heard that I never wanted to again. I shouldn't have come back home." He sighed, pushed his drink away from him and grimaced. Then he was looking squarely at Declan. "You know, I saw you and your siblings, out on Main Street when I was in town once. The triplets were tiny, loud little things. Inseparable and a spectacle all in one. Everyone paid attention to them because of how rare triplets are, especially in Overlook. I admit, I was one of them. To this day I've not met another triplet set. But you? The eldest brother and singleton? No one paid you any mind. You weren't special. Not like they were."

Declan's hands had balled into fists. He couldn't look away from the man who would have been his father's age, staring at him without an ounce of fear of the consequences to what he was saying.

Dean Lawson didn't waver one bit.

Even when what he said next changed absolutely everything.

"That's why I paid him to kidnap you, instead. But he didn't listen to me, did he?"

Chapter Nineteen

Surprised wasn't the right word.

Angry wasn't, either.

Remi watched as Declan's face hardened into an emotion that made her feelings fall somewhere between the two. Fear didn't even register. Why would it?

Dean Lawson was just a sad man in a bar with a drink never that far from his fingertips.

A sad man who'd just said he had paid to have Declan kidnapped which, as history showed, hadn't worked out.

"Come again?" Declan's voice was ice.

Lawson sighed. The hunch he'd already been sitting with became more pronounced.

"Michael Nash was one of those hard-nosed detectives you see on old cop shows. The ones who never lose. If he'd gotten ahold of Justin, he would have gotten ahold of me. There was only one thing in the world that could have distracted him. Taking his kid." He pointed at Declan and shook his head. "But…" He glanced at the bartender. The older man was staring as he wiped a glass dry. Remi wondered if he had heard the patron's admission. "Things escalated. And now we're here."

Declan moved his blazer. She knew beneath it was his gun. They'd come here to get more insight into Justin Redman, and here they were sitting with the man who had paid to make the abduction possible.

"Who did you pay?" Declan's voice was unrecognizable.

Lawson shared a look with Remi. Or at least she thought it was with her. Instead, his eyes skirted to the person on the bar stool to the right of her. He had been in a conversation with a woman on the other side of him when they'd first sat down. Now the couple had gone silent and still. The bartender had also changed states. He placed a still-wet glass on the bar top and kept his dishrag in hand.

The hair on the back of Remi's neck started to stand.

Declan was understandably focused on Lawson, just as she had been, but now other details were blaring. The music that had been somewhat loud when they walked in had now softened. The movement of the bar's patrons eating, drinking and talking had lessened. The bar was quiet enough for her to hear the TV at the other side of the room.

Now that her focus wasn't homed in on Lawson's every word, Remi could tell something was off. *Very* off.

And Lawson was a part of it.

He wasn't answering Declan's question, even though he'd just incriminated himself by supplying information he hadn't really needed to give.

Surely he knew that Declan and the sheriff's department would go at him full force now?

Why did he suddenly seem so hesitant?

"I asked a question," Declan thrummed.

Again, Lawson kept quiet.

Something hit the floor between Lawson and Remi. She glanced down, body already taut with nerves.

Nerves that escalated so quickly it was a struggle not to openly gasp.

Blood.

That was what had hit the ground.

And it was coming from beneath Lawson's blazer.

"Coconut." The word came out before Remi could stop it. Then she chanted it. "Coconut. Coconut. Coconut."

Declan tore his eyes away from Lawson. Remi shook her head. The man between them chuckled. He finally took a long look at her.

That was when Remi *really* saw it. The pale skin, the pain.

The acceptance.

Now she knew why he'd freely admitted to what he'd done.

He was already dead.

"You can't escape them," he said. "He blamed me for complicating his life. He blames the Nashes for ruining it."

"We need to leave," Remi whispered across him, urgency making her heartbeat take off in a gallop.

"For over two decades he planned a way to find his justice." Lawson shook his head. "You'll only leave this place if it's a part of that plan. And, boy, is he big on plans."

Declan was off his bar stool in a flash. The movement seemed to be tied to every person inside the bar. Chairs scraped against wood and glasses clinked against tables as the entirety of Waypoint stood. They all had their guns out before Declan could pull his.

And they all were aimed at Remi.

Lawson was the only one who remained seated.

He turned back to his drink.

Remi, wide-eyed, looked at Declan.

He was furious.

"This was a trap. One we set up ourselves," he said through gritted teeth. "I should have never brought you."

Remi had opened her mouth to say she was sorry for pushing them to come since it had obviously been a bad plan after all when she was interrupted by a man breaking away from a group in the middle of the room. He was dressed in an expensive suit and smiling.

"We didn't give you much choice, now did we?" the man said. "After we realized the value of Miss Hudson, we knew that an attack against her would only make you stick that much closer to her side. Even taking her to a bar for a seemingly insignificant meeting." He stopped a few feet from them. Then he held out his hands and lowered them. Every patron around them put away their guns and sat back down.

Then it was just the three of them standing.

"If you hadn't brought her, then we would have. And killed every innocent person we had to to do it," he continued. "*This* was the best option you could have hoped for."

"I've been looking for you for a while now," Declan said. "The man with the scar on his hand who seems to pop up when us Nashes are involved."

Remi looked down at the man's hand. Sure enough she could see the scar in the shape of an X on it.

He was the leader of the Fixers.

And they were apparently in their den.

The man kept smiling.

"Maybe it's you all who keep popping up in my business. Did you ever think of that?"

Declan's hands were fisted. Remi wanted to hold them, but didn't want to move and start a fight.

"You're too young to have carried out the abduction," he said. "What's your part in all of this now? What do you want with us?"

The man's smile twisted into a nasty smirk.

"*I'm* here to give you some choices. Some hard choices. Then we'll be leaving and you'll never see me again."

Declan wasn't pleased with that answer.

"Let her go and I'll make all the choices you want."

The man shook his head. Then he looked at Remi.

"She's the one who has to make the first choice."

Declan started to move toward her to, she guessed, shield her from the man, his words and the consequences they'd bring. The man in the suit didn't have to lift a hand to stop him. Half of the bar raised their guns again. Declan held up his hands and stopped.

He actually growled.

"It's okay," she said. Then to the man in the suit, she said, "You clearly like the sound of your own voice so why don't you go ahead and give me your bad-guy spiel so you can hear it some more." The man's eyebrow rose. "Sorry, do you want me to sound more like a damsel? Do you want me to cry?"

"Huds," Declan warned.

I'm sassing because of pregnancy hormones and straight up fear, she wanted to explain. Instead, she tried to simmer down.

The man actually sniggered at her.

"I guess it shouldn't surprise me that you have some bite. You *did* manage to escape my men yesterday."

"After I shot one," she added, failing at keeping her sass in check.

The man nodded, conceding.

"You did, and it was such a bold decision given the odds. Which makes this next part interesting for me." He cleared his throat and clasped his hands behind his back. "This entire organization was made with the sole purpose of destroying the Nash family. From root to stem, every job taken, every connection made, has been a means to an end…for some of us. Myself? I'd like to think we're worth more than a revenge plot. But, for now, here I am to get us all to the next stage." His smile dropped and suddenly he was the image of a consummate professional. "You, Remi Hudson, can do one of two things. You can either come with me willingly to be bait for Declan and the triplets to come save you later, or you can refuse and I'll kill Declan and you'll still be bait for the triplets later. The choice is yours."

Remi went ramrod straight. Declan cussed and started telling her no.

She didn't listen.

"So I can either die now or die later? Not much of a choice."

The man shrugged.

"Think of it like this, if you leave voluntarily *he* won't die now and might even save *you* later. It's probably your best option."

"She's not going anywhere with you," Declan yelled. The man paid him no mind again.

"If I go with you, what's to stop your happy helpers from killing him the moment we leave?"

"Nothing, but we'd like his help for this next part. He's the best candidate to convince his siblings to meet us all at Well Water Cabin. Alone."

A shiver went down Remi's spine.

"Why do you want to go there?" Declan had to ask.

"Because it's poetic, I suppose. Because we can. Now, Miss Hudson, make your choice."

Remi looked at Declan.

Beautiful, soulful green eyes. Smart and cunning and, most of all, kind.

Declan Nash was a good man. He would be an even greater father. But to be that, to have that chance, Remi had to keep herself alive. Just as she had to keep him alive, too. Since she wasn't in law enforcement, didn't have a weapon and was standing in a room filled with at least fifteen people who weren't afraid to use theirs, making her choice was laughably simple.

"I'll go."

EVERY MAN AND woman had their weapons back up.

Some were itching to use them.

Declan knew the feeling, but reality was biting him in the backside. He made a rough estimate that there was no way he could get Remi out before one of the fifteen or so guns went off and bullets rained down on them both. Even if he became a human shield, the odds weren't in their favor that he could get her out without being hurt. He also figured there was no way he could get her safely out the back door behind the bar which, he assumed, led to a kitchen or office and eventually to an exit.

In fact, any way he sliced it, there was no good option to save Remi.

Rage boiled beneath his skin. Helplessness only made it hotter.

He should have never sought out information on Justin Redman. Going to Well Water to look for the note in the first place had been a mistake. Just as going back with Remi to find it had been.

He should have locked Remi and him up in his room.

Stayed together beneath the sheets.

Definitely not brought her along to Waypoint Bar.

"There's no way in hell you're going," he told her, chancing a slight movement that angled him between her and the man in the suit. She smiled. It made every part of him wish he could protect every part of her.

"I am. And you're going to let me." She lowered her voice to an almost-whisper. "Who knows Well Water better than you do?"

It was a question that hung in the air as the distance between them grew. Declan watched helplessly as his future family walked away from him.

Remi stopped at the man's shoulder. When she spoke, there was fire in her words and she let the entire room hear them.

"I may not have a badge or a gun but if I find out anyone so much as touched him after we left, you will never see me coming. I'll rip you and your cute little suit to shreds."

The man in the suit chuckled and nodded. He motioned to a woman at the table nearest him. She made her way over and then led Remi out.

Remi didn't look back at him.

Which was good.

Declan was doing all he could to keep from running after her and taking out as many guns as he could along the way. And maybe the Fixers around them knew that. Some pulled their guns higher.

When Remi and the woman were out of the bar the man in the suit moved closer. The smile he'd given Remi's sass was gone. His tone reminded Declan of a tired teacher.

"You will bring Madi, Caleb and Desmond to Well Water Cabin at midnight. You will tell no one else where you are going or why. You will lie if anyone asks where Remi is and you will do it convincingly."

"And if it's just me who shows up?"

The man in the suit shook his head.

"That's not part of the plan."

"And that's not a good answer."

He shrugged.

"I'm not here to give you what you want, Declan. I'm here to tell you the only chance you have at saving one family is to sacrifice the other. Like Remi, you have a choice here. Show up at Well Water with your siblings or don't."

"You're just going to kill us all when we get there," Declan said, trying to tamp down his anger. He motioned to Lawson behind them. He'd seen the blood after Remi had started yelling "coconut." Then he'd pieced it all together. They'd done something to Lawson, hurt him. Now he was dying. "Did you give him the same ultimatum? Show up and die, or don't show up and have someone you love die?"

"No," the man answered, voice clipped. "He never had a choice."

Declan flexed his hands, uncurling and curling them into fists.

"If you're really going to let me go, then let me take him with me."

Dean Lawson was a walking and talking answer. He'd paid for the abduction, which meant he knew the man with the scar who'd done it. Because Declan didn't for one second think that the man across from him now would tell him. And, honestly, if he did Declan would have a hard time believing him.

Lawson was the only silver lining of everything that was happening. A small, barely there sliver.

The man in the suit's lips curled up into a grin.

"Like I said, Dean never had a choice," he said. "He was always meant to die here surrounded by us, an empire made from nothing."

Lawson must have known that.

That was why he'd told Declan and Remi what he'd done.

And that was why he hadn't told them who he'd paid. He couldn't. Not with a room filled with Fixers.

He might have been dying, but he hadn't wanted to die yet.

Neither did Declan.

"I'll go," he said, repeating Remi's words.

The man in the suit nodded. He didn't flinch as Declan moved toward him and instead walked him out of the bar. Remi's car was still parked in the same spot they'd left it in, but she and the woman who had gone after her were nowhere to be seen. In fact, there was no one around at all.

It was just him and the man in the suit.

Declan could take him right then and there. Could pull his gun out, could tackle him, could dish out a punch that splayed him out on the concrete, but Declan found that he believed in the man's sincerity about what would happen if he didn't show up at Well Water Cabin.

He'd lose Remi.

He'd lose his baby.

Nothing was worth that.

Instead, Declan decided to throw himself into the next part of the plan he was being forced into. He started to walk away, but the man in the suit had some last words for him.

"You've seen us over the years. You've seen what we do and you know how good we are at doing it. There's also a lot you haven't seen. There's a lot you don't know. Don't underestimate us, Sheriff." It wasn't bragging. It was a warning. One he recapped. "If you or your siblings tell anyone about what's going on, we'll know, and it won't end well. For any of you or your families."

Declan almost decked the man then.

"I've met a lot of criminals in my life," he said with barely contained rage. "Do you know that most of them have a code? Have *some* honor?"

The man in the suit sighed. He actually sighed. Then he met Declan's eyes with a pensive stare.

"You've seen us over the years, and I've seen you Nashes over the years, too. I've seen you drown. I've seen you shot. I've seen you run into the darkness, run into flames, and run into places where the odds were never in your favor. You may think of yourselves as a normal family dealing in bad luck, but me? I see you as survivors, even if it's by the skin of your teeth. I wouldn't bet against you Nashes. You shouldn't, either."

Declan felt his eyebrow rise. The man in the suit gave a brief smile.

"I may not have *honor*, Mr. Nash," he continued. "But I am smart. Putting all four of you in one place while threatening your partners and children? Well, anyone would be a fool to believe with certainty that you'd lose in the end. I'm just trying to remain realistic."

Pride stirred in Declan's chest at that, but he made sure not to show it as he asked one last question.

One that he already knew the answer to.

"Your client, the one who hired you to orchestrate all of this—he's the one who took the triplets, isn't he? He's come back for them."

The man in the suit was solemn as he answered.

"He's come back for all of you."

Chapter Twenty

Declan went to Caleb's house first.

It was on the Nash Family Ranch and had been rebuilt with the help of the siblings. There was a wraparound porch with a swing on it that Declan himself had hung. That was where he found his brother sitting with his wife, Nina, and their son, Parker.

It was just after supper and they looked content.

When they saw Declan they all smiled, even Parker.

It tore at his heart as he lied.

"Hey, Caleb, I need your help on something," he said after they greeted each other. "Do you mind coming with me?"

Nina was readjusting Parker who had started to squirm, so she didn't see her husband's look of concern. Declan didn't have that triplet telepathy but he knew Caleb could feel something was majorly off. He ran his hand over his wife's back and dipped in for a kiss against her temple.

"Sure thing," he said to Declan. Then to her, Caleb said, "Nina, why don't you two go over to Mom's while we're gone. It would be the perfect time to put together that plastic play set she's been needing help with for the kids."

"Oh, you mean the one you boys were supposed to put together but always seem to have something better to do?" she responded, teasing clear in her voice. She sighed, all dramatic. "I suppose I always knew us ladies were the more capable ones. Plus, Parker took too long of a nap today and I don't see him going to bed anytime soon. Maybe this will tire him out."

Caleb and Declan helped her get Parker and his things into the car. While he gave Nina a quick kiss, Declan ruffed up Parker's hair and then gave him a tight hug. Caleb, seeing this, spent more time with the goodbye.

It wasn't until they were in the car and heading to pick up Desmond that Caleb turned to him.

"When you went to that bar you told us all to watch our families because they weren't safe. What's going on? And where's Remi? Why are we in her car but she's not here?"

"I can't tell you yet," Declan said with the stiffness of holding on to a world of worries for far too long. "We need to get Desmond and Madi first."

Caleb didn't argue. He didn't question. He listened to his big brother and Declan loved him for it.

Desmond's house had been built behind the main home they'd grown up in and their mother currently lived in but, from Declan's earlier instructions, he and his wife were at the main house. Nina got to the house a few seconds before they did and Caleb jumped out of the car to help her and Parker into the house. Desmond came back outside with him as Declan hung back.

He loved his mother dearly, but if Caleb was picking up on his tension, then their mother would, too.

Desmond's limp only made Declan feel worse. It must have shown. Both brothers shared a look between them after seeing Declan.

All three got into the car in silence.

Then they were on Winding Road and heading toward Hidden Hills Inn.

"Julian will know something's wrong," Desmond said

without prompting. "He won't let her leave without an explanation. Not unless he knows she won't be in any danger."

Declan gritted his teeth.

"Then she'll have to lie."

"It's that bad?" Caleb asked.

"It'll be worse if anyone thinks something's wrong."

That was enough to keep the boys quiet until they made it to the bed-and-breakfast Madi and Julian lived at and ran. There were no guests currently at the inn, but as soon as they cut the engine Julian appeared in the doorway of the house.

"Let me go get her," Caleb said, grabbing Declan's shoulder to keep him from getting up. "I'm closer with Julian than you two."

Declan didn't argue that. Julian had saved Caleb's life and, since then, the two had become close. In fact, Parker's middle name was Julian. Something that had made the older Julian tear up when he'd found out.

Their friendship was put to the test that night. Declan and Desmond couldn't hear what they said, but it was clear that Julian knew something was wrong, too, and wasn't about to let Madi be a part of it. Then Madi appeared. She joined the conversation and must have strengthened whatever argument Caleb had been making.

Then all three went inside.

Only Madi and Caleb came back out a minute later.

Caleb slid into the back seat and Madi buckled into the front.

They left Hidden Hills Inn and were quiet until they got to where Declan hadn't been in years.

He parked next to the river he had drowned in once. It was on land that no one currently lived on. He got out and the triplets followed.

The night was peaceful and cold.

Declan looked at his watch and began.

"I'm about to give you a lot of information really fast. Information that will be a lot to understand, but we're running low on time so I need you all to take it with a nod and let me keep going. Okay?"

They nodded in unison. No one was smiling. They wouldn't be after he was done, either.

"Justin Redman was supposed to meet Dean Lawson. That meeting was supposed to be secret. Lawson has been, as far as I can guess, dealing with drugs to make his fortune. Or, at least, he was back then. Justin got into a fight with one of his suppliers and then said Lawson's name in an official report. Lawson said he knew if Dad looked into the attack at all that Justin would eventually lead him to what Lawson had been doing and everything he worked for would be taken away. So, he decided to pay someone to abduct me to distract Dad. Lawson said that the man he paid didn't listen and, well, we know what happened instead."

Guilt surged through Declan. Guilt so strong he nearly stopped talking. He should have been the one taken. Not them.

"It's not your fault," Madi said, picking up on his thoughts. "Keep going."

Declan sighed.

"Lawson only told me this because he was dying and he was only still alive to get me and Remi to the bar. It was filled with Fixers." At this part he hesitated. Three pairs of true-blue eyes searched his face.

They were adults now. They had children and spouses. Careers, mortgages, and dental insurance.

Declan had walked Madi down the aisle at her wedding in the backyard of the inn she'd made into a home and business.

He'd been at Caleb's graduation and then sworn him in when he'd become a detective.

He'd stood, arm around Desmond, and looked up at a building that had been erected for the foundation he'd created that helped thousands of people daily.

Declan knew they were adults.

Knew that they could handle themselves. Knew they'd grown into thriving individuals.

Yet, standing there looking at them so close to where their father used to take them all fishing as a family, Declan saw only the little kids who had snuck out to a park to play a game of hide-and-seek and had reappeared three days later all grown-up.

How he wished with all his heart and soul he could have changed their fates.

He took another breath and then ripped off the bandage.

"The man who abducted you is back and he wants us to go to Well Water Cabin tonight to die."

There was a moment where no one said a word.

Then that was the last silence for a while.

"Who is he?" Caleb asked.

"I don't know. Lawson wouldn't say."

"He hired the Fixers, though?" Desmond asked.

Declan nodded.

"Apparently they've been in his back pocket for years. All the bad stuff that's gone down with us all? Them, at his order. I don't know why he's coming after us all now, but he is. The man in the suit, the leader we keep running into, said they'll kill everyone we love if we tell a soul about the meeting."

Madi took a small step forward. She put her hand over her heart.

"You want us to go," she said, voice soft, "because they have Remi, don't they?"

He nodded.

"They know something I should have told you yesterday." He gave them a small smile. Happy for the news, angry at how he had to give it. "She's pregnant...with my kid."

Madi was the first to move. She threw her arms around Declan. Caleb and Desmond weren't far behind.

"Oh, Declan, I'm so happy for you," Madi said into his chest.

"Same here, big guy," Desmond said.

"You'll make an awesome dad," Caleb finished.

"Thanks, guys."

The warmth of familial love spread through him at the words. At the group hug. At the way the future seemed brighter with the thought of a baby in it.

Then that warmth cooled until it was ice.

The Nash children stepped back and all joy was gone.

"I'm not like the Fixers. I'm not going to force you to come to Well Water with me. My best guess is this man wants to talk and then he'll kill us all. But there's no guarantee he won't kill us all the moment we drive up." Declan felt the resolution in his heart before the words to back it up left his lips. "But I'm going. Even if it's only to give Remi a better chance at escaping. I just—I wanted you all to know. You've deserved answers for most of your lives. I wanted you to at least get some of them."

The triplets didn't even look at each other.

Madi spoke first.

"You're wrong," she said with bite. "Saving your family, getting our answers, and finally giving that son of a bitch what's coming to him. We deserve it all."

"She's right," Desmond said with vigor. "We're going and we're going to save Remi and we're going to finally put this mystery to rest."

Caleb nodded. Declan was surprised to see him smirk. In fact, he was surprised to see all of them so calm. The man who had scarred them, locked them up and changed all of their lives because of this was waiting for them.

Waiting to kill them.

Yet, there they were.

Suddenly those three children looked exactly as they should have to him.

Two men and a woman ready for justice.

Caleb captured the sentiment well.

"Whoever this man is, whatever his reason is for wanting us, he's overlooked one devastating fact. We're grown-up now and we won't be as easy to push around."

Madi and Desmond agreed.

Declan smiled at this brothers and sister.

"Then it's settled," he said. "Now, we have less than three hours to come up with a plan to find justice for our father, bring peace to our mother, get answers for us, and save the woman I love and our kid. Any objections?"

Not a one of them made a peep.

THE BASEMENT WASN'T as bad as Remi had pictured. In fact, in any other circumstance, she would have thought it was cozy.

A few steps from the stairs was a door that led into a spacious room with a kitchenette in the corner and an open door that showed a bathroom on the other side. The light fixtures were nice and did a good job of lighting up the place, and even the kitchenette was pleasing to look at.

What changed the feel of the room in such a sudden and violent way was the three small cots against the wall and the four locks on the door, reminding her just what the triplets had gone through all those years ago.

When the woman in the pantsuit locked all four locks,

Remi quaked in fear. She was alone in the room and leaned into the privacy. She cried. She hoped she hadn't left Declan to die and she hoped she hadn't just led herself and their child to do the same.

She felt exhausted.

She felt helpless.

And then she felt sick.

Remi ran to the bathroom with tears blurring her vision and threw up in the sink.

Because of course morning sickness didn't take a break. Not even when she was being held captive. She tried to compose herself after the deed and instead was hit with another wave of nausea.

This time she threw up in the toilet.

After that she leaned against the wall and cried some more.

It wasn't until a man cleared his throat that Remi realized someone was in the doorway.

The man in the suit from Waypoint was holding a bottle of water and a packet of gum.

"There might be power now, but there's no running water in the house, I'm afraid," he said. "And if you die tonight I'd bet it would feel nicer to die with somewhat fresh-feeling breath."

He stepped back to let her out of the bathroom and shook the bottle when she didn't take it.

"Both are in sealed containers. Not taking them is only going to make *you* more uncomfortable. Not me."

Remi was thirsty and her mouth tasted awful. Denying either point didn't make them go away. She relented and took both, but not without a severe look she hoped hurt the man.

"Being kind to a pregnant woman you're about to kill doesn't make you a good person, you know," she said hotly.

The man shrugged.

"Who says I want to be a good person?"

That sent a shiver of fear down Remi's spine. Whether she wanted to feel it or not.

"But, if it makes you feel better, I won't be the one killing you. That's not part of the plan."

Remi opened the bottle, breaking its seal, and went back to the bathroom to wash her mouth out. When she came back she took a long drink of water and popped two pieces of gum.

Both made her feel light-years better.

So did her barb at the man.

"For someone who thinks they're so clever, it's interesting to find out you're nothing more than someone else's bitch."

The man snorted, trying to seem like he'd blown off the insult, but Remi saw it.

She saw the nostrils flare, saw the anger pass over him. She'd hit a nerve.

Because she'd spoken the truth.

But the man was more disciplined than she had hoped. He was back to smiling.

"For being the bait that's going to lead almost an entire family to slaughter, you sure are cocky."

Remi wanted to say something clever, something that hurt him, but she didn't have his discipline. She kept quiet and went to one of the cots, and he eventually left without another word.

Then there she sat for hours.

In that time she thought about her father, her brothers, her mother and stepfather, her job, and the Nashes. She thought about Declan and their unborn child the most.

By the time the door to the basement opened, Remi had

come to a decision. The only catch was that they all had
to survive the night.

Remi didn't recognize the man who walked in but she
recognize did the scar on his hand.

The man who had taken the triplets.

The man who wanted them all to die.

And he'd come to see her first.

Chapter Twenty-One

There were at least twenty men and women wearing suits surrounding the cabin. It was such an odd sight to Declan. For the last decade Well Water had been forgotten by most of the world, a desolate structure that was visited by him only for the occasional maintenance. Before that it had been his father visiting. Before that it had been a circus.

Now the abandoned cabin in the woods had too many people in and around it. People dressed for the boardroom with guns in hand like they were going to war.

"If it all goes sideways I'm doing everything in my power to get Remi out," Declan said after he found a place to park among a cluster of inconspicuous cars and trucks. "That includes dying. And you're going to let me if that means you can get out, too."

No one rebuffed him, but Desmond tried to be reassuring.

"This will work. I know it will."

No one backed him up but no one disagreed.

They'd had three hours to come up with a plan to save Remi and themselves without weapons, without help, and without knowing how many people would be at the cabin.

Their plan was at best risky; at worst it was downright idiotic.

And it was all they had.

A man came to the door as Declan got out. He was sneering. It was the one man he'd chased across Main Street. He ran a hand through his red hair, exposing the holster and the gun in it against his side.

"Howdy, Sheriff. If you'd be so kind to allow my associates to check you all for any knives, guns, bombs, *et cetera*, that would be mighty kind of you." He was mocking them but Declan allowed the search. Just as his siblings did. The redhead seemed surprised that none of them had any weapons of any kind on them. No cell phones, either.

Those were back at the river, GPS on, and each holding video recordings for their families and law enforcement. They were hoping their plan would work but prepared if it didn't. Watching his siblings make their videos for their kids and spouses tore Declan apart. They'd noticed and told him again this was their choice to make and they'd made it.

Tonight, for better or worse, one nightmare would end.

Redhead led them inside and cut right to the living room. Declan felt the tension coming off the triplets. This was the first time Madi and Desmond had been back to Well Water since they'd escaped. For Caleb it had been a few years, but that didn't matter.

This place was their personal hell.

One that was filled to the brim with strangers waiting for them.

Among the crowd was the man in the suit. Still the fanciest in the group. He smiled when they stopped in front of him.

"You didn't bring any weapons and you didn't ask for any help. I don't know if you aren't that smart or if you all are just a bit too confident."

"You gave us terms and we followed them," Declan said. "I'd say that makes us, at least, respectful."

The man in the suit nodded. He was pleased.

"It does make everything go smoothly when you follow the rules."

Declan looked around the room. He knew where she probably was but still had to ask.

"Where's Remi?"

The man's smile faded. He became the ideal image of a businessman.

"She's downstairs with the man of the hour." He held up his hand to stop Declan from saying how much he didn't like that. "She's fine. We can go see her now."

He nodded to the people around them. Most stayed but Redhead, a woman with a sneer and three others followed. They walked behind their group as Declan followed the man in the suit to the only place that was ever an option for this horrible meeting.

Declan turned to his siblings as they got to the top of the stairs to the basement. He lowered his voice.

"You're not little kids anymore."

Caleb nodded. Desmond and Madi grabbed hands and stood straighter.

Then the Nash children followed the man in the suit down into the room they wanted to go in least. Right up to the smiling face of a man Declan had never seen.

Yet the triplets had.

Madi made a guttural, primal growl.

Caleb balled his fists.

Desmond lowered his head but kept eye contact, jaw clenched.

Declan looked past the man at Remi.

Then he yelled.

Guns came out and up from the man in the suit, Redhead and the woman. Declan stopped in his tracks.

Remi was lying across one of the cots, blood visible across the side of her face.

"She's not dead, not yet," the man said. "She got a little too mouthy so I showed her what that gets you in my house. I hit her a little too hard, I suppose. She fell right over like a twig in the wind."

Declan was absolutely seething. His chest was rising and falling in rage-fueled pants. He turned to the man in the suit.

"You said she was fine," he roared.

The man in the suit shared a look with the other. He didn't seem too happy, but he offered Declan no explanation or apology.

Then Declan was staring back at the man he was going to kill.

The triplets had tried their best to describe what their abductor looked like after they were rescued. Madi had talked about his eyes so dark they looked black and made you feel cold when they were on you. Brown hair like dry mud and messy like mud, too. Caleb had focused on his stature. He wasn't too tall but was wide. Strong but slow. Not overweight but not rail thin. Average. Desmond, on the other hand, had gotten more emotional with his descriptions.

One had always stuck with Declan.

"He was quiet but looked like he wanted to break us just because he could," eight-year-old Desmond had said. It was a statement that had held more weight than the others, considering that same man had badly broken his leg during the initial attack and then made him suffer with it for days.

Now, standing close enough to strangle him, Declan saw what young Desmond had seen.

The man wanted to break them. All of them.

And Declan was over it.

"What do you want?"

The man kept smiling.

"My name is William Gallagher," he started. "And I tell you that to remind you that you won't be leaving this cabin, so having my name does nothing for you. As for you, well, I'll never forget you." He looked past Declan's shoulder and listed the triplets off as he looked at them. "Desmond, Madeline and Caleb. It's been a while, hasn't it? I've been keeping tabs on you three. Late congratulations on your marriages and children. Your careers are also touching. Not what I would have picked had I had a choice, but it doesn't really matter in the end, does it?"

Declan had to breathe in slowly through his nose and let out a breath through his mouth. It was the only way to keep from running at William.

He seemed to sense Declan's struggle with his rage.

"Dean wanted me to take you. Did you know that?" William said. "But if Dean wanted a distraction by taking one of Michael Nash's kids, boy howdy at the distraction taking three would be." His smile twisted upside down. Anger flashed across his expression. "I had everything planned out. But what I hadn't foreseen was how much heat taking you three would be. And after you escaped?" He shook his head, anger apparent on his face. "Dean decides not to pay me. Skips town. So what do I have to do? Go underground. Give up *my* life to hide as the entire country looks for my face. My scarred hand. *Me.* And all because I *gave a damn about you dying.*"

At this he looked at Desmond.

What was more famous than the abduction itself was how the triplets had escaped. After having his leg broken and untreated, by day three Desmond was in immense pain and in a bad way. Madi and Caleb knew that if they didn't get him help soon he could die. So, in a last-ditch effort, they'd decided to have him play dead.

Up until this point William had only ever brought them food. But when they started screaming and crying, saying that Desmond had stopped breathing, he'd run in to check. The moment he was trying to find a pulse was the moment everything changed.

It didn't matter who you asked, neither Madi, Caleb nor Desmond could remember exactly what happened next. The best they could describe it was that they'd simply synced up. Become a hive mind. They'd attacked William as one unit and gotten to the other side of the door to lock it. Together they'd run into the woods, bloody, broken and scarred.

When Caleb had brought the cops back to the cabin after they'd been found, William was gone.

"We couldn't have done it had you not broken my leg in the first place," Desmond shot back.

William let out a low, tense laugh.

"You don't understand the danger you're in, son. For years I missed out on the life I wanted, living in the shadows, waiting. So I decided to spend those years building something that could do what I'd been forced to do. All for the purpose of destroying everyone who forced me to abandon what I'd loved."

"You started the Fixers," Caleb said.

William nodded.

"And I used them to torment you all the last few years. Help those who despised you, who wanted to harm those you loved." He shared a look with the man in the suit. It wasn't a kind one. He didn't explain it, either. "You might have prevailed each time but you also were waiting. Waiting for the other shoe to drop." William extended his hands out wide. "Now it has."

"Why now?" Madi asked, voice sharp.

"I wanted you to build your lives. Make careers. Fall

in love. Create families. I was getting restless waiting for our dear sheriff to find someone. But then his truck broke down and, well, the mouthy one behind me came into the picture. That was enough for me to start."

"So, Lydia, she's a Fixer." Declan said it because he already believed it to be true. "She used Jonah to get to Remi."

William snorted.

"You want to know a fun thing about small towns? You get a happy coincidence once in a while. See, Lydia was brought in only to do whatever plan I saw fit. She was supposed to blend in first and build up some grace with the locals until I had that plan. And what better family to attach to than those who ran the Heartland Ranch? Childhood friends to the Nashes? It was a shock to us all when we realized that, not only were you and Miss Hudson no longer just friends, that she was pregnant with your child." His grin was sickening. "Having Lydia and the others try to take the mother of a future Nash child, even though it didn't work out the way I wanted? Well that was almost as fun as planting a note in a wall, knowing that just the mention of it would drive you mad. Watching you Nashes obsess has become a fun pastime of mine throughout the years. I think, when this is over, that's what I'll miss most."

William took a small step forward. Not close enough that Declan could lunge at him but close enough that Declan's muscles started tensing up, ready for anything. His mirth was gone. He had gotten to what he really wanted to say. "I want you all to know that your violent deaths will become a horror story every man, woman and child will know. A nighttime terror that will haunt your families, your loved ones, your friends, your coworkers. Strangers. I had to live in the shadows and you'll never leave the spotlight. Not even in death."

He turned to the man in the suit. He nodded, but neither man made a move. William looked at Declan as he
added one last thing.

"Any last words before *all* of you meet horrible ends?"
Declan took a quick breath.

Then he turned to the man in the suit and made sure
his words were absolutely sincere.

This was it.

"I want to hire you."

The man in the suit raised his eyebrow. Redhead and the
woman laughed. So did William. The man didn't.

"Come again?"

Declan turned to face him completely, angling away
from William. So did Madi, Caleb and Desmond.

"My father was a good man," he started. "But when he
couldn't find who was behind the abduction, he became
obsessed. Every day, every night. Weekends. He worked
the case until it was all he did. Holidays, birthdays. He
started to hate every special day that families are supposed
to enjoy together. They were reminders that the years were
going by and he was no closer to figuring it out. He pushed
my mother away first, and then, when we all started to
move on, he dug in so deep that he sacrificed himself to
it. The obsession. Then he died, and even though I knew
not to become him because I'd seen what it did, I still followed his example." Declan motioned to the room around
him. "I own this place. This hell pit. Because *he* did and
he willed it to me. No explanation. No note. Just a deed
and an unspoken direction." That was something no one
in his family knew. He could feel six baby blue eyes look
in his direction. He kept on. "And I went into law enforcement and I started to obsess. I started walking that line
between doing what I wanted and doing what he wanted."

Declan glanced at William. He still looked smug.

"When William took the kids, he ended whatever chance we had at a normal life. That includes you." This part was a gamble, but it was a theory they had kicked around before coming to Well Water.

Declan motioned to his hand. To the scar that matched William's.

"You were right earlier. I don't know much about you, but I *do* know you follow contracts. You never betray them. *That's* your code. And since William is your father, I'm going to assume he doesn't have a contract, does he?"

A pin could have dropped and they would have heard it.

The man in the suit didn't dispute a word he'd said.

Which meant they had been right. The man in the suit wasn't the boss, he was their abductor's son.

"You want to hire me to kill my father?" he asked after a moment.

Declan shook his head.

"I want to hire you and the Fixers to get Remi, take her to the hospital and tell them she's pregnant, and then do what you all do best. Disappear." Declan looked around the room to the suits ready to mock such an outrageous idea. He pointed to William, who was looking less smug. "At his prime he was bested by three eight-year-olds. Then he spent most of his life plotting against them when he could have easily killed us time and time again. You've been around here. You know who we are. We're fathers and mothers and husbands and wives. We're law enforcement. We're charitable and charming and kind. This town loves us. If you kill us? All because an old man's pissed he messed up a job by not following orders in the first place? You'll be hunted to the ground by our loved ones. And if they don't find you, they'll have kids that will grow up and hunt your kids down. The cycle will never end."

Declan went back to the man in the suit.

"Let's show our fathers we're stronger than they ever were."

William made a noise. A snort that clearly said he thought Declan was crazy.

But he wasn't paying attention to the suits. Their expressions had turned thoughtful and their gazes had turned to the man in the suit.

He considered Declan. He considered his father. Then he looked at the scar on his hand.

That was when Declan knew.

"There's money in the trunk of the car, where the spare tire is. I don't know your going rate, but it should be enough."

The man turned back to him. He nodded.

"Your contract has been accepted."

"What!" William was livid. His son paid him no mind.

"We'll take Miss Hudson to the hospital and let them know she's pregnant. Then you won't ever see us again." He nodded to Redhead and the woman. They went to Remi and scooped her up. Declan wished it could be him, but the Nash siblings had already guessed that while the man in the suit might accept their contract, he wouldn't go so far as to interfere with his dad.

The other suits seemed to agree and, just like that, the man in the suit became the real boss of the Fixers. He saw to Remi being taken to the stairs and only stopped at the door. He turned around and looked his father up and down. His last words before he left the room, however, were for them all.

"There's a gun in the middle kitchen drawer. Good luck."

The door shut and the sound of it locking became the background noise to a whirl of motion.

William was faster than Declan would ever give him credit for. He couldn't grab him in time. None of them could though they tried.

Madi got to him just as he flung the drawer open. She grabbed at his face, lashing out with her nails. It tore at his skin, making him yell so loud it hurt Declan's ears. Still he pulled the gun out and turned. Desmond gave his own battle cry as he hit the man in the gut with a devastating tackle. He, Madi and William slammed backward into the wall. The gun hit the ground and skidded away but William kept struggling.

Caleb joined the fray next with a punch that hit William's face so hard it echoed.

Declan scooped up the gun. He aimed it at William but there was no reason to use it. William had gone slack from the hit even though Madi held one arm, Desmond held the other, and Caleb had his hands against his chest so he wouldn't move an inch from where he was.

Despite everything, Declan smiled.

The Nash triplets had, once again, bested their abductor.

He wasn't dead but, this time, there wasn't a chance in hell that he was getting away.

Chapter Twenty-Two

Remi was shocked.

By many, many things.

First, she was shocked to wake up in her car being driven by the man in the suit. They were alone, which made her feel such an intense wave of anger and anguish that she nearly got sick again. The throbbing headache from being knocked out by his boss in the basement wasn't helping.

"Declan hired me to take you to the hospital," he'd said when she moved. "From there you can call for help to go out to the cabin. It'll only be the Nash family and one other man."

Remi hadn't known what to say or believe but, sure enough, he'd dropped her off right outside the hospital doors. Then he'd gotten out of her car, which apparently Declan had driven to the cabin, and stepped into one that had been following them.

And then he'd left.

The second shock was, after sending almost every member in law enforcement to Well Water Cabin, she got a call from Declan. Remi blamed the pregnancy hormones on how hard she cried at hearing his voice.

The shocks only got better after that.

Remi was seen by a doctor alongside her mother, who

had finally made it to the hospital. Together they learned something that made them both freak out and squeal at the same time. After that Remi found out her father was awake and asking for her.

She hugged him fiercely, told him what she'd just found out and then the decisions she'd come to while being trapped in the basement. She'd cried again as he'd teared up. Josh and Jonah were next on the list for some familial love and the good news.

Then Declan arrived as she settled into a seat in the lobby to wait for him.

He ran in, saw her and was upon her before she could stand. He only broke their kiss to ask a volley of questions.

"Are you okay? Why are you out here? How's the baby?"

Remi laughed.

"I have a headache but am okay. I came out here to wait for you." Remi took a deep breath, then let it out. "And the babies are fine."

Declan's eyes tripled in size.

He smiled like a wild man.

"Babies?"

Remi held up her fingers.

"It's still too early to really tell anyone but, there are two sacs, Declan. *Two.*"

She laughed, unable to stop the giddiness.

Declan shook his head, then was laughing.

"I'm guessing that means you're okay with the idea of having twins?"

"Are kidding me? I'd love it!" He laughed again, throwing his head back. Then he wrapped his arms around her. "Man, my family is going to flip. The singleton Nash might have twins?"

He pulled away from her and dipped low for another kiss.

Then those green eyes she loved were on her. Suddenly his expression changed to a serious one.

"Huds, we said we were going to have a talk about the future and here's what I'm thinking. I want to move to Colorado with you," he said. "I want to raise our kids together, in the same place. I want to wake up next to you and go to sleep with you in my arms."

That was the second biggest shock of the night.

"You'd give up being sheriff? You'd leave your family?"

Declan put his hand on her stomach. Remi could have melted.

"You're my family, too. And I'd cross oceans for you if that's what you wanted."

Butterflies dislodged and had a frenzy in her stomach.

"Well, look at that. My wild cowboy ready to hang up his hat for me." She ran a hand across his cheek. Every part of her softened. "I suppose this is a good time to tell you my new life plan. I have a feeling you're going to really like it."

ONE CHRISTMAS PASSED.

And then another.

By the third Christmas, so much had changed.

And so much hadn't.

Declan sat on his horse wearing his cowboy hat. Desmond and Caleb wore theirs while Madi was sitting on the fence next to the stable wearing her boots. She was pregnant again and her bump was the reason she'd decided to sit on the fence rather than a horse. Still, she wanted to hang around her siblings until Julian showed up so they could go home.

"You know, Ma is bringing a date to Christmas Eve dinner, right?" she asked, no hard feelings in the words. Between Desmond and Riley becoming parents, Caleb and Nina expanding the retreat, and Madi and Julian preparing for their fourth child, spending time together had lessened. They still had Sunday dinners together, but that was at their mother's, which meant gossiping about her hadn't been ideal.

"It's about time," Desmond said with a smile. Caleb mirrored it.

"Y'all do know she's been seeing Christian in secret for over a year, right?"

Declan laughed.

"Yeah, it's not like you can keep a secret in this town. I'm glad she's making it public, though. Now we don't have to pretend like we have no idea why he keeps showing up around the ranch even though he lives in Kilwin."

Madi laughed and bounced her foot in the air. She rubbed her belly.

"I think Dad would approve, despite him and Christian's differences from back in the day."

They all agreed. During what felt like a lifetime ago, their father had believed Christian was connected to the triplets' abduction. It had put a wall of resentment and discord between the men and the Nash family. That was until Christian had proven he was a great man after helping Madi survive the family's first brush with the Fixers. Since then he'd become friends with the family. More so with their mother. Dorothy Nash had been nothing but happy the last year or so and they knew it wasn't all because they'd put William Gallagher behind bars for good. Though, having him locked up had definitely helped.

For a man who had spent years cultivating a group who would rather die than spill their secrets, William became a very talkative man once in handcuffs. He said he did so to take Dean Lawson down with him, detailing their arrangement and what had really happened all those years ago. Lawson, who had passed away at the bar that night, lost the reputation he'd built for years, as well. And that had been William's goal.

He was big on trying to hurt people, even after death.

As for his son, the man in the suit, he mostly stayed true to his word. A month after everything had settled down, he visited Declan outside of the grocery store of all places.

"I don't think you understand what 'I won't see you ever again' means," Declan had greeted. The man in the suit had smirked.

"Don't worry, this is a quick social visit."

Declan knew the man wasn't good, but he couldn't bring himself to be wary of him, either. Especially since the Fixers had been rumored to have disappeared from, not only Overlook, but all of Wildman County.

"For what it's worth, I'm sorry about your dad," Declan had found himself saying. He'd later blame the kindness on the fact that the man had taken Remi to the hospital and, honestly, had saved all of their lives by taking the contract in the first place.

"For what it's worth, I'm sorry about yours, too."

They'd shared a small companionable silence. One of understanding. Then they were back to their normal roles.

"You know, this is the only time I'll let you go free," Declan had said. "So after you leave my sight, you better stay out of it."

The man in the suit had laughed.

"Remember how we agreed that you don't know me?" he'd asked. "Well, let me enlighten you on something. While my dad was amassing money to help with your destruction, I was stealing and saving it. The second I'm out of your sight I'll be heading to a private airfield and on my way to a beautiful, remote beach somewhere very tropical. And *then* I'll disappear."

"Still, very brazen of you to show back up here again."

The man in the suit started to walk toward a car near them.

"I can afford to be brazen, Sheriff. I bet you still haven't found *any* record of my existence, have you?" He'd said it with a smile and he'd been right. No one had been able to find any hint that he existed, not even his name. "Don't feel bad. While my father spent decades waiting to reveal himself when the right time came, I spent the same time waiting to disappear."

The man in the suit had pointed to Declan's truck.

"Consider that an early baby shower gift," he'd said. "For what it's worth, I don't hate that you Nashes might now have a shot at a happy ending. And consider this the only time I'll ever break a contract."

He'd already been gone by the time Declan saw what he'd left in Fiona's front seat.

It was the bag of money he and his siblings had collected to pay for their contract with the Fixers back at Well Water. On top of the bag were two ribbons. One pink, one blue.

Declan and Remi had received another gift after they'd married that he believed to be from the man. It was a postcard of an island with well wishes and an exorbitant amount of money that they'd decided to give to charity. The card had been signed "the Whisperer."

Other than that, Declan hadn't seen or heard of the man in the suit or the Fixers since.

"I think Dad would have liked this, too," Caleb said, bringing Declan back to the present. He motioned to the four of them. "Us, I mean, but, especially you."

Declan was surprised to see those three sets of baby blues turn to him. Caleb continued.

"We realized this morning when we were helping set up the Christmas lights that we somehow have been idiots and haven't told you this outright and in clear words. So, get ready for the mushiness."

They all shared a look.

Desmond spoke next.

"Thank you, Declan."

He didn't understand.

"For what?"

Madi's smile was small but true.

"For giving us peace."

It was such a simple statement but it did something Declan hadn't thought possible. A weight had been lifted. The guilt, the heartache… It all blew away in the nice December breeze.

Movement caught his eye at the edge of the field.

"You guys are going to make me cry in front of my wife," he said with a genuine smile.

Madi laughed.

"Like you didn't blubber when Michael and Lysa were born," she teased.

"And don't forget that tearing up you did at the wedding," Caleb added with a grin.

Declan laughed and didn't deny either accusation. Other than his kids being born, his wedding to Remi had been one of the best days of his life.

It had been a small, perfect ceremony held in the no-man's-land between the Nash Family Ranch and Hudson Heartland. To show they approved of Declan, Gale Hudson had officiated while Josh and Jonah had walked Remi down the aisle of flowers and grass. Her mother and stepfather had held the twins while his mother and Christian had distracted the rest of the grandchildren. Every Nash sibling and spouse were either groomsmen or bridesmaids.

"Don't act like you didn't drop a tear or two," Desmond said to Caleb.

Caleb in turn swatted at him, which riled Desmond up. Soon they were racing around the barn and up toward Caleb's house. A car started up the drive and Madi waved Declan off.

"That's Julian," she said. "You can go on to your wife now, Sheriff."

"If I could, I'd swoop down and kiss you on the cheek, little sister," he said, half-mocking. She laughed.

"And if I wasn't the size of a beach ball I'd stand up and accept it."

Declan laughed and soon he was off riding. He slowed as Remi did, meeting him in the middle.

She was as beautiful as a sunset and he told her as much.

"You keep sweet-talking me like that, Mr. Nash, and we might be catching up to Madi and Julian's kid count tonight."

Declan chuckled.

"We did say we'd start sometime after the kids were walking," he pointed out. "Though now I can't see where the sense in that is."

"We're attracted to adventure, I suppose. Why else would we be building a house with a set of twins and two stressful jobs?"

Declan ticked the reasons off on his fingers as he listed them.

"Because my house was too small. We're sentimental fools who thought it would be nice to live on the same stretch of land we got married on. We didn't plan to get pregnant with twins, though I'm over the moon it happened. *And* because we actually love our jobs."

Remi, who was now chief financial officer at Desmond's foundation, nodded at each point.

"Don't you come at me with answers that make sense."

"Oh, I'll come at you with something all right, cowgirl."

He winked at her, which made Remi throw her head back as she laughed again.

Then she was all smiles.

"Only if you can catch me, cowboy."

Remi was off on her horse, pointed toward their home, faster than Declan could whistle.

Before he followed after her, Declan turned around and looked at his family and the ranch he'd been born on and would probably spend the rest of his days around.

Caleb, Desmond and Madi were still hanging around, laughing, talking and riding. His mother was up at the house, not five minutes away, singing Christmas carols and baking gingerbread cookies, he had no doubt.

Declan had spent years worrying about his family. Worrying that they'd never be whole again. That they'd never *truly* find happiness. That life wasn't as kind as it was mean.

Yet, sitting astride his horse in a field he used to ride with his father, Declan Nash *really* did feel it, too.

Peace.

* * * * *

COLTON 911: DETECTIVE ON CALL

REGAN BLACK

For Mark, my personal hero.
I'd be lost without you, my love.

Chapter One

At the reception desk of the women's prison, Pippa Colton waited, smothering her brewing impatience under a professionally unflappable demeanor. Probably the most important lesson of law school: never let them see you sweat.

Though *she* wasn't sweating in her charcoal slacks and tailored jacket, it was impossible to ignore the ripe smells of the countless bodies that had passed through. Thanks to its overcrowding and pervasive violence, she could not consider the prison system as anything other than inhumane. No matter how clean on the surface, every prison had a distinct odor of fatigue, resignation and stress that never faded. Her client would have likely thrown a fit and demanded air freshener upon arrival.

The guard on the other side of the window frowned at her credentials, shifting his gaze to a computer monitor and back to her. "You're not listed on the visitor log today."

"There must be a mistake." She reached into her briefcase for the confirmation she'd printed out after registering this meeting through the online portal. This wasn't her first trek to a prison. "I have the details right here."

She slid the page through the gap in the protective

window, and on the other side, the skinny man's thin upper lip curled. He seemed bent on turning her away, but jumping through hoops was part of the job. Soon she would be heading deeper into this monstrosity of a facility, and the attitudes aimed her way from both inmates and guards were likely to get surlier along the way.

With a put-upon sigh, the guard keyed in the number at the top of the page and waited. Shaking his head, he pushed the paper back to her, along with her credentials. "Nothing here, ma'am."

"But—"

He shrugged. "There's nothing here. You'll have to reschedule."

She reined in her temper. No one in the legal system wanted to befriend the lawyer trying to overturn a conviction. Especially when that conviction meant freeing the woman everyone loved to hate, Anna Wentworth, who had been transferred to the prison two weeks ago after a jury found her guilty of murdering her lover, David Hicks.

Public opinion had been working against Anna from the start. A prominent married socialite in Grand Rapids, Michigan, Anna had been dubbed the Queen of Mean long before being labeled as a killer. Oddly enough, no one cared that she'd been unfaithful to her husband, Ed, only that she'd allegedly offed Hicks when the younger man ended the affair.

"Could you please double-check?" she asked with a polite smile. Her mind was envisioning outrageous methods of getting to her client. But she wasn't an action hero, just the least popular attorney in Michigan today.

The guard walked away without a word, paper in hand. She had no idea if the man would return to the window or how long it would be until someone else stepped up to return her credentials.

She'd never been outright denied a visit. To get Anna released, she had to give the court the real killer and proof to clear her client. Unfortunately, the case file and collected evidence had yet to point her in the right direction. Why was she the only person who could look at the evidence and see it was too neat and tidy to be true? Her hope was that Anna would cooperate today in ways she hadn't done with her original defense team.

At the time of her arrest and trial, Anna had been certain being innocent—and wealthy—would be enough to get the charges dismissed and the case thrown out. No one could convince her of the severity of the evidence against her. As a strategy, being too wealthy to go to prison was terrible. As a lifestyle it was worse. Though Pippa had also been raised in a wealthy family, she detested Anna's elitist and privileged attitudes. But no one deserved to be in prison for a crime they didn't commit.

The skinny guard returned, looking annoyed that she hadn't given up. "Sorry, ma'am. I double-checked." He pushed the paper and her credentials back across the counter for her. "You can't see your client today. In the future you'll need to schedule an appointment with the new form."

"I scheduled today's appointment with the current form," Pippa said. She pulled up her phone and opened her email app. Briskly, she read aloud the dates of her emails and the positive responses from the prison. "Shall I forward these to you?" she queried.

"No, ma'am. I can't accept that as authorization." His

gaze fell and he looked a bit sheepish, and she pounced on the first sign of weakness.

"What can you accept? I've driven over two hours to see my client after filing everything properly. You do know she and I have a legal right to confer."

"Yes, ma'am—"

"Great." She cut him off. "In the past, I've been able to fill out visitation paperwork right here. Is that an option today?"

"No, ma'am. New policy is in effect. I can't let you in without the correct paperwork, completed twenty-four hours ahead of the requested time. Sorry. Ma'am."

His diligent use of "ma'am" struck her ears like nails on a chalkboard, and she was sure that's why he kept it up. She pressed her lips together and started over.

"I respect your position and the system," she began, ignoring the guard's sneer. The anti-Anna movement was in full force today. Again, she mentally scolded her client for making this all so much harder than it needed to be. Clearly, the woman's superiority complex wasn't making her any friends in prison either. Only more enemies.

Elizabeth, Anna's daughter and Pippa's good friend, would be terribly disappointed if Pippa couldn't get inside today. *For Elizabeth*, she reminded herself, infusing her voice with steel. "You, *sir*, are hindering the legal process," she snapped. "May I speak with your supervisor?"

"No, ma'am. He's at lunch."

One more snarky "ma'am" and she would come dangerously close to committing a crime herself. She lightly rested her folded hands on the counter. If she had to wear prison orange, it should be for a better reason than losing her temper. She smiled, absolutely certain the expression was less than friendly. "Is Warden Birrell available? Although we haven't spoken in person since my father's funeral, it would make the trip worthwhile just to say hello and catch up for a few minutes."

Name-dropping wasn't her thing, and she typically avoided throwing around Colton family connections and influence this way, but she was growing desperate.

The guard closed the panel so she couldn't push any more papers at him. "The warden and my supervisor are having lunch together."

"How wonderful for everyone," Pippa said. "I'll wait right here for their return." She planted herself in the plastic chair across from the window.

And didn't that plan shine a spotlight on the differences between her and the prison inmates, including her client. She had the luxury and freedom to stay or go as she wished. It shouldn't have surprised her that the speculation in the press had reached the prison. Calling her the Queen of Mean, the general consensus was that she'd taken on the Queen's case for immediate notoriety. While it was true that getting Anna's conviction overturned would allow her to progress her ideal career path, Pippa was here to right a wrong and to help Elizabeth, her friend.

Twenty minutes ticked by, then another twenty. Although it made sense for both the supervisor and the warden to return through this entrance, closest to their offices, it was clear someone had warned them off. She knew when she was defeated.

Using her phone, she drafted an email to the warden, who really was a family friend, and sent a text message update to Elizabeth on the day's failure. Pulling out her portfolio, she opened it to the notepad printed with her firm's formal letterhead. With her best penmanship, she wrote a friendly little letter to Warden Birrell, praising his staff. She folded the note and slid it into an envelope also printed with the firm's logo. There was no sense pretending the note wouldn't be read long before it reached him, if it reached him at all. Thus the reason for the more direct and candid email she would send once she was outside.

She stepped up to the window once more. "I'd like to leave this note for the warden, please."

"Fine. I'll take it," the guard said.

It didn't escape her notice that he didn't say the note would be delivered. "Thank you." She pushed the envelope across the counter, up to the closed slot. At least he'd laid off the "ma'am" routine. "Have a wonderful day." Chin in the air, she turned and marched out, feeling only marginally guilty that she could leave the prison behind.

Prisons were a necessary piece of the justice system. Defense teams were essential too, and not just to stand up for those wrongfully accused. She knew she was on the right side with the Wentworth case, but it was going to be a hard road to help this particular client.

The crisp autumn air and bright sunshine were welcome and she breathed deeply, closing her eyes briefly when she reached the relative security of her vehicle.

After unlocking the car, she opened the back door and set her briefcase on the floor behind the driver's seat. She paused to send the email to the warden, then shrugged out of her suit jacket and draped it over the hanger in the back. Settling behind the wheel for the drive home, she started the engine, then sat back, checking her phone one more time, just in case the warden had seen her email.

Having dawdled as much as she dared, she backed out of her parking space and drove away.

THE PRISON GUARD kept an eye on the security monitors, waiting until the gates closed behind the snooty attorney. He waited a few minutes more until she pulled out of the parking lot. Then he called someone to cover him so he could go have a smoke. Outside in the employee parking lot, he stared out at the line of trees blocking the prison yard from the rest of the world.

He lit his cigarette and took a long, deep drag. The persistent woman had been almost as annoying as the inmate she wanted to see.

Pulling out his phone, he called the number he'd been given. It rang three times before anyone picked up.

"Go," said the voice on the other end.

"She's gone," he said. "No meeting with her client."

"Got it."

"And the daughter?" the guard asked. It was going to be a whole lot harder stonewalling that one, but he could find a way if it meant extra cash. "Hello?" He checked his signal and saw the Call Ended icon flashing on his screen.

"Whatever," he muttered, tucking his phone back into his pocket. He'd done his part. If the money wasn't in his account when he got home tonight, he'd do things the right way next time.

DETECTIVE EMMANUEL IGLESIAS checked his phone as he finished his lunch outside the GRPD headquarters. One of his favorite food trucks had parked nearby today and it was too beautiful outside not to soak up the fall weather. He dealt with the less appealing facets of Grand Rapids most days and last year, on the verge of burnout, he'd promised himself to focus on the nicer elements as often as possible to balance the scales.

Seeing the text message from his friend Griffin Colton, he hesitated. The preview on the app mentioned Griffin's sister, Pippa. Emmanuel tried not to groan out loud. Why had he agreed when Griffin asked him to keep an eye on his sister?

Because friends stepped up.

He opened the full text message. No word from Pippa today. No answer at her office or condo. It happens when she's focused, but I'd feel better if you have time to check.

Apparently Pippa had a reputation within the family for being a little too reckless in the pursuit of justice. As a business, founded by Griffin's older brother Riley, the siblings worked together as Colton Investigations and they had their hands full with the escalating RevitaYou situation.

RevitaYou, a daily "miracle" supplement, promised to make a person look ten years younger after only one week of use. With rave reviews from consumers and falsified medical endorsements, a new business had exploded with investors and distributors. But something in the formula was off and turning into deadly Ricin. One death had already been linked to the supplement and everything indicated there would be more.

The GRPD and Colton Investigations were cooperating to prevent more untimely deaths, though Emmanuel knew a top priority for the Coltons was locating Brody Higgins, a young man they considered part of

the family, who had borrowed money to invest in RevitaYou. Unfortunately, he'd borrowed from Capital X, a
loan shark operation disguised as a legitimate financial
group. The Coltons were determined to find Brody before the Capital X enforcers hurt him—again.

Changing directions, he headed for his car to swing
by Pippa's condo and office. He'd keep his word and
try to find something to ease Griffin's mind.

Emmanuel knew Griffin worried about Pippa getting caught up in Brody's mess, since his last direct
contact had been with her. Now that she was the new
lead attorney for a convicted killer, Emmanuel had other
concerns. He wouldn't define Pippa's choice to defend
Anna Wentworth as a reckless pursuit of justice. In his
mind, it was more like career suicide.

Having worked the Wentworth case, he knew it
was solid. He'd testified at the trial and walked the
jury through every piece of evidence he'd found. Pippa
hadn't been on the defense team then, but now resentment was brewing against her in the GRPD. No one
liked having good work picked apart in the search for
a technicality that would set a criminal free.

Anna Wentworth was guilty, Emmanuel was certain
of it, and promise or not, he wouldn't let one idealistic
attorney unravel everything so a murderous socialite
could get back to her mansion.

ONCE PIPPA WAS out on the deserted stretch of road that
eventually connected with the highway, she finally let
out the scream of frustration that had been building for
over an hour.

Feeling better with just that simple, primal release,
she found a radio station playing heavy metal music and

turned up the volume. People usually took in her conservative wardrobe and professional manner and decided she was a prim, entitled lawyer with musical tastes that didn't veer from serene and classical. They couldn't be more wrong. She was more than willing to dress the part and play the game to get a job done, but she wasn't afraid to get her hands dirty. Blame those traits on her mother, a woman who had died before accomplishing all her big goals to help people who struggled in their community. With heavy bass pounding through the speakers, Pippa rewound and reviewed every detail of her interaction with that guard.

Obviously he'd been instructed to block her at all turns. Who on earth had the influence to prevent her from meeting her client? More important, who had a reason to do so?

She'd initially kept up with the Wentworth trial to support her friend, believing from the start Anna wasn't a killer. It was only after Elizabeth had hired her that Pippa had pored over the case page by page. After two weeks, she had the case pretty much memorized from the first emergency call to the reading of the verdict. For the life of her, she couldn't come up with anyone close to the victim who could successfully frame Anna.

Pippa firmly believed in the theory that every crisis held the seeds of opportunity. If she couldn't speak with her client, she was back to square one with the overwhelming evidence that was too perfect. It wasn't enough that Anna wasn't the sort to do her own dirty work. And making it clear she didn't consider the victim a threat had backfired during the trial. What was her next move?

The warden, assuming he'd actually been in his office, wasn't interested in helping her. The guards didn't seem to like Inmate Anna. No shock there. The woman wasn't easy at the best of times. Used to having her own way on her own terms, she was probably raising a stink over having her days controlled by others.

According to the last count, only Elizabeth; Elizabeth's father, Ed; and Pippa truly believed Anna was innocent of the Hicks murder. Unfortunately, Ed was so frustrated and angry over his wife's indiscretions and arrogant behavior during the trial that he was content to let her stew in her own mess, offering little in the way of support.

Anna's unswervingly self-centered choices and her habitual delegation of everything from car pool duty to signing Christmas cards would never win her awards for best wife or mom of the year, but she wasn't foolish enough to kill a man and leave a piece of her stunning bespoke jewelry near the body. Yes, shock and rage affected the mind and impaired critical thinking, but even if Anna had been capable of those extremes and had managed to fire the two bullets that stopped David Hicks's heart, she wouldn't have tossed the gun into her beloved rose bushes less than three feet from the body.

In Pippa's opinion, if Anna had been bothered enough to want a person dead, she would've hired someone to handle the job. For as long as Pippa had known Elizabeth, that's how Anna Wentworth operated. The vast majority of her volunteer hours were handled by assistants. Anna wrote checks and dressed up in glorious gowns and gems, but she *never* got her hands dirty. Trouble was, she didn't have anything concrete to prove Anna's innocence.

Using the controls on the steering wheel, she muted

the radio and called her office, leaving a message for her paralegal about the derailed meeting. When she was back home, she would review her notes on the case one more time to find a way forward. At last, she called her twin sister, Kiely, and let her know she was on the way back to Grand Rapids. That left her with two hours of uninterrupted drive time to figure out how she could effectively circumvent the prison to interview Anna.

Last week, she'd spent an entire day with this case file in the evidence room at the Grand Rapids Police Department. She could arrange for the evidence to be reviewed by an independent lab, but it was a pricey option that was unlikely to be helpful since there were no glaring gaps in the chain of evidence.

It would have been nice if Pippa could back up a theory that Anna had been railroaded, but it just wasn't true. The detectives on the case had been thorough and cautious, refusing to give the press anything that might color the investigation or the trial. They'd also come to the wrong conclusion.

Whoever had framed Anna had done an excellent job.

If the prison system wouldn't allow her to have reasonable meetings with her client, she would just find another way to get any helpful information out of Anna. As Hicks's lover, she might not even realize what she'd learned about him and any enemies who might have motive to kill him and frame her.

Pippa was still working her way through the transcripts of the interviews and depositions. At some point there must have been a different suspect, yet somehow the GRPD investigation had decided the motive and evidence fit and pinned the murder on the wrong person.

Yes, Anna had been having an affair with Hicks. Yes, Hicks ended it before Anna was ready, and he'd reportedly threatened to tell her husband if she didn't pay him off. But Ed had known about the affair. At some point Ed and Anna had agreed to break their wedding vows. Infidelity was one weird cog in the machine that kept their marriage working. Pippa had heard of stranger things. Her parents' marriage hadn't been nearly the picture of perfection that the public assumed. What worked for the Wentworths shouldn't make any difference to the case or to anyone else, though it fed local gossip columns for weeks.

The sound of a big engine behind her drew her attention back to the roadway. An SUV painted in the blue of Michigan State Police troopers was bearing down on her, lights flashing. Her pulse kicked up a notch as she checked her speed—within the limit—then she eased closer to the shoulder to give him room to pass.

He blew right by her. Relieved, she merged back into the lane. For several seconds she'd thought her botched trip to the prison was going to get worse. She was jumpy. Only ten days on the job and she'd had her fill of the press hounding her for interviews and explanations.

Well, as her dad would have said, the right choice wasn't always the popular choice.

Grand Rapids wanted to enjoy the implosion and downfall of the society Queen of Mean. They weren't interested in the more pertinent facts about David Hicks. The victim was more than a decade younger than Anna, and from what Pippa could see, he'd shown a distinct pattern of risky behavior. He chose to be seen publicly with wealthy and influential married women.

There were plenty of pictures and videos of him caught in unmistakable displays of affection and intimacy.

Pippa figured any number of husbands wanted him dead, and probably a few ex-girlfriends too. She was sure Anna wasn't the first woman, single or married, that he'd tried to blackmail in the course of a breakup. She just hadn't been able to prove it yet. The man enjoyed an active dating life, and he thrived on rubbing elbows with society's elite. Sleeping with Anna had provided Hicks with a serious boost of notoriety. And when he'd been ready to move on, he'd probably been shocked Anna didn't care enough about his threats to pay him off.

Shocked, yes, but he hadn't shot himself in the chest.

As Elizabeth's friend and a familiar face, Pippa held out hope that Anna would be more forthright about what she knew of Hicks's habits, instead of dismissing those questions as irrelevant. Pippa needed a kernel of truth to run with, something that would turn that case file upside down.

She sang along with the radio for a time, her mind still sorting out the pieces and players.

The prosecution insisted the insult of being dumped combined with the threat of blackmail pushed Anna to kill and to make mistakes in the process. That might have been enough with anyone else. Although Anna was self-absorbed, she wasn't stupid.

Her defense team had been caught in a sticky web. Everyone in the area had an impression and opinion of high-profile Anna Wentworth. If her defense made her seem too smart or too into Hicks, that only made it easier to believe she could commit murder. The prosecution portrayed their case as a crime of passion and claimed the damning evidence had been left almost in plain sight because she'd been overwhelmed and enraged.

Naturally, Anna's fingerprints were on her jewelry but they hadn't been on the gun. No gunshot residue on her hands, either, but those facts hadn't swayed the jury.

Bottom line, no one wanted to believe Anna's side of the story. It would've helped if she'd had a decent alibi, but she'd been working from home that day and the timing of the messages she'd left her assistant weren't enough to clear her. It didn't help matters that during the trial Anna had referred to Hicks as a dirty rat whose only redeeming quality had been his handsome face.

The defense team recognized they were finished, though they'd fought right up to the closing arguments and sentencing.

What they'd needed—what Pippa still needed—was another valid suspect, another theory about the motive. The threat of blackmail sounded like enough, until you dug into the Wentworth marriage. So far the only chink in the prosecution's armor was the lack of an interview with Ed. Or even Elizabeth. She'd found the notes from the detectives working the case that confirmed those alibis, but shouldn't they have taken a closer look at the cuckolded husband?

That fishy detail wasn't enough to reopen the case, but it was something she wanted answered by Sergeant Joe McRath and Detective Emmanuel Iglesias, who had worked Anna's case.

She muted the radio and dictated more notes into her phone, brainstorming ways to get the GRPD to cooperate with her. Her family had connections in the GRPD from her sister Sadie, a crime scene technician, to Detective Iglesias, a good friend of her brother Griffin.

She had to tread lightly because this case was polarizing, and win or lose, she still had to live here when it was done.

Pippa was absolutely certain the real killer was still out there, and she needed to convince the police, but so far no one would speak with her about it. Since taking on the Wentworth case, she'd been dealing with a rash of threats on her office voice mail and one nasty postcard delivered to her home. All par for the course these days when representing an unpopular client. While she logged each incident, she knew a few random threats wouldn't inspire anyone to take a second look at what appeared to be a solid conviction.

Another death would do it. Her stomach cramped at the thought.

She had been tempted to use her siblings as a sounding board or even ask for some hands-on help. All of them supported and lent their professional expertise to Colton Investigations, the family business investigative agency. But the team had its hands full at the moment, and the press ganging up on her was bad enough. No way would she drag that public relations quicksand closer to her siblings.

The music wasn't helping anymore. Restless and feeling idle, she cued up a recording of the trial provided by Anna's defense team and picked up where she'd left off, listening to the smooth, mellow voice of Detective Iglesias on the stand.

She remembered that day in court. He'd worn a charcoal suit and his wavy hair had been brushed back from his face. Short stubble had defined his jaw and the steady confidence in his warm brown eyes never wavered. Not even under cross-examination.

It was easy to understand why the jury had gravitated to him, taking his every word as unassailable truth. Even though Pippa knew better, it was easy to believe his testimony. He'd been the star witness for the prosecution, all but guaranteeing Anna's conviction.

Her phone suddenly interrupted the flow of his voice, announcing an incoming call. She used the control on her steering wheel to answer. "You've reached Pippa Colton. How may I help you?"

"Hi, Pippa. It's Elizabeth." Her friend sounded miserable. "I'm sorry to bug you. I just couldn't wait to hear how it went. Did Mom cooperate?"

More than anything else with this case, Pippa regretted that a mother-daughter relationship, already under pressure, had been nearly destroyed by the trial. Elizabeth and her father had been in the gallery every day to support Anna, but it hadn't impressed the jury. And Elizabeth's testimony as a character witness during sentencing had hit a sour note, giving the impression that she was fabricating a few good moments with her mom just for the hope of leniency. Her strident belief in her mother's innocence came across as too little, too late.

It broke her heart to say it, but she had to be truthful. "I didn't get to meet with her," Pippa replied.

"Why not?" The worry in Elizabeth's voice was sharp as a blade. "Did something happen?"

"Your mom is fine," Pippa assured her. "They told me it was a system glitch on their end," she hedged. "I'll reschedule."

"So she still doesn't know I believe her."

Elizabeth sounded utterly defeated. Pippa had seen this struggle between Elizabeth and her mom practically since day one of their friendship. The Wentworth mansion was impressive for all of the architecture heir-looms and history, but it would never be called a happy home during Anna's reign.

"She knows it," Pippa insisted. "You go out there every day."

"Not today."

"Well, no." Because they'd thought one visitor per day was enough. Maybe if Elizabeth had been with her, she would've gotten inside. Too late to second-guess things now. "But you'll be there tomorrow."

"And every day after until this is over," Elizabeth agreed.

Pippa swallowed her irritation with the runaround she'd been subjected to. "I'm glad to hear that. You may have to be the go-between right now." The conversations wouldn't be protected legally, but she didn't see another option.

"What do you mean?"

"I think she's annoyed the guards," Pippa explained. "Which means they aren't inclined to do anything that works in her favor. Or mine."

Elizabeth grumbled. "I've warned Mom to cool it."

Pippa laughed, though the situation wasn't funny. "You really think your mom is going to listen to any-one right now?"

"A daughter can hope."

"Agreed," Pippa said. "I want you to hang on to that hope. I need you to hang on to that hope. Yes, it would be easier if she could find a measure of humility and soon, but I'm not holding my breath. In the meantime, please do what you can to reassure her that the guilty verdict isn't permanent."

"I'll do my best."

"And if possible, get her talking about Hicks. The man had another enemy, and your mom might not realize she knows who it is."

"You think he talked to Mom about someone else he was seeing?"

"Probably not, but we have to ask. Maybe he talked with her about other interests. I can't find any signs that the police looked very closely at anything beyond his relationship with her, but we both know there's more to the story."

"I'll do my best," Elizabeth repeated.

"Same here," Pippa vowed, more motivated than ever to speak with Anna. The woman needed to understand how committed Elizabeth was to her mother's cause. Most likely Anna had never been an easy person. Somewhere along the way she decided that being the wealthy Mrs. Wentworth meant avoiding everything she found uncomfortable or distasteful. She prioritized her idea of perfection over personal relationships, preferring to nurture power and influence rather than people. Having watched all of the heartache and strife through the years, Pippa worried that no one would ever convince Anna how much her daughter loved her.

"You sound so sure of yourself."

"This is one small setback, that's all," Pippa said. Far bigger challenges awaited them.

Overall, Pippa preferred the challenges. *An easy sea never made a good sailor.* So she had embraced every speed bump and roadblock on the way to her goals. She didn't mind when people underestimated her focusing on appearances and ignoring her grit and steel spine until it was too late. She considered that her secret advantage.

"I'll be back in town soon," Pippa said. "Let me know how it goes with your visit tomorrow."

"I will. Thanks for everything you're doing, Pippa."

The call ended, but Pippa was still unsettled. Since she'd agreed to tackle the task of proving Anna's innocence, talking with Elizabeth was no longer easy. There was too much weight loading down every conversation. She didn't regret helping a friend; she just hadn't expected the burden would be so heavy.

Chapter Two

Emmanuel hadn't had any luck during his brief search for Pippa. She wasn't at the office. The place had been locked up tight and all the lights were out. Though he'd been told she worked from home, she hadn't answered the door when he stopped at her condo. He'd cruised around her neighborhood but didn't see the woman or her car.

He wasn't eager to tell Griffin he'd failed, but he had to give his friend something. Once he'd returned to the GRPD, he sent a text that he would keep looking.

His phone rang before he could get out of his car. He expected Griffin and instead, the Caller ID showed his mom's number.

Smiling, he picked up the call. "Hi, Mom."

"Emmanuel. I'm sorry to bother you."

"Never." She was always a bright spot. He and his siblings knew how lucky they were to have warm, involved parents. No matter where their careers took them, they all knew the door was always open at home. "What's up?"

"I had lunch with Sofia today."

His mother, Lucia, and her younger sister were both

retired and had lunch at least once a week. "How is she doing?"

"Amazing." Lucia didn't sound happy about it. "She went on and on about how great she felt."

His stomach dropped. *Please don't let this be about RevitaYou.* "And that's a problem?"

"She's taking that new pill."

"RevitaYou."

"That's the one," Lucia said. "You told me it wasn't such a miracle, but she looks good and says she feels better."

"Stay away from it, Mom. Please. It doesn't work so well for everyone," he added. "They haven't figured out what makes it effective for some people." And deadly for others, but he wouldn't say that to his mom.

The scientist who developed the formula had disappeared, but what Emmanuel had learned from Griffin's fiancée, Abigail, was enough to convince him he didn't want anyone he cared about taking a chance. "If you can, try to get Aunt Sofia to give it up too."

"I see."

And he knew she did. Lucia understood there were limits to what Emmanuel could share and when. "Thanks, Mom."

"I'll make sure she throws away her supply and doesn't buy any more. You'd best get back to work," she said. "Come for dinner soon."

"I promise. Love you."

"Love you, too."

As he walked into the station, he was more determined than ever to put an end to this RevitaYou case. Whatever it took.

FINALLY HOME, PIPPA parked in her assigned space behind her building. She couldn't wait to get upstairs to her condo and pour a glass of red wine. After a hot, steamy shower she might even think about food as well as other things before she sat down with the case again.

And she'd had plenty going on in her personal life recently. Her foster brother, Brody Higgins, had gone missing. But he'd recently gotten in over his head with a health supplement company that carried a single product: RevitaYou. The product supposedly reversed the signs of aging by at least a decade. Unfortunately his no-fail investment didn't pay out as soon as promised, and now he was hiding from Capital X, a loan shark operation posing as a legitimate finance company.

Brody had agreed to a loan with impossible terms, and after he was unable to meet the repayment timeline, enforcers had been sent out to motivate him. He had the information that would put an end to Capital X, but only if CI could find him first. Pippa had been texting with Brody, relieved they were about to get him into a safe house, when he stopped responding. At least they had a new plan to help him. After much debate and discussion, she would be putting in a loan application tomorrow night with Capital X in an effort to draw out the enforcers. That would enable the Coltons to track them back to the bosses behind the operation.

She gathered up her phone, jacket and briefcase and hurried into the building. Autumn put a bite in the air tonight. Turning, she aimed for the mailroom and fished out her key, hesitating before she opened her box.

Threats had been trickling in since that first press conference following the verdict, when Elizabeth announced Pippa's addition to the legal team. Calls to the office were typical when an attorney took a stand on a polarizing public issue. But the postcard a few days ago had thrown her off, made her nervous.

DON'T BE A FOOL. SHE IS WHERE SHE BE-LONGS.

The note had been written in all caps, with a blood-red marker. The picture on the front was an iconic shot of the Wentworth mansion at Christmastime. It hadn't been stamped or postmarked, either, which indicated the sender had delivered it personally.

Although unsettling, it happened with prominent cases. The general sentiment matched the tone of the phone calls the office staff had screened on her behalf. Although she'd worked on other wrongful conviction cases involving women, the timing of the note and the photo of the mansion tied it clearly to Anna. No one wanted to see this particular murder conviction overturned, because everyone was so damn sure the woman was guilty.

Why couldn't anyone understand the potential trouble of having the *wrong* person behind bars?

The postcard wouldn't have bothered her nearly as much if it had come to the office. Her home address wasn't exactly well-known, but it was public record. She'd bought the condo in her own name, never imagining a time when someone would turn against her.

Standing here wringing her hands wasn't her style. She was being silly, letting herself be bullied by one piece of disturbing mail. She hadn't reported it to the police, only her twin. Kiely understood she didn't want to cause an upset when little could be done at this point. She had placed the card in a plastic bag labeled with the date and time it had arrived and locked it away in her safe with the other materials she was gathering on the case.

Working against public opinion wasn't fun, but it was the job. An attorney who took only popular clients would eventually get burned. There had been a few cases in her father's career as district attorney when he'd made decisions that resulted in public backlash. No one appreciated lawyers, but at some point every person—even if only as part of a community—needed legal expertise or advice.

She opened her mailbox and stuffed the correspondence into the side pocket of her briefcase without looking at it. Better to wrestle with anything unpleasant in the privacy of her condo than get upset here, where a neighbor might walk up and ask too many questions.

Assuming, of course, her neighbors weren't the ones sending nasty cards.

She'd never taken much time to socialize. As one of six kids in the Colton family, Pippa had grown up with plenty of company on any given day and enjoyed her solitude now. She knew the other residents on her floor and wouldn't be at all surprised if they'd sided with the rest of Grand Rapids against her decision to help Anna Wentworth. And with her current caseload she didn't have much time to meet anyone.

Her shoulder strap slipped as she climbed the stairs to the third floor, and she slowed to adjust the load. Although the elevator would have been easier, she wanted movement after the hours in the car. One of the perks of her building was the fitness center. She was considering a quick workout before the shower and wine as she tapped the code into her electronic door lock.

The gears gave a soft whir and the dead bolt slid back.

Home at last. The day's frustrations started to dissolve as she crossed the threshold. She halted when the strange smell hit her. Bitter and powerful, the scent stung her nose. Wondering if she'd missed a message from maintenance about a repair, she set her briefcase and jacket down just inside the door.

The lamp she'd left on low this morning was turned off. Uneasy, she reached for the light switch near the door. The overhead lamp in the entry came on, and the glow spilled out into the front room.

"What in the world…"

The strange odor was spray paint. She took a step closer to the vicious message scrawled across her wall in red: *DO-GOODERS END UP DEAD.*

She couldn't comprehend this. Who would have done this? Why? How? Her door had been secure. How had the vandal found a way inside?

She turned in a circle, her temper rising. The threat and stench were bad enough. Her home had been searched. Ransacked. For a specific purpose or just to hurt her?

At the other end of the hall, she heard a door open. Concerned, she shut her own front door quickly. She leaned back against the door, one hand still on the door handle, knowing better than to go forward and contaminate the scene.

Now, when it was too late, it occurred to her she should have stopped on the other side of the door. What if the intruder was still here? She thought she was alone, but it was hard to hear anything over her pounding heart and the blood rushing through her ears.

She nearly dropped her cell phone as she scrambled

to pull it from her pocket. After two failed attempts to unlock it, she tapped in the nine and one before she stopped herself. Was this a true emergency? She wasn't actually in immediate danger. Maybe better to just call her brother Riley. But that would wreck his evening. She started to dial the primary police line when she heard another sound in the service hallway.

Anger and fear bounced through her system and jumbled her thoughts. Wishing she could avoid the inevitable chaos and questions, she pressed the three numbers into her phone and waited for the emergency operator to answer.

Every second seemed to last forever until a woman with a firm voice was taking her information. Relaying her address and the situation, Pippa followed instructions, staying on the line as instructed while she exited the condo to meet the police downstairs.

With each step away from her front door, her anger ratcheted higher. Someone had invaded her home, her private sanctuary, and caused havoc. Scrawled a threat across her wall. Had they just gotten lucky that she wasn't home, or was someone keeping tabs on her? Would they have done worse if she'd been there?

The note in her mailbox suddenly felt far more sinister.

Assuring the operator she'd reached the front door and would not go back upstairs without police, she ended the call and quickly dialed her twin sister. If anyone could help her unravel this mess without any extra fuss, it was Kiely. She was one of the best freelance private investigators in the region. Highly sought after, she frequently worked with police, FBI and Colton Investigations, going wherever she was needed.

Pippa needed her now, but once more she had to leave a message. She took a deep breath. Kiely was probably caught up with an urgent case elsewhere. Trying to calm herself, Pippa turned to watch the sunset. Days were getting shorter and cooler. Autumn was usually her favorite time of year, with the trees changing color and the college football season underway, but she was struggling to find anything restful in recent days.

Her phone rang in her hand and she jumped. Irritated at being so flighty, she spoke sharply when she answered.

"Easy, sis. You called me."

Kiely. Their connection steadied her, took some of the sting out of the lousy day.

"Pippa? What's wrong?"

"Nothing. Well, a little bit of everything," Pippa admitted before she got control of herself. "I was hoping you could come by. Just for a few minutes."

"This is a bad time." Kiely said with regret. "I'm sorry. I'm following a lead on Brody. Can you call Riley or Griffin?"

"No worries," Pippa replied brightly. She didn't want to face either of her brothers tonight. Not while she was so rattled. "This can totally wait." The case involving Brody was a much bigger priority. "Stay on that lead and track him down."

"Pippa? Are you there?"

"Yes."

"I swear I'll come as soon as I can."

Flashing lights appeared at the end of her street. "Don't worry, Kiely. It was just a bad day."

"All right," her sister sounded less than convinced.

"You can unload tomorrow afternoon when we deliver the materials for that seven o'clock appointment."

"Great." She forced cheer that she didn't feel into that single word. That didn't give her a lot of time to get her house back in order. Tomorrow evening it was her turn to do her part for Brody and the investigation. It was the last thing on her mind right now, but she couldn't admit that to her twin without raising more concerns. "Keep me posted."

DETECTIVE EMMANUEL IGLESIAS and his partner, Daniel Gomez, were heading back to the police station with burgers for a working dinner when they heard dispatch send officers to a possible home invasion. Recognizing the address, he felt a prickle of unease between his shoulder blades.

"You mind if we drive over and check it out?" Emmanuel asked.

Daniel shook his head. "Works for me. Saves the patrol a call if it's serious."

"Right." Emmanuel hoped it was a coincidence rather than something serious. He turned on the emergency lights and headed away from the station.

"Want to tell me why it's an issue?" Daniel asked.

Emmanuel shrugged, shifting in his seat. "No issue." Not definitely, at any rate. "A friend of mine has a sister living at that address."

"I'm in." Daniel swiped a french fry out of the bag and then tipped it so Emmanuel could do the same.

"Thanks." He appreciated working with a man who wasn't afraid of long hours and unexpected detours.

They were only a few minutes away from the neighborhood, giving Emmanuel time to consider his approach. He might not approve of her newest client or agree with the hopes to overturn the conviction, but she had a reputation for being good at her job. All of the Colton siblings had a keen understanding of the law, thanks in part to being raised one of the best DAs to ever serve in Michigan.

"So what's her name?" Daniel queried in a voice that promised relentless teasing.

"Philippa Colton," Emmanuel replied.

"Oh." Daniel gave a low whistle. "Safe to assume she's not your biggest fan. I guess you want me to do the talking?"

"We'll see."

Daniel made a snorting sound that might have been a laugh. "That we will."

Based on her serious demeanor in press conferences, he doubted she'd lay into him when she heard his name. Not with witnesses, at any rate. He had no intention of hassling her about her lousy taste in clients. He was only driving out to help at the request of her brother, but if she had an obvious problem with him, he'd leave.

The responding patrol officers, Jeffries and Simmons, were already there when Emmanuel parked on the street in front of Pippa's building and notified the station of their arrival.

"Nice place," Daniel said. "I've always liked this one."

Emmanuel agreed. The developers had restored the brickwork and kept the arched windows that made this building a favorite subject of photographers. The neighborhood had a low crime rate, despite its proximity to the city center, and this particular repurposing of an old factory had been met with full support from the community.

The detectives joined the two officers speaking with Pippa on the sidewalk near the stately front entrance. She stood with perfect posture. Her briefcase strap crossed her trim body shoulder to hip, and a coat was draped over one arm. It was chilly enough tonight that she should be wearing that coat properly.

Their paths hadn't crossed often, but he'd always found her pretty and tonight was no exception. Her silky brown hair was down, skimming her shoulders and framing her face. Her big blue eyes were somber and there was no sign of the usual smile on her soft pink lips.

The urge to step in and usher her away from the crisis hit him like a punch to the gut. He was supposed to keep an eye on her for Griffin, not get drawn in like a moth to flame.

He caught the nervous gesture as her hands clutched her cell phone while she explained the situation. "I walked in and found my home trashed. Vandalized. That's when I called you."

Her voice was flat, each word precise. Either she was processing things quickly or this was the first sign of shock. Her expression didn't give anything away; that serious, sweet face could've owned a poker table in Vegas.

Officer Jeffries, a slender woman with several years of police experience, seemed to be taking the lead. "You didn't see anyone inside?" she asked.

"No," Pippa replied.

Emmanuel watched as her gaze skimmed over his partner and locked onto him. Her eyebrows flexed into a frown, but in an instant, her face was a neutral, emotionless mask. Emmanuel wasn't fooled. He'd been recognized.

"Did you notice any problems at your door? Scratches on the lock or door jamb? Maybe your key didn't work as well," Jeffries continued.

"No problems," Pippa said. "Everything appeared to be fine when I walked up."

"If you could lead the way," Simmons suggested, opening the front door. He'd been on the force for as long as Emmanuel could recall. They were both good officers.

Emmanuel and Daniel were likely overkill here, but he'd stick it out. The four of them followed her to the elevator in the lobby, and she pressed the button.

"Did you take the elevator earlier?" he asked.

Her gaze snapped to him and the scowl returned. "No."

"If you don't mind," Daniel said, drawing her attention. "We'd prefer you followed your earlier footsteps."

Pippa checked with Jeffries and waited for her agreement before turning to the wide stairs and marching up the three flights. She stopped in front of her door. "I entered my code—" she pointed to the keypad "—and the lock opened without any trouble."

"Go ahead and unlock it again," Jeffries suggested.

Emmanuel couldn't see anything out of place on or around the door and lock. "Miss Colton, you can change that code at any time, correct?"

"Yes, of course." Instead of a frown, she wrinkled her nose. "It was the smell that tipped me off first," she said.

The smell?

The door swung open, and they all caught the unpleasant odor of fresh paint. Emmanuel expected her to step aside, but instead she walked in before Jeffries or Simmons could insist on taking the lead.

"What did you do when you smelled the paint?" Officer Simmons asked.

"I stopped right here and set down my briefcase and coat. My first thought was that maintenance had entered to make some repair. But then I turned on the light."

Daniel pushed a hand through his hair. "And you saw that."

"Yes."

All of them were staring at the threat scrawled across her wall. *DO-GOODERS END UP DEAD*.

Pippa's attitude was too cool for Emmanuel's comfort. Granted, everyone dealt with shock in different ways, but victims of home invasion usually exhibited more fear or outrage or bafflement. Griffin warned him she was tough as nails, but smothering intense reactions could backfire. One more thing to watch for as he fulfilled his promise to her brother. "Pardon me if you've already answered this, but how long ago did you come home?"

She ignored him, addressing Officer Jeffries. "I didn't touch anything other than the light switch and my door."

"Good." Jeffries used her radio to request a team to process the scene for evidence.

"Is there a neighbor you can stay with while we clear the home?" Simmons asked Pippa.

She shook her head, her lips a firm line. "I'll wait right here."

At Jeffries's pained expression, Emmanuel insisted they step out into the hallway.

Daniel pulled his gun and followed Simmons and Jeffries. It was unlikely the intruder was lingering even if they had been in the condo when Pippa walked in. Still, they needed to find the point of entry. Normally, he'd knock on doors, but he didn't want to leave her alone. And he sure didn't want her to join him in that endeavor.

"I know Griffin sent you," she said in icy tones. "He overstepped."

"He's just—"

She cut him off with a sharp look from those green eyes. "It might be best if I work with the other officers."

Before he could comment, the officers called an all clear, and she darted inside. He never expected everyone to like him, but her clear distaste was grating on his nerves. If this was about Wentworth, he'd only been doing his job. Like it or not, the case had been straightforward, and they'd left no stone unturned.

"Over here," Daniel called out. "We have a print."

They followed his voice to the back door of the condo.

"Whoever it was came in right here." He pointed to a boot print far too big for Pippa. "A man, most likely. Used a key. Judging by the scratches, I'm guessing it gave them some trouble. Or they were nervous. Simmons is looking for a trail or anything that might identify the perp," Daniel continued. He returned his gun to the holster on his hip and pulled out his phone. "I'll try to get ahold of any surveillance in the area."

Emmanuel's mind wandered, and he was distracted by her small foot tucked into a stylish black shoe with a low heel. In the charcoal slacks and soft blouse, she dressed like a lawyer with a superb sense of style. He supposed it was a type of armor, like his badge, but the shadows deepening under her eyes concerned him that she couldn't hang on to the facade much longer.

"All right," Pippa prompted. "What next?"

"Is anything obvious missing?"

Pippa scanned the room. "Nothing obvious, no."

"I'm going to speak with your neighbors," Jeffries stated. "Detective Iglesias will take over and stay while the technicians do their thing. When they're done, you can take a closer look. We'll be as efficient as possible," she promised.

Although he appreciated having an official reason to stick around, he could tell Pippa wasn't happy about it.

Emmanuel cleared his throat. She shot him a look that could have melted concrete block, confirming her low opinion of how things were working out. Crouching for a closer look at the lock, he asked, "Who has access here?"

"It's the service hallway." She spoke with deliberate emphasis on each syllable. "Anyone with trash going out or large deliveries coming in would be back here. If a concern is outside of building maintenance, most service men and women use this access too."

"Who has keys to your door?"

She closed her eyes for a moment, clearly struggling to hold on to that rigid composure. "There are only two keys. The maintenance staff has one, and I have the other. They send me text messages in the building app to schedule appointments or to let me know when they need to come inside."

Standing, he scowled at the footprint and took a picture. "After you." He gestured for her to lead the way back into the condo.

"Will the CSI team need to go through my entire place?"

"Wouldn't hurt," he said. "Is there somewhere you can wait or even stay over tonight?"

She set her coat and briefcase on the peninsula countertop in the kitchen. "I'm not leaving."

Emmanuel recognized that arguing was futile at the moment. He walked away from her to gather his thoughts and take pictures of the scene with his cell phone. The candid shots gave him perspective to use as they worked a case.

She trailed after him this time, documenting the damages herself until Jeffries and Simmons returned to finalize their report. Emmanuel just listened, considering what he would ask about when they were alone.

And they would be alone, because he wasn't going anywhere tonight. Griffin would kill him if he left her here by herself. Frankly, as he walked through the scene, Emmanuel's concerns multiplied.

The crime scene unit arrived and went straight to work. While they gathered any available evidence, Emmanuel called one of his cousins to change the lock on the back door. He wasn't sure if Pippa was relieved or frustrated that her sister Sadie, a CSI with the department, wasn't on duty. It would have been a conflict of interest, anyway. For that matter, where were the rest of her siblings? He'd been told time and again the family was close.

If this had happened to one of his sisters, he'd be here in the thick of it, officially or not.

He was about to call Griffin with an update when

Daniel returned. He could tell by his partner's face they hadn't had any luck finding tracks or a witness.

"Whoever did this didn't leave a trail," Daniel said. "Ready to call it a night? We have two cold burgers waiting for us downstairs."

Emmanuel ignored his rumbling stomach. "Can you catch a ride with Simmons and Jeffries?" he asked quietly.

Daniel's eyebrows shot up toward his hairline. "Seriously? That's fast work. I got the impression she didn't like you much."

"She doesn't like me at all," Emmanuel said. As Wentworth's new attorney, she probably thought she had good reason. "Regardless, I'm sticking around until the place is secure."

"She's staying here?" At Emmanuel's nod, Daniel whistled softly. "Stubborn and cute is a bad combination."

Just as he'd thought, the teasing had begun. "Shut up, Gomez. It's not like that." Besides, cute didn't fit Pippa at all. Sophisticated. Smart. Lovely. And a tendency to make cutting remarks, at least when she interacted with him.

Daniel grinned, unrepentant. "Good luck. I'll get the paperwork rolling."

"Great. See you in the morning."

He closed the front door behind his partner and prepared for a series of awkward conversations. Griffin would be hot about the trouble here but grateful Emmanuel planned to stay over and keep things under control. Pippa would likely be equally furious that he'd called her brother without discussing it with her. And he was pretty sure she'd post a strong argument against his plan to sleep on her couch.

He looked at the couch, with its torn-up cushions, and decided he'd sleep better on her floor. Smiling to himself, he thought she might agree with that idea.

Chapter Three

Progress, the man thought as he continued his disposal of anything that could tie him to Philippa Colton's sleek condo. No wonder the Wentworth bitch hired her to try to flip the unanimous decision of a good jury. They were two of a kind.

How did the daughter of a top DA wind up defending arrogant killers? Good thing Graham Colton hadn't lived long enough to see this. Her father would've been heartbroken.

He hadn't meant to do more than search for her case notes and leave her that message to scare her off. But he'd unloaded a few frustrations in the midst of his search.

The call from the guard out at the prison had come at the perfect time, helping him focus on the first priority: sidelining the misguided lawyer.

Unless there'd been trouble on the highway, she should've found the mess he'd made by now, but he kept the radio off. That way he wouldn't have to worry about being surprised when they talked about this at the station.

And they'd talk. There was always plenty of gossip when the upper crust of society was involved.

Overall, he was pleased with how today's effort would shake out. By the time the cops got to looking, all of the evidence of his visit would be destroyed or disposed of in areas no one would connect to him or her.

The gloves he'd worn to keep from staining his hands with paint were stuffed in his pocket, inside out, until he could drop them in a public restroom well away from the scene. He'd wiped down the can of spray paint, too, tossing that into a big garbage can behind a community theater several miles from her fancy address. The service coveralls were generic enough and already deep in the collection box for a local charity group. Although he was in his own car, he wasn't worried about being spotted or identified. He had friends all over Grand Rapids, in law enforcement and in various communities. He had the friends that came along with years of public service.

He'd worked his butt off to build his stellar reputation. Sure, there had been a misstep here and there, but no serious blemishes on his record. Nothing actionable. He'd keep it that way. No lawyer with uppity artwork and impossible idealism would trash his reputation.

After nearly three decades of solving crimes, he knew how to commit most of them. More important, he knew how to avoid getting caught.

When he'd heard that Wentworth had some eager new lawyer trying to overturn her conviction, he'd experienced a blinding panic. But that had been a clean case from start to finish. Anna Wentworth wasn't 100 percent guilty of killing Hicks, but she sure as hell wasn't innocent. Behind bars was the best place for her. Everyone involved knew it. Hell, everyone who'd ever met her knew it.

He hadn't expected anyone to raise much of a ruckus. Standard appeals, nothing more. Wentworth had money, but few friends. Throughout the case, it felt like everyone in Grand Rapids wanted to share their story of the woman's rude behavior. No one had any doubt she'd been hiding murderous tendencies behind her charitable fundraising and flashy jewelry.

If only the woman's daughter had shut her trap, things might've blown over after the verdict. If only. Unfortunately, the daughter had hired Philippa Colton, vowing that the real killer would be found, true justice served.

What the hell did she think he and the rest of the cops in this city did all day, eat doughnuts?

He and his fellow GRPD officers weren't bumbling hacks. He wore a sergeant's stripes and had received commendations for various actions in the line of duty. Neither he nor anyone in the department deserved the glare of media scrutiny they were under now.

Hiding an annoyance that edged toward anger, he'd been cautious, careful not to overreact and draw unwanted attention. No one was happy with the wrongful conviction rhetoric, and he kept his trap shut, letting the chatter flow around him.

Waiting, watching, he mentally lined up his moves to prepare for the worst if the new lawyer convinced a judge to reopen the case. An appeal was one thing, with all the legal posturing and arguments. What the new lawyer proposed was entirely different.

The Wentworth conviction was rock-solid from the detectives arriving on the scene to the testimony given in court. He smiled now, just thinking back to Detective Iglesias on the stand. That man had the kind of face people trusted, along with a steady gaze and pleasant voice. The jury had been hooked, leaning forward in their seats, hanging on his every word.

It had been perfect. Done. It should've stayed that way too.

A niggle of resentment crept over his skin, raising goose bumps the length of his arms. Thanks to a daughter's refusal to accept her mother's true nature, it wasn't done.

That fresh-faced lawyer had come for the evidence box. Par for the course and nothing too worrisome. He knew what was in there. She'd spent a few hours poring over a case they'd worked by the numbers for weeks. They hadn't taken any shortcuts, hadn't skipped a single step. Hell, they'd been working to convict one of the most notorious people in the city.

Still, the lawyer made her notes, took pictures of what they'd found and gathered at the scene. Hindsight was always perfect, an impossible standard. He'd seen eager, bleeding hearts who believed a convict's sob story turn a case inside out on the basis of a misplaced comma in a report. The second-guessing from people who didn't have a clue how real police work was done was one of the worst aspects of his career.

As if all that time in a classroom and libraries full of court rulings was somehow better than real-life, on-the-street experience. No way would the world improve by legally manipulating the system to get one snobby socialite out of prison.

Colton certainly wasn't winning any friends in the GRPD, or the city at large, but she wouldn't quit. A couple of witnesses attached to the original case had told him she'd reached out, asked questions.

She'd forced his hand. If Pippa Colton wouldn't stop, he wouldn't either.

Damn idealists.

He had to move with care. The media was all over her. He'd thought the negative press would be enough, yet she persisted as if she was the key to righting some tragic wrong.

With a little planning and a couple of phone calls, he'd set things in motion. Having so many friends in and around law enforcement came in handy, giving him a heads-up about Colton visiting her client in prison. They'd happily agreed to make that visit problematic.

His next stop was to pick up a case of beer for the pal who'd kept Colton out there, stringing her along that she might actually get into the conference room. After making the purchase, chatting up the clerk behind the counter, he loaded the beer into his trunk, sliding it between two plain cardboard boxes.

The entire Wentworth case was right there. Stealing the paperwork from the cage without getting caught had been a stressful nightmare, despite the rush of making sure Colton would be out of luck if she came back for another look. He'd taken the case files out of her reach, but now he was stuck. He needed the right disposal solution for the contents of those boxes. He considered planting the entire mess in her office, but that was too obvious, and everyone coming and going made the timing complicated.

Getting rid of a can of spray paint was easy. Hell, breaking into her condo had been a cake walk. Wearing a ball cap, keeping his head down, and walking with a group made it easy to avoid the security cameras that were mostly useless. Would've been nice to find something though. He'd searched as long as he dared and hadn't found the first page of all those notes she'd taken on the case. He hadn't expected her to haul it all to the meeting.

For tonight, the nasty message and damage would have to suffice. He could take things up another notch if the home invasion didn't make her reconsider her attempt to set Wentworth free.

With one last look at the boxes, he closed the trunk and headed out to deliver the beer and shoot the breeze with an old friend. He'd figure out something; he always did.

PIPPA WAS HUNGRY and well beyond weary. She hadn't had the wine or the shower she'd been counting on, but she still had plenty of unwanted company. And plenty of cleanup to tackle as soon as everyone cleared out.

Detective Iglesias wandered back to the kitchen after another chat with the technicians processing her home. "You'd probably be happier elsewhere. Can I drive you someplace?"

"No, thank you." It took all her willpower to keep her gaze away from her wine rack. But that left her looking at either the mess or the detective. Both views rattled her for different reasons. The mess reminded her someone harbored enough hatred for her—or her work—to invade her home. Iglesias…well, with that confident swagger and trim beard, he was far too sexy for her comfort. She saw through his friendly, supportive demeanor. He was *not* her friend.

She supposed hiding in her bedroom until this was over was unacceptable behavior, especially in front of him.

Bedroom. Detective Iglesias. Her pulse kicked. Best to never think about those two topics at the same time again.

"Can you tell me a little bit about your active cases?" he asked.

As if he didn't know what this had to be about.

He tapped his pen to the small notebook in his hand, waiting. It was such an old-school motion, and yet somehow it captivated her. He intrigued her on a level that had nothing to do with crime scene procedure. She had to get him out of here, quickly.

"I'd rather give a statement to your partner," she said.

"He isn't here. He went back to the station to start on the reports."

Would nothing go right today? "You should probably join him," she said. "There's no need to stay. If you have more questions, just call."

"But I'm here now." He aimed that pen at her office. "Looks to me like whoever did this searched your office. So again, tell me about your cases. Please."

The man was insufferable. She'd had a dreadful day, spent hours on the road, made zero progress on her most important case, and now she had to deal with the man who had almost singlehandedly put Anna behind bars.

Her gaze cycled from wine rack to ransacked home to detective. "I'm sure you feel some obligation or whatever to my brother," she stated. "It isn't necessary." She'd told Griffin she didn't need a babysitter. And yet here he was.

"Even if I agreed with you, I'm not leaving just yet." He smiled.

On another man, that smile would warm her right up, maybe tempt her to kiss the deep creases bracketing his lips. "I think we both know that this incident has everything to do with my representing Anna Wentworth," she said at last. "That message doesn't fit my other cases." She turned her back on all of it, on him, too, going to the refrigerator to pour water from the pitcher she kept chilled.

Being rude, even to him, made her feel small and petty. "Would you like a glass of water?"

"Yes, please."

She filled a second glass and carried both back to the counter. For several minutes he was quiet, sipping his water and watching the crew finish. When her doorbell rang, she groaned. "That's probably my twin."

"Let me get it," he offered, striding away.

Why argue? At least his absence, however brief, gave her a reprieve from more questions. And from this vantage point, she could enjoy the view without getting caught ogling the enemy. The man was tall and well built, and his dark jeans fitted his long legs and firm backside perfectly.

Detective Iglesias walked back into view with another man at his side, slightly older, a few inches shorter and thicker through the middle. But the twinkle in the older man's eyes and the wavy brown hair gave her the impression they were related.

"Pippa, this is my uncle, Carlos. He's here to replace the lock on your back door."

Carlos held out his hand. "A pleasure," he said, beaming as she shook his hand. "A few minutes and I'll be out of your way."

"Um," she stared at the locksmith, then at his nephew. "I thought maintenance handled this kind of thing."

Carlos glanced at his nephew, and getting a go-ahead nod, scooted down the hall.

"Detective Iglesias," she snapped. "You can't just do that."

"What?" he asked, the picture of innocence.

She wasn't buying it. "Take over." Griffin had put him in her way and her brother would hear about it. "This is *my* home."

His dark brown eyes swept over the kitchen behind her. "I'm aware. Do you still plan to stay the night?"

"Yes." She pressed her lips together, seeing the trap as it snapped shut.

"Then let Carlos handle the lock. If the building requires something different, you can deal with it in time, but I can't allow you to stay if your home isn't secure."

"Because of Griffin."

He shook his head and motioned for her to sit down at the counter. "Because when everyone clears out, you need to be able to rest with confidence."

Her mouth fell open. She only knew because he tapped her chin to close it. Of all the reasons he might have provided, that was the only one that guaranteed her cooperation. "Thank you," she managed. That point where his finger had touched her chin tingled pleasantly. It took significant effort not to rub the sensation away. Definitely overtired.

"Were you at the office all day?" he asked.

This question didn't feel like an interrogation, especially not with the warmth in his gaze. "No. I..." She looked up and her gaze collided with his, the words getting lost between her brain and her mouth. He seemed genuinely interested in her responses. In her.

What was her problem? Of course he was interested.

Anything she said would reveal too much about her attempt to overturn Anna's conviction.

"I drove to the women's prison to see Anna Wentworth."

"How did that go?"

She studied him. Was he playing dumb? "Seriously? I'm not about to discuss anything about that with *you*."

Whatever he might have said was cut short by the CSI team packing up to leave. They assured her she could clean up the house and that the detectives would get the reports as soon as possible.

While Detective Iglesias walked them to the front door, Pippa refilled her water glass and pulled up the app for her insurance company. She could get started on the claim right now and have her agent come by first thing in the morning.

"Pippa," he called out. "Have you reset the code?"

She wanted to snipe at him for making himself too much at home, but his uncle was still in earshot, and that would just make her look bad and confirm the rumors that Anna was rubbing off on her.

Joining the detective at *her* door, stubbornly ignoring the state of her home, she stared at the electronic panel, trying to choose another code she and her twin could recall with ease. Making a decision to use her mom's birthday, in reverse order, she tested the new code a couple of times.

"That feels better, right?"

"A little," she admitted. Her gaze drifted back to the message, and she did her best to view it as a compliment. She was a do-gooder, and she wouldn't apologize to anyone for living out her values.

"I feel obligated to tell you not to give that code to anyone," he said.

"Someone has to have it. What if my plants need water?" All of her plants were silk and would stay that way until she was ready to make more time for her personal life. Only the aloe vera in the kitchen managed to thrive, despite her neglect.

"You can program multiple codes. We recommend you only hand out one spare key and only when necessary."

"The whole safety lesson is great, but the intruder didn't come in this way."

"We'll sort out how he got into the building as we review the video from the security cameras," he promised. "Now can you talk me through this, please?"

"Detective—"

"Call me Emmanuel."

She would *not*. That was too familiar, too normal. As much as she might appreciate the potential of him on a personal level, he was a threat to her case. To her career goals. If she thought the media attention was difficult now, it would be impossible if it came out that she was on a first-name basis with the detective who put her client in jail.

"Pippa—" He raised his hands in surrender when she glared at him. "Miss Colton. I'd like to pin down more details while things are fresh in your mind."

She feared the wrong details were crystallizing while the important things were becoming a blur. All the urgency to find the intruder that flooded her system an hour ago was gone now that the adrenaline rush was over. "Let's finish this in the morning. I'll come to the station." She looked around at the mess and somehow managed not to swear or cry. "I have too much cleaning left tonight."

"Emmanuel will help." Carlos had a sparkle in his eye when he volunteered his nephew. "My sister raised you right," he said to Emmanuel. "You can ask your questions while you are helping." With a broad smile, he handed Pippa two keys. "One for you and one for the building staff. Assuming you trust them."

"I do." Or she had. Still did. Maybe. Good grief, her brain felt like oatmeal. "Thank you. Do you take checks?" She started for her office, picking her way through the debris to the drawer where she kept her checkbook. Pulling it open, she was relieved to see everything still there, if not as neat as she'd left it, confirming the motive for someone making this mess wasn't fraud or theft.

"You okay?" the detective asked.

"Yes," she lied through the fatigue. "How much do I owe you?" She looked up when Carlos didn't answer. The older man was gone, leaving her alone with his nephew. "I didn't pay him."

"He said he'll send an invoice."

"I didn't hear that."

"You zoned out for a minute." He approached her as if he thought she might fly apart at any second. He might be right. "When was the last time you had something more than water?"

She shook her head. "I have no idea." Where was the grit that had carried her through the death of her parents, long nights of law school and that nasty breakup just before she sat for the bar exam?

Her siblings were an invaluable source of support, and she loved them for it, but she couldn't rely solely on them. Not when they were all consumed with Brody, RevitaYou and the Capital X investigation.

"You don't want me here, but I'm not leaving you alone."

She had the absurd urge to thank him. "I'll be fine."

"Of course you will. But my uncle will flay me if I leave you to handle this by yourself." He shrugged out of his jacket and draped it over a stool at the counter. His button-down was open at the collar, and she was mesmerized as he rolled back the cuffs, revealing strong, tanned forearms dusted with dark hair. "Go change clothes or whatever. I'll figure out food."

What was happening? "Your family is big on service?"

He shot her a look. "You could say that."

She'd touched a nerve, but she was just too tired to understand which one.

Chapter Four

Emmanuel put his focus on feeding Pippa, hoping she'd wander off while he rummaged through her kitchen for something fast and hearty. She needed fuel. The woman was running on fumes. But still running, which was impressive.

He found cereal in the cabinet and milk in the fridge along with some fresh fruit and orange juice. As if a stranger hadn't done enough invading tonight, he kept digging and came up with a better meal plan when he found frozen vegetables, eggs and some precooked sausage patties.

He didn't want to like her. She sure didn't like him. He was fine with her as just Griffin's sister. And he understood her work was important to the legal system overall, even when that meant second-guessing good police work. When he heard the water in the pipes between the walls, he had to force his mind away from the images of her stripping away her professional clothes and stepping into the shower.

All woman, no pretense. And completely off-limits.

Not just because he valued his friendship with her brother and wanted to keep the peace with her sister in the crime scene unit. Pippa was also several years younger and a whole lot less jaded.

The sausage was sizzling in one skillet, and he had another pan heating while he whisked up eggs in a bowl, adding ground pepper and the vegetables. When she walked in, her hair was down, the light brown waves brushing her shoulders, and she'd changed into faded jeans and a soft blue T-shirt. His pulse tripped over itself, his fingers itching to discover if her hair was as soft as it looked. He caught himself and pointed to a glass of orange juice. "That's for you."

She stared at him, her lips tight and her brow furrowed. "You're cooking?"

Was that bristling reaction her default with everyone or just him? "As I said." He poured the egg mixture into the pan.

"You said you'd figure it out."

"I did. This is faster than delivery."

"If you say so." She picked up the juice glass and drank it down. "This smells good."

His shoulders relaxed with the compliment, and he hid his smile. Hopefully the meal would fortify her for the many questions as well as the cleanup ahead of them.

Loading up two plates, he brought them to the countertop. She set out the napkins and forks while he refilled their water glasses. "Did you want coffee?"

"No, thanks," she replied. "I had more than enough caffeine during the drive today."

The drive to the prison. He had questions about that, but he didn't want to ruin the meal for her.

At her first bite of the omelet, she sat back and closed her eyes. "This is amazing. Thank you."

It beat the cold burger and fries waiting for him in the car. With so much going on with the RevitaYou crisis, he hadn't taken much time with friends and even less trying to date. He'd almost forgotten how nice it was to share a meal with a pretty woman.

When her plate was clean, there was more color in her cheeks and the spark was back in those big green eyes. Turning to face the office, she crossed her legs, and he noticed her feet were bare. They were slender, like the rest of her, and her toenails were painted with a deep rosy pink. What a contrast to her sleek professional image. The simple awareness took on the weight of a privileged secret.

"What a mess," she muttered.

"Definitely a focused effort there," Emmanuel agreed. He started to clear the dishes, but she stopped him.

"You cooked. Let me do this." She cleaned the dishes with an efficiency his mother would appreciate.

"Where are the cleaning supplies?" he asked.

"Hall closet." He found what passed as her laundry room with a stacked washer and dryer, a pull-down drying rack and a shelving unit. "You'll want to put shoes on before you go in there again."

"Hey, Detective?" She was behind him, paused at her bedroom doorway. "I don't need another big brother."

Right. He wasn't feeling brotherly. Uneasy with his not-at-all-fraternal reaction to her, he gave her a nod and then pulled out the broom and dustpan along with a couple of trash bags. He started in the living room so she wouldn't think he was trying to interfere with her work.

He was carefully sweeping up broken picture frames

when she joined him. For a second he thought the scowl was for him, but her gaze was on the wall.

"I can't believe you walked into this," he said quietly.

"Me neither." She tiptoed over to the wall and swore. "I thought so."

"What is it?" He helped her lift up a large framed painting of a sunset over a lake.

"The jerk tagged this too," she said, clearly disgusted. "Can you put it near the door? I'll take it for repair and reframing tomorrow."

He did as she asked, taking a closer look at the piece. It was definitely a statement by size as well as subject. The soft-focus blur of trees, vibrant with autumn color, tucked up close to the edge of the lake was calming. In fact, her home must have had a comfortable vibe before the vandal blew through. The colors and fabrics she'd decorated with were gentle and soothing, and nothing he would've expected from the stern and stressed woman from a few hours ago.

"It's not quite as bad as I thought," she said.

"Is that a joke?" he wondered.

She gave him a genuine smile and the unexpected rush left him momentarily speechless. "I thought the cushions were destroyed, but the upholstery is only unzipped," she said, wrestling foam back into the fabric. "You have no idea how long it took me to find this couch."

"It's a big decision," he agreed. "When I bought mine, I could've skipped squats for a week with all the ups and downs."

"Exactly!"

She brought out the vacuum and cleared away any

small bits of glass, and they soon had the couch back to normal.

"I can work in here if you'd rather get started on your office," he offered. Maybe she'd have an easier time with his questions if there was a bit of distance and distraction. "You need to be sure nothing's missing."

"You mean like my files?"

"Yes." The glass clinked as he swept it into the dustpan. "I assume you took your computer with you."

"I didn't," she replied. "But my laptop and all of my case notes are secure."

He glanced across the room. "At the office?"

"No, in the floor safe."

"Seriously?" He was impressed by her security measures. Maybe he shouldn't have given her a hard time about the lock.

"Yes." She was distracted by a stuck drawer in her desk. "This piece was my grandmother's," she muttered. "This drawer is a bear to reopen when it gets closed all the way."

He walked over, about to offer an assist, when the drawer gave and she stumbled back, right into him. His hands spanned the sweet dip of her trim waist, and he breathed in the faint citrus fragrance of her hair.

"Thanks," she said, an adorable rosy color rising in her cheeks.

"Anything missing?"

"Not so far, but the vandal was definitely searching."

He retreated to the other room, unable to hold back the flood of questions any longer. "Did you call the police immediately?"

"Sort of. At first I tried to talk myself out of dialing the emergency line due to the lack of imminent danger.

Then I called Kiely. She's a private investigator. But she was tied up with another case tonight."

"I've met her," he said. "Never had the pleasure of working with her."

"Your loss. Should've called her in on the Wentworth case when you needed a hand."

He bit his tongue rather than wreck a few positive steps by snapping at her. They hadn't needed any help on that case. The evidence had been clear, all of it leading to one specific guilty party. "Who knew you were headed to the prison today?"

"Kiely, my clients and my paralegal at the office." She'd cleared her desktop and was wiping it down.

He dragged his gaze away from the little flash of skin that showed between her shirt and jeans when she stretched. "By client, you mean Anna Wentworth?"

"Yes. Along with her daughter, who is overseeing this effort and footing the bill."

He had all the big pieces of glass picked up and was now vacuuming the smaller bits.

"You don't have to do that," she called out over the sound. "I'll call a professional cleaning crew tomorrow."

He ignored her, determined to make the space around the couch safe for her bare feet. "Why did you take Anna Wentworth's case?" he asked when he finished.

"Aside from the retainer?"

"It's okay to be financially motivated," he said, unfazed by her sarcasm. "You're not the only lawyer making more money by taking on a wealthy lost cause."

The bristling and scowling returned in force. "She is *not* a lost cause, and I *will* prove it."

He spread his arms, as frustrated as she was with all of this. "Do enlighten me."

"Fine." She leaned back on her clean desk. "First of all, Elizabeth is a good friend from school and I've known the family for years. Anna might be an awful snob who is happier writing a check than investing any real energy, but she isn't capable of murder. Plus, I don't take on loser cases. Not even for a friend."

"At least tell me Wentworth is grateful you're on board."

"I wish I could." Her gaze dropped to the floor. "I'm sure Elizabeth told her about hiring me, but today was supposed to be our first meeting about the case."

"Supposed to be?" he echoed.

She looked him dead in the eye. "We didn't get to speak at all."

"Was there trouble? It wasn't your first time meeting a client at the prison?"

"No and no." She sighed. "I had all my ducks in a row, even printed the confirmation of the scheduled appointment. They should've walked me right back to the conference room." She chewed her lip, lost in thoughts she wasn't sharing.

He wanted to know everything and not just because of the home invasion. "But?" he prompted.

She snapped out of it. "When I arrived, they claimed the paperwork was missing, that there was no record of my appointment in the system. I tried the waiting game, then name-dropping. The warden is an old friend of Dad's. That didn't work either. The guard claimed Mr. Birrell was away at lunch and couldn't spare a minute to help me straighten things out."

"That's weird." Normally Birrell was very helpful and professional. Then again, Emmanuel came in as a cop, not a defense attorney seeking to overturn a conviction. He bent down to pick up a pencil that had fallen near the baseboard. Turning, he studied the message on her wall. She'd clam up or get mad if he pressed on the Wentworth issue. "What else have you been working on lately? Any chance this is related to another case?"

"I don't see how. Aside from the RevitaYou investigation I'm working with my siblings, Anna Wentworth is my only open case."

"All right." He handed her the pencil, and she dropped it into the cup on her desk. Then he strolled back toward the kitchen.

"That's it? You're leaving?"

"You don't have to sound so excited about the prospect." He refilled his water glass, watching the disappointment come into her eyes.

"I like my space," she said.

He filled her glass too. "You'll have plenty of it. After a few more questions."

Her jaw clenched, but she drank down half of her water. "Go on and ask," she said.

She was defensive again, and he needed to change tactics. "Griffin and I go back, like you and Elizabeth. He's a good friend." Based on the deepening scowl, he'd made things worse. "He gave me a heads-up about the loan shark operation Colton Investigations is trying to take down and your part in it."

"That," she flung her hand toward the wall, "has nothing to do with the Capital X case."

"You sound sure." He admired her confidence.

"It's too soon. I haven't done anything significant with that case yet."

Yet. That one syllable seized his full attention. Griffin had said she'd play a key role in bringing down the loan shark operation. Colton Investigations and the GRPD were quietly working together on cases involving Capital X and the RevitaYou vitamins. Several people in the city had become sick, and one death was already attributed to the product. According to the research Abigail had conducted, more deaths seemed likely. On top of that, Capital X enforcers were the prime suspects in a recent murder in Heritage Park, since the victim had suffered eight recently broken bones in addition to the fatal gunshot.

"I don't believe this has anything to do with Capital X," she continued. "When they go after someone, they hit direct and hard and leave behind broken bones, not graffiti."

She wasn't making him feel any better. "Your sister is in the thick of that investigation already," he reminded her. "And the two of you share a strong resemblance."

"You're implying someone from Capital X followed me by mistake or even followed Kiely when she stopped by."

"It's possible, right?" He could almost see the wheels turning in her head. "Just don't want to leave any stone unturned."

"Because you're trying to impress me with your thoroughness." She wrinkled her nose. "Being thorough now doesn't mean you didn't overlook something on Anna's case."

Insulted, he had to agree with Daniel. Cute and stubborn was a bad combination. When his jaw unclenched enough to speak, he said, "Did Elizabeth mention she also was a questioned as we worked the case?"

"At the time, she told me you spoke, that's all. I assumed it was to clear suspects or verify an alibi. She's no more a killer than Anna."

"She was a concern," he reiterated. "And far too vocal about her mother's innocence."

"Because she knew Anna didn't kill anyone."

"The point is, I turn over every stone and I work my cases with integrity. Her alibi was solid and she had no interaction with Hicks before or during the time he was seeing her mother." He leaned close, noting the way her eyes widened at the apparent revelation. "And I'm good enough at my job that your friend didn't realize what I was doing."

Her gaze narrowed. "If she was a person of interest, why isn't that noted anywhere in the case file?"

"It is."

"Not." She shook her head.

He nearly repeated himself, but that sounded too much like a sibling argument and he had no desire to lump Pippa in with his sisters. "I filed everything. We looked at Elizabeth as well as her father, Ed."

"Anyone else?"

"Of course. We worked the case, Pippa. Followed the evidence and motives."

She was quiet a long time. Then she walked around him to pour herself a glass of wine. "It would've been nice to see some indication of that in the case file."

What was she talking about? His notes and reports had to be in there. He didn't appreciate the insinuation that he'd been inept or even slack about that particular case. Everything had gone to the prosecutor's office for the trial preparation. Maybe something got mishandled, but it had all been there.

She settled back on the stool, watching him. "Tell me something before you go."

He wasn't going any farther than her couch or floor tonight, but that argument would come soon enough. "What's that?"

"Why are you so sure Anna is capable of murder?"

It was a fair question, one he had asked himself often since catching that case. And one he was thankful he'd never had to answer in court.

WHILE PIPPA WAITED for his reply, she had to give Emmanuel points for being helpful this evening. And she couldn't criticize his manners or his cooking, though she did *not* want to like him. He was patient and neutral. Professional. Even Elizabeth had commented on how warm and kind he'd been during their conversation about the relationship between her mother and Hicks and when it had soured.

She wondered if he'd taken that warm and friendly approach while interrogating Anna or if he'd been cold and tough when facing off with a suspected killer. It was hard to sort out tone in the dry written transcript, and she hadn't yet listened to that recording provided by Anna's defense team. She'd been focusing her time and energy on the peripheral interviews and witnesses, looking for anyone else who had a real motive to kill Hicks.

"I'm surprised anyone believes that self-centered socialite is innocent," he said quietly. "In court I only spoke the truth."

"That's not much of an answer."

His head fell back for a moment. "Can I have another glass of water?"

"Help yourself." She watched him refill his glass from the pitcher in the fridge and ran out of patience after the long day as the silence stretched on. "Stop stalling, Detective."

His lips twisted to the side, his eyes on the water in his glass. "Anna was her own worst enemy long before the trial. It didn't require any extra help from the GRPD to put her behind bars where she belongs. She killed a man."

Pippa tensed at the certainty in his tone. Too bad for him she was equally certain the police and the jury were wrong. "She did not kill David Hicks. From what I've seen and heard, your mind was made up before you asked her the first question."

"Not true. Every case deserves good police work. Due to her standing in the community, we were even more thorough on the Hicks case."

She bit back another protest. He couldn't have been too thorough or an innocent woman wouldn't be in jail right now. They were clearly entrenched on opposite sides of this issue. "You've met killers. Caught them and seen justice served."

"I have," he verified.

"What does Anna have in common with those criminals?" She was pleased to see that question put a dent in his pervasive confidence.

What if the person who had trashed her home was the real murderer? She rubbed the sudden chill from her arms. Dwelling on that with someone as observant as Emmanuel nearby was a one-way ticket out of here. No way would she run from such an obnoxious and cowardly act.

"Not much on the surface," he admitted after a moment. "There are exceptions to every rule."

She waved that off. "Don't try to sell me the 'crime of passion' line. Anna isn't capable of extreme emotions with people."

"We found her jewelry near the body," Emmanuel said. "Maybe she killed Hicks because he tried to steal it."

She motioned for the wine bottle, pouring just a bit more into her glass. They shouldn't be talking about this. "I'm asking about you, personally," she stated. "Forget the evidence. Why were you so convinced she could take a man's life?"

"First of all, everyone is capable of doing terrible things."

He wasn't wrong. "This is murder we're talking about, though."

"I know. A big crime with big players and big stakes. I'm not going to lie—there was pressure to solve the case quickly. From the Hicks family as well as the Wentworth family. There was also pressure to do it right, coming from the mayor and the GRPD brass."

She folded her arms across her chest, refusing to let him off the hook. It was impossible to reconcile the considerate professional he'd been tonight when he'd had such negative tunnel vision about Anna Wentworth.

"She was mean," he finally said. "A mean and cruel woman. I'm aware that sounds childish."

"It is childish."

"At the heart it's the truth," he said. "You can't sit there and tell me Anna Wentworth is a nice person." She opened her mouth, but he cut her off. "Charitable contributions do not make someone a nice person. She's rude to her staff, aloof with her family, and she can hardly make eye contact with anyone with a smaller net worth than her husband."

He had a point. "Go on." There was more to this, more he clearly didn't want to talk about. Pushing at his hair, he muttered something under his breath, possibly in Spanish. All that did was make her want to ruffle his hair too. The untimely and inappropriate distraction irritated her.

"This is irrelevant," he said with a patently false smile. "But you win." He planted his hands on his lean hips. "We worked the case properly. Whatever I thought of Anna, I worked the evidence that was there."

"The evidence was compelling," she admitted. That was part of her problem. It was *too* compelling. Seasoned detectives like Emmanuel and Sergeant Joe McRath should've recognized that.

"If you believe the evidence, why are you convinced she *didn't* do it?"

"You first." More muttering in Spanish. "Detective Iglesias, would it help to consider this an exercise in my due diligence?" she asked. "I needed to speak with you, officially, anyway."

"Not much."

"But some?" She slid her wine glass aside and rested her elbows on the countertop. "Nearly every day you ask others, witnesses and suspects alike, to talk about uncomfortable and potentially embarrassing situations."

"Fair point."

"I'm not going away. You told Griffin you'd keep tabs on me anyway. Might as well get some work done too."

"You're impossible," he said. "My mother was a maid in the Wentworth mansion when I was little. Mrs. Wentworth didn't have children then. Maybe things would've been different if she had."

This wasn't the bias she'd been expecting at all. "Different how?" An image flashed through her mind of him as a little boy with tousled brown curls and big brown eyes sliding down the polished oak banister of the central stairway while his mother worked. Assuming that kind of thing would have been allowed.

"I never talk about this." His voice was a deep, unhappy rumble that heated her skin. "Mom had to take me to work one day. I guess the babysitter was sick and Dad was working. Who knows? I can remember her making calls, frantic to find someone to take me. I was too young to stay alone, and my brothers and sisters were in school."

"You're the youngest in your family?" she asked.

"I was then." He paused, his dark eyes knitting together over his straight nose. "Mom must've been pregnant, though it was probably too early for anyone but Dad to know." He stalked back and forth, as if he couldn't settle.

"It wouldn't have made a difference to Anna," Pippa admitted.

He raised an eyebrow and then continued. "So, yeah. I was the youngest. Mom was pregnant. She must've been sure Anna would fire her if she called in sick, so she took me with her." A faint smile hovered at one corner of his mouth. "That house."

"I know." Pippa had been equally awed when she'd seen it for the first time as a ten-year-old. Truth be told, the mansion was still an impressive and intimidating museum of a house.

"Whatever." He paced away and back again. "Mom

let me bring along a toy truck and a small teddy bear. The same quiet toys she let me take to church on Sundays. The three of us trailed after her, room to room, as she did her work." He shoved his hands into his pockets and refused to look at her. "I was quiet," he said, grumpy again.

Her heart ached for that little boy he'd been, and she was sure he'd behaved perfectly. "Just like in church?" she asked.

His lips curled up into an all-out grin. There was a fresh tingle to go with her heated skin. What was wrong with her? She couldn't indulge any of this curiosity or interest, not with him.

"Just like Sundays," he said. "We learned early and were reminded often of the penalties of outbursts or tantrums in church."

"I assume your mom issued the same reminder before you entered the Wentworth mansion?"

"She did." He met her gaze, and the earnestness in his eyes floored her. "I swear to you I wasn't making a sound when Mrs. Wentworth noticed me. She fired my mother on the spot."

He'd been a child, though she didn't doubt the whole thing must've been an ordeal. "In the interest of playing devil's advocate, are you sure she didn't give your mom a chance to explain?"

"I'm sure. I remember Mom pleading to be allowed to gather her things." His eyes locked on her once more. "Did you hear me? She didn't plead to keep the job—she begged for access to *her own belongings*."

Pippa groaned. "That sounds like Anna."

"So how can you sit there and *not* believe that a woman so cruel and selfish is capable of murder?"

Because she knew Anna better than most people. "Being a terrible human being doesn't necessarily make her a killer."

It was like striking a match to paper. Emmanuel erupted. "My mom barely got out with her own purse and her car keys. She didn't get a reference or severance or even that day's pay. She drove halfway home and then pulled over. I sat in the back seat and watched her *cry*. Totally helpless."

She wanted to cry for him, for them, all these years later. She wanted to drive right back to the prison and yank the woman out of her cell and shake her until she apologized.

"The woman was heartless. *Is* heartless. Was I doing anything to harm her? No. Was I keeping my mother from her work? Again, no. Anna Wentworth forgot my mother's name the moment we were gone." He paused to gulp in air. "But Mom getting fired sent *my* family into a tailspin. Mom had to scramble for a new job without a reference. Very few positions paid as well as the Wentworths."

It was all Pippa could do to keep her voice even, calm. When she finally spoke with Anna again, she'd… well, she didn't know what she'd do, yet. "So you've been angry all this time."

"Yes," he admitted. "Yes, it's been years. My mom got another job and my family survived and I'm *still* angry. That doesn't mean I didn't do my job." He drilled his finger into the granite countertop. "Everything I said in court was true. I didn't embellish any of it. I didn't have to. The dead body, the murder weapon, that outrageous brooch in the grass, splattered with the victim's blood. Add in all of her rude, unkind and outright mean antics through the years and it's not a big leap from Queen of Mean to murderer."

"I know it looks that way from—"

"Looks that way?" he echoed. "Pick up a tabloid, grab a newspaper, scroll through the gossip blogs. It *is* that way."

"You're helping my case if you're admitting online gossip influenced your investigation," she warned.

"Go ahead, try to pick my work apart. It'll hold up."

It couldn't. Pippa knew deep in her gut that Anna had not killed David Hicks. A grave mistake had been made, some detail had been overlooked or purposely suppressed and a murderer was still roaming around free. In her mind, the proof was scrawled across her wall. She needed Emmanuel to understand.

"You might be her daughter's friend, but you'll never convince me that Wentworth values you for anything more than your last name."

"I wouldn't try," Pippa said. She was suddenly exhausted again, her second wind gone. "I'm fairly sure she doesn't value me at all. But as Elizabeth's friend I have seen a different side of the woman everyone loves to hate."

He raised an eyebrow and rocked back on his heels. "Give me one instance where she exhibited compassion."

Well, that was a tough one.

"With more than a checkbook," he clarified.

Now she was stuck. "I've never seen an instance of hatred or anger hot enough to be deadly," she countered. "Taking a life requires effort. Hicks was shot in the heart. I'm not sure Anna has even held a gun."

"The lab decided she'd worn gloves and wiped the gun down."

Pippa waved that off. "Whoever killed Hicks wore gloves and wiped down the gun," she insisted. "You know Anna Wentworth doesn't lift a finger if she doesn't want to."

"So she hired someone to have it done."

"And asked the killer to drop the gun in her prized roses to frame herself?" She snorted. "Give me a break." Restless now, she stretched her arms overhead and then walked over to her desk. "More important, she would've had to care about the man enough to want him dead. He was convenient, but she didn't need him."

"She needed him to keep quiet about their affair," Emmanuel said.

"The prosecution was wrong about that," Pippa said. "I'm telling you blackmail wasn't a problem. Ed knew about the affair. He knew about all of her affairs before Hicks. No one would've paid him off."

"You're serious?"

She nodded. Emmanuel's disbelief was no surprise. "The Wentworths' marriage wasn't typical." Or maybe the happy-ever-after sort of relationship was the exception. She and Elizabeth had grown up in wealthy families with unconventional dynamics, and they had adapted differently. They'd both chosen personal accountability over convenience, one of the hallmarks of their friendship. Pippa understood that wasn't always the case. Money might open doors, but unlike Anna, Pippa and Elizabeth valued the hard work and kindness that built lasting connections.

Pippa understood she'd grown up with opportunities many kids didn't get, but she'd taken on Anna's case as a matter of righting a wrong. Much the same way her father had taken an unpopular stand to see that Brody wasn't wrongly convicted.

Life had crazy rippling effects on people. Elizabeth still believed in love and true devotion and all of that, despite the poor example set by her parents. And Pippa struggled to trust anyone outside of her siblings.

Clearly she and her siblings had adapted differently even under the same roof. It was still odd to think of her brothers partnered up with women who made them wildly happy. Riley and Charlize would soon be parents, and Griffin and Abigail, with their foster daughter Maya, already were. New examples of family dynamics rooted in love and hope.

But life had taught her that what worked for others wouldn't necessarily work for her. Dating was pointless when she was too busy to feed herself, much less find a few minutes to have coffee with a stranger from an app. She was happiest when she was up to her neck in a challenging case.

"Pippa?"

She blinked, rearing back as he waved a hand near her face. "What?"

"You checked out," he said. "It's been a long day. Let's pick this up again in the morning."

"Right." She pressed her hands to her eyes. "I do understand." She dropped her hands and caught the flare of concern in his gaze. The urge to step into the warmth and strength of him was nearly irresistible. "At least you have a valid reason to hate Anna, beyond the tabloid antics."

"I handled her case objectively," he said quietly.

She really wanted to believe him.

"Mom got a better job eventually," he continued. "A better boss. I should be over it."

"It was a defining moment." She forced her lips into a smile. "It's also late." Scooting past him, she aimed for the front door, but he didn't follow. "As you said, we can pick this up in the morning."

"I'm staying."

"No." She couldn't have the detective who'd testified against Anna stay here. "Locks are all new and I'm safe, so thanks again." She motioned for him to head out. He didn't budge. "I don't care what my brother asked you to do. I'm thirty years old and I can take care of myself."

"Normally, I'd agree." He tipped his head toward the nasty message on her wall. "That implies you need backup."

She swore under her breath and pushed a hand through her hair. Pointing at the screaming red paint, she said, "That mess is on my wall because the GRPD made a mistake." No more warmth in his eyes now. He was cold, his entire body braced against her. "In your opinion."

At the moment, the home invasion was the closest thing she had to hard evidence. "It's more than that. I'm getting threats and stonewalled at every turn because I understand there's a killer loose in Grand Rapids."

"Threats?" He took a step closer. "This isn't the first trouble you've had."

She wanted to bite off her own tongue. "Why won't anyone try to see this my way?"

"Because everyone else believes the evidence."

"I know how it must have looked," she allowed. "If you want to solve this home invasion, then you might have to rethink that. People in general might not like what I'm doing on the Wentworth case, but only the real killer has motive to drive me off of it."

Her heart thudded against her ribs as they stared at each other.

"There are other explanations, other cases past and present," he said. "I'm only being objective and doing my job."

"That's true. So am I. I will see you tomorrow." She opened the front door. "I'll discuss this with you and your partner then."

His expression stony, he grabbed his jacket and walked out. Almost. He paused in the doorway. "Be careful, Pippa." Something resembling doubt flashed in his eyes. "If we need anything more, we'll come to you." He cleared his throat and bent his head close to her ear, his breath fanning her cheek. "Tomorrow I'll review the Hicks murder case one more time. With fresh eyes."

Then he was gone, pulling the door closed behind him. She locked it, and for several long minutes she simply marveled over the fact that she had finally gotten through to someone…especially that infuriatingly handsome detective.

Maybe the day wasn't a total loss after all.

Chapter Five

Emmanuel took the stairs down to the street two at a time, his mind spinning as he exited the building. Pippa truly believed in Anna Wentworth's innocence. Based on her brother's descriptions and anecdotes, he'd thought she was levelheaded. He'd assumed she was just helping a friend exhaust every legal option.

But she really believed it. Worse, her dogged determination had him rethinking everything. What if she was right and there was a killer on the loose, ready to stop her before she exposed the truth?

As a detective he'd seen more than his fair share of homicide victims through the years. Picturing Pippa snuffed out and lifeless gave him a chill he couldn't shake. Even without the promise he'd made to Griffin, he wouldn't have left her alone tonight.

Antsy, he wasn't ready to settle into his car yet. He walked around the block while he called Daniel to check in. "How are things there?" he asked when his partner answered.

"Slow tonight, thankfully," Daniel replied. "Are you on your way in?"

"Not until morning." He'd reached the back of her building. The parking lot, drive and a walkway leading to the main sidewalk were all paved, but there was grass on either side of the walkway and landscaping around the residential rear doors. Daniel had already searched the area for any prints or other evidence, but another glance never hurt anything.

Fresh eyes.

"Did you get our prickly victim delivered to her brother?" Daniel asked, distracting him.

"No." He sighed. "She's staying the night."

Daniel chuckled. "She didn't strike me as the runaway-from-trouble type."

"No," Emmanuel allowed. "I wouldn't classify her as cooperative either," he added.

"Stubborn and cute."

"Don't start that," he said. "She's a victim." That status alone should nix any personal interest. Having sisters of his own, he could just imagine Griffin's reaction if he voiced any of the observations swirling in his head.

"But what if she wasn't?"

Without any caveats, Pippa would be a woman he'd want to know better. Intelligent and witty and independent was a heady combination, even before he factored in her beautiful eyes and figure. His palms warmed, recalling that moment when she'd lost her balance.

"A shame she's leading an investigation that could cause the department big trouble," Daniel said.

"Stop." Daniel had just made everyone on the GRPD a potential suspect for the home invasion.

"Have you even had a date in the last six months?" his partner challenged.

"Of course I have." He must have gone out with someone lately. It just hadn't been memorable. "Have you found any security cameras that might help us find the perp?"

"The church nearby has a few cameras covering the doors and the street, but no one answered when I called. I left a message and will follow up in the morning."

"Good." Emmanuel moved toward the street until he spotted one of the church's cameras. It was placed high enough it might help them. "What about the building?"

"I spoke with the head of maintenance for the building. He confirmed there were service teams in and out all day and we'll get the footage. More to the point, everyone coming in is supposed to use those paper shoe covers."

"That explains one partial," Emmanuel said. Maybe the paper cover had torn or slipped and the perp hadn't noticed. "All right. If you need me, I'm keeping an eye on things from the car tonight."

"For your friend?"

"Yes," Emmanuel replied. He managed to catch himself before offering more excuses that Daniel would only use to tease him later. "I'll be in first thing in the morning," he said. "Call if you need me before that."

He ended the call and walked back toward the building, right up to the service entrance. The motion-sensor floodlight came on and he stopped, searching for any kind of clue. Red spray paint had been used, by a man, based on the size of that partial boot print in the hallway. Whatever the man had walked through, Daniel hadn't seen any evidence of it in the building, and he hadn't picked up any trace of prints out here.

No surprise. Everything at the service entrance was paved.

Emmanuel kept thinking about that lone partial

print, just inside Pippa's back door. How long would the sole of a boot stay damp enough to leave a mark? He searched the landscaped areas around the residential door, then followed the walkway to the parking lot. Coming up empty, he returned to the door and started over, this time examining the opposite end of the wide paved steps.

His light caught on a bit of crushed ornamental grass and displaced mulch. Jackpot. Well, *maybe* a jackpot. He took a couple of pictures, using his hand as a reference for scale. The depression wasn't really clear enough to warrant making a mold, but someone had stepped off the path recently. It was a big leap to assume this mark was made by the same boot heel they'd found upstairs, though he was happy to have a target, something to watch for when they reviewed the videos from the security cameras on both buildings.

If the intruder had come in or left through the residential exit, did that mean they were looking for one of Pippa's neighbors in disguise?

It was plenty to think about. He could run a preliminary background on the other residents from the computer in his car. Rounding the building, he unlocked his car and settled in for a long night.

PIPPA STOOD BACK, pleased with cleaning efforts. The office was back to its normal, organized state. She'd even pulled her laptop and the Wentworth file from the floor safe so she could dive right in first thing in the morning.

She went to the hall closet and found a reusable grocery bag. Carefully, she loaded up the pieces in need of new glass. Hopefully the framing shop could help with that too. Some of them had been purchased during her travels and weren't easily replaced.

The mess on the wall gave her a fresh rash of goose bumps every time she walked by, as if the person who'd put it there was still watching her, challenging her resolve.

"Not for long," she decided.

Opening the app on her phone, she reviewed the list of service providers recommended by her insurance company. She would definitely complete her claim, but whether or not they paid didn't matter. She couldn't leave things like this. Having done volunteer work around the city scrubbing graffiti off public buildings, she knew that red spray paint wasn't going to be covered with a simple coat of paint. Or ten.

The cleaning and restoration company at the top of the list had a five-star rating and offered a twenty-four-hour answering service, so she called to schedule an appointment for tomorrow afternoon. Within minutes arrangements were made, and she'd uploaded the pictures she'd taken of the damage through the link at their site.

It wasn't until she was out of things to do that it all hit her. Someone had been in her house. She stared at that message. Someone had entered her home intent on intimidation, threats and destruction.

The trembling started in earnest, and no amount of calm breathing eased the pressure. Her knees shaking, she double-checked the locks at the front and back doors. Everything was secure.

She was safe.

She clasped her hands together to stop the shaking. How long would it take for her to believe it? Her fingers itched to pick up her phone and call her twin. But Kiely was working and her other siblings were likely settled in for the night. She could handle this and discuss it calmly tomorrow.

Frozen in the hallway, she wrapped her arms around herself as a dozen worst-case scenarios ran through her head. What if she'd been home when the man who'd left the boot print came through the back door? She often worked with her earbuds in and the music volume cranked up high. Would she have heard anything in time to protect herself? With surprise on his side, he might have done far worse than trash a room and ruin a wall.

"Stop!" Her intended shout emerged a hoarse whisper.

Nothing dreadful had happened. This type of vandalism was the work of someone who didn't want to face her. The person had come when she had been away, intent on scaring her off the case. She'd been inconvenienced by the property damage, that's all.

It was over. She was alone and safe. No one could get in without her knowledge. Not her sister, not even maintenance until she gave them the key.

Still, her hands shook as she walked into the kitchen to wash the glassware.

She didn't have to stay here tonight. There was plenty of room in the house where they'd all grown up, the house where Riley still lived and where they conducted Colton Investigations business.

And if she ran away to Riley's house, which was how she thought of it now, she'd be interrupting his new life with Charlize. Once she told them about this her siblings would circle the wagons and try to protect her. Griffin would raise more concerns about her involvement with the Capital X case.

She couldn't let them down. They were all worried enough about Brody. She would tell them in the morning, when she felt strong enough to overcome any discussion.

The fact was she was safe. She was just overtired and frustrated because her home had been trashed. But that would be set right again soon. Topping off her water glass, she retreated to her bedroom with her laptop.

There was absolutely no indication the intruder had bothered with anything in here, though everyone from Officer Jeffries to Detective Iglesias had taken a look around.

Before she'd left, Officer Jeffries explained the prevailing theory was an intruder had slipped in with a work crew, gained entry with a master key stolen from the maintenance office and slipped out again with no one the wiser. With a little luck the police would find something helpful from the security cameras around the area.

If she kept dwelling on the trouble, she'd never get to sleep. Changing into her softest nightshirt, she added some extra moisturizer under her eyes and then settled into the bed to watch a movie on her laptop.

As the streaming site loaded, showing her what was trending and what she'd been watching, she smiled a little. The intruder had most likely been searching for information on the Wentworth case, but having her search history on this site exposed would've been really embarrassing. Her reputation as a tough, serious and cerebral lawyer would take a hit if anyone discovered she was a sucker for sweet romance movies and shows.

She treated herself to these light, pleasant hours because it was the only time a happy ending was guaranteed. Although one of the reasons she worked so hard for her clients was to reach a happy conclusion, sometimes making things right didn't make things whole.

Too tired to focus on something new, she turned out the light and chose an old favorite with plenty of humor to scrub the worst of the bad day from her mind. The hero reminded her a bit of Emmanuel. Confident and smart, he took charge unapologetically, yet kindly. While she didn't always appreciate it when her brothers forgot she was an adult and tried to step in and protect her, she did appreciate Emmanuel's efforts tonight.

He stirred her up inside, despite all the reasons she shouldn't let herself be distracted. It was more than his sharp good looks. She didn't have any regrets about prioritizing a case over a man when it was all superficial, but add in the intelligence and the life experience that gave interest and depth to his face and she felt like a bee in a field of blooming flowers. She dozed off, her mind on Emmanuel, her imagination spinning movie-caliber scenes of quiet walks in the park and deep, drugging kisses.

Hours later, her alarm clock sounded, and Pippa discovered she'd spent another night with her laptop on the pillow next to hers. Another secret no one needed to know.

Except today, as she rolled to her back and stretched her arms overhead, her muscles were as soft as pulled taffy and she was warm all over. Oh, no. She'd dreamed of Emmanuel—Detective Iglesias—all night long. Even in bed alone, the ridiculous dreams of romance and tender intimacy mortified her. She covered her face with her pillow. This was *not* good. The man was a trained observer. How would she face him today? Ever?

She leaped out of bed and headed for the bathroom, avoiding her reflection. A cold shower and a cup of coffee would clear her head and body. People had sex dreams all the time with inappropriate partners. It wasn't as if she had to discuss it with anyone. Clearly it was a fragment in her subconscious linking her biggest stressors.

The dream was an outlet. No need to make herself crazy about it. As soon as she saw him today, she'd remember the man was the opposition. He was the biggest enemy to her making the case, even if he had gone above and beyond to help her last night.

The bracing shower helped, and drying off, she caught the scent of fresh-brewed coffee. Today was going to be so much better. Pausing at her closet, she quickly decided on dark cropped jeans and a more casual white tunic blouse since she'd be working from home between meetings with the adjuster and cleaning crew. And if she had to go to the police station?

Emmanuel said he and his partner would come here.

Dressed, her hair pinned up in a loose knot, she took her laptop into the kitchen, setting it on the counter. Once she filled a mug with fresh coffee, she added a spoonful of sugar and carried it back to the bathroom to apply her makeup.

Feeling almost normal again, she went to work. The threat staining her living room startled her. It shouldn't have. Though it would've been nice, she'd known it wouldn't miraculously disappear. Determined not to let herself fall into another fearful paralysis, she deliberately turned her gaze to the desk and her thoughts to Emmanuel.

She hadn't expected him to help her clean up or see that her locks were changed. Was that all out of some obligation to Griffin or was that just his way?

Watching her parents' marriage fade into too much silence, diverging interests, and separate bedrooms had eroded Pippa's faith in the institution of lifelong partnerships. She could count on her siblings, but she didn't want to rely on anyone else. Didn't want to need anyone else. Her insistence on handling life's challenges on her own created some friction with her siblings, who only wanted to protect her. Between her stubborn streak and her tunnel vision when it came to a case, relationships didn't stand a chance.

The system had worked for her. Right up until tonight. Something about Emmanuel made her want to rest, to share theories on a case or the burdens of a bad day. He made her want to lower her guard.

He couldn't possibly take care of all the victims he met the way he'd cared for her. She had assessed his recent caseload. He worked like a man with no hobbies.

Not unlike herself.

She wanted to admire that despite his testimony sending the wrong person to prison. And now she knew beyond any doubt he held a grudge against her client.

This obsession with him wasn't healthy or practical; it was dangerous territory. She had to get the man out of her mind.

Would he really look at the case with fresh eyes today? Was it even possible for him to remain truly objective?

With her second cup of coffee in hand, she opened

the curtains, just enough to let in some light without giving anyone outside a view of the nastiness on her wall. That just couldn't come down fast enough.

On the street she noticed an unfamiliar car. Nerves struck immediately, and she was reaching for her cell phone when the person in the driver's seat moved. She recognized the jacket and the curl of hair around the man's ear. Both belonged to Detective Iglesias.

Had he spent the night out there? That was ridiculous. He'd left his business card; she could just call him. Concerned there had been more trouble, she decided to go down and talk to him. She wouldn't know if she should be charmed or irritated by his presence until she had some answers. Whatever his reasons for being here at this hour, she would get further if she was nice.

Filling a travel mug with hot coffee, she walked downstairs. Stepping out of the building, the first thing she noticed was the frown on his mouth as he spoke into his cell phone. Cautiously, she looked around for more law enforcement. If there was an immediate crisis, she couldn't imagine he'd be here without backup.

She crossed the street and tapped on his window, regretting the bold move when his head jerked up and around in surprise. She hadn't meant to startle him. His brown eyes darted from her condo and back to her, as if he couldn't make sense of her being in the wrong place.

He rolled down the window, and she saw his eyes were red rimmed. She could almost feel the distress pouring out of the car.

"What's wrong, Detective?"

"Just tired." He smiled, but she wasn't fooled. "Long night."

"Were you out here all night?"

"It was the right place to be," he replied.

Everything about him was strung tight, from his smile to his white-knuckled fingers curled around the steering wheel. Something was terribly wrong. "You're upset," she said, stating the obvious.

"No. Just tired."

That time she heard his voice crack. "I brought you a coffee, but maybe you should come upstairs and talk it out. This time I'll fix breakfast."

"That's…generous, Pippa," he said. "I couldn't possibly eat, but thanks all the same."

Why couldn't men just share rather than waste time in denial? "Come upstairs anyway."

"I'm fine. Really."

She hung on to the coffee she'd brought for him. "Maybe I'm out here because someone else is up there."

His gaze narrowed, and he reset his grip on the steering wheel. "That isn't funny."

Probably not, but she wouldn't let him sit out here alone with whatever was troubling him. She could analyze her reasons later, but seeing him so unhappy troubled her. "Ask anyone who knows me, I won't give up."

Grumbling, he rolled up his window and got out of the car.

She handed him the coffee she'd brought downstairs. "It's black," she warned. "I wasn't sure how you take it, but—"

"Caffeine is caffeine at this hour."

That's exactly what she would've said. "Right." She crossed the street, and he got the door half a step before she could, holding it open for her. "Thanks."

Upstairs at her condo, she did a double take when

her lock wouldn't open. Her palms went damp and her pulse skittered.

"You changed the code," he said, his voice rough.

She paused, drying her palms on her jeans before she tried again. More than forgetting the new code, the flash of fear rattled her. This was her home, and until yesterday walking inside had been a comfort. She'd been gone only a few minutes, and she was afraid that she'd catch someone in the act when the door opened. What would happen when she came home again after being gone all day?

"It's just us," Emmanuel said, as if he could read her mind.

His certainty soothed her as much as it embarrassed her. She'd invited him up to talk about his troubles, not to rehash hers. The door opened and she stepped inside, studiously ignoring the damaged wall as she went straight to the kitchen.

Behind her, Emmanuel closed and locked the door.

Striving for a breezy hospitality, she said, "If you want to clean up or anything, go ahead. The guest bath is fully stocked." He knew her place as well as she did after last night.

"Seriously?" He took a drink of the coffee. "I'll just be a minute. Thanks," he said, excusing himself.

He wasn't the only one who knew how to be thoughtful. When he returned a few minutes later, she had bacon in the oven and water simmering for poached eggs.

"What's all this?" he asked.

"Breakfast." She grinned. It was basically the same thing he'd prepared for them last night. "Most important meal of the day."

"I've heard studies that contradict that," he said. "And I really need to get going."

She wasn't sure how to read his expression. His gaze was haunted, but since leaving his car, he seemed intent on being cheerful. She'd earned her reputation for being pushy, and right now she thought he needed a push to open up. Maybe even a shove. "You have time for coffee."

His expression turned mulish. She'd seen it plenty when her brothers were trying to avoid an uncomfortable topic.

"I don't give up," she reminded him for the second time in five minutes. "Did something happen at home or with your family?" She dropped the eggs into the water, stirred gently and covered the pan.

"Please don't do this," he said.

"You don't like eggs?"

"Pippa. I don't want to talk."

"You helped me last night," she pointed out.

"So pestering me today is how you say thanks?"

She didn't reply, just checked the bacon and dropped slices of bread into the toaster.

With a sigh, he sat down on a counter stool and laced his fingers together, thumbs pressing back and forth. "I got some really bad news. An email landed in my inbox a few minutes ago."

"I'm sorry."

She set down plates and silverware, napkins and condiments.

He fiddled with the utensils. "Two more deaths have been linked to RevitaYou."

It took all of her self-control to hold back a tidal wave of questions. News had spread that the miracle vitamin was making some people ill, and one death had already been attributed to a toxic element in the proprietary formula. Yet people were still taking it, choosing to roll the dice for the sake of feeling and looking younger.

"Do you know the victims?" she asked, plating the bacon, toast and eggs.

He stared at the food for a long moment, then pinched his eyes closed before he looked up again. "Thanks."

"You're welcome." Taking a seat at the end of the peninsula, she started to eat, but Emmanuel kept staring at his plate. She knew he wasn't seeing the food, but rather someone who had been important to him.

"I only know one victim directly. Ingrid Glucksburg." His lips canted to one side and he sniffed. "She was a GRPD informant. The report listed her as fifty years old."

That sounded far too young to Pippa for someone to be buying antiaging supplements, but that was exactly why the market was huge. The sadness in his voice made her heart ache. Tempted her to reach out and soothe him. She kept her hands busy with her breakfast.

"Before she became an informant, she was a petty thief." A smile flitted across his lips. "I can't tell you how many times she joked that all she needed was a good facial and a day at the spa to erase the years. She swore if she could look young enough to turn my head, she'd ask me out."

"She sounds like a real character," Pippa said.

"You have no idea." Emmanuel sighed. "She was ornery and spry and smart as a whip, despite the bad choices she once made."

Nothing she'd read or heard in the trial transcripts prepared her for these facets of Emmanuel's character. Last night's generosity and his compassion today were a surprising counterpoint to the yawning grief that seemed to be threatening to swallow him whole.

"I'm really going to miss her," he said, pushing his eggs around his plate.

Pippa wished he would eat his breakfast. He needed to keep up his strength. "How did you become friends?" she asked.

"Catching Ingrid in the act was kind of a rite of passage in a way." He tore his toast in two, and buttered one piece. "She would give new patrol officers a run for their money on the street. There were times when her interactions with officers gave us better insight than any formal training or evaluation."

"What do you mean?" she queried.

"You know the *Star Wars* movies?"

Not the question she was expecting. "I'm offended you have to ask." When he only stared at her, she took a bite of her bacon, hoping to trigger a mimic effect. It worked. He took a bite of his bacon, as well. Hooray for those psychology classes she'd aced in college.

He chewed and swallowed and his smile seemed a little stronger. "Remember when Yoda pesters Luke after he crashes in that swamp?"

"Of course. It was an attitude test." She ate a bit more, and he did the same.

"The first of many," Emmanuel agreed, chasing a bite of eggs with more coffee.

"Ingrid was like Yoda," he continued. "She often knew right away who would turn into a good cop and who would be problematic or quit at the first sign of adversity."

Fighting the strangest urge to pull him into a comforting hug, Pippa cradled her coffee cup in both hands. A dozen more questions zipped through her mind, but he was eating well now and she didn't want to interrupt him.

When he finished, he stared at the empty plate as if he wasn't sure what had happened.

"More coffee?" she offered. "There's more bacon too."

"I'd better not." He checked his watch. "Daniel's expecting me any minute. Thanks for breakfast. And for listening."

"My pleasure." And it had been. Most of the time when she remembered to eat, food was only functional. Feeding Emmanuel had felt far more personal and filled her with a new and delightful satisfaction. She enjoyed sharing meals with her siblings, even pitching in with the cooking or clean up. And she often found helping others energized her. This was different; it created a fluttering sensation around her heart. She couldn't quite put a label on it. Wasn't sure she wanted to. She hadn't enjoyed the topic, but she had enjoyed his stories and insights about his friend. The man was dangerous territory, indeed.

"I am sorry for your loss," she said, walking him to the front door. "It's all the more reason to put an end to this RevitaYou nonsense and the Capital X enablers issuing those impossible loans. I'm glad I'll be part of the solution when I apply for a loan tonight."

She pulled the door open, but he shoved it closed, his face clouding over. But this wasn't sorrow, it was anger.

Chapter Six

He couldn't have heard her correctly. Taking her by the shoulders, he turned her away from the door, held her firmly. "What did you say?"

"Let me go."

Her green eyes blazed. She was angry. He understood that. "Answer me first." She could *not* be entertaining the idea of deliberately putting herself in harm's way. Griffin hadn't mentioned how she would work on the Capital X case, only that she was determined to make a difference.

He stepped back and rubbed at his gritty eyes. He hadn't slept well. It wasn't possible to truly rest in the car with his body braced for trouble and his mind preoccupied with the woman in front of him. And now Ingrid. He was overwhelmed, that's all.

Her death would take some time to get over. He pressed his fist to the ache deep in his chest.

"Are you okay?" she asked.

"Yeah. Fine." The coffee would kick in soon and all of this would make sense. "Repeat that last thing, please."

Her brow flexed, then cleared. "Oh. I'm going to apply for a Capital X loan tonight. Colton Investigations is putting the final touches on things today." She bounced on her toes, and he noticed her feet were bare. "We're all set to go at seven o'clock tonight."

"That's crazy." Couldn't she hear how crazy that sounded? "Those people are dangerous. Why would you set yourself up?"

"The loan isn't for me," she said. "They've been working on an alias, complete with identification, a background, the works. I'm just the one filling in the details online."

"No." He couldn't let her do that. He turned away from her, his gaze slamming into the threat on the wall. What if that hadn't been about Wentworth? And she'd implied there had been other threats too. "You can't."

He'd shown up to help a friend, but something about her made him want to do more. A lot more. The idea of her in danger scraped at his frazzled nerves like a burr in a sock. "I'll talk to Griffin. You'll make a new plan."

Her gaze grew hard. "That's not your place."

"It should be," he shouted. "It's too easy to trace IP addresses," he said, forcing his voice to behave. "Capital X will come after you—"

"That's what we're counting on. But not me, not here," she added in a rush. "Relax, Detective." She reached out, rested her hand on his arm. "We're professionals at Colton Investigations. They did some masking thing to make it harder to find this laptop."

He did know CI's good reputation. At the moment all of his attention had zeroed in on the place where her hand touched him. He could feel the heat of her through the layers of his shirt and jacket. He wanted to take that hand in both of his and—

"Maybe you should go home and get some rest."

Great, now she thought he was inept. Or too grief stricken to work. But work was what got him through. "I'm not doubting the expertise. I'm pointing out that you're planning to apply for a loan from a bank that doesn't only charge late fees. This company," he used air quotes, "is vicious. They break bones."

"I'm aware." Stepping back, she folded her arms over her chest, taking away the sweet-hot contact. "We have a foster brother out there hiding from Capital X enforcers while his broken bones heal. We can end this. I'm not walking away because it's risky."

Damn it. There was plenty of room between walking away and walking right into the line of fire. "I'm not asking you to walk away. Can you tell me what precautions you're taking?"

"I'm afraid that's confidential."

This was the worst morning he could remember in a long time. He'd promised Griffin to watch out for her, and he intended to do so despite his caseload and that she wouldn't want him underfoot. One threat was already painted on her wall. He understood the desire to help; he'd go the distance for his siblings too. But he didn't want her setting herself up for more trouble.

"I'm sure you have a busy day ahead, Detective Iglesias. I do, as well." She reached for the door again. "Take care."

"Pippa, come on. Aren't you dealing with enough right now?"

"I like to stay busy," she said. "If you and Griffin are so worried about me cracking under pressure, come on back tonight and hover however you see fit. I'll be submitting the application at seven."

Clearly she didn't want him to accept. She would have to be disappointed in his diligence. "That's pretty specific."

She shrugged a shoulder. "Part of the background they've created for me," she said. Her expression softened as she studied his face. "You really don't need to worry, Detective."

"Emmanuel," he corrected. He wanted her to think of him as a friend, not the detective who'd testified against her client. "I'll see you at seven. Earlier," he said before he could change his mind. "I'll bring dinner."

Her lips parted, and he was tempted to silence her protest with a kiss. Instead, he walked out, closing the door before she could utter a word. Before he could make a fool of himself.

He wasn't buying that lie about her limited involvement in the Capital X investigation. If Griffin had believed she was only going to tap a few keys anonymously, he wouldn't have mentioned it to Emmanuel at all.

In his car, he called Griffin. "What are you thinking?" he demanded as soon as his friend answered.

"And good morning to you too. Did Pippa shoot you or something?"

"Sorry." Emmanuel pulled himself together. "And of course not. It's been a long day, and I'm not even to the station yet."

"Pippa can do that," Griffin said with a chuckle. "She's a junkyard dog when she sets her mind on a task."

Emmanuel bristled at the unflattering description. He didn't mind her feisty side. Grit and determination were positive traits in his book, especially in the pursuit of justice. On that they were agreed, even if they had different approaches and opinions on how that should be accomplished. He was far more troubled by the way her green eyes flashed when she was mad and she nibbled her lip when she was lost in thought.

"Iglesias?"

"What?" He'd lost track of the conversation.

"I asked if she demanded you recant your testimony."

"No." Though, like her brother, he expected her to suggest it at some point. "She did convince me to take another look at the evidence."

"Seriously?"

"You heard me," Emmanuel said, resigned. "I'm almost to the station. Need to double-check the report from her break-in last night and then—"

"Is she doing all right?"

"Seems to be. Is she always so stubborn?" Emmanuel asked.

"She prefers the term *independent*, and yes. Pippa and Kiely have both been that way since the day I met them. That's why I asked you to step in."

He remembered the story about Griffin, a couple of years older than Pippa and her twin sister, being adopted into the family when he was eight.

Emmanuel drove past the station, deciding he wanted a shower and a change of clothes before dealing with anything else this morning. "Independent or not, she's taking a hell of a risk with this plan to get a loan."

"I'm sorry you disapprove," Griffin said, his voice cool. "Again, that's why I asked for your help. She's mad at me because I insisted we take the time to work up a solid alias. She was willing to handle it under her own name."

Stubborn and cute. It was a fascinating combination. Was the fierce independence rooted in the awareness that her siblings always had her back? But that kind of stunt could've wrecked her credit, put her at risk with the Michigan bar, not to mention practically a guarantee of physical harm. Her blatant disregard for her own welfare was shocking. "Anything for family?"

"Pretty much the Colton motto."

Despite the awkwardness and inevitable pitfalls ahead, he was weirdly grateful that Griffin had involved him. "I'll keep you posted," Emmanuel said.

"One second. You can't leave me hanging," Griffin said. "How did she convince *you* to take another look at the Wentworth case?"

He couldn't tell her brother the whole truth, that he was worried for Pippa's safety. Neither could he voice his concern that the man who'd trashed her apartment would try again if she made any progress on overturning the conviction. He sure wasn't ready to admit that Pippa's fierce faith in a woman no one else liked had made him question himself.

"It's the only way to prove I'm right about Wentworth," he replied.

"Good luck, then."

"Thanks, Griffin."

Emmanuel ended the call as he pulled in to the driveway. He dashed inside, cleaned up and changed clothes in record time and, feeling like he'd hit the restart button, headed to work. Through it all, he thought about how she challenged his view of Anna Wentworth. Maybe he had been too quick to dismiss alternate suspects.

The mood was somber as word spread about Ingrid's

death. All of them thought the world of her and no one could believe she was gone. It was almost a relief when he sat down at his desk and found a stack of paperwork that needed his attention.

"You okay?" Daniel asked, peering over his computer monitor. "Tough night, tough news this morning."

"I'm fine," Emmanuel lied. "Rather not talk."

Instead of cooperating, Daniel came over and dropped into the chair next to Emmanuel's desk. "I was hoping you'd have more of a glow after spending the night with the cute attorney."

If only. "Not the time," Emmanuel said, keeping his head and voice down. And not the right woman, since Pippa considered him a roadblock to her goal of freeing Anna.

He flipped open the first file on the stack. "This is the report from the break-in at the Colton condo?"

"Thought you'd want one more look before I filed it."

"Definitely. Thanks." Emmanuel read it, taking his time because he knew he was tired. "The paperwork looks good." He sat back. "Does it bother you that everything was so clean?" Other than the partial boot print, they didn't have anything to go on. "Did you get anything from the security video?"

"I haven't been through it all yet, but so far I haven't spotted him." Daniel leaned an elbow on the corner of the desk. "Do you really expect us to solve this one?" he asked. "She's trying to free a woman the city loves to hate. If she gets Wentworth released, all of your cases and all of McRath's cases will come under review. We'll need a whole new department just to deal with the attorneys and their dreams of legal glory."

So Daniel did realize that anyone on the GRPD with

the right shoe size was a potential suspect. And that was in addition to everyone in town who viewed Wentworth as the wicked witch and Hicks as an "innocent" victim of her wrath.

"I'm aware."

"So how much effort are we putting in?"

"As much as it takes," Emmanuel replied. "I can't believe you'd even ask. We're the good guys, remember?"

"Does she remember?"

Emmanuel tipped his head back and stared at the ceiling. "Yes," he said, though he wasn't sure Pippa wasn't bearing her own grudge against the department at the moment. "Let's focus on the break-in." He righted himself and drummed his fingertips on the report. "That's our job."

"All right. Setting motive aside, the method doesn't match any open cases or recent complaints."

"Any other pesky trouble in the building?"

"Not so much as a stolen package," Daniel answered.

Zero crime news should be cause for a victory dance, but Emmanuel felt defeated. "That's one bored building security team."

"It's all remotely monitored off-site. They have one guy on the desk for packages and stuff, but that's it. When he's off duty, the maintenance supervisor is expected to step up."

"Have you talked to him yet?" Emmanuel asked.

"Meeting him in an hour."

"Good. Do you need help getting through the video files?"

Daniel snorted. "I've gone through everything from the building. Twice. I focused on the hours after I saw Miss Colton head out to her car. At this point, I'm wondering if it's someone in the building. Maybe Wentworth or Colton pissed off a neighbor or the condo association."

Emmanuel tried to laugh it off, but it sounded false to his own ears. "Did CSI go back to that boot print I found in the grass?"

"Sent it to them this morning. Not enough to make a mold," Daniel said.

He'd been afraid of that. "What about the message itself? I'll look for a similar MO in the files of other vandalism cases. Maybe something will match up."

"I'll see what I can find from the church cameras. Unless the man was inside, he didn't just fly away."

Emmanuel stood and walked to the break room for more coffee, Daniel right behind him. "Take a closer look at her neighbors," he suggested. "I don't trust myself to talk to anybody for a couple of hours yet, and we need to find a lead."

"All right."

"I'll review the security footage too." Tired as he was, watching the modern-day equivalent of silent movies was about the safest use of his time. "Maybe I'll catch the intruder coming in earlier in the day with one of the service crews."

"Good luck. I saw a few strays, but nothing helpful. Most of the deliverymen came and went within minutes. What happened in her condo took some time."

Fresh eyes. On a new case and a closed one.

"Divide and conquer it is," Daniel said.

By midday Emmanuel caught his second wind, though he had yet to pinpoint which of the people entering Pippa's building could possibly be the vandal.

It was beyond frustrating. Most people weren't this

good at hiding in plain sight. Especially not people angry enough to deface a wall and ransack a home. He'd almost convinced himself it must have been someone on the building maintenance staff who had gone in, done the damage and returned to work. He texted the list of names to Daniel so his partner could follow up after visiting with her neighbors. They would have to look into the backgrounds for everyone on staff in her building.

Daniel texted back immediately, confirming they were on the same page. He reported that the maintenance staff spoke well of Pippa and none showed much more than a passing curiosity about Anna Wentworth.

Though he didn't want to label the break-in unsolvable, it was lining up that way. Worse, he knew if it had been reported by anyone else, they would've filed the report and put it aside after a day's cursory investigation. With no injuries and no missing items, it wasn't a GRPD priority. Under typical circumstances, they would watch and wait for the perp to strike again and a pattern to emerge.

He couldn't set this aside and wait. Not just because he'd promised Griffin, but because his gut was telling him Pippa was in danger. When he gave his word, he kept it. That integrity was vital to him, ingrained into him and his siblings practically from birth. His parents raised them all with a strong work ethic. His mother had given her word to show up when she was scheduled to work, even when it wasn't easy. Even when her employer had no compassion.

Although Pippa wasn't as well-known as her newest client, she did have a good reputation in the area: generally viewed as a chip off her father's block in terms of the types of cases she took on…except for this one. Attorneys made enemies, just like cops did. It was part of choosing a specific side of an issue. He would definitely ask her again about her other recent cases, but he agreed that this was likely tied to Wentworth. The timing, the high profile, all of it tracked.

Who would have known she was headed to the prison?

People in her office, probably an assistant, and if she did her job properly, she would have notified the prison of her intent to visit. After only a few hours in her company, he had no doubt Pippa had done things correctly. He believed her when she'd said the forms were received and approved.

Yet they'd denied her upon arrival. That was skirting the line, especially when it came to attorney and client meetings. He didn't care for the doubt creeping in, bringing him right back to the conclusion that the best way to protect her was to remove any question of Wentworth's guilt.

If he had made an error during the case, it wouldn't be the first time a legal professional was swayed by belief more than facts. Same for her. She might claim to know Anna Wentworth better than anyone outside of the family, but he'd caught a peek of her heart on her sleeve when she'd talked about Elizabeth.

Pippa had been genuinely startled when he told her they'd looked at Elizabeth for the crime. But while working background on the victim, it had become apparent that Hicks dated a lot of women. Jealousy was a powerful motivator. Emmanuel and Joe needed to confirm Hicks hadn't been the center of a love-triangle between mother and daughter. He accessed the case file on his computer and started reading. The details came flooding back. Hicks had been found by one of the landscapers in a rose garden behind the house. Detective Joe McRath and Emmanuel had caught the case. Joe took the lead when they arrived, questioning the landscaper while Emmanuel assessed the scene.

Hicks had taken two bullets in his chest, and Emmanuel found the two casings a few yards away. No stray bullets were found. Closing his eyes, Emmanuel could see it all perfectly. The man's clothes had been mussed and his shirt wrinkled, as if someone had grabbed him during some mild altercation. No powder burns had been found on the clothing, so the killer must have fired from several yards away. They'd noticed a bruise on his face as if he'd been slapped hard. During the trial, the prosecution provided witnesses to several instances of Anna slapping people who'd offended or angered her.

A gun had been located immediately under a rose bush next to the body and later confirmed to be the murder weapon. The most incriminating evidence, one of Anna's unique sapphire brooches, had been discovered under the body by the coroner.

The photos were there organized as an attachment to the file, but Emmanuel didn't particularly need them. He read through Joe's raw notes and his own. No one remembered hearing gunshots around the time of death. The GRPD had found the car Hicks had driven to the scene and the blackmail note addressed to Anna's husband in the glove box, but no witnesses who could put the two of them together that day.

While the grounds surrounding the Wentworth mansion were monitored, there were plenty of ways to get in and out without being too obvious, and Hicks, her lover of at least four months, would've known the gaps in the security coverage.

Wentworth had verified that Hicks had visited her more than once in that rose garden. She denied seeing him on that day, though she admitted to escorting him into the mansion through the sunroom to a guest suite where they could be alone and undisturbed on prior occasions.

He and Joe had spoken with everyone who worked at the Wentworth mansion and everyone who'd been near the mansion on the day of the murder. No one had seen Hicks or had contact with him. No one with easy access to where the body had been found had a motive to kill him. Emmanuel skimmed the original interviews with the family. Ed Wentworth had been out of town and Elizabeth had been away from the house. Neither of them had even heard a whisper about any blackmail threats.

Hicks's new girlfriend, Jenny Dawson, gave a statement that he'd gone over that day to break up with Wentworth. Again. Because Anna hadn't accepted the fact her ex-lover had broken up with her, that it was over.

Emmanuel stopped and read through that interview transcript again. Joe had spoken with the distraught new girlfriend initially, and they'd gone back later, together. Jenny's theory was Hicks had broken up with Wentworth and she'd then shot him when he threatened to tell her husband if Anna didn't leave him alone. The girlfriend hadn't provided any evidence or tangible examples to back up her claim that Wentworth had been harassing Hicks to come back. And she claimed no knowledge of Hicks trying to blackmail Anna.

Naturally Wentworth denied all claims that she'd wanted Hicks back. She'd said he was a grifter and had dumped her when she refused to invest in some new business venture. She swore she'd never touched a gun, much less purchased the one used against Hicks. Fortunately, the prosecutor hadn't needed the new girlfriend as a witness or gun receipts during the trial. The evidence at the scene combined with other witnesses and Wentworth's snobbish outbursts had zipped the case up tight.

He couldn't see a mistake. Couldn't identify a place where he'd allowed his bias to color his decisions or his testimony. Would it have been nice to have found gunpowder residue on Wentworth's hands or her prints on the gun? Sure. But they'd found gloves similar to those the staff used in the trash in her private bathroom, and the crime lab analysis backed up everything found at the scene. It was Wentworth against the state of Michigan.

Neither public nor private opinion had come into play in any significant manner.

And still, Pippa was adamant the wrong person was doing time for the crime. If she was any other defense attorney, he might think she was posturing to sway the media, but not Griffin's sister. She'd insisted the GRPD hadn't looked for anyone else. Obviously they had, since the records were right there in the system database. He was half tempted to invite her in to look for herself, but a detective cooperating with the attorney trying to undo his work would stir up too much trouble.

It bothered him that she hadn't noticed how thorough they'd been when she'd studied the case file in the evidence room.

Pushing back from his desk, he headed downstairs.

The case was recent enough that all the documentation would still be here. He'd feel better when he could confidently tell her that Wentworth was the only person with motive and access to commit the crime. Then she could drop that case and he would only have to shelter her from the less direct threat of Capital X.

Considering how that "bank" operated, it would be more than enough to keep him busy.

He signed in with the officer on duty at the evidence desk and was allowed into the cage. When he reached the shelf where the Wentworth box should have been, it wasn't there. He double-checked the case number. "Must be misfiled," he muttered to himself.

He verified that the cases boxed up before and after were in place, but there was no sign of the box he needed. A chill skated over his skin. This didn't have to mean anything suspicious. Someone had probably checked out the box, or shoved it out of place when they were looking for another case. Happened more often than anyone in the department wanted to admit. Sometimes people were just in a rush.

Like he was today. This was supposed to be quick. Over and done.

The lack of sleep made him grumpy, and he started dragging boxes off shelves to check the contents. The Wentworth case had to be here. Feeling frantic, he stifled curse after curse when he kept finding cases unrelated to the Hicks murder. Where was it?

All the noise he was making brought young Officer Swanson from the front desk. "Detective Iglesias, do you need a hand?"

"Please," he replied. "Bring over that ladder."

"Sure." Swanson complied in a hurry.

"Who's at the desk?" he asked over the obnoxious metallic rattle as the young officer dragged the rolling staircase closer.

"No one right now," Swanson said. "I locked the window to come check on you."

Emmanuel stomped up the ladder to the top shelf, a sick feeling in his stomach. He could hope forever, but the Wentworth case file wasn't up here.

"Which case are you after?" Swanson asked. "I can help."

Ignoring him, Emmanuel moved every box on the top shelf, checking inside each one, careful with odd shaped objects and paperwork so he didn't compound his current problems. "No, thanks." He would not say the case name aloud. "There's nothing matching the case number I need. It's not here."

From the floor, Swanson gazed up at him earnestly, like a puppy eager to please the big dogs. "Let me run it and see who checked it out," he offered.

Emmanuel bought himself a minute to think while he descended the rolling stairs and pushed them back out of the way. "I guess that's the smartest next step." Though he did *not* want anyone knowing he was looking at this. The rumors alone would be problematic, especially after he responded to the call at Pippa's condo last night. He took his time, making sure every box was in the right place. Little comfort when the effort only made the absence of the Wentworth case more obvious.

"Wow, thanks," Swanson said. "I really appreciate that, Detective. You must have worked down here."

Emmanuel had never had this job, but he believed keeping things organized helped everyone. "Are you calling the GRPD a bunch of slobs?" he joked.

Swanson cleared his throat. "Well, coming back and straightening up is part of the routine."

He clapped the kid on the shoulder. "I'll try to remind everyone to do better," Emmanuel said as they walked back to the front of the secure area. He slid the paper with the case number on it across the counter. "Can you let me know who checked out this file?"

Swanson entered the case number into his computer, and they waited for the system to respond. With a little luck, the kid didn't follow gossip columns or the upper echelon of Grand Rapids society.

Luck was not on Emmanuel's side today. The kid gave a low whistle and shot Emmanuel a look. "Wentworth?"

"That's the one." He was paging through the log of recent visitors. Any officer or visitor had to sign in with their name and badge number, and the visit was entered into the computer system, as well.

Swanson studied his computer screen, a frown tugging the corners of his mouth. He typed something else and then used the mouse, scrolling up and down. What Emmanuel wouldn't have given to see what had upset him.

"What's the matter, Swanson?"

"No one has checked out the box, Detective. It should be there." His fingers pounded the keys again. The poor kid looked like he might burst into tears. "I don't have any record of it being signed out."

"Do you recall anyone asking about Wentworth besides me?"

"No, sir."

Pippa implied she'd been here. "I thought I heard

something about her new attorney stopping by." Had she lied to him?

"Well, yes," Swanson said. "Her new attorney called and set up an appointment. She came in ten days ago."

The sign-in log in front of Emmanuel went back only seven days. He pulled out his phone and opened the app he used to take notes. "What day?" he asked. "Were you here?"

"Yes, sir," Swanson confirmed. "She was very polite."

No doubt. He suspected Pippa could turn on the charm when it suited her purposes. Not that he blamed her. He did the same thing at times.

"I carried the case file to the back table for her," Swanson said. "She was here for hours."

"Do you have the sign-out time?" Emmanuel made another note of the kid's answer. "Did you put the box back or did she take it?"

"I don't know. She was still here when the shift changed and Officer Mitchell replaced me." Swanson tapped a pen rapidly on the counter. "He would've put the box back for her."

"Anything else?"

"No." That pen kept tapping. "I don't have any requisitions for the file or notes. This is bizarre."

"Agreed." Emmanuel sighed heavily, thinking of Pippa's floor safe. She'd never opened it in front of him. Because she didn't want him to know she'd taken the evidence box without permission? Would she have pushed the line that way? If someone believed she had the documentation on the Wentworth case that would explain the break-in and search.

But not the message. It was a rare burglar who came

armed with spray paint, just in case he needed to leave a threatening message.

He jerked his thumb toward the security camera over the door. "How far back do we keep surveillance footage?"

Swanson shrugged. "I'm sorry, Detective. I don't know."

The feed was monitored by someone. If his lieutenant didn't know, the captain would. Or one of their administrative assistants. "Thanks for your help," Emmanuel said. "I'll take it from here. I'm sure there's a logical explanation."

"Any suggestions on how I should write this up?" Swanson asked.

"I'm guessing there's a form." The kid nodded. "Just fill it in to the best of your ability," Emmanuel continued. "It'll work out. Most likely we're dealing with a clerical error. No one likes to admit it, but we all know those happen."

"Am I in trouble?" Swanson wondered.

"Not from where I'm standing. Just fill out the form."

Fired up, Emmanuel went straight to Lieutenant Tripp McKellar's office to get a look at the security footage. If Pippa had walked out of this station with the Wentworth case file, he was going to lose his mind. His thoughts ticked back and forth like a metronome, sure she hadn't been so foolish and certain she'd taken the risk to save her client.

Then again, if she *had* taken that risk and the box had since been removed from her possession, he couldn't imagine her waiting it out in her condo last night. She would've leaped into action of some kind.

Unless she'd had the box in the car—the one place no one had checked.

At the lieutenant's open office door, Emmanuel knocked. "A minute, sir?"

McKellar waved him in. The lieutenant was a rising star in the department who'd earned the trust of the officers he supervised. When Ingrid had met him, she'd told Emmanuel that McKellar had promise and a good character.

"What's on your mind, Iglesias?"

"I was doing some research and just found out an evidence box is missing from storage."

The lieutenant's eyebrows lifted. "Not misfiled?"

"No, sir. We've searched top to bottom," Emmanuel said. "It's possible the box was removed by the last person who accessed it. Any chance you have access to the footage from that camera over the door?"

McKellar scowled. "Can you narrow that down with a date?"

"Yes, sir." He gave the date of Pippa's visit and the time Swanson's shift ended.

"Let's take a look." McKellar invited him to watch the monitor over his shoulder.

When the footage for the right day came up, Emmanuel caught a high-speed view of Pippa signing in. Just as the young officer had said, she stayed for hours and the shift changed. When she exited the room, she had only the briefcase she'd brought in.

Emmanuel hadn't realized he'd been holding his breath until it all came out in a whoosh of relief. Why did he care so damn much if she was guilty or innocent?

"See something helpful?" the lieutenant asked, pausing the video with Pippa frozen at the door.

"Yes and no," Emmanuel replied. If Pippa hadn't taken the file, then who? And when?

"That's Sadie Colton's older sister, right?" McKellar asked.

"One of them, yes."

"Right. Graham Colton had four daughters." He didn't sound entirely thrilled by the fact. "Hope she found whatever she was looking for. I'm not entirely comfortable with having Colton Investigations so involved with the Capital X and RevitaYou situations."

Emmanuel agreed wholeheartedly. "I would've thought you'd have a bigger problem with her trying to find something to reverse the Wentworth verdict."

McKellar laughed. "Let her dig. We all know that case is airtight."

It helped to hear it from his lieutenant. "Thanks for the assist," Emmanuel said on his way out of the door.

Relieved in one aspect, he was still twisted up over too many other unknowns. If Pippa hadn't taken that file to support her efforts to overturn Wentworth's conviction, who had?

He kept running into the same dead-end conclusion. With the evidence box missing, the break-in and search at Pippa's condo, and her inexplicable trouble at the prison, the culprit was likely tied to the GRPD. He would need to find a way to keep reviewing the video footage.

His stomach cramped, and the discomfort had nothing to do with being overtired, grief stricken or hungry. Someone in this building—or at least someone with access to it—was determined to keep the truth under wraps. He checked his phone for any word from Daniel that might be better news.

Nothing.

Did he dare tell Pippa and fuel a hunch she was surely entertaining? The woman was too smart not to think her client had been set up by someone on the force. Might be better to do more digging first. Notions wouldn't free her client, only facts. He smothered an oath, thinking about her reaction if she ever learned he'd kept this to himself.

"Trouble, Iglesias?" Joe McRath asked, pausing as he walked through the bullpen. "You look like hell."

"Ingrid," he said. He couldn't tell Joe what had him really upset. Emmanuel wasn't in the mood for a lecture on career longevity right now. The sergeant believed that working a case, solving it and moving on was the best way to avoid burnout. Only the cold cases were worth dwelling on in Joe's opinion.

"We're all gonna miss her." Joe swiped a hand over his eyes. "Heard anything about the service or final arrangements?"

"Not yet." Thanks to the RevitaYou connection, he wasn't even sure when the body would be released for burial.

"Go on home, Iglesias. Get some rest."

Not a bad idea. "Is that an official order, Sergeant?"

Joe smiled. "It is."

"Thanks."

Emmanuel grabbed his cell phone and headed out, but his mind kept stewing over the real problem. If someone on the force was interfering with Pippa's review of the Wentworth case now, it was a short hop to assume that same someone framed Wentworth at the time and he and Joe had overlooked someone who hated Hicks that much.

Furious that he might have been duped then and was being sent on a merry chase now, he sat in his car and sent Pippa a text message. He didn't dare talk about any details over the phone. Not this close to the station.

In a few hours, he'd be face to face with her and they could talk candidly. Or argue. He smiled despite the hellish day. The simmer in his veins whenever he thought of Pippa was an unexpected bright spot in this twisted mess. While he wasn't looking forward to explaining what he'd found, he was definitely eager to see her.

Chapter Seven

After Pippa met with her insurance adjuster, assured the claim would be paid in a timely manner, she'd deliberately turned her back on the violent message scrawled across her living room wall. The morning hours ticked by as she resumed her work on Anna's case.

Around noon, when her suspect list was as weak as it had been yesterday, she reached for her coffee cup and found it empty. She stood up to stretch a bit and give her eyes a rest, debating whether or not to have one more cup of coffee. Probably better to switch to water and a healthy snack.

With an apple in hand, she walked out to stare down that message on her wall. "We all end up dead," she said aloud. "Personally I'd rather go out knowing I did something right."

In the meantime, it might be better to stop talking to walls.

It still annoyed her that one of her favorite framed prints would have to be redone. She returned to her desk and flipped to her calendar, reviewing her schedule for the rest of the week. After tonight's appointment with the Capital X loan application, she didn't have any set appointments. As some point she needed to get back to the prison and have a face-to-face with her newest client.

Excitement simmered through her system whenever she thought about what she was going to do tonight. Her part in helping Brody—and who knew how many others—might be small, but it was crucial. Griffin and Riley had wanted to shut down the unscrupulous loan operation for a long time.

Though she tried, she couldn't suppress a thrill of anticipation that she would see Emmanuel again tonight too. But that was hours away.

She answered several emails and dictated a few more notes about how to approach the witnesses tied to Anna's case before the cleaning crew arrived at the back door. Just like this morning, opening the door took more effort than it ever had in the past. She couldn't stand being afraid. Though it hadn't even been a full day, she wondered how when she would feel like herself again.

Craig and Rachel Norris were a brother-and-sister team and equal partners in their small business that specialized in cleaning and restoration. "When we saw the pictures, we thought we'd better handle this one ourselves," Craig said when introductions were made.

"This is a great building," Rachel added.

The pair put Pippa at ease immediately, and she caught herself smiling as she led them into the living room.

"Wow," Craig said. The siblings exchanged a long look.

"This is going to look worse before it gets better," Rachel warned Pippa.

"I understand it's a process," Pippa said.

"All right." Craig cocked his head as he studied

the wall. "Might be faster to cut out the drywall and start over."

"He's kidding," Rachel assured her with a confident smile. "We'll take care of it and make it as good as new."

"Thanks." She wondered if even with a clean slate she'd ever *not* see those words.

Her phone rang as they started unpacking their supplies. Seeing Elizabeth's number, she picked it up right away. "Good morning," Pippa said brightly. "I'm sorry I couldn't get back with you last night. Things got a little hectic once I got home."

"What's that noise?" Elizabeth asked.

Pippa moved away from the cleaning efforts, but regardless of their friendly, bonded and insured status, she wasn't willing to leave them unattended. At the moment she didn't trust anyone outside of family. And Griffin was on thin ice for planting Emmanuel in her life.

"Nothing to worry about. I'm just having some professional cleaning done."

"Really? Your place is always so perfect. Well, I just wanted to let you know I'm going out to see Mom this afternoon."

"Good," Pippa said. "Be careful, Elizabeth." She hoped they wouldn't change the routine and give Elizabeth trouble now too.

"Is there anything you want me to tell her?"

"Officially, no." Elizabeth's conversations with Anna wouldn't be legally protected. "Just let her know I'm sorting things out. If she's had an epiphany about who might have wanted to kill Hicks, that would be great, but otherwise, just enjoy your visit."

"All right. I was going to let her know you had

trouble getting through yesterday, if that won't cause any problems."

"Please tell her about that," Pippa said. "I'm hoping to have an explanation before the next time I go out." That task had topped her to-do list today, but so far her calls to the warden and the prosecutor's office asking for clarification had not been returned.

None of that would comfort Elizabeth, and any extra burden on her mind would make her visit with her mother more of a challenge. "You can also tell her I'm requesting another look at all the physical evidence in the case."

"I thought you'd done that," Elizabeth said.

"I've been through the reports and transcripts and I've taken pictures of the evidence, but I want to see it firsthand again." She wasn't ready to share her concern that she'd overlooked something. Last night Emmanuel had been surprised that she hadn't seen any record of the interviews he'd conducted with persons of interest, and that bothered her.

"Drive safe," she said. "And please let me know how your mom's doing." With just over two weeks in prison, Anna would either be adjusting or melting down.

"I promise," Elizabeth said, ending the call with another thank you.

Pippa wished she'd done something to earn her friend's gratitude. So far this case seemed to be one high brick wall she kept slamming up against. There had to be a way over, around or through because Anna was innocent.

Curious, Pippa made the mistake of peeking into the front room. She couldn't stifle her subsequent groan of dismay. The wall was definitely worse. An ugly, wet mess of grayish-red. She snapped a picture with her phone, not even sure why it mattered to have documentation of the cleanup process. This wasn't something she planned to share on social media.

She returned to her work, doing her best to stay focused, but the smell of solvents soon got the best of her. Craig and Rachel had set up a big fan and an air purifier, but she cracked the window to bring in some fresh and crisp autumn air. Maybe she should just go to the office, but it made her ridiculously uncomfortable to have strangers alone in her house after last night. She grabbed her favorite sweatshirt and was pulling it over her head when her phone chimed with an incoming text.

It took her a second to realize the number was Emmanuel's. He was reaching out already? Maybe he'd come to his senses and was canceling his plans to join her tonight. She was an adult and she didn't need supervision to fill out an online form, no matter what her brother believed.

Just because Griffin trusted Emmanuel didn't mean she had to. Although…no, that was her sexy dreams talking. He'd been nice last night, but one good deed didn't change the role he'd played in Anna's conviction.

She scolded herself for demonstrating the same kind of bias she'd accused him of applying to the Wentworth investigation. So the man rubbed her the wrong way; that wasn't the end of the world. She'd learned that it was impractical and impossible to get along well with everyone. There were days she didn't even get along with her twin sister. And none of them thought much of Sadie's fiancé.

While she didn't appreciate that it was primarily his testimony that sent Anna to jail, she'd found no indication that he'd done anything inappropriate or incorrect as he worked the case. Plus, Griffin had excellent instincts about people. Whether or not she liked the detective, she would find a way to deal with him politely. The first step was probably not to think the worst or turn surly at the sight of his name.

Bracing herself to be a mature professional rather than a snarky little sister, she opened the app and read his text.

Digging on this end.

Suggest you look for connections to top players within the GRPD.

She stared at the message, reading the brief lines over and over. Was he kidding? He hadn't struck her as the type of man to have much sense of humor about Anna Wentworth. Which left her with the obvious conclusion that he was serious. What had he found?

She deleted the text message. He hadn't recommended it, but it seemed like the practical move in light of the crap she'd dealt with yesterday. Anyone in the GRPD would likely have ties within the prison system. But ties high enough to prevent an attorney-client meeting? That was a serious problem.

Phone in hand, she paced the hallway, thinking. Yesterday he was thoroughly convinced of Anna's guilt and the department's faithful execution of the investigation. Today he was telling her to take a look with an eye for new suspects in his own police force?

She couldn't ignore it, and honestly it had occurred to her. Going in guns blazing without any proof would only backfire, hurting her, her client and her family.

Colton Investigations currently enjoyed a strong partnership and mutual respect with the police department, so she'd been tiptoeing around that research. And at first glance, the case was so cut-and-dried that the number of people who could affect the outcome was limited.

With a clear direction in mind, she sat down and opened the file, printing out a list by hand of every name connected to the case, from the 911 operator who took the call to the responding officers, Detectives Iglesias and McRath, and everyone who touched the scene in some way or another.

Sitting back, she smiled. Detective Iglesias was now on her official interview list. Maybe it was immature, but it amused her greatly to think of the roles being reversed on Anna's behalf. It also forced her to consider how he and McRath would have built their own list in search of witnesses and suspects in the case.

They'd interviewed Ed, which made sense. The husband was always a top suspect in such a case. And they'd interviewed Elizabeth, covering every angle. Pippa was determined to be even more thorough. Anna was in jail, in part, because the real killer had not had an obvious motive or connection to Hicks.

Next, she segmented the list based on duration of the person's involvement. That would make it easier to clear people. And she repeated the process based on their possible connection or opinion of Anna Wentworth. As she'd learned from her siblings, working a case properly meant considering everyone as suspect, even the most unlikely.

Craig called her over before she could start eliminating anyone. "How does this look to you?" he asked.

Beside him his sister smiled as she turned on an industrial fan to help dry things out.

It looked like the most beautiful blank wall she'd ever seen. The wall needed primer and paint, but the ugly message was completely gone. "That's a vast improvement," she said. "Thank you."

"Are we painting this for you?" He reached for his clipboard with her service order. "Once it's dry, that is."

"I elected to handle the repainting once it was clean," she said. "I'm considering changing things up with a feature wall rather than just a coat of paint."

Rachel studied the wall, turning a little to take in the entire space. "Can I make a suggestion?" At Pippa's nod, she continued. "You wouldn't want to go too rustic, but you could do something natural that still marries modern and homey. Bamboo would work well, and beadboard could be interesting too."

Pippa tried to envision her suggestions. "I always think of beadboard in country kitchens or revamped attics converted to bedrooms or sweet nurseries."

"Him too," Rachel replied, elbowing her brother. "It has more uses, I promise." She handed Pippa a business card, pointing out the link to her design pages on a social media platform. "I have several idea boards that might spark things for you."

"She wants paint," Craig said. He tilted his head at his sister. "She wants to be a designer," he explained.

"I *am* a designer," Rachel countered with a grin. "He gets grumpy because at some point he's going to have to find another partner to put up with him."

Pippa understood all too well the push and pull of siblings. She tapped the card. "I'll take a look."

"Whatever you decide," Craig interjected, "you'll

need to wait twenty-four hours for everything to dry completely. We'll pick up the fan and dehumidifier tomorrow evening."

"Great. Thanks again."

She closed the door behind them as they left. Huddling into her sweatshirt, she realized the droning sound of the equipment was going to make it a long night. Why did people appreciate white noise? Again, she could escape to her brother's place, but she didn't want to send the message to whoever had done this that she couldn't hack it when things got tough.

The restored wall and clean carpets, free of every bit of glass and debris, filled her with a sense of peace. It was almost like moving in again. A blank slate full of potential. She pulled up Rachel's website and the social media idea board.

"Wow." The woman had good ideas, and although the beadboard pictures still struck too close to paneling for her taste, she saw the design merit. Distracted, she scrolled through several other idea boards on the page. Maybe she did want something more dynamic than paint after all.

She was hip deep in bamboo options, of varying colors, textures and layouts, when a text message from Kiely came through. Her twin and Riley would arrive at her place within five minutes, just as they'd planned. Pippa was glad she'd scheduled the cleaning crew when she had. Her siblings didn't need to worry about her, especially when the trouble had nothing to do with a CI case.

As she'd done with each of her previous visitors today, she felt the nerves building, and she waited until her sister and brother were right outside her door before she unlocked it. In the past she would've left the door unlocked or even slightly ajar. After the break-in that seemed foolish. More risk than necessary.

When Riley and Kiely entered, their gazes immediately went to the clean, bare wall and the drying equipment.

"He tagged the whole thing?"

"He did." Pippa tucked her hands into the long sleeves of her sweatshirt.

Riley turned, hot anger blazing in his eyes. Then his expression softened as he pulled her into a tight hug.

Kiely set the bag she was carrying on the floor and nudged them apart. She held up a boxy device and, with a look, asked for Pippa's permission to sweep the condo for listening devices.

Her stomach cramped as she gave a nod. Why hadn't she considered that earlier? She hoped she hadn't said anything during her chat with Elizabeth that would come back to bite her later. Riley chatted with her about the plans for the new wall until Kiely gave the all clear. "No bugs," she announced.

Pippa released a breath in a rush. "Thank goodness. Unless the police have found something more, the intruder somehow evaded the cameras around the building and in the hallways."

"Someone who knows security systems," Kiely mused.

"Still a pretty big suspect pool," Pippa said, thinking of the list she'd made. "We have one partial boot print near the back door, so I'm sure we'll narrow it down."

Riley deliberately moved toward her office. "Nothing was taken?"

"You know I'm careful," Pippa said.

"I need coffee." Kiely handed Pippa a bag from a nearby electronics store. "Go on and start with that."

Pippa looked into the bag and saw a new laptop. Taking the box out of the bag, she started to unpack the device. "How long do I have to wait to find out who you've turned me into?"

"Not you," Riley said. "We're not *Mission Impossible* with the masks here."

"Much to your dismay I'm sure," Pippa teased. "This is exciting." She plugged in the laptop and followed the prompts for the initial setup.

When Kiely had her coffee, the three of them gathered around the desk. At the point where the computer wanted personal information, Riley opened up an envelope. She was surprised to see what looked like a very real ID and a credit card. "Excellent work," she said, as she carefully entered the details for the persona CI had created for this fake Capital X loan application. "Did you make a passport too?"

"Not quite enough time to pull that off the right way," Riley said. "The loan application doesn't ask for that anyway. You need to remember her schedule. With the background we worked up, it would be out of character for her to do a loan application during business hours.

"We gave your alias a comprehensive employment history and banking records and one not-so-successful independent business, along with a shopping history on that credit card."

Pippa made mental notes as Riley talked, but it helped to know Kiely would have this all written out for her, as well. When she finished, Riley tucked the credit card into the envelope she would keep for reference. "The laptop was purchased with that card, and you should probably make one or two more purchases in person or online this afternoon."

"Maybe dinner," Kiely suggested. "Something special for two?"

Pippa did *not* appreciate the glint in her twin's eyes. Or the way her words brought back the inappropriate dream from this morning.

Riley, who had been relaxed in the chair beside her, sat up straight, his gaze locked onto Pippa. "What's she talking about?"

"Nothing," Pippa said.

"Nothing with serious potential." Kiely held up her hands when Pippa glared. "Okay, okay. Harmless teasing, sis. But that look on your face tells me I'm on the right track."

Pippa denied it. "You've jumped the track and crashed in a glorious blaze." There were times when having an excellent private investigator as a twin was a curse.

"One of you better start talking to me," their brother demanded.

The twins turned on him. "You do know we're adults?" Pippa queried.

"Yes, I noticed. For the record that only makes brothers worry more."

"That is the dumbest non-rule," Kiely protested.

"Too bad." He folded his arms and returned his attention to Pippa. "Is she talking about Iglesias?"

"She is," Pippa said immediately. A denial would only mean a more intense interrogation. "Ridiculous, really. We met last night for the first time. I'm sure he's seeing someone." A flicker in Riley's eyes alerted her to the misstep. She dragged her thoughts back into line. "We're on opposite sides of a critical case for my friend and my career." She continued ticking off each relevant point on her fingers. "And while I appreciated his help cleaning up—"

"He helped you clean up?" Kiely's eyebrows jumped up and down.

"I don't need his supervision or whatever Griffin asked him to do," she finished.

"Griffin disagrees on that," Riley said softly.

It was a challenge to argue with Riley whenever he did that quiet-voice strategy. "I do know Capital X is dangerous." She pointed to all of the precautions they were taking. "It's obvious we're doing everything the smart way."

"Pippa, I know this feels anonymous," Kiely said. "And it is. To a point. There shouldn't be any possible way to connect you to the application you'll put in tonight. But a little backup never hurt anyone."

"Is there some new detail you're not telling me?" she asked. "I'm not fragile, and you both know I won't back out."

"Of course you won't," Riley said. "That's why we're all so concerned about the break-in."

Her sister rested her hands on Pippa's knees. "I'm not sure you're concerned enough."

"Trust me, I was upset," Pippa said. She clamped down on the admission lodged in her throat. They didn't need to know how wary she was about answering her door. That would pass. "It was creepy to know someone had been in here long enough to trash the place and…" Her voice trailed off as she stared at the fresh, clean wall. "And try to intimidate me," she finished, resisting the urge to rub the chill from her arms.

"You should come stay with us for a few days," Riley said. "At least until we get some movement on the loan application."

"No." She shook her head. "Thank you, but I need to stay put."

Riley swore.

"There's more to life than reputation, sis," Kiely said.

"I'm aware." Though she hadn't indulged in much of that life lately. "Beyond reputation, it's a matter of principle. I've never been afraid to take controversial cases."

"Right," Riley agreed. "But the cases you take on are rarely as high-profile as Wentworth. I think serial killers get more love than that woman."

"Pleasant or not, I won't leave an innocent woman in jail for a crime she didn't commit. This break-in won't put me off the case, no matter what the vandal intended. All of this protectiveness is appreciated but unnecessary."

Her brother and sister exchanged a look. "Is that code for get the hell out of your way?" Riley asked.

"It's probably more like code for I'm tired," she admitted with a smile. What was the use of having family if you didn't lean on them in problematic times? "I'm not trying to be obstinate. I'm trying to stay focused on what I can control."

"That's our Pippa," Riley said, hugging her again. "You're all right to keep working here today?"

"Pretty much. Some of my framed art was damaged, so I'll run that over to the frame shop for repairs." She tilted her head toward the drying equipment. "Looking forward to getting out for a bit. That fan is not my friend."

Riley was glaring at the wall again. "Sadie sent us pictures the police took last night."

"Somehow I doubt a common criminal also knows how to evade all the security precautions in and around the building," Kiely said.

Pippa agreed with her. "If we could get back to why we're really here? I'll log in at seven and fill out the application. Any trip wires I should be aware of?"

"We haven't found anything like that. Only that Capital X likely does a personal check on the applicants." Kylie walked her through the day-to-day patterns for Alison Carrington, an administrative assistant for a fake insurance company, per the alias they'd created.

"We're going to save lives," Pippa said as anticipation strummed through her bloodstream.

"We'll definitely save people the pain of broken bones," Riley agreed.

"Have you heard anything about Brody?"

Kiely frowned. "My last lead fizzled out. He's running scared. Until he makes a mistake or wants to be found, I'm afraid we're going to keep chasing our tails."

"I'll let you know if he sends me another text message," Pippa said. The idea of Brody out there alone, trying to stay one step ahead of violent enforcers, made her sad. In instances like this she took it for granted how lucky she was to have the support of her brothers and sisters.

"It won't be a problem once we shut down Capital X," Riley said.

"Count on me," Pippa said. "I need to get over to the frame shop for these repairs." Her siblings helped her carry the pieces down to her car, and they parted ways there after she promised to be cautious. She tuned the radio to a station with classical music. As she drove out of the parking lot, she noted the unmarked car across the street, and when she reached the frame shop, she sent Emmanuel a text message about her errands and expected return time. Assuming she didn't meet any traffic delays, she would have time to do some more digging into that new list of names before he arrived to watch her enter the loan application.

Overkill. Then again, Brody was in hiding and Griffin had another friend who'd been burned by Capital X. Enforcers had broken two of Brody's fingers. It was possible the woman playing the role of Alison could be hurt. Pippa could very well be at risk for retaliation too if Capital X discovered she'd duped them.

She had to focus on the positive, the potential to break open the loan shark operation so Brody could come home. The earlier excitement returned while she considered the big leap forward her efforts would make in a few hours. Nothing made her happier than doing the right thing and making a difference in the process.

EMMANUEL PULLED UP, pleased to find an open parking space on the street in front of Pippa's condo. Hopefully he wouldn't need to spend the night out here again, but just in case, this gave him a great vantage point. He slipped his cell phone into his pocket and then reached for the grocery bag and the bakery box from the front seat. He'd offered to bring dinner, but she'd told him she had that under control, so he'd selected one of his favorite desserts.

With his car locked, he walked over and checked in with the teams in the unmarked cars also on duty. Knowing Pippa's plan for the evening, he'd asked Lieutenant McKellar for a second unit on her place, a little surprised by the immediate agreement. Apparently it had been a quiet day. No one sketchy lurking around the building, and everyone who had gone inside as part of a service crew had a legitimate tie to their company. Maybe it was over-the-top, but his gut wouldn't let him back down.

In the building lobby, he pressed the call button, though he'd looked up the emergency access code provided to the police. Pippa buzzed him through the interior door, and he took the stairs instead of the elevator, wanting another casual look at how an intruder might still bypass every basic precaution in the building.

From the hallway in front of her door, he heard the drone of a fan and wondered how the cleanup and repairs had gone today. She hadn't mentioned any of that in her two texts. She hadn't responded directly to his first message. Probably smart, all things considered. He'd only received the two texts about running errands and dinner. Technically, she didn't owe him anything, and she had plenty of siblings in the immediate area, but it would've been nice to be kept in the loop anyway. Especially after he'd taken such a big chance solely on her hunch today.

That wasn't fair. It was his hunch, too, along with his persistent integrity that had forced him to search the evidence room.

His heart gave a kick in his chest when she opened the door. She was dressed simply in a white top and trim pants, with heels that put her in easy range of a kiss. If only this was a different kind of dinner. Her hair was down, and at the open collar of her shirt, a turquoise pendant in a silver setting drew his attention. The woman was giving him a fever.

He held up the bakery box between them. "Peace offering," he managed.

"What is it?" Her nose twitched as she accepted the box. She stepped back so he could walk in.

"I guess you'll have to wait until after dinner to find out," he teased, closing the door behind him and turning the dead bolt. To his astonishment she faked a little pout. It was dangerously sexy.

"Dinner is a simple stew," she said. "I hope you don't mind."

Something smelled delicious, and the equipment drying out the repaired wall pushed the aroma throughout her condo. "Wow," he said, taking in the expanse of clean wall. "They did a good job. And fast. You sure didn't waste much time."

"No one did," she said. "It was a long day, and the fan is getting on my nerves. I'm focusing on how delighted I am that the message is gone."

"I bet."

She stopped at the kitchen counter, her fingertips tracing the string tie on the box. "Don't tell me you're a white-noise type of person."

"Not a bit. Would you rather take this somewhere else?" His apartment was available. And far more disconnected from the Colton Investigations case than anywhere else in the city. No one would expect the new Wentworth lawyer to hang out with him.

She clearly wanted a peek at what he'd brought, but she deliberately averted her gaze. He admired that kind of discipline and couldn't help wondering what it would take to break it. In a good way of course.

Straightening her shoulders, she flicked a hand toward the stove. "Beef stew," she said. Her teeth sunk into her lower lip. "I'm having a really hard time not jumping all over you."

The admission caught him off guard, and he floundered for an answer, wondering what she expected. He wouldn't mind being jumped by Pippa.

"About the case," she clarified. "I know you couldn't tell me more via text earlier, but why should I be looking into any GRPD connections?"

He smothered the sudden disappointment that her thoughts hadn't matched up with his. This was the moment of truth. Sharing what he hadn't found in the evidence room could change everything. Correction: it *would* change everything. He'd wrestled with this moment all day. It wasn't exactly his job to tell her the evidence was gone. He had active cases that should trump her effort to undo solid police work. But treating her like the enemy wasn't working for him. If he'd ignored it, he wouldn't be able to look himself in the mirror. "There is no reason for what I'm about to say to become public knowledge. In fact, you can't tell anyone yet. Do you understand?"

"I know how to be discreet." She folded her arms over her chest. "And I can keep secrets locked down tight when it helps my client."

"This will help your client," he muttered. "I don't suppose you have a beer?"

"Once we're officially off duty," she said.

"I clocked out," he said. "Besides, aren't we officially having dinner?"

"Dinner before tackling a CI assignment," she reminded him.

"I happen to know Griffin has a beer, even when he's on an active investigation for CI."

"Fine." He must've passed some test. She went to the refrigerator and pulled out a beer. Before she handed it over, she said, "Tell me why you sent that message."

"Because the evidence box for your case is gone. Missing."

She was speechless and pretty adorable, her mouth hanging open in pure shock. He had a serious soft spot when it came to Pippa Colton.

"Who signed it out?"

He used the bottle opener she handed him and popped the top off the beer bottle. "No idea. That's the problem. Your name is actually the last one tied to the case, per the logs. I know you don't have it," he hurried to add when she started to protest. "I searched all over for the box and the contents. Nothing has been misfiled or shoved into the wrong box. Everyone who's been in and out of the evidence room since your visit is accounted for."

She sat down on the counter stool, her gaze drifting back to the wall that had been vandalized yesterday and was clean today, if drab and plain. "So how did the box go missing?" She turned to him, her eyes intent as she sorted through what he'd said. "I can see how the contents might be smuggled out, but the whole box?"

"Right?" He shook his head, feeling as if he'd let her down. Ridiculous, but true. "I can't see anyone outside the GRPD managing it."

She pursed her lips. "I'd have to agree."

He waited for her to shout at him that this proved Anna Wentworth had been set up, but Pippa only sat there, her brow furrowed in contemplation. What was going through her mind? Did she suspect he was feeding her a line to impede her progress?

"That's it? You're not going to gloat or taunt me about the missing evidence box?" He'd expected…well, he didn't know what he'd expected. Definitely not easy acceptance.

"Did you take it?" she asked.

"Hell, no. I don't have anything to hide."

"Then why waste my breath shouting at you?" She shrugged. "Obviously, the disappearing evidence is a compelling problem. I'll work from what her defense team had during the trial and what I can glean from the notes I took before the box went missing. I will overturn that conviction."

And he would help her, whether she wanted him on board or not. He'd spent the majority of his day doing just that already. "What happened with your art?" he asked, changing the subject awkwardly. "I assume that was the errand you ran this afternoon. Was anything damaged beyond repair?"

"No, it will just take time to clean." She smiled up at him. "Thanks for asking. The framing shop thinks they can have the pieces cleaned and reframed and the glass replaced within a week. The cleaning crew told me I could repaint and redecorate as soon as everything dried out." She rubbed her temples. "Theory is, the fan will be gone by tomorrow night." She checked the clock. "You must be hungry."

She moved through her kitchen in the same way she did everything else, with an economy of movement that was streamlined and graceful and with a sense of purpose. Tonight she didn't seem to be braced for battle as she'd been when he'd shown up last night.

Filling two bowls with stew, she brought them over to the counter and then set a basket of thick slices of brown bread between them. She poured water for both of them and a glass of wine for herself.

The stew was a flavorful blend of savory beef, red potatoes, onion, carrots and celery. The aroma was amazing, and a spicy kick of heat surprised him. "This is delicious, thank you."

"My pleasure." She eyed him over her wine glass. "You sound surprised."

Another opportunity to prove his integrity. "I didn't expect you to cook. Not for me."

She pointed at him with her fork. "I'm going to play nice and not take any offense at that."

"Because I brought you something from the bakery?"

"Maybe a little," she confessed, amusement dancing in her green eyes. "Really, it's because my parents held us to a high standard of hospitality. On top of that, you brought me information that can change everything about how I work Anna's case." She took another bite of stew, chewing slowly.

Why did he find her every move appealing? He focused on the food, hearty and warm and comforting.

"I'm sure it's occurred to you that you've become a person of interest." She broke a piece of bread in two and dipped it into the sauce.

"It crossed my mind," he said. Unfortunately it was chased by the thought that he'd rather earn her interest on a personal level. Based on his role in the Wentworth conviction, that was likely just a pipe dream. "I had to be on your list even before I told you about the missing evidence box."

"Yes, but you were at the bottom of the list."

"Why?"

Being at the bottom of her list felt like a personal attack, though he knew she was speaking of the case. The chemistry he sensed between them was apparently one-sided, and it would be better if he could ignore that slow simmer in his bloodstream. He was eight years older than her, so maybe "seasoned detective" wasn't her type.

He'd seen formal pictures and candid snapshots of the Colton siblings during his visits to Griffin's place and the office located in their family home. It always seemed as if Pippa, a notorious workaholic, vacationed with equal focus and intensity by choosing hiking or sailing or otherwise off-the-beaten-path adventures with friends like Elizabeth Wentworth. "I felt too strongly about you," she said.

He smothered another flicker of that persistent attraction.

"In court, you were too sure of what you'd found," she was saying. "I didn't want to talk with you until I had a better handle on who you were as a detective and a man."

"You were going to ask Griffin about me," he said, seeing the truth in her eyes. "To find an angle."

"Yes." Her chin came up, unapologetic. "But then he declared that you were going to be my bodyguard, and I was too irritated with both of you."

"So when will the interrogation begin in earnest?" he asked, taking a second slice of bread. The stew was good enough that he wanted seconds, but his stomach was too jittery over what they might uncover as they discussed the Wentworth case.

"I'd really like to hear your thoughts on the evidence

you found." She pushed her fork around her bowl and then set it aside. "I've read the report and listened to your testimony in court, and I'd like you to walk me through that whole mess again, but not tonight."

"What do you want from me tonight?" His body had an opinion and Griffin wanted him to stick close, but Emmanuel was more interested in her wants and opinions.

"Other than whatever you brought from the bakery, I'd like you to help me eliminate a few names from the long list of GRPD personnel tied to Anna's case."

He checked his watch. "We have a few minutes before you're scheduled to start that loan application, right?" He was pleased he kept his opinion on that to himself.

She nodded as she gathered up their dishes and rinsed them at the sink. He followed her, loading the items into the dishwasher. "Thanks."

He thought they'd move into her office, but she retrieved her laptop and a manila folder with notes from her case file. With everything in place, she changed seats so they were side-by-side. "After your text, I created this long list of names. Of course your name is here, too, but I don't believe you're a killer any more than I believe Anna Wentworth is."

"Thanks?" The low undercurrent in her tone put him on alert. "Are you thinking I'm protecting the *real* killer?"

She propped her chin on her fist and studied him. "Not intentionally."

"Are you always so hard to win over?"

"Probably." She fidgeted, tapping her pen against her knee. "I won't apologize for having high standards."

He smiled. "I'd never ask you to lower your expectations." Leaning forward, he scanned the list of names. "I will say I've learned through experience that good people are capable of doing bad things under the right circumstances."

"Anyone there have the right circumstances to frame Anna?"

"No one is leaping out at me," he said after a few minutes.

"Me either," she said with a gusty sigh.

It looked as though she'd listed everyone on the force. With good reason. The Hicks murder had been high profile from the first moment his body was found on the Wentworth estate. The case shook up the entire city, and no one involved was above scrutiny as they worked the evidence and interviews. He figured Sadie's name would be on that list if she'd been with the CSI that day.

"Is it chocolate?" she asked, her gaze on the bakery box again.

"Yes."

Another sigh that left him wondering how that soft breath would feel against his skin. Whoa. He yanked his thoughts back into line. Pulling out his cell phone, he took a picture of her list. "We have the same information on the computer at the station," he said. "But there, access to the files is also tracked."

"Which means possibly alerting someone to your search." He nodded, and she continued, "Off the record, does anyone on the list have a reputation for mishandling evidence or steamrolling suspects?"

"No one jumps out." He returned to the top of the list. "Let's clear out some of the easy ones. Not these two," he said, pointing at the names of the responding officers. Though they had answered several calls at the

Wentworth mansion, that team always came back to the station more amused than bothered by Anna's nonsensical claims of thieving maids and scurrilous chefs.

"You're sure they don't hate her in secret?" Pippa asked. "Maybe we should check their social media for any latent despise-Anna tendencies."

Emmanuel shook his head. "Even if they did hate her, those two officers have other things going on in life. Little league, soccer practices. They aren't the kill-somebody-to-get-even type."

"I'll take your word." She pulled the list closer and crossed off those two names.

"Really?"

"Is there a reason I shouldn't?" she asked.

"No." Her acceptance felt as awkward as her resistance had last night. "I just... I don't understand you," he blurted it out.

"You don't need to." Her lips curled into a smile. "Last week, I did my best to pin down the last time Anna wore the brooch that was found under Hicks's body. Neither of those officers was near her bedroom suite in that time frame."

"So that was a test?" he asked, irritated.

"Not at all," she assured him. "I considered the outside chance of them having an accomplice within the mansion staff. Your confidence in their character is enough for me."

Pressure eclipsed the irritation. "Anna Wentworth was the prime suspect from day one. Moment one," he amended. "Before the brooch was discovered."

"Being under a microscope didn't make you feel rushed?"

"Of course it did, but McRath and I worked the case

beat by beat. We didn't jump to conclusions. We followed the evidence."

"You followed *planted* evidence."

Good grief. He hoped not, but he understood why she was devoted to that theory. "You have no evidence to support that theory. Look, no one likes your client, but she has serious influence in this town, not to mention the charitable donations. The prosecutor wouldn't have followed through with this case if he'd thought we half-assed any aspect of it."

"You're aware the prosecutor and Mr. Wentworth are friends."

"Everyone tied to the case was aware," Emmanuel confirmed. "The man was out of town with a rock-solid alibi," he reminded her. "You think the prosecutor was helping a friend get rid of his wife?"

Reaching up, she rubbed the back of her neck. It was all he could do not to jump in and help. "The prosecutor would have the means to manipulate things within the department." She shook her head, as if to clear it of the troubling thoughts. "I don't think Ed cared enough about Anna's flings to set her up for murder, but maybe I'm overlooking another reason."

"I doubt it," Emmanuel said. "Mr. Wentworth was solid in the interview. More embarrassed about a body turning up on the grounds once he learned it wasn't anyone he'd known. That sounds callous, but knowing the family, you get it, right?"

"I do. One of Ed's top priorities is protecting the reputation of the Wentworth name." She rolled her eyes. "For Elizabeth's future."

If Pippa succeeded in overturning this conviction, it would be all kinds of trouble for the prosecutor as well as the GRPD. Enough trouble that maybe the prosecutor hired someone to drive Pippa off the Wentworth case. Emmanuel couldn't put that doubt in her head, not when she had CI business to deal with.

Pippa's gaze returned to the paper in front of them. "Perception is a tricky thing," she said. "You arrived at a crime scene and saw things a certain way. When I look at the pictures, I see it all so differently. Who had reason to paint the picture you saw?"

"Let's take a different tack," he suggested. "Rather than consider who wanted to frame your client—"

"Because that's half the city," she interjected.

He cocked an eyebrow.

"Fine. It's ninety-eight percent of the city."

He liked the twitch at the corner of her rosy lips. "Who in the GRPD had any reason to get rid of Hicks? As soon as we found his intent to blackmail her, we knew Anna had means and motive. Combined with evidence at the scene…"

"Slam dunk," she finished for him. "I've been looking at this angle, too, though not within the GRPD." She open several windows on her laptop. "I need to get set up for the loan application, but go ahead and take a look at those articles. It's all from gossip sites and society pages. I'm going to compare his known dates and lovers. Let me know if any names have ties to GRPD or the prosecutor's office."

She went to her office while he tried not to groan over Hicks's dating history. The man liked to party with the rich and slightly famous. He ran across one name and nearly swallowed his tongue. It couldn't be related, and yet it had to be connected.

"Here," he said, his throat suddenly tight. This had

never come out before, and they'd interviewed every-one recently tied to Hicks. Or so Emmanuel thought.

"You found something?"

"Someone." He dragged the mouse and highlighted the name for her.

"Leigh McRath." Her eyebrows climbed toward her hairline. "Is she related to Detective Joe McRath?"

"His daughter." Emmanuel pinched the bridge of his nose. This looked bad, but it had to be a fluke. Joe couldn't be involved in this debacle. He was a decorated cop who took real pride in the work he did for the city. He was a mentor, an inspiration.

The sergeant pushed hard at times, but he closed cases and didn't cut corners. Years ago there had been rumors that he'd gone off the rails on a case involving the death of a little girl, but no disciplinary measures or formal complaints had resulted.

Joe couldn't have known about Leigh's ties to Hicks when they landed the case. If he had, he would've re-cused himself or spoken with the lieutenant about the distant connection to the victim.

"You never spoke with her?" Pippa asked. "I don't have any record of either you or Joe interviewing her."

"I didn't question her." He shook his head. "We did the divide-and-conquer thing on several peripheral con-nections." His stomach cramped, and he was glad he hadn't had more stew. "Joe took most of the prior re-lationships."

"On purpose?"

"No. No reason to think so at the time." What if Joe had taken the relationships to keep Leigh's name out of the investigation? He pushed back from the counter and swore low and long in Spanish. His mother would wash his mouth out with soap even now if she'd heard him. This was bad.

"Hey. Relax," she said, suddenly offering comfort. "It's a connection. One probably random link you didn't know to explore. Just because Hicks and Leigh dated doesn't mean she did anything wrong." Pippa nibbled on her lip again. "Maybe he just wanted to spare his daughter some embarrassment."

"You don't think a father would go to any lengths to protect his daughter and keep her out of jail?"

She opened her mouth to reply and snapped it shut again. "I'll grant you, that's a fair motive. But only *if* that's what happened. It gives me a new potential suspect, a new direction to check on, which is something I didn't have before."

No comfort in that for him. He had years of police service. Enough experience that he shouldn't have missed this piece of the puzzle. His career combined with his upbringing gave him a double dose of that protective instinct that made him a good cop.

Or so he'd thought. Had he been lazy that day at the scene, looking only at the evidence laid out for him? As a detective's daughter, Leigh might have a good idea of how to stage a crime scene if she'd tagged along with her dad and studied his cases.

"Clearly, you need to follow this thread," Pippa said. "What if it was Leigh? Look at the dates. They broke up six months before the murder. If she was brokenhearted, why wait six months and then frame Anna?" Pippa crossed her legs and drummed her pen on her knee.

"As Joe's daughter, she might have easier access to a gun, but how would she have accessed Anna's jewelry?"

He didn't have those answers. A good detective would've asked those questions at the time, not weeks after the prime suspect was sentenced to life in prison. "Pippa, the evidence box is missing. No one else on your list has such a clear connection to Hicks or such a substantial motive.

"Leigh McRath has both. She has access if her father helped. Who knows what he might have done to keep the heat off his daughter?"

"Those are questions I can pursue," she said. "Thanks to you."

As if that made him feel any better. This was definitely a rock and a hard place kind of situation. When Joe caught wind of this, he'd turn on Emmanuel for helping Pippa. Missing evidence box or not, the entire GRPD was likely to turn on him for helping a lawyer working "against" them. He wanted to ask her to be careful, and yet he had no right.

"I won't throw you under the bus, Detective," she promised. "But first, it's time for me to infiltrate the Capital X system. I can't afford to be late on this."

Naturally, helping Brody was the only thing that would momentarily divert her attention from exonerating Wentworth. Through the years, Emmanuel had listened to Griffin vent about Brody. Everyone in the family agreed the kid meant well, but it often bothered Griffin that Brody usually looked for quick fixes to his troubles rather than putting in the tough hours to get where he wanted to go.

Days ago, Emmanuel thought overturning the conviction was a lark and the real threat to Pippa was moving close to Capital X. Now it felt as if both cases had grown teeth and claws and there was no clear path to safe ground.

For either of them.

Chapter Eight

Pippa opened the new laptop and followed the directions provided by CI's resident tech expert, Ashanti Silver. She'd created a step-by-step list so Pippa could find her way to the Capital X site and loan application portal on the dark web.

Emmanuel was hovering, as promised. It wasn't easy to ignore him, and she wasn't even sure she wanted to try. The sizzle she felt when he was close was addictive. If she was reading the signals correctly, he felt something more than a passing cooperative interest.

Not that they could do a thing about it when she was neck deep in two cases, one of which he was far too entangled with.

"Wow, that's not what I expected at all," he said.

He was leaning close enough that she could smell the crisp scent of his cologne. He must have gone home at some point during the day, because the fragrance had been faint this morning and was much fresher now. She had no business being tempted or enticed by that smell.

"It looks as slick and clean as any other legitimate bank."

"Which is probably why they get away with what they're doing," she pointed out. She scrolled through the site, taking a look at products and account options. "If I didn't know how they operated, I'd think this was a great answer for a loan, especially to get a business off the ground."

"You're smart enough that you'd come to your senses when you saw the terms," he said.

His compliment warmed her. "True." She sat back, staring at the screen and giving herself some needed distance. From the man more than the assignment.

"Second thoughts?"

"A few," she admitted. And all of them were about him. She really hadn't expected to like Emmanuel after what he'd said in court, and she didn't know quite how to proceed since he'd shown himself to be a person of high integrity. "It's hard to imagine a person being so underinformed or so desperate that they'd agree to such exorbitant interest rates," she said.

"Not to mention the repayment schedule." Emmanuel stood up and pushed a hand through his wavy hair. She thought he could probably use a trim, then decided that was something Anna Wentworth would say. Pippa found him ridiculously attractive just as he was. The hairstyle wouldn't make any difference. She really needed to find a boyfriend or dive back in to the dating-app scene.

She shivered. During her last attempt, she'd lost patience with the whole messy system. She didn't mind casual hookups, but at this point in her life she was looking for something different. Something more substantial. The men those apps wanted to match her with didn't meet that criteria. Even when she changed her preferences, looking for someone a little older, she'd never been matched with anyone half as intriguing as Emmanuel.

Sliding away from her dangerous thoughts, she focused on the task at hand. There were big buttons on the loan screen for preset loan amounts. She chose the $25K button, the amount Kiely had determined her alias needed and would easily qualify for. Not that any of them believed Capital X turned down an opportunity to suck in a consumer.

Emmanuel was leaning close. "You don't have to watch every keystroke," she said, trying to be cool when she really didn't mind the warmth of him at her back.

"I'm curious you referred to this as an infiltration," he said.

"It feels that way," she admitted, her blood running hot with the excitement. Excitement over the role she would play in saving Brody, *not* over the man at her back. She couldn't possibly let those little flutters of attraction grow into something more. Even if he hadn't been Griffin's friend, they were on opposite sides of a case that was important to her heart.

"Why is the time so specific?" he asked.

"The timing fits with the background my sister and brother created for this person I'm pretending to be."

It was no shock when he reached over and flipped through the papers, quickly getting a read on the fake Alison Carrington. She was thoroughly distracted by his hands. A flat, long-healed scar wrapped under his right thumb, disappearing into his palm. During her single semester of art in undergrad, the professor had devoted a solid week on the mechanics of human hands. With a subject like Emmanuel, she might've aced that section.

Shifting her focus back to the application, she finished entering the personal information, including a social security number and driver's license. Then she added in the details about work history. If she screwed this up, Riley would never forgive her and they might never save Brody. She double-checked all of the basic information and then clicked the arrow to go to the next part of the application. Here she inputted information about her finances, including current debts and any collateral.

After that it was a page about the loan itself, confirming how much she was asking for and how she planned to use the money. She filled out those fields per the paperwork provided and clicked the button to continue.

"You sure about that address?" Emmanuel asked when it was time for her to review everything one last time before hitting Submit.

"This is the address they gave me," she replied. "Can't change it now. Why don't you approve?"

"I don't disapprove," he said. "It's just pretty darn close to this neighborhood."

"No one can connect me to Alison Carrington. That's the whole point of a new computer and the IP magic Ashanti cooked up."

"Right, right." He tucked his hands into his pockets and took a step back.

She appreciated his attempt to give her space, even if he wasn't much good at it.

She checked the box confirming she'd reviewed all of her materials and that it was all correct. As if Capital X would bother going after a loan applicant for a fraudulent application. Satisfied, she pressed Submit.

They only got aggressive with clients who didn't pay them back in accordance with the absurd terms.

"Done?" he asked.

"Looks that way." She hesitated, since the loading wheel was still spinning. There. She pointed to the screen and the flag that said her application was successfully submitted.

The scowl on his face was evidence of his concern. "What next?"

She signed out of the program and shut down the new laptop registered to the Alison Carrington persona. "Time to relax," she said. "As much as possible anyway. According to the site, the approval process can take up to forty-eight hours for a decision."

She wasn't sure why butterflies were suddenly doing aerial stunts in her belly. It wasn't her credit or her person on the line. She had only used the materials provided by her sister and brother. They hadn't even told her who would be playing the role of Alison at the address she'd provided. Someone had to perform day-to-day tasks in case they were being observed, but Pippa's was still the face on the fake ID. There was no reason it should come to that, but Pippa accepted that she might have to step in and be familiar with the identity if there was an unforeseen emergency. She wasn't trying to be a slacker, but so far, all she'd been was a convenient pair of hands who'd completed a few online forms.

She carried the laptop and its charging cord to the office, where she knelt down near the floor safe. Having pulled back the rug, she entered the combination and tucked the equipment away. At Emmanuel's quizzical expression, she explained that she could check the email through an incognito window on her own device if necessary.

"I guess that's it." Pippa straightened the rug and dusted off her hands. What happened now? "At least we're making progress on one case." Even if her contribution was minimal.

It was nice to have that task done. No more wondering. Assuming the Carrington application would be approved, they would soon be drawing the ire of Capital X enforcers. Maybe even the same team who had broken Brody's fingers. Maybe she hadn't come up with the fake identification and background, but she was definitively helping. Thanks to Brody's ties to the family, Capital X would be smart to avoid the Coltons, but by taking on this alias, she was contributing for her siblings, Brody and everyone else Capital X would bilk if they weren't stopped.

"You do carry a strong sense about right and wrong," he said.

The look he gave her was pure appreciation, and she felt overheated in an instant. "Never tried to hide it. Besides, you've got plenty of the same traits."

"As character flaws go, I'll take it," he said.

"Same. Though I don't believe the pursuit of justice is a flaw." She turned to the wall, determined to ignore the noisy fan and dehumidifier. "What do you know about interior decorating?"

"Only what I can't forget when my sisters are chatting," he replied. "Why?"

"I might make this a feature wall instead of just repainting." If he wasn't going to leave, she had to find some common ground. She folded her arms and tried again to imagine floor-to-ceiling beadboard. "Bead-board or wallpaper or…"

"You're too modern for beadboard," he said absently, looking around the space.

She was inordinately pleased by that observation. "That was my thought. I'd invite you to sit down and toss around ideas, but—" She gestured to the fan. "And you probably want to get going."

"Only if you're kicking me out," he said. "We haven't opened that bakery box yet."

She'd almost forgotten about the treat during the thrill of making a stand online and the presence of the man who'd been thoughtful enough to bring over something special. "You can't possibly be worried about Capital X striking tonight."

"Let's just say I'm overly cautious about several things," he said.

"Does that include chocolate?"

"It's in the top five," he teased. "Can't go around indulging in mediocre chocolate."

She enjoyed the sparkle in his brown eyes, as if he might give way to honest laughter any minute. "Thanks for all you've done already," she said.

"You want to keep working on that list?"

"Not tonight." She was tired of thinking about the best approach to Anna's case. Trying to isolate someone within the GRPD without hurting careers and feelings would be a delicate proposition. "I need some time to let things mull in the back of my mind."

He didn't seem all that thrilled with her reply. "Let me know how to support you when you make a plan."

She tilted her head. "You mean that?"

"Of course."

"You continue to surprise me, Detective." One more new development in her life to mull over when she was alone. "Let's celebrate a job well done tonight."

EMMANUEL FOLLOWED HER back to the counter that seemed to serve as her primary dining area. Pippa looked so damn proud of herself, as she should. She'd just laid a trap that could result in a significant leap forward on the CI investigation into Capital X.

The sassy glint in her eye and the tough set to her delicate jaw were an intriguing and irresistible combination. He didn't quite understand his infatuation or why she fired his blood this way. Technically, this was only their third interaction, yet he felt as if he'd known her for years. Sure, Griffin talked about his family, but this was a deep, certain awareness he couldn't shake.

Didn't want to shake.

She was younger, not an insurmountable difference when he thought about it, and he was aware, through his ties to her family, that she'd been through hard times just like he had. Yes, he'd come from a less privileged background, but the Coltons had been community-oriented parents, and their children understood the value of commitment and service.

Her optimism, especially as it related to her pursuit of overturning the Wentworth conviction, should have annoyed him. Pippa's blind faith in a convicted killer should have been a turnoff on its own. He was well aware that he wouldn't be going the extra mile for any other lawyer representing Wentworth. Yet here he stood, reluctant to leave her alone in her secure home, and it had nothing to do with his promise to her brother.

"What are you thinking about?" she asked.

Nothing he should be thinking. Her lips looked soft and kissable and his fingers twitched, eager to learn the feel of her hair. Though he tried to think of Griffin, he couldn't slam the door on his meandering thoughts. "I'm thinking I should stay the night," he said.

She pulled the tie loose from the white box. "That's ridiculous. I'm perfectly safe here. You have an unmarked car downstairs."

"Two," he clarified. It seemed important. "Front and back."

Coiling the length of string around her fingers, she said, "And no sign of anyone, right?"

"Not so far. That can change." He'd draped his jacket over the counter stool earlier and reached for it now, drawing the panic button from the pocket. "I brought this, too, but that doesn't change anything. I still want to stay."

"What is that?" she queried, eyeing the device.

"A panic button," he replied. "I've set it up so it sends an alert to my cell phone and the teams downstairs."

"That's…thoughtful," she finished.

He chuckled. "You think it's too much."

"Thoughtful and too much don't have to be mutually exclusive. You saw me update the electronic locks last night," she said. "The building is secure, and everyone is on alert now. What makes you think any Capital X enforcers would even try to get in here? I used an alias."

He wasn't as worried about the bogus loan operation right now. As she'd said, she used a pseudonym and masked the true IP address, though he believed the company could still find her. No, he was far more concerned about what the missing evidence box meant and the inexplicable red tape she couldn't cut through at the prison. Why couldn't she see she was painting multiple targets on her back? It made protecting her that much more difficult for everyone.

Which was exactly why Griffin had asked him to keep an eye on her. He decided to play the brother card. Family meant everything to the Colton siblings...and to him.

"Griffin insisted I stay close," he said.

"So you said last night." Her voice frosted over. "I'll remind you that he doesn't get to speak for me." She drummed her fingertips on the granite countertop in front of the bakery box. "I appreciate you answering the break-in call and helping so much. Thank you, in case I didn't say that last night."

He couldn't recall if she'd said it either, his mind on other things, primarily how to keep her safe from a distance. "If my partner and I hadn't caught that case clean, I would've come by as a courtesy."

"To Griffin."

Of course. He hadn't even met Pippa. Her tone was as crisp as the leaves falling from the maple trees lining her street. No sense massaging the facts. "Yes. As a courtesy to Griffin, I came by to check out the trouble and see if I could help."

"Or to see if you could worm your way into my world?"

There was a vulnerability in her voice he wasn't sure how to handle. "No. Not the way you're implying."

"Maybe you wanted to keep tabs on my progress during the Wentworth case."

"That's not how I operate," he said with all the calm he could. Maybe twenty-four hours ago he'd had different motives. More self-focused intentions. But not now, not after seeing that threat scrawled across her wall. "If the situation was reversed and I couldn't be sure my sister would be careful enough, I'd expect Griffin to uphold his promise. Even if my sister didn't like it."

"Careful enough?" She swore under her breath, folding her arms. "I don't like it. I don't need a babysitter or a watchdog or whatever you want to call yourself."

"It's a panic button. A precaution." Should he have expected her to give him any grace or cooperation? His testimony in court had pretty much nailed the Wentworth case shut. Clearly her friendship trumped the obvious—the *only*—conclusion the jury could have made. The defense had not provided an effective counterargument to all of the evidence he'd found.

Planted evidence. Her words echoed in his head. If she was right and someone in the GRPD had framed Anna, Pippa needed this panic button and *him* more than she realized. "You are taking strategic risks, and you deserve the best protection against any unpleasant consequences."

She wasn't swayed. "This is who I am. I can handle my consequences."

"Pippa, I understand. I'm not here to change you, or because your brother doubts your ability. Just call me the safety net. That little bit extra you ignore until you need it." He didn't care for the description, but it was accurate.

"I'd rather call Griffin and give him a piece of my mind."

"You can do that," he said. "Why not wait until after?"

"After what?"

He tipped up the lid of the bakery box. "After chocolate."

"éclairs," she said, her tone full of all the reverence the pastries deserved.

He admired her unapologetic enthusiasm, and his mind detoured straight into a fantasy of Pippa demonstrating that kind of eagerness for a lover. For him.

Whoa. That was a big leap. He needed to dial it down. She might not be off-limits precisely, but the woman was prickly, and he suspected she wouldn't appreciate an ill-timed advance. No, Pippa would likely enjoy an all-out seduction with plenty of finesse.

What was wrong with him? He wasn't here to sort out what she did or didn't enjoy on an intimate level.

She bounced on her toes a little as she grabbed two plates from the cabinet.

"Forks?" he asked, sliding a napkin closer to her.

"Are you kidding? These are the best éclairs in the city. They deserve fingers." She wiggled hers, urging him to hurry.

He was doomed. She had no idea of her effect on him. He could quickly become addicted to this charming, playful side of her. It was a lovely counterpoint to her grit and drive. He enjoyed her serious intensity. It was one of the first things they had in common, a passion for justice and seeing that what was right prevailed.

"No forks," he agreed, placing an éclair on each plate.

"I'd suggest relaxing on the couch, but the fan is too loud."

"I'm fine right here." Her grateful smile hit him square in the chest.

"Would you like coffee?" she offered.

"Milk, if you have it."

"Done." She pointed a finger at him. "That kind of thinking gives me hope for you."

She poured them each a short glass of milk and they

sat at the counter, neither of them willing to wait a minute longer to dive into the decadent éclairs.

The flavors of rich chocolate, perfect pastry and thick, sinfully smooth cream melted in his mouth, but the experience was enhanced by Pippa. Pure joy bloomed across her face at the first bite. Closing her eyes, she licked a dot of chocolate from her lip.

Emmanuel was hard in an instant, wondering how her unique flavor would make the éclair even better. He had to get his mind off sex before his reaction to her made it impossible. She would never let him stay if she noticed how stirred up he was.

He paused between bites. "So, Pippa Colton, a.k.a. Alison Carrington, you've set a trap for a notorious loan operation. What will you do next?"

"This." She took another bite of her éclair. "Better than any amusement park vacation," she said. "I might even have a second one."

"I'm glad I made the right choice," he said. He'd thought about calling Griffin for advice, but that had felt like cheating. Making the right call on instinct made this moment even sweeter.

"Did Griffin mention these éclairs are my kryptonite?"

"No," he said with pride. "All my idea."

"It was a good one." Her brow puckered over her pert nose. "How did you and Griffin meet?"

"Through a community event for the foster system years ago," Emmanuel said. "We hit it off and have been friends ever since."

She didn't ask any follow-up questions. Was she uninterested or just processing things while she enjoyed her dessert? When she finished her second éclair, he stacked her plate on top of his and carried both to the sink.

"You don't have to do that," she said.

"You weren't raised by my mother," he replied, laughing a little.

Pippa leaned back against the counter, and he felt her gaze like a touch as he rinsed the dishes and loaded them into her dishwasher. "I've had plenty of time to find the balance," he said. "Although most days you can still eat off my floor."

She laughed, and the merry sound along with the happy glow on her face rendered him speechless.

"Tell me something else about your mom," she said.

"Why?" He needed a few more minutes to gather his wits.

Her gaze lifted to the ceiling, and he catalogued every detail in that brief moment. Her wistful expression made him wonder about her past. He'd heard a few details about the difficulties between their parents from Griffin. The idyllic image the Coltons had projected while in public had not translated into a perfect home life. Apparently once close, the couple had drifted apart due to Graham's career and Kathleen's focus on raising their children and her charitable endeavors in the community.

"The way you talk about your family..." Her voice trailed off. "You make it sound as if your parents were happy."

"They *are* happy," he said. Closing the dishwasher, he waited on the other side of the kitchen, curious about the change in mood and topic.

"Sometimes I wonder what happens to people who don't have good examples to follow."

"In marriage?" he asked.

She met his gaze and one slender shoulder rose and fell. "In anything."

He knew she meant personal relationships. "I think, at a certain point, we have to make our own choices about what we want and how we'll get there."

"Right," she agreed. "That's being an adult. But do you think people without a solid example in one thing or another are doomed to struggle? Maybe it's a hurdle no one knows how to recognize," she said.

He was pretty sure psychiatrists knew how to recognize and fix those hurdles. "What about your friend Elizabeth?"

Pippa's eyebrows lifted. "What about her?"

"From the sound of it she's a kind person. She shows up in and around Grand Rapids helping out and doing good things. As far as I know, she's never once called the police to accuse anyone in her employ of any kind of crime."

"That was her mother's MO, the example she was raised to follow. Anna Wentworth shows up in the right places for the photo op, does good work in name only and often harasses her best employees without any true cause."

"You're of the opinion that we're more than what we've seen in life."

He closed the distance between them, drawn to her by a force he could no longer deny. Fast or not, he didn't want to hold himself back from something that had the potential for a life-altering shift. "I'm saying what you already know. Experience shapes us and informs us, but we can choose how to interpret those experiences, how we grow from them."

Slowly, giving her plenty of time to move or otherwise signal him away, he nudged a lock of her hair behind her ear. Hair soft as silk against his fingers; the shell of her ear warm to his touch. Those small discoveries heated his blood, not at all insignificant.

She held her ground, her eyes locked with his and his pulse kicked with anticipation.

"I've seen bad people come out of good families," he said. "And I've seen people do remarkably good things amid dreadful circumstances."

Emmanuel traced the pale skin on the inside of her wrist, pleased to feel her pulse pounding as hard as his.

"We have choices," she agreed. "I know that. We can choose to learn and grow." Her gaze dropped to their joined hands, and her fingertips trembled as she traced the shape of his hand.

Choose me. He couldn't resist her. Was there a chance she felt the same inexplicable draw to him? When she looked up at him again, he slowly bent his head toward her. He wanted her to have the time and space to say no to a kiss, even as he prayed like hell she wouldn't.

She met him, her lips brushing lightly across his. The spark that sizzled out from his lips through his whole being was lightning in a bottle, a flash too powerful for the moment. The fleeting, brief contact left him craving more. Everything. All of her. He wanted to be her choice. Would happily beg for the honor.

Her fingers laced with his, but she didn't seem eager for another kiss. How would he exit gracefully now?

"Emmanuel," she whispered. Her hands came up to frame his face, her thumbs rasping against the grain of his short beard. Ever so gently she brought his mouth back to hers.

The sweetness of her was like a balm to that first jolt of electricity and power. Her lips were firm and sure. No surprise she knew what she wanted. Him. He nearly crowed in victory.

Gripping her hips, he boosted her to the countertop, standing between her knees. She giggled, and when her lips parted, his tongue stroked across hers. She tasted of the rich chocolate icing and the sweet cream filling of the éclair, and the taste that was hers alone.

It was a sugar rush of a completely new variety.

He tugged her to the edge of the granite surface, letting her feel what she did to him. This time there was no giggle, just a moan that nearly sent him over the edge. "Pippa," he murmured against her lips.

She wrapped her legs around his hips in response, holding him close. Close but not close enough. There were too many barriers keeping him from everything he wanted to learn about her.

Her lips and teeth scraped against his jaw and down his throat and he gripped her hips, fighting for control. "Pippa," he said again. Her name was the full extent of his vocabulary right now. Everything started and ended right here.

With her.

He speared a hand into her hair, angling for a deeper kiss. Her fingertips curled over his shoulders, then dragged down his chest until she tugged his shirt free of his jeans. Her hands slipped under the clothing, skimming his ribs and waist, around to his back.

"*Mmm*, you're so hot." She smiled against his lips. "I like it."

He was on fire for her without a doubt. He jerked

when she touched a ticklish spot under his rib cage, and a peal of her bright laughter surrounded him.

"You're ticklish," she said, clearly delighted.

"Don't tell anyone."

Her eyes sparkled with pure mischief. "They'll never hear it from me," she vowed. "Just here?" Her fingers danced over the spot again.

He growled, sliding his hands under her skirt and gripping her thighs. She was burning up just like he was; he could feel it through the thin fabric of her pants. Feel the strength in her legs. "Pippa," he warned. His thumbs dipped low, following the curve of her inner thighs, teasing them both by staying well away from the most sensitive areas of her body.

Everything about her made him more aware, more sensitive to *her*. Every inch of her fascinated him. The entire fleet of police cars might come screeching to a halt outside her door, sirens blazing, and he wouldn't notice.

She wriggled under his touch, her hands working at the buttons of his shirt. "Off," she commanded, pushing at the panels. "Let me see you."

He grinned, skimming kisses along the shell of her ear. If she wanted to make demands, it would be his pleasure to fulfill her every wish. Standing tall, her knees still snug around his hips, he cast his button-down shirt to the floor and the undershirt followed.

Her eyelids were heavy, her lips flushed and plump from their kisses as she stared at him. They both watched her hands, small and fair against his deeper complexion, explore his torso.

He couldn't recall ever being quite this desperate to hear a woman's opinion of his body.

Her palms flattened over his pecs, smoothed across his shoulders and down his arms. With a firm grasp, she leaned closer and kissed his chest right over his heart. He couldn't bear it but didn't dare move as her tongue and mouth flicked a sigh-inducing path upward until at last they were kissing again, lips fused as tongues dueled.

He breathed her in, filled himself with her scents, orange in her hair, chocolate on her lips, and the arousal swirling thick in the air between them. His hands wandered over her delectable curves, from her breasts, to the dip of her waist, to her hips. Slowly, he dragged his touch back up until his thumbs were resting just below her nipples.

She was making soft, needy noises that tested his resolve. "Touch me." She rubbed her breasts against his hands.

"My pleasure." He teased her nipples, pinching lightly through the fine fabrics of her shirt and bra. With an arm around her waist, he bent her back a little, giving him better access as he kissed a path down around that gorgeous pendant and lower to her breasts. He hesitated, unbuttoning her shirt slowly and keeping his kisses light. Her bra was sleek satin, but the glow was nothing compared to her skin. He could happily lose himself in her for the rest of his days.

"Emmanuel."

"Mmm?"

"Put your mouth on me before I die."

He cupped her breast and met her command, suckling hard on her nipple and then blowing lightly across the moistened peak. She held his head close, moving against his mouth, crying with pleasure when he used his teeth lightly.

The woman was a marvel of demands and responses. He dipped a hand lower, pressing his palm to the heat at her center over her pants. Her hips bucked, and he grinned against her breast, learning what she enjoyed.

"Stop," she whispered, her hands dropping from his head to his shoulders as she nudged him back so she could sit up.

He did, easing back as far as she would allow. She still held him with her legs. She was adorably disheveled, and whether or not they went any further with this, he was staying the night. In her bed, on the couch or on the floor in front of her door. He wasn't taking chances with her.

"You…" She paused, her throat working as she swallowed. "We, *um*…we shouldn't do the rest of this out here."

Despite a critical lack of blood flow to his brain, he could think of several reasons why they should. "Okay?"

"Any of my siblings could walk in on us."

Us. He liked the sound of that. The rest of that, not so much. "Really? I told you not to share the code."

"Really?" she mimicked his tone. "Scolding me here and now?" She arched a golden-brown eyebrow. "You'd rather explain *this*," she circled her hand to indicate their state of undress, "to Riley or Griffin?"

"Well, no." Although she'd be worth the inevitable broken nose or bruised jaw. "Be clear," he said, stroking the length of her thighs, teasing them both. "Do you want me to take you to the bedroom and continue *this*?"

"Yes." That sparkle was back in her eyes. "And hurry."

His heart rate kicked into overdrive and desire flooded through him. They were on the same page. "You got it."

Chapter Nine

Pippa couldn't suppress a shocked squeal as he plucked her right off the counter. She wrapped her arms around his neck and kissed him. His lips were a fantasy and she couldn't get enough of his taste. She might already have an irreversible dependency. Sliding her tongue over his, she pressed herself to him. Couldn't get close enough to his heat and strength.

She never lost control. Was never desperate. And where on earth had the courage to snap out demands come from? Until right now, her sexual experiences had all been very practical. Definitely satisfying, but practical. She'd never felt anything like the joyful abandon she felt tonight with Emmanuel.

He carried her out of the kitchen, but they'd made it only a few paces down the hall before he stopped to feast on her breasts again. Good grief, she was perched on the edge of an orgasm already. She'd prefer to be naked, with him buried deep inside, when the wave crashed over her.

"Wall is good," she decided.

"Next time," he said, continuing the journey into her bedroom.

Next time. The idea held tremendous appeal. Especially as he eased her to the floor, the backs of her knees bumping the bed. He shoved off her shirt and tossed it to the floor before he cupped her aching breasts once more.

They were leaving a trail of clothing anyone could follow. She started to giggle and stopped short when he removed her bra and covered her with his hot palms. "Oh, yes." His thumbs flicked over her hard nipples.

Reaching between them to work on his belt, she got it open and unbuttoned his jeans, carefully lowering the zipper. "Take those off."

He complied immediately, a sexy smirk on his mouth as he pulled a condom from his pocket and dropped it onto the nightstand. When he was naked, she just stared. Her skin felt too tight, too hot, and she craved his touch. Everywhere.

But first she wanted to kiss every inch of that glorious body. His fitness had been apparent from the start, but now, seeing every ripple and ridge, every firm plane, her mouth positively watered. She couldn't decide where to kiss him first.

"Pippa, you're killing me."

She looked up and saw the raw hunger, the blatant need, in his brown eyes. Tiptoeing, she gave him a searing kiss. "I don't know where to start," she whispered against his mouth. "You're so beautiful." She'd been spewing orders, and now she just wanted him to take over. Sliding her hand over his length, she delighted in his deep groan.

He covered her hand with his, let her stroke him a few times, then he knelt down to remove her pants. "Pippa." His breath teased the sensitive skin of her inner thigh, now bare to his view, exposed to his touch.

His next words were incoherent as blood pounded in her ears, and when his mouth met her center, her thoughts scattered. He tasted and teased her with his tongue and intimate kisses. He spoke in a flow of Spanish that made her feel like the sexiest woman, the most valuable treasure, on the planet.

Her legs trembled as he brought her to a shuddering climax and he caught her, held her close, so she couldn't escape the full rush of sensation. Tears welled in her eyes and she blinked them away, desperate to get herself under control. Easing back onto the bed, she barely had time to catch her breath before he was prowling over her, grabbing the condom he'd left on her nightstand.

"You are glorious," he murmured against her belly. "Amazing." His tongue circled her breasts. "A beautiful joy."

She couldn't muster a protest or find shelter from the emotions bombarding her. He'd stripped her bare, inside and out. Did she regret it? Too soon to know, especially when there was more to discover. All she could do was stare at his striking form as he rolled a condom over his jutting erection.

She took comfort in his kisses and touches, finding her way back to those playful and tantalizing moments in the kitchen until she was on the verge of another orgasm. Poised at her entrance, he pressed in just enough to make her crazy. To make her crave.

"More." She lifted her hips. He complied, but not enough, then withdrew. "Emmanuel," she pleaded, her hands gripping his lean, sculpted arms. "Please, Emmanuel."

He drove deep in one full stroke and her body soared, the physical demands and bliss blotting out everything but him. She clung to that pleasure, chased it as he did, looking for the touches and adjustments that made him growl and moan in pleasure.

When the next orgasm crashed over her, she was lost, then found as her gaze met his. A moment later he reached his release on a shuddering groan. They were both spent, but she didn't want to let him go, wishing she could hold him all night.

No. That couldn't be right. She didn't do the all-night thing. She wasn't the cling-and-cuddle type. So why did she nearly protest when he left to dispose of the condom?

She didn't have time to sort out the reactions spiking through her system before he was back and stretched out beside her, pulling the sheet over their cooling bodies.

Pippa was in shock, the bliss of moments ago shattered by the reality of what she'd done. There were consequences, and now she had to face them. But how? She didn't leap into physical encounters and to hell with the aftermath. Not like this. The worst part, aside from being speechless and breathless, was the intense desire for an encore.

Emmanuel had just gifted her with a series of orgasms that should have kept her satisfied for years. She was here, tucked up beside him, feeling greedy and wanting more. It would be comforting to think he had merely unlocked some previously unknown Pandora's box of passion. She knew better.

And it scared her.

"Wow," she whispered in the direction of the ceiling. "That was…"

He rolled to his side and propped his head on his fist, watching her with those deep brown eyes. He traced her lower lip, and she was afraid he would catch the tremor. There was a certain knowledge in his gaze that went beyond the physical. A deepening warmth that made her edgy and nervous.

This wasn't supposed to go down this way. She didn't fall into situations that left her ruffled or unsettled. She stayed in control. Always. He was waiting for her to finish, so she tried again. "That was…" She couldn't find the words that made sense without exposing this strange fear prodding her to run away and leave her own bed.

"Amazing," he finished for her. His smile was almost shy, and he seemed to be as much at a loss for words as she was. Maybe in another time and another place with another man that would have been comforting.

Emmanuel had come into her life as a definite enemy to the case. Tonight changed all of that. Irrevocably. But not publicly. Not yet. She could still deny any inappropriate connection to the detective who'd sealed Anna's fate. Her gaze drifted down his torso, and her hand followed before she could stop it. *Enemy* was such a strong word, a divisive word, not at all suitable after what they'd just shared. Honestly, he'd been winning her over since this morning when she'd found him grieving over an informant. Add in his guidance for her top case and determination to keep a promise made to her brother and she could so easily become a lost cause.

He eased her over, nuzzling her neck, murmuring nonsense about her beauty.

Finally, common sense kicked in, or maybe it was a jolt of self-preservation. Her hands on his firm shoulders, she pushed him away. "Yeah, okay. You should get going," she said.

"Pardon me?" His dark eyebrows disappeared under

the wave of hair that fell across his forehead. "We agreed I'd stay the night."

Had they agreed? She couldn't remember, and that wasn't the point. "I've changed my mind. The panic button is enough."

His chin dropped. "Pippa, what—"

"You heard me." She scooted out of the bed and grabbed her robe, cinching the tie tight at her waist. "You heard me. Please go."

He sat up, the sheet falling low across his hips. "Pippa, talk to me."

She shook her head. How could he sit there in the middle of her bed, naked and unaffected?

"Talk to me," he urged. He indicated the pillows they'd just been resting on. "This was something special."

"Right. Sure." She stopped herself before she started wringing her hands. "Whatever it is or isn't, this is over," she said. "No sense rehashing every little detail." Though she already knew she'd do just that as soon as he walked out. The real thing had been infinitely better than her heated dreams last night.

"For tonight?"

She couldn't make herself say forever. Not when her body refused to accept this was a one-and-done thing. "Emmanuel, please leave." If he kept pressing, she might cry, and that would not be tolerated.

She didn't need a flood of foreign emotions right now, not with two major cases demanding her time. "This was fun. Amazing," she used his word. "It was an excellent experience." She folded her arms, her skin heating as his gaze cruised over her cleavage. "Clearly we were both in need of a physical outlet for our stress."

"This was more," he snapped, cutting her rambling short. "Why are you making it cheap?"

She didn't reply. Couldn't.

His next words were a string of Spanish, spewed so fast she had no idea if he was swearing or praying. Probably the former. Whether he was swearing at himself or at her, it didn't matter, as long as he left.

If he stayed, the temptation would be too big for her to resist. She held firm, held herself back from his enticing body as he gathered up his clothing, following the trail back to the kitchen. Good grief, the man was beautiful.

The neediest parts of her body begged her to reconsider, to take it all back and kiss him until his heat surrounded her again and gave her that rush of feeling so cherished.

Madness.

He was far too reasonable. Too easy to talk to. She was kicking him out of her bed and out of her home, and he didn't rage or rant. Of course not. Emmanuel Iglesias was suddenly everything calm and cool. A complete flip from the desire and passion not fifteen minutes past.

EMMANUEL REMINDED HIMSELF this was her choice. If he wanted her to choose differently, to choose him, that was his problem. He'd honor her decisions. Didn't mean he wouldn't fight for more—for her—but this wasn't the time for that battle.

He was in the kitchen, tugging his shirt over his head, when her phone rang. It was there on the counter, impossible to miss the caller ID screen showing Elizabeth Wentworth's face.

Perfect.

Pippa rushed out of the bedroom to answer the phone while he slipped back in for his shoes and socks.

From what he could glean from Pippa's vague responses, Elizabeth was chattering on about something. Pippa paced up and down the hall; the tension of her kicking him out of her bed had faded into a friendly warmth for her friend. Whatever was going with Elizabeth, Pippa was all for it.

She nearly plowed into him at one point, and in her excitement over the call, she apparently forgot her anger. Pointing to the phone, she put it on speaker.

"Thanks for listening, Pippa. When I told her you were on the case, that I hired you, she smiled. Like, a *real* smile. Finally, it's sinking in that I'm in her corner."

Emmanuel managed not to roll his eyes.

"Well, you always have been. I'm glad something good has come of this mess." Pippa's tone was warm, but her eyes were cool as she watched him.

"Truly," Elizabeth gushed. "We haven't had conversations this open and sincere since before middle school."

It was hard to imagine Anna being an open and sincere mother at any stage of the parental process. Emmanuel knew a series of nannies had raised her daughter. But listening to the friends talk, he was forced to rethink his certainty about Anna's guilt in the Hicks murder.

The two people who knew the woman best were clearly aware of her inherent flaws.

"It's like she finally believes me," Elizabeth said. "I know you couldn't meet with her personally that day at the prison, but just knowing you tried to come out has given her some confidence. I've told her I believed in her innocence from the start, but I guess hiring you was the sign she needed to believe *me*."

"We are making progress on her case," Pippa promised.

He glared at her. That was a big stretch.

"Thank goodness. I'll let you go. I just wanted to tell you about the RevitaYou issue."

"I'll see what I can do from this end. That supplement is dangerous," Pippa said. "I'm so glad she's interested in being your mom again."

"Me too. It's more than refreshing." Elizabeth sniffed. "I'm such a baby. But…"

"I get it," Pippa assured her. "You deserve to have the best of your mom."

"You don't think it's the vitamins?"

Pippa laughed. "No. I think your mom is learning from a tough experience." She said goodbye and ended the call, and they both stared at her phone.

"What about RevitaYou?" he asked.

A lesser man might be offended that her attention had so wholly shifted away from him. He couldn't exactly call himself the bigger person here, but he wasn't offended. That tightness in his gut told him he'd rather have her attention, and he definitely wanted her body under his again. Or over. Being kicked out of her bed made his motions as jerky as his thoughts while he finished dressing.

"Apparently Anna has bribed someone in the prison system to deliver RevitaYou and other things to keep her comfortable and youthful during her incarceration."

"Of course she has." But if Anna had a cooperative network inside and she'd wanted to meet with Pippa, who had blocked that meeting?

"Elizabeth warned her. She's worried about the risks with the illnesses and deaths tied to the product," Pippa added, pacing again.

"Understandable. But if Wentworth won't listen, that's on her."

Pippa's nostrils flared as she whirled around to face him. "Manipulating a system doesn't make her a killer."

At last he had her attention. For the moment. "Did I say that?" He stared her down, waiting for her to argue. She didn't. "Remember to use the panic button," he said, with a little too much bite as he tapped the device. Her eyebrows arched in challenge, but he didn't back down. If she wanted to limit their conversation to the cases, it was fine with him.

"There are two unmarked cars on the street," he added. "One up front and one out back." And he would be close too. "Just in case Capital X figures out that application is bogus and originated with you."

"They won't." Her chin lifted. "Colton Investigations is better than that. Honestly, Griffin is your friend."

Yeah, and his friend would be pretty pissed off to learn Emmanuel had slept with the sister he was supposed to be protecting. "Pippa..." He just didn't know what else to say. "Forget it. We can talk tomorrow."

"Thanks for the panic button," she said. "Even though I know how to take care of myself."

Far safer to keep his mouth shut rather than be a jerk and remind her she'd let him take pretty good care of her in the past hour. No, he definitely was not the bigger man tonight.

Insulted, with no real cause, he stalked downstairs to his car. He'd known another night in the car was probable, and still it stung that she'd booted him out. He trusted the teams in the unmarked cars, but he couldn't leave her safety to others. He didn't want to pinch her independence, but that didn't mean he couldn't have her back.

Yes, Griffin was counting on him, but more than that, Emmanuel felt like he owed her. Especially after hearing Elizabeth and Pippa talk. He'd interviewed enough family members to know the difference between bluster and belief. He understood that believing wasn't always the right character assessment.

Elizabeth probably hadn't missed the signs of murderous tendencies. On the other hand, he'd let an unpleasant interaction color his view of the crime scene and the prime suspect. Anna wasn't a nice person, but thanks to the inconsistencies in the case, he was starting to think Pippa was right about the woman's innocence.

He looked up toward Pippa's window, half hoping he would see her watching for him. Of course, she wasn't there. Being there would imply he mattered to her. She had made it painfully clear he did not. What had she called it? A physical outlet.

And why was he so damn upset?

He dropped his head to the steering wheel and waited for his common sense and normal detachment to return. He wasn't the guy who got hung up on the girl. Especially not when the girl was a woman eight years his junior and had tossed a grenade into one of his closed cases.

He wasn't anyone's role model; he didn't want to be a hero. When it came to relationships, he wanted a woman willing to be warm and open. A woman to enjoy, who wasn't afraid to admit she wanted him back.

"Pipe dream," he said to the empty car.

Years ago, he'd proposed to a woman he thought fit those criteria, and he'd been burned. A reporter, she'd used his body and his connections to make a name for herself so she could move up to a bigger market. At least he discovered the truth before they were married. In his family, divorce wasn't an acceptable option. *For better or worse* was taken as a formal commitment.

It really sucked that the best sex he'd had in years would dredge up those old painful memories. Noticing that his battery was low on his phone, he plugged it in and turned on the car to charge it. The radio was tuned to an oldies station, and Elvis was singing a ballad about love. One of his mother's favorites. He switched off the radio and reclined his seat, closing his eyes and letting the hum of the engine lull him into a drowsy sleep.

Not much point in worrying about how Pippa affected him. When her brother found out, Emmanuel knew he was a dead man.

PIPPA COULDN'T TAKE the droning white noise anymore. She turned off the drying equipment and all the lights on her way back to her bedroom. She left her phone and the panic button on her nightstand while she got ready for bed. She stared at herself in the mirror over the sink, daydreaming about those sweet moments in Emmanuel's arms.

What had she been thinking? Too bad she couldn't blame the sugar high of the éclairs. She turned her back on her reflection, ashamed by the satisfied smile that kept flitting over her lips.

She had jumped Emmanuel as if he were the last slice of bacon on the platter on Christmas morning.

Oh, how the man could kiss. And do everything else

with a master's touch, as well. That hadn't been good sex; it had been life altering. And she kicked the man out. What a fool. She walked out of the bathroom and stared at the rumpled bed. She should change the sheets, erase all traces of what they shared. Instead she caught herself hugging a pillow, breathing in his scent.

Why had she sent him packing?

Fear. A simple, if uncomfortable, admission. She was afraid of her feelings, afraid of losing herself and losing sight of her goals within the happy fog of a relationship. She'd watched her mom's goals and dreams get smothered by her dad's career. Her dad had subscribed to the theory that ambitious men deserved women who would support their goals. The rift and underlying unhappiness had left a lasting impression on her young heart. She loved both of her parents, and it was so sad to watch their marriage spiral out of control, to watch them fall out of love. She couldn't give that kind of support to Emmanuel without sacrificing herself, and she didn't expect him to adjust for her. It wasn't fair to either of them to pretend otherwise.

Pippa knew what she was capable of, knew how she dialed in on a case to the exclusion of all else. A man like Emmanuel wouldn't stick around for long when she had to cancel dates or change plans for the sake of a case.

Banishing all thoughts of "next time" from her mind, she straightened the bedding and traded her robe for her normal nightshirt. It wasn't nearly as warm as his skin or as comforting as having his arms around her.

He was a beautiful distraction, but she couldn't afford to become attached. Not to the man who had convicted Anna in the first place and definitely not to the man her brother had sent to keep tabs on her.

She battled back a blast of panic that Griffin would find out, but there was no way Emmanuel would volunteer any personal details of their evening. He didn't have a death wish, and deep down, aggravated or not, she knew he wouldn't want to embarrass her.

She appreciated his sense of fair play when he'd told her about the evidence box. If only it didn't feel as if she'd thanked him with sexual favors.

Eventually her sister would figure it out. That was going to be an awkward conversation, unless she could delay chatting with her sister for several days.

Considering how best to avoid her twin in the days ahead, she turned out the light and snuggled down into the bedding. Breathing in Emmanuel's scent, she closed her eyes and tried to sleep. She would have herself under control when she faced him again.

She wasn't sure of the time when a soft beep in the hallway brought her almost all the way out of a sweet dream of her body tangled with Emmanuel's. Ignoring the sound, she rolled to her side, trying to get back to the dream.

A squeak that sounded like the dry hinge at her front door brought her fully awake. She reached for the panic button on her nightstand while she listened for any confirmation that she might be in danger.

Maybe Emmanuel had let himself back in. Something to be mad about later. She was tempted to call out his name, but if someone was inside, it might be her sister Kiely. Sometimes her twin crashed in the second bedroom, so Pippa had given her a new code for the front door.

She must have dozed off waiting for another noise, because the next thing she knew, strong hands suddenly landed on her throat, cutting off her airway. The heavy body looming over her, a shadow in the dark room, made a low grunting sound as he choked her.

Gloves, not skin. She registered the different texture as she bucked and twisted away from the assault. Her hand gripped the panic button fob, fingers squeezing in a dazed hope that she'd pressed the right button and the signal was getting through.

She fought, twisting one way and kicking another, raking at the arms holding her. He wore some kind of coat and something over his face too. All she caught in her fingernails was fabric rather than skin. The man had her pinned down, and the bedding impeded her ability to escape.

Desperate, with bright sparks of light dancing at the edges of her vision, she planted her feet into the mattress and drove her hips up. The move loosened his grip, and she sucked in a short breath, but it wasn't nearly enough for her oxygen-depleted lungs.

She struggled against the inevitable while her lungs burned. Pain and panic filled her in equal measure under his crushing grip. She gave up on the key fob and managed to get an arm free of the bedding. Her hand landed on the stack of books on her nightstand, and she pummeled him with the nearest hardbound edition.

He grunted, then knocked the threat away, jerking her around as if he were wrestling with a small, crazed animal instead of a full-grown woman. The movement freed her legs and she kicked out wildly. Every time she threw him off a bit, she got a little more air. Another minute to live.

She heard a crash, followed by shouting and then the attacker was gone, off of her. Dragging in a ragged breath, she coughed and sputtered her way to the floor, crawling toward the safety of the bathroom. Behind her, she saw the shadows of two people fighting, one of them swearing in Spanish.

The room shook as the men slammed into a wall and then out of her bedroom and into the hallway. More voices were shouting now, but only one she recognized: Emmanuel. Disoriented and afraid, she huddled in the dark bathroom. Before she could remember she'd left her phone behind, she heard Emmanuel calling her name. Was it over? Her body quaked as she inched closer to the comforting sound of his voice. He hadn't gone home. He'd stayed close and come to her rescue, charging in to save her from that deadly, choking pressure. Was he all right?

WINDED, HIS HEART pounding in his ears, he couldn't tell if he was clear yet. He was getting too old for this crap. Rounding a corner, he paused, relieved that no one was on his tail. He removed the stocking cap and stuffed it into his coat pocket, exposing his graying hair. Yanking off the coat, he turned it inside out so the bright color showed, and concentrated on walking normally, despite the knee going stiff after wrestling with Iglesias.

The car he'd borrowed from his brother-in-law was still several blocks away. But at least now he wouldn't match the alert that was being broadcast for a perp in all black.

He took measured breaths, as more aches and pains lit up various points in his body. That little scrap of a lawyer had landed a couple of solid blows. He might have to call out tomorrow if the tenderness at his temple turned into a visible bruise. No way would he take a chance that Iglesias added up a defensive injury with the man in Colton's condo.

He'd been sure she was asleep, but her reactions had been too quick. And that panic button had been a mean surprise. Iglesias must have left that with her after the break-in. He'd given his daughter something similar when she'd gone to college. Just a little extra precaution in a dangerous world.

Stupid thoughtful detective. He knew his caring streak really should be fading, after all his years with the GRPD.

Iglesias was smitten, that was all, he decided. Hanging out and watching over the friend's little sister, it was natural. Hopefully he'd see through her before she burned him. The lawyer was surely as manipulative as her client. No decent person would help a conniving bitch like Wentworth.

He wouldn't be surprised if he peed blood for a day or two after that kick to his kidneys. Whoever taught Iglesias to fight dirty did a good job. Under other circumstances he might be impressed. Now, out of breath and afraid he was going to be scooped up any second, he hated the detective almost as much as he hated Hicks and Wentworth.

He'd heard the woman was tossing money around the prison, doing her best to pretend she was in charge. The guards would take the payoffs and consider it hazard pay for dealing with the Queen of Mean. No one inside got paid enough. He just hoped they took her money and didn't deliver on her silly demands.

When would she learn that the world didn't turn on her whim?

Insensitive people like Hicks and Wentworth deserved each other. He typically didn't judge others, but bullies? Never could stand one.

He pressed a hand to his aching side, wondering if Iglesias had cracked a rib. He hadn't seen that kind of skill and aggression coming from a smooth one like Iglesias. The man had been on him so fast he'd barely made it out the back door. Damn lucky he hadn't been exposed right then and there.

When he reached the car, he tossed the coat into the passenger seat, further distancing himself from the description Iglesias would be handing out. He wasn't hungry, but he needed more of an alibi, so he rolled into a drive-through for a burger, fries and a milkshake, not outside the norm.

Heading home, he contemplated the real trouble: the lawyer had survived.

He had to get her to drop this nonsense about finding the real killer. The jury's verdict had been good enough for everyone else—why not her? The sad daughter just had to accept that her mother wasn't a good person.

He'd give her forty-eight hours to come to her senses and drop the case. If she didn't, well, he'd think of something. Going back to her condo wasn't an option. Iglesias would surely up the security measures again. Hell, they'd probably add a dog to the patrol and put a bear trap on the back stairs.

He choked on a fry when he thought about what a scent dog might pick up. Had to ditch these clothes, the shoes, all of it.

Wentworth and her lawyer were costing him big-time, making this entire mess worse.

He swore as he turned a corner, his back and shoulders already so damn sore. He couldn't go to his normal doctor, couldn't file the claim with his insurance through the department.

If he couldn't finish this, who could he trust to take over and make sure the Hicks case stayed closed and Wentworth never stepped out into the free world again?

That would take some thought, some finagling and more than a case of beer.

Before he invested another cent in this endeavor, he was going to dive deeper into the lawyer. If she wouldn't come to her senses for her own sake, maybe she'd make the smart choice to protect someone else.

Unlike Anna Wentworth and that sleazy David Hicks, the Colton family had a solid reputation in Grand Rapids, and everyone knew how tight they were, especially after their parents were killed.

There was an angle worth digging into.

"Pippa, honey?" She heard Emmanuel's voice, soft and close, just on the other side of the bathroom door. "Pippa, it's me. Can I come in?"

Instantly she felt calmer and took her first deep breath in too long. She tried to answer him, but her throat was too raw. He turned the doorknob and she squeaked in fear. On an oath, he slowly nudged the door open until he could come inside. "You're safe now," he said, crouching in front of her.

He had a split lip and a smear of blood on his cheek. Otherwise he looked just as he did when he'd left. He held his hand out to her and waited as if he didn't have anywhere else to be for the rest of his life.

Emmanuel. She put her hands in his palm, steadier just from that simple connection.

"That's my girl. Come on with me now."

Yes. His girl. She wanted to be his. Needed to be his. When she tried to stand, her legs quaked and wobbled, but he caught her around the waist and kept her upright.

Her bedroom was a series of tumultuous images as he guided her through and out to the hallway. She saw scuff marks on her walls, from the fight no doubt, and her back door was open too. Her condo was full of people, including the officers who'd been stationed outside and paramedics arriving with their bags and a transport chair.

She clung to Emmanuel's hand and shook her head. She didn't want to go to a hospital.

He pulled her into his arms and cuddled her close to his chest. "You're safe now. He's gone." He murmured more words in Spanish, too fast for her to understand.

"Wh-who," she stuttered. Trying to speak without pain was impossible. "Who was it?" she asked, wincing.

"Hush. Don't talk. Let the paramedics take a look."

She knew Emmanuel and the others had questions for her. She had questions of her own. But interviews had to wait until the paramedics were satisfied about her condition. They covered her bare legs with a blanket and gave her oxygen while they checked her vitals. Her blood pressure was up, as expected, but her lungs sounded clear.

"Do you want me to call Griffin or Kiely?" Emmanuel offered.

She shook her head. She wanted only him right now.

Emmanuel brought her tea laced with honey so she could answer a few preliminary questions about the assault. He drifted out of reach at one point, giving a statement or guiding the responding CSI to the crime scene. Thankfully, it wasn't her younger sister Sadie. She didn't want anyone else to see her while she felt so fragile. It occurred to her then that her bedroom was a crime scene, and tears rolled down her cheeks.

"Keep breathing," one paramedic said. "Easy and smooth."

She tried to comply, but it was easier when Emmanuel was close again, his hand stroking through her hair. When she refused a trip to the hospital, the paramedics left her with a cold pack and instructions, urging her to follow up with her doctor as soon as possible.

"You should go," Emmanuel said. "They can give you something for the pain."

"The cold pack is fine," she said with a croak.

"Please, don't talk." He escorted the CSI to the door, and finally it was just the two of them in the condo.

"Who was it?" she asked.

"*Shh.* I don't know," Emmanuel replied. "He wore a ski mask."

"And gloves." She turned the cold pack. "Did you catch him?"

"I couldn't get that mask off before he made it out the back door." His scowl was fierce, and it remained so even after he scrubbed at his face. "You sure you don't want a doctor?"

She shook her head. There was more he wasn't saying, but she didn't have the energy to press him for answers or theories.

Gently, he tipped back her chin and moved the ice

pack to examine her throat. "The scene is processed," he said. "You can change clothes and take a shower if you want. I'll keep watch out here."

"Gloves," she repeated. "No prints."

"I'm begging you, Pippa. Please stop talking."

The worry on his face made it all so much worse. She had to talk to communicate, but when she flinched with pain, she saw it reflected in his eyes, so she kept her mouth shut. Her body felt stiff and sore as she headed down the hall. At her bedroom door, she halted, unsure if she could walk in alone.

Emmanuel was right on her heels, and she turned into his arms. His hands moved up and down her spine, comforting and gentle. "You saved me," she said, unable to hold it in any longer. She'd nearly become a statistic tonight. "Thank you."

"They took pictures and bagged most everything in your room," he explained. His cheeks colored. "Faster that way. I had to tell them I was here too."

It wasn't ideal, but it was better to volunteer the information than try to hide it and raise more questions. "How did the man get inside?"

Emmanuel grumbled something incoherent. "Somehow he sneaked past the unmarked cars and bypassed your electronic dead bolt with a key."

So she wasn't safe here anymore. Without the panic button she probably wouldn't be alive. The tremors of shock started in earnest, and Emmanuel picked her up and carried her back to the couch, wrapping her in a quilt. "I'll make more tea."

When he returned, she sipped the tea, letting the honey soothe her sore throat while he explained the events from his perspective. "I got the alert that the panic button went off," he began. "As I told the others, I charged up here to help. Your door was unlocked, not open. I followed the noises to the bedroom and knocked the man off of you. We went a few rounds on the floor and down the hallway. He was clearly aiming for the back door."

So the man knew the condo layout, if not her condo in particular.

"He seemed pretty familiar with the layout," Emmanuel confirmed her unspoken question. "In the back hall he knocked me into the fire extinguisher, and was down the steps before I recovered. I knew the other team was out there so I came back for you."

"Thank you," she whispered.

"There may be some follow-up questions by tomorrow."

This time she nodded, rather than worry him with the sound of her voice. When she looked at him, she wanted to cry all over again. Bracing against that, she stood up. "Shower."

This time she would make it all the way to her bathroom. She needed to wash away the memory of those horrible hands. It felt as if the attacker's breath through the ski mask had stained her skin. Stale breath and sweaty wool were not a good combination.

"Do you need help?" he offered.

She desperately wanted to say no, to be the independent woman she'd been before the assault. But at her bedroom door her feet froze again. The attack was too fresh. She turned toward the guest room. "I'll use the second bath." It had the supplies her twin sister preferred, but it would work for tonight.

"I'll get some clothes for you," he said.

She pointed at him. "Not leaving?"

"No."

The simple answer did more good for her than a longer explanation. "Thank you."

He pressed a finger to his lips. *"Shh."*

Everything was neat and tidy in the guest room and a stark contrast to the mess she knew was waiting in her bedroom. For right now, all she could manage was getting clean enough to feel safe in her skin. After that she'd figure out how to feel safe in her home.

When she stepped out of the shower, her hair dryer was on the counter along with a glass of water and a bottle of ibuprofen. Cozy flannel pants in a deep green plaid, a thermal shirt and thick socks were stacked neatly for her, as well. She didn't even care that he'd gone through her drawers to find the clothing.

"You okay?" he asked from the other side of the bedroom door.

The man was standing guard for her in the hallway. Her heart tripped and fell. He'd seen her naked hours ago, but he didn't presume that gave him the right to hover too close now. Still, he guaranteed she could feel safe. Were they back to the original detective and attorney status or were they walking at the fringes of friendship?

"Yes," she said. Although it hurt, she pitched her voice loud enough that he could hear. Was it vanity or fear that had her wondering how long it would take her voice to recover?

Dressed and ready for another cold pack, she opened the door all the way, grateful for his respect of her privacy. She stared up at him, knowing he didn't want her to speak, but needing to show him how much his kindness mattered.

She wound her arms around his waist and rested her head on his chest.

He let her hang on, his arms banding around her carefully, as if he was afraid she might break.

"You'll let me stay tonight? Inside," he clarified.

She nodded, her cheek rubbing against the warm, solid wall of his chest. She was so thankful she didn't have to be alone.

Chapter Ten

Emmanuel understood Pippa's restlessness. She wasn't ready to rest, despite the pain and exhaustion plaguing her. He knew there were things she wanted to talk about, and there were things he needed to say. Once she'd relaxed a bit, he guided her back toward her living room.

"Do you want coffee?" she asked.

She didn't sound at all like herself. Her smooth, often prim voice was rough and damaged. "I'll make it," he said. "Do you want more tea?" She shook her head. "How about hot chocolate?"

He was relieved when she nodded her answer. Her throat needed time to rest, but she would want to hash through a few more details before she could settle.

When the coffee and hot chocolate were ready, they sank into opposite ends of her couch. She seemed steadier since her shower, but the signs of shock were still there. What he had to say wouldn't make it any better.

"I think I know who broke in tonight."

She raised her eyebrows, waiting with more patience than she'd ever shown before.

"Joe McRath." It didn't sound any better out loud than it did in his head. He was potentially accusing a decorated cop of doing the unthinkable. He wanted to catch the perp and he wanted to be wrong about the suspect. Maybe CSI would find evidence to lead them to a different conclusion. Catching his friend and mentor in an attempted murder was too bizarre to process.

Her brow flexed into a frown. "Saw his face?" she queried in her raspy voice.

"No." He sighed and leaned forward, bracing his elbows on his knees. "I've worked with him a long time. Trained with him, gone through various qualifications and exercises. The man under the hat and gloves and coat was built the same as Joe." Not enough for a confrontation or to take to the lieutenant. Just enough of a similarity that Emmanuel would have to take a closer look into why Joe might've done this.

"Not a Capital X attack?"

"No." He appreciated her brevity, though he had to hide the urge to cringe. Every word was a source of pain; he could see it in her eyes and the tension in her hands. He wished he'd insisted on a visit to the hospital.

He shook his head. "As you said, it would take some pretty speedy work to connect you and the alias loan application. They have no reason to suspect the application is a trap anyway. To hear Griffin tell it, the company has been operating outside of the law for years, and they're quite confident in their ability to keep it up."

"W Plenty of men are built like Joe."

He turned to catch her gaze. "Then call it instinct. Attacking you is minor compared to evidence tampering. It smells fishy, his daughter dating Hicks and Hicks dying at the home of his new lover, Anna. Joe has access to the evidence room, and I'm sure he has friends and ties to every prison in the state."

"To keep me away."

He nodded.

"But kill me and stage the scene?" Her gaze was skeptical.

Though he admired her willingness to be objective, Emmanuel was all but certain McRath had been under that ski mask. The sergeant had access to the building codes, and assuming he'd painted the threat on her wall, he would've had time to make a copy of the key for her front door that bypassed the electronic code.

"Who else?" he said. "He must have framed Wentworth. He knew about my dislike for the woman and complained frequently about her frivolous calls." He couldn't prove Joe was the culprit. Yet. "Nothing else adds up," he continued. "That evidence was laid out too neatly. You've said so yourself."

"A few times." She gave him a weary half smile.

Looking back, he could kick himself for following the breadcrumbs like an idiot newbie. And now all that perfectly planted evidence was gone.

Joe had access, and if he was guilty, he had motive to steal it out of the evidence room and threaten the lawyer determined to expose the real killer.

"Pippa, I'm going to dig deeper into McRath's connections to Wentworth and Hicks," he said. "He's been on the force long enough that she could have pissed him off a thousand times. Maybe it was just too much and he snapped."

Her eyes were still a little red from the attack and the subsequent lack of sleep. The stress was evident in the way her hand gripped the quilt over her lap. "She's difficult."

"More than difficult," he said. "Wentworth's calls

tied up good police officers, wasting time. Not something Joe would appreciate."

The marks on Pippa's neck were already deepening, and tomorrow Emmanuel would have to answer to Griffin. He was here to protect her, from herself and any outside threat. So far, he was failing in grand style.

"Emmanuel." Her hand slid over his, and the coolness of it slayed him. She was always so warm and vibrant. "Did you hear me?"

"Sorry, I was lost in thought."

She tapped her own brow. "I noticed." The smile she gave him was a shadow of her typical self. He wanted to bolt out of here, or just hold her all night long. Neither seemed like an acceptable solution.

"Be careful," she said. "If we're off track, we could wreck his reputation. Won't send another innocent person to jail."

"I get it," he said, pushing to his feet. He paced behind the back of the couch. "I still have to take a closer look. No one else on that list has access, ties or motive." He couldn't believe he was saying these things. "He was my mentor, Pippa. I don't want to wreck a good man or a good friendship either."

"Motive," she said. Her voice cracked and she coughed, her eyes tearing up. "Never motive in this case."

"And who should've found that motive the first time around? Me."

He couldn't bear the pain clouding those beautiful green eyes. "You need to get some rest. Voice and body. Even if it's not deep sleep, you need to rest," he said when she started to protest.

She opened her mouth again, and he cut her off

again. "Hush. If you lose your voice, you'll be more upset than you are now."

She glared at him.

"Finish your hot chocolate."

"Dictator," she whispered, once she'd polished off the warm drink.

He took the cup to the kitchen and came back for her. "Bedroom or couch?"

Her teeth sunk into her lower lip. "Couch."

"All right." He went to the guest room for pillows and a blanket and proceeded to tuck her in. "I'll take the chair." He kissed the worry that puckered her brow. "It beats the car," he joked.

When she was comfortable on the couch, he turned the lights down and settled into the chair, stretching out his legs. In the morning he would have another briefing with the officers who let the intruder through. And he would take another hard look for any evidence outside.

As much as he didn't want it to be Joe, he knew in his gut the sergeant was guilty. As Pippa said, he just had to figure out why, and then he could figure out the best path forward.

WHEN PIPPA WOKE AGAIN, early-morning sunlight was filtering through the front window. She wondered why she'd fallen asleep on the couch, and then all the chaos from last night came rushing back. Tears pricked the back of her eyes, but she would not start today as she ended yesterday. Sitting up, she rolled her stiff shoulders and gently stretched the battered muscles of her neck. Nothing a hot shower wouldn't fix.

Her cell phone was on the coffee table, but there was no sign of Emmanuel. The chair where he'd slept was empty, the pillow and blanket he'd used folded neatly in the seat. He'd probably gone home or even gone into the station early to get a jump on his new personal investigation.

His absence inexplicably irritated her, and she scolded herself for being out of sorts. She hadn't wanted a babysitter, and yet now that he was gone, she missed him. The man was entitled to live his life, regardless of the promise he'd made to her overprotective brother.

She checked her messages, mildly disappointed that he hadn't left her a text. Come to think of it, no one had reached out to her. The way information moved through the GRPD, Sadie must have heard about the attack. Pippa knew she could reach out, any of her siblings would happily give her a shoulder to cry on. But with everything going on, that comfort would surely turn protective and hiding wouldn't resolve this. Annoyed with her uncharacteristic neediness, she took a long, deep breath and slowly stretched her arms overhead. Getting to her feet, she padded to the half bath down the hall. She still wasn't ready to face her bedroom all by herself.

Had it been blissful ignorance or an ostrich mentality to believe things couldn't get worse after the break-in? That incident paled in comparison to last night's direct and violent attack. That man, whoever he'd been, was determined to silence her forever. To kill. She was alive thanks to Emmanuel's quick response. She should spend today celebrating being alive, rather than revisiting events that couldn't be changed.

Of course she felt violated and vulnerable, another stain on a home she loved. That was a basic human reaction to being attacked by a stranger in a familiar place. Once the wall was reset, she'd invite Kiely over and break out some champagne, reclaiming the space as hers. That was her approach to a setback: brazen it out and keep moving forward.

To hear her mom tell it, she'd been that way from the womb. While her twin sister might be more deliberate, once Pippa decided on a course of action, she ran with it. She had never seen the value in holding back.

This wouldn't be any different, no matter how hard her enemy came at her. Anna Wentworth was innocent, and she should not be in prison. If the process of freeing her caused Pippa some distress, so be it. This too would pass.

Ready to exit the bathroom, she heard footsteps in the hallway. Another intruder? Her heart raced and her fingers curled into fists. Damn, she didn't have her phone in here to call for help. She looked around the small space for anything she could turn into a weapon. As she tried to silently remove the heavy porcelain lid from the toilet tank, blood rushed through her ears, making it hard to distinguish the noises on the other side of the door.

At the knock on the door she had to stifle a scream, and the tank lid dropped back into place with a bang. Thankfully, it didn't break.

"Pippa? Are you okay in there?"

Not an intruder, Emmanuel. He hadn't left. She should've known better. Dropping her head against the door, she tried to catch her breath while her heart rate resumed a pace closer to normal.

"The shower's free," he said. "Sorry about that. Pippa?"

"I'm okay." Cursing her trembling hands, she unlocked the door and opened it. His smile smoothed the rough edges of her jangling nerves. "Good morning."

He winced at her voice. "Still hurts?"

She nodded. Somehow he looked as handsome as ever in yesterday's clothing. She just enjoyed the view with his damp hair curling at his collar and his beard neatly trimmed.

"I made a fresh pot of coffee, but I don't have time to do a full breakfast."

"No problem." She couldn't have eaten if she'd wanted to; her throat was so raw and tight it hurt to swallow more this morning than it had last night. Depending on how the coffee cooperated, she might try some soup later when her stomach woke up.

She followed him to the kitchen, where he clipped his badge to his belt and put the gun in its holster at his hip. "You're sure you're okay?"

Not at all, but she wouldn't be one more worry for him. "Go on," she insisted. "I need to go into the office today."

"All right." He dropped a quick kiss on her lips, the movement so easy and domestic it rattled her all over again. "Keep me in the loop about where you are today."

"You too."

"I promise." His sexy smile left her feeling feverish.

Normally she'd head straight to the shower, but she didn't want to reveal the weakness that she wasn't ready to face her own bedroom. For now, she had the excuse of seeing him off. She perched on a counter stool and watched him make a cup of coffee in a stainless travel mug, a little baffled to discover having him in her space felt so right. Something else to analyze later.

When he was all set, he came around the counter

and kissed her again. "Whatever you need, ask," he said. "There are two teams watching the building, and they have instructions to follow you today, so behave."

Obviously she was putting out a seriously strong victim vibe, and that wasn't at all who she was. It certainly wasn't the type of person she wanted to be. "I'll behave."

His phone hummed in his pocket. Checking the display, he groaned. "I forgot. My uncle will be here in about an hour to change the lock on your front door. I notified your siblings and assured them you were fine and had it under control. I'll check in on you throughout the day. Don't bother getting mad about any of it."

She laughed, but the sound was more of a rusty snort.

"Lock up behind me." He paused at the front door, indulging in one more kiss before he walked out.

Knowing he was waiting to hear the lock tumble, she flipped the dead bolt right away. Would it make any difference to the man with a copy of her key? Fear swamped her and her knees buckled. She slid to the floor, hoping she could drag herself up again when his uncle arrived.

She pushed her hair back from her face and tugged hard until her scalp stung. The discomfort cut through the fear and she stood up. It was either sell the condo or start reclaiming it as her own. Running was the coward's way. She would not let the person behind these attacks change her life.

She turned the fan and dehumidifier back on and then paused in the kitchen for a few careful sips of coffee. Next stop, the bedroom. She would never claim her steps were steady, but she made it to the doorway.

She expected to see remnants of the attack. The tangled sheets, the overturned lamp, the books from her nightstand she had used as weapons.

Tears dribbled down her cheek, but this time it was a wash of gratitude. Somewhere between tucking her in on the couch and making coffee this morning, Emmanuel had changed her sheets and made her bed, minus the duvet. He'd cleaned up the broken lamp and stacked her books in an orderly pile. Other than the missing lamp and duvet, everything was in its place. Her entire body relaxed; the sensation was almost as effective as having him here.

The man was a saint. She never thought to associate that term with the name Emmanuel Iglesias. From the moment she'd read the transcript of his testimony, he'd been her enemy. Now he was her partner in this convoluted pursuit of justice.

Her partner in more than that, if she was honest with herself.

Shoulders back, she marched through to her bathroom and turned on the water for a shower. Scrubbing clean again helped restore a sense of self and purpose. When she was dressed for the day in a cozy turtleneck that hid the bruises and makeup was deftly applied to blur the signs of her rough night, she took a cup of coffee into her office.

The original plan was for her to work from home while she waited for the approval on the Capital X loan application. The break-in and attack had cost her enough time and confidence. Anna was counting on her to make real progress, and fast.

Every minute alone, despite the precautions, her agitation grew until it was an itch down to her bones. It was ridiculous to look over her shoulder in her home.

She had to stay until the lock was repaired, but she couldn't work here all day. She'd just come back when the cleaning crew was ready to reclaim their equipment.

Technically she needed to open the computer only long enough to check the progress on the application and look for the approval email. Still alone, she opened her floor safe and withdrew the laptop. It booted within moments, and she confirmed there were no issues with her application. She just had to wait. She'd locked it away again when her phone rang.

Glancing at the caller ID, she saw it was Elizabeth. It was tempting to ignore the call and send her friend to voice mail, but that would only delay the inevitable. "Good morning, Elizabeth," she answered brightly to hide the rasp in her voice.

"I know I'm being a pain," Elizabeth said. "But is there any news?"

Since last night? Pippa stroked the soft fabric of her cashmere turtleneck, searching for patience. "Nothing definitive," she said, thinking of Emmanuel's theory. "It takes time, but as I said last night, we are making progress."

"Be honest, Pippa. Do you really think you can get her out?"

Pippa reminded herself that Elizabeth was a good friend. Her best friend, in fact. But she couldn't offer any guarantees. She had to stop and sip her coffee to soothe her throat. "Every step forward gets us a little closer." That much was true.

"Thank you." Elizabeth sighed. "I don't know what I'd do without you."

It gave her a boost to hear those words. "I do understand. You're worried, and I know this is urgent." Even more so now that Anna was taking RevitaYou.

"I'm going to see her again today," Elizabeth said. "At this rate, I might be better off buying a place near the prison."

"Don't go looking at real estate just yet," Pippa said.

"I don't trust the prison to tell me if she gets sick off that junk she's taking. She claims the supplement is offsetting the lousy food. You'd think prison would be a wake-up call, but she's as appearance focused as ever."

Despite everything, Pippa laughed. "When it comes to your mother, I wouldn't expect sweeping changes. She's far from typical, and you love her for it."

"True enough," Elizabeth said. "What's wrong with your voice?"

"Just allergies," she fibbed.

"Uck. I'm sorry my high from yesterday didn't last long."

Pippa searched for reassuring words. The police certainly hadn't been inclined to help her. Everyone on the jury was willing to think the worst of Anna. She wanted to meet with her client and ask the questions no one bothered to ask the first time around. "Has she talked at all about Hicks's connections? It's possible he confided in her about someone else wanting to hurt him."

"No," Elizabeth replied. "It's on my list of topics to tackle today. She is a little more approachable these days. Or maybe it seems that way because she can't dash off on her own agenda. Most days she seems genuinely happy to see me."

That was a different kind of progress all together and one long overdue in Pippa's opinion. Anna was never a touchy-feely kind of mother, though she was devoted to Elizabeth in her own way.

"I'll keep up the visits," Elizabeth said. "Maybe they're doing some group-therapy thing. It can't be the RevitaYou that's giving me a nicer version of mom lately."

Pippa chuckled. "I'm sure it's not."

"I'll let you get back to work. Take care of those allergies."

"Thanks. I'll keep you posted," Pippa promised as they ended the call.

In the silence that followed, Pippa's skin started to crawl. Thankfully, Emmanuel's uncle showed up. While he worked, she admitted defeat and packed a bag to go to the office as soon as he was finished. Better to make some progress there than stew over all the things she couldn't control here.

Once the new lock was in and working, and programmed, she paid for both new locks. Then she notified Emmanuel and let him tell the teams about her change in plans. She made it to the car without hyperventilating, and as she drove out of the lot, she decided that being in the car gave her a good reason to look over her shoulder.

On the short drive across town, she got a call from Kiely and answered using her voice commands.

Naturally the car didn't recognize her voice, and the call went to voice mail. Her sister called back immediately, and Pippa tried again—and failed again—to pick up. She listened to the voice mail as soon as it came through.

"Hey, Pippa. Just checking in on you. On *you*, not the case," Kiely clarified. "Griffin told us there was more trouble at your condo overnight. Call me back when you get this."

Pippa unwrapped a hard candy to soothe her throat, sucking on it for the duration of the drive. When she was parked in her space at the office, she called Kiely back.

"Pippa!" Kiely sounded relieved.

"Hi," she croaked.

"Oh, no. What happened?" Unlike Elizabeth, her sister picked up on the trouble in her voice immediately. Pippa reminded herself she was thankful for a big family. "If I told you I had a cold, would you believe me?"

"Not a chance. You're never sick," Kiely replied.

"Well, first of all, other than the voice and a few bruises, I'm perfectly okay," Pippa assured her. "There was another break-in, yes." Best to give Kiely the facts only. "We did not catch the intruder, and the GRPD has all the available evidence at their lab."

"We?" Kiely had that tone, the one Pippa knew she couldn't avoid. "Was someone staying over?"

"For a private investigator, you pick up on the wrong details," Pippa said. "And you're completely off track."

"Stop dodging the question."

"I said *we* as it refers to the protective detail Detective Iglesias assigned to watch the condo." It was only half a lie. A fib, really, and mostly for the sake of privacy.

"They did a lousy job if an intruder got past them," Kiely pointed out. "I'm coming over."

"Then turn around. I'm at the office." It was probably a good idea. "Come to the office anyway. The lock at my front door is completely new. There's no key option. And I have your new code."

She chose to wait at the car rather than face her sister in the office, where they might be overheard. Opening the app on her new door lock, she used the remote option to set a code for Kiely. The rest of her siblings would have to knock for a while.

Kiely parked and hurried to Pippa's car. Naturally her sister saw straight through the makeup and clothing as she climbed out from the driver's seat. "Pippa! What happened? You look like hell." She pulled Pippa in for a gentle hug.

"Thanks. I feel worse."

"Then go home," Kiely said. "Oh. I get that."

Pippa was grateful she didn't have to say a word for her twin to understand the higher stress of staying home. "The attack last night was direct. Emmanuel called it attempted murder when he gave his statement. No real damage to the condo, just me." She pulled down her turtleneck, showing the bruises on her throat. "At least I can talk today."

"If sandpaper could talk, maybe."

Pippa chuckled, then coughed. Just telling the watered-down version of the story face-to-face made her feel weak. She cleared her throat.

Kiely straightened her collar. "You need a security system."

"I had electronic locks in a secure building. I have better smart locks now. With a doorbell camera." Pippa didn't explain Emmanuel's role in the quick and expert lock service.

"Good." Kiely looked to the office, then at some point behind Pippa's shoulder. It was all she could do to stand there and not panic. "You have to let the Wentworth case go," Kiely declared.

That was the last thing Pippa expected to hear.

"You know I can't do that." Her throat burned, but she wouldn't let Kiely run roughshod over her life and career. "I won't drop a case or unpopular client just because things get dicey."

Kiely sighed heavily. "I know." She smiled. "Can't blame a sister for trying. At the very least you have to bring in some sort of personal protection."

"A bodyguard?" Pippa rolled her eyes. "Griffin already did that."

Kiely laughed. "The detective?"

Pippa nodded. "I should get inside and do some real work. Can we talk about this more later?"

"You're into him," Kiely stated. Then she beamed. "Tell me everything."

"Stop." Pippa wanted to smack that look off her sister's face. "This is not the time or place."

"Fine. But I will find out. From you or another reliable source." Kiely pulled her keys from her pocket. "Any word on the other case?"

"Still early, but you and Riley will be the first to know."

"Sounds good." She gave her another hug. "Call me if you need anything. And don't overdo it."

Pippa wanted to be snarky, but between her sore throat and her sister quickly dashing back to her car, the opportunity was missed. She hauled everything into the office and settled in behind her desk. She felt so much better here than at home.

In the privacy of her office, she pulled out the laptop for Alison Carrington and checked on the email account. No alerts from Capital X, only a customer service survey from the store where Kiely had purchased the laptop.

Satisfied she couldn't do more on that front, Pippa shut down the alias's laptop and stowed it back in her bag under her desk. Then she resumed her search for the real killer in the Hicks case. How close could she get to Leigh McRath without alerting the father? Pippa reviewed all of the personal details she had on Hicks. According to the prosecutor, Anna had been jealous of a different lover as well as threatened by his blackmail attempt.

No other lover was ever identified in the court proceedings, but the prosecutor only needed to create doubt. Hicks had a reputation as a player in high society, and that had been verified over and over again with a parade of witnesses that Anna had glowered at during the trial. Hicks's credit card history backed up an active and extravagant dating life. It seemed as if he blackmailed one lover to finance lavish dates and entertainment with another.

Definitely a slimeball, although handsome enough and connected enough to tempt Anna. She adored handsome men; moreover, she thrived on being the center of attention. Pippa wondered if anyone from his family would speak with her about his social life. It wasn't exactly a breach of protocol, and Emmanuel couldn't be the only one taking risks here.

She reached for the phone just as her older brother Griffin filled the office doorway. His expression was thunderous. "What in the hell are you doing here?"

"I beg your pardon." Thanks to the sore throat, she couldn't work up a proper snippy tone. "This is a place of business," she said. "You're out of line."

He stepped inside and closed the door behind him. Rather than take a seat in a visitor's chair, he rounded to her side of the desk, crouching in front of her. The temper brewing in his eyes softened to concern. "Show me."

"You're not my boss or my doctor."

"Technically, I'm sort of your boss."

She latched on to the only excuse she could think of. "This is related to a situation that you are not the boss of."

"Pippa. Show me."

She wanted to argue, but her throat hurt. He'd get his way eventually. "It will only make you mad."

"I'm already mad." He rested his hands lightly on her knees. "Come on. I don't want to see you hurt."

"Then I definitely shouldn't show you."

"Stop talking like a lawyer." His lips twitched. "I mopped the floor with you in debate club."

"That was high school." He'd been two years ahead of her and far more experienced. "Only once."

"I need to know that you're okay."

"It's not enough that I'm sitting right here, the picture of health?"

"Your voice sounds like you're chewing gravel even when you're speaking softly."

Resisting wasn't going to get him out of her way, and she had work to do for Anna and Elizabeth. Choosing efficiency, she drew the turtleneck down so he could see the marks on her neck.

Griffin cursed. "I'm so sorry."

"Not your fault." She adjusted her sweater and stiffened her spine. "I appreciate your concern, but this has no bearing on you as a protective big brother or CI partner." She shooed him back to the other side of the desk. If this concerned-brother routine went on much longer, she might burst into tears, and that would be a disaster.

"Did you see a doctor?" Griffin asked.

"No need. The paramedics checked me over."

"Let's get you a protective detail."

"You already did that," she said. "And before you suggest it, I'm not walking around in bubble wrap, body armor, or with a full entourage of bulky men in dark suits and sunglasses. Detective Iglesias and his unmarked cars are enough."

Griffin's lips tilted at one corner. "What about stretchy velvet tracksuits and sunglasses? You can choose the color they wear."

"Get out of my office," she said, thoroughly exasperated. If he was cracking jokes, he was confident she'd survive.

"I thought Emmanuel could handle this," Griffin muttered.

"He did." She felt heat creeping into her cheeks.

Without Emmanuel she would not be sitting here today. She'd be in a hospital bed at the very least, more likely the morgue if the intruder had had his way. None of that was safe to say around her brother. She hadn't mentioned it, not even to Emmanuel, but she'd recognized the deadly intent in the man's breath, not just his grip.

"Emmanuel said you didn't get a description of the assailant." Griffin shoved his hands into his pockets.

Of course they'd talked in detail. "Emmanuel and the responding officers had better notes about his size and build. All I saw was the black ski mask, gloves and coat."

Griffin sank into a chair. "I heard. I came over hoping to get more to go on."

"Trust me, I'd love to give you more, but the man

wasn't kind enough to attack me in daylight without a mask."

"Riley and I talked. It's best if you move back into the house until this blows over."

"No." She wanted to shout and yell at her brother for being an idiot. Out of respect for the resulting pain, she checked the urge. She smiled instead, an expression she knew her brother would recognize as false. "I'm an adult. My home and the new safety measures in place are sufficient." How could she explain that if she left, she'd only be more afraid to return? "And I'm staying on the Wentworth case until that innocent woman is out of jail."

He started to protest, but she cut him off. "Save your breath. Have you seen or heard from Brody?"

"Still in the wind," Griffin said, honoring the change of subject. "Let's all have dinner at the house. I'll get everybody together and—"

"No, thank you," she said. "I really can't cope with that. I'm tired," she confessed. "There are a few tasks I need to check off my list, then I'm going home, having soup and going to bed early."

Griffin opened his mouth and wisely snapped it shut. "All right. But you've got all of us at your back. Remember that."

He came around the desk again and helped her up so he could hug her. She didn't resist; in fact, she let herself lean just a little. "You are an excellent big brother," she said. "Bossy and overprotective, but excellent." Stepping away from him she added, "I'll let you know when the approval comes through from Capital X."

She could see how badly he wanted to say that didn't matter, but neither of them would believe it.

"I'll leave you to it." He paused at the door. "One last thing? Don't be afraid to ask for help."

"I promise."

With the office to herself again, she was just digging into her case file, making a plan, when Sadie stopped by, followed soon after by Riley. A veritable parade of siblings needing to see her with their own eyes.

In between, she fielded text message check-ins from Emmanuel. Somehow those didn't bother her. By the time she actually succeeded in dialing the number for Hicks's mother, she was almost grateful no one picked up. She left a voice message with her name and number anyway, assuring the woman she only wanted true justice for her son by making sure the right person was behind bars.

Only time would tell if that call had any impact or value for Anna.

In the meantime, she returned to the task of evaluating the victim's credit card records and banking history, matching the dates he'd been out with other women to the gossip columns in the local papers.

She couldn't call the man discreet, but he didn't seem prone to drawing undue attention when he was out at events or on casual dates. There were several pictures of Hicks with one particular woman around the holidays last year. But that was the closest she could come to finding anything that might qualify as a relationship. Nothing criminal in that. Unfortunately it gave her no leads.

Her stomach growled, and she remembered she hadn't eaten anything today. It was already past six. She checked her phone for any updates from Emmanuel, but he hadn't reached out since three, when he told her things were slow during his time on the tip line the GRPD had set up for information on the key players in the RevitaYou crisis.

Though they hadn't made any formal plans or declarations, she assumed he would show up at her place at some point this evening. Too weary to cook, she looked over the menu online of her favorite sandwich shop. She could pick up a meal for him and soup for herself and be ready to feed them both, or have extras for tomorrow.

Deciding to check one last time for any news on the loan application, she turned on the laptop and logged on with the alias's information. Once she opened the email, she saw the message from Capital X. Apparently they were moving through the approval process with lightning speed.

She opened the email, and her hand immediately touched her throat as she read through the information. They had approved Alison Carrington's loan request for $25,000 at a 30 percent interest rate. For the life of her, she didn't understand how people fell for such outrageous terms.

The schedule showed the first payment would be due in three days. Not a lot of time for an initial, legitimate investment to yield a return. A smart applicant would hold back the amount of the first payment from the original loan amount or risk getting in deeper.

All she had to do was click Accept. The money would be transferred and the clock would start ticking. It wasn't even real. She was doing this to protect real applicants, people who didn't know better and felt as if they had no other solutions beyond the Capital X financial abuse.

She checked the box to accept the repayment schedule, and the screen changed. The next section was an acknowledgement that, in the event of a missed payment, Capital X had the right to adjust the interest rate, call in the entirety of the loan, and take any and all required action to recoup their investment.

A chill iced her skin. Understanding the Capital X tactics, she knew that any sincere applicant who accepted the terms was setting themselves up for broken bones at best. With Capital X so adept at eluding investigators and criminal lawsuits so far, Pippa could imagine what they would do if they figured out she had fooled them with an alias.

She reviewed all of the sections one more time, agreeing to the disastrous terms and accepting the loan. For Brody. For all the others who had been hurt or injured. CI would close down the Capital X operation permanently.

Another email came through within minutes so she could provide the routing number and specify where she wanted the deposit placed. In the case of this alias, the money would sit idly in an account, only to be used later as proof against Capital X.

Turning off the computer, she packed it back into the bag. She sent a group text message to Riley, Griffin and Kiely, with the full update and first payment due date. The reply came back in record time; the woman fulfilling the role as Alison Carrington was in place. Somehow Riley and the GRPD had come to terms about using an undercover officer to impersonate the alias and give Capital X enforcers a physical target.

The woman was bait. Trained and willing, but still bait. Her job was to reel in the enforcers so the police had an opportunity to turn those brutes against the people calling the shots at Capital X.

She tidied her office, per her habit, putting everything in its place before she left. With a little luck the CI team could soon have actionable leads on Capital X and Brody could come out of hiding.

Chapter Eleven

When Emmanuel met Pippa at her condo that evening, they compared notes, and he learned his day hadn't been much more productive than hers. He hadn't had visits from siblings, but he'd bumped up against dead end after dead end trying to track the attacker's escape from her building. Such expert avoidance of traffic cams and the unmarked cars only fueled his theory that the intruder was indeed Joe McRath.

The sergeant had called out sick that day, all the more suspicious in Emmanuel's mind, though it made it easier for Emmanuel to return to the evidence room. No surprise the Wentworth case box was still missing. With the lieutenant's permission he had been reviewing the video footage of the evidence room, and he'd found discrepancies that warranted a closer look. On two occasions, Joe showed up on the video when he hadn't officially signed the log. It wasn't enough to take to the lieutenant, but he added it to the file he was building.

Over a sandwich piled high with thick slices of juicy roast beef for him and a bowl of vegetable soup for her, he shifted to simpler topics. The good news was the repaired wall was dry and the noisy equipment was gone.

The quiet was clearly a relief to her, but he could tell she was sore and tired.

"I need to decide if I'll repaint or try something new."

"Go new," he suggested. "It can be a fresh start."

She tipped her head, considering. "I know feeling shaky is par for the course after what happened, so I don't want to rush that decision."

"It is a big wall," he teased. Personally, he thought doing something different was a good opportunity to put a division between the bad that had happened and moving forward.

Her amusement faded, and she pushed the remainder of soup around the bowl with her spoon. "I'm glad you're here." She took a deep breath and lifted her gaze to meet his. "I'm really glad you were close last night. Thank you," she finished, her voice cracking.

"You want me to stay over again?"

She nodded. "Please. If you want to."

"Whatever you need." He'd packed an overnight bag just in case. Reaching out, he covered her hand with his. "I really don't want to be anywhere else, sweetheart."

She bit her lip and her eyes misted, though she blinked before the tears could spill over. He decided his thought about the two of them could wait until a better time. Feeling vulnerable was unfamiliar territory for her, and he didn't want her confusing his feelings with the circumstances.

"The deli threw in a dozen cookies," she managed after a sniffle. "Chocolate chip."

"What do you say to cookies and milk and reruns?"

She smiled, that sparkle faint, but evident in her green eyes. "I'm in."

They demolished the cookies and milk and she snuggled next to him, quickly drifting off as they watched a series of mindless reruns on television. When she was sound asleep, he carried her to bed and stretched out beside her, pleased beyond reason when she curled into his body, holding him close.

He stared at the ceiling, thinking of the next move for both of them, creating a mental timeline for himself. Everyone would be counting down the hours to the missed Capital X payment. While Pippa had to stay away from all of that, Emmanuel planned to be close to the undercover officer when that deadline approached.

Until then, he had nothing but time to figure out how to get some kind of proof that Joe was involved with the attack last night, and the framing of Anna Wentworth months ago.

PIPPA COULD PRACTICALLY hear the clock ticking toward the first payment deadline. All she had to do now was stay away from the Alison Carrington address, keep the laptop turned off and focus on the rest of her life.

If only it was as easy to do as it was to say.

It helped to have Emmanuel as close as a text message throughout the day, and she appreciated his presence keeping the nightmares at bay while she slept. As much as she valued her independence, he managed to give her support and care without stifling her. A strange and rare combination that she could get used to.

Would he want that, or was this closeness between them just a fluke of an ongoing investigation?

A final decision would have to wait. Elizabeth was still calling before and after every visit to the prison, and try as she might, Pippa wasn't making the strides necessary to pinpoint an event that led to murder.

An attorney for Hicks's mother had returned her calls, strongly suggesting she leave the family alone. She had to believe that closed door only put her closer to the right path.

Who had wanted that man dead, and why commit the crime on the Wentworth estate?

As much as Emmanuel believed McRath was involved and continued to pursue proof through his channels at the GRPD, Pippa wanted to find the real killer. Was it Leigh? Parents notoriously went to extremes to shelter their kids from consequences. Evidence tampering could be a felony. Would Joe risk his career and reputation to protect Leigh? If he had manipulated a case as publicized as the Hicks murder once before, it couldn't be his first. Everything had been set up too perfectly to frame Anna.

Her stomach churned. Did practice make perfect? Finding proof he'd mishandled previous cases would definitely bring the Wentworth case up for review. That helped, but still left the real killer unpunished.

Hicks had dumped Leigh McRath for Anna. Betrayal could cut deep, especially when compounded by a broken heart. But why would Leigh wait six months to act out? Crimes of passion usually merited an immediate reaction. Pippa couldn't see Joe having a motive for the murder. Most fathers would be relieved to learn that a man as slippery as Hicks was out of a daughter's life.

SHE DIDN'T HAVE enough to take to a judge or anyone else for a new trial. A press conference would be a flimsy publicity stunt at this point, and it could backfire in spectacular fashion. Trashing her reputation was one thing. Pippa didn't want Emmanuel getting twisted up in her pet project, especially if they were wrong. The whole point of this effort was to find the real killer, not drag another innocent person through the mud.

Her cell phone buzzed against the surface of her desk, and she smiled at the text message from Emmanuel. He was on his way and bringing food. Feeling better, she probably should have cooked, but that would have to wait for another night.

Listening for him, she opened the door before he could knock and was rewarded with the savory aromas of salsa and hot spices. The bag in his hand was from one of her favorite Mexican restaurants. Her mouth watered in anticipation of the meal and the man.

His smile was temptation and a handsome distraction from her swirling, go-nowhere case. She stepped back, and her stomach rumbled loud enough that he laughed in response as he walked inside.

"Didn't you eat at all today?" He strode directly to the kitchen.

How had he already figured out that she often forgot to eat? "I had a good breakfast." The breakfast they'd shared before he'd gone into the station.

He arched an eyebrow. "Pippa," he scolded lightly.

"I know, I know." She lifted her hair up to the top of her head, then let it fall. "I went into the office, then drove by the Wentworth estate. I would've eaten if I'd made it to the gym," she added, hearing the excuses. "My appetite is just—"

He cut her off with a kiss, and her appetite for food evaporated again. She pressed her body close, her fingers curling into his jacket, as she took the kiss deeper. For the past two days, he'd been treating her as if she was fragile, but she felt strong enough for anything right now.

"Take me to bed," she said.

"The food?"

"Can wait." She unbuttoned her blouse as she darted down the hallway. He was right behind her, catching her as she turned. His gaze skated over the lingering marks on her neck, then lower to her breasts. She shimmied out of her skirt and stood before him in only her bra and panties, stockings and heels. Only this man made her feel so bold.

"Hold it," he said, his voice rough with desire. "This is a fantasy I intend to enjoy."

She whispered his name, over and over, as they came together in a whirl of passion and tenderness that overwhelmed and empowered in turns.

Only him. Only him with her. Only them together, reclaiming her bed and restoring her confidence. She soared under every touch and reveled in every sigh. When at last they were sated, she knew her world had changed.

She was falling in love.

She should tell him. If the last days had proven anything, tomorrow wasn't a guarantee. But if telling him drove him away, the challenges in the days ahead might just drown her. She needed him like she'd never needed anyone else.

HOURS LATER, AFTER a long and steamy shower for two, Emmanuel and Pippa made it back to the kitchen. He reheated the food and she poured wine. It was so natural, so easy and comfortable that he nearly blurted out the only three words on his mind.

He was falling for her.

Impossible, but true. However it had come to pass, he couldn't deny it anymore. She'd slipped under all of his preconceived notions and shifted something deep inside him. He couldn't wait to see her at the end of the day, and whether they spent the evening debating suspects or watching cartoons, he'd never been so content.

Could he tell her? Should he?

Not yet. Hell, it had only been days. And a rough few days for both of them. Would she be this willing to have him around once the Capital X and Wentworth cases were done?

There was the crux of it. He didn't dwell on fear often, but he couldn't shake it this time. She wouldn't be safe while the person who killed Hicks walked free.

After two straight days of trouble, the person harassing her—had to be Joe—had gone quiet. Was he injured or just planning his next move to reduce the risk of another failure?

He had to find a way to flush out the killer.

LATE THE NEXT MORNING, Pippa followed Leigh McRath to the juice bar with a pang of envy that the younger woman managed to look refreshed after leading the intense spin class. She'd signed up only as a way to get close to the woman without raising suspicions.

Pippa counted herself fit, but after this first spin class she never wanted to repeat the experience. Her legs felt like jelly, and she couldn't wait to get home and shower off the sweat and soreness. "Thanks for agreeing to chat with me," she began while the person behind the counter prepared their order.

Leigh's chin came up. "Talking with you is the last thing I want to do," she stated.

"You want justice for David," Pippa reminded her gently.

Leigh's lower lip quivered. "I miss David so much." She pressed a dollar bill into the tip jar when her smoothie was delivered. "Why are you so sure that Wentworth bitch didn't kill him?"

Pippa managed not to wince. Most people referred to her client in those terms or some variation. With good reason. "Well, there are actually several reasons. Unfortunately, I'm not at liberty to discuss them in detail."

"I was in that courtroom," Leigh said, her voice low and hot. "Difficult as it was, I listened to all of the testimony."

And along with everyone else, Leigh had seen those arrogant and careless above-it-all gestures from the defendant.

"The motive has always bothered me," Pippa explained with far more patience than she felt. "I've known Mrs. Wentworth for many years. She's certainly capable of being cold, rude and, yes, mean, but I don't believe she murdered your friend."

"He was *more* than a friend," Leigh sputtered.

"Yes, he was," Pippa agreed. "That was obvious from my research into the case. It's exactly why I came to see you."

Leigh's surprise was obvious and genuine. Nearby, she noticed Emmanuel walking past. Not close enough to be recognized by Leigh, but enough to remind her he was there. When he'd heard what she had planned, he refused to let her deal with it alone.

"They claimed he was blackmailing her," Leigh said. "He wasn't."

All of Pippa's preplanned questions dried up. Fact or fiction, she wondered as Leigh rambled on about everlasting love and all the plans she and David Hicks had been making.

"He didn't need her money," she insisted. "Well, fine. No one turns down easy cash, but he didn't *need* it."

"Regardless," Pippa interjected, "Anna wasn't afraid of his threat."

"Because he never threatened her," Leigh snapped. "You've got him all wrong."

Pippa refrained from mentioning the blackmail note that had been entered as evidence along with Hicks's previous patterns of bilking money from women. "I only meant Mr. and Mrs. Wentworth had an understanding about her extramarital affairs."

"Oh." Leigh blinked, her outrageous false eyelashes adding to the effect.

"Did you lend money to David when you were together?"

"Not a loan, an investment," Leigh said. "We had plans for a boutique fitness club until…" She pressed her lips together. "Until…"

Pippa had never understood how some women could cry so prettily.

"This is so difficult," Leigh managed, fanning her face. "I admit sometimes it annoyed me when David blatantly admired other women. But I was the one he came back to."

Pippa prodded Leigh a bit more until she had a couple of more names of women Hicks had "admired" while out with Leigh. Thanking her, Pippa took her smoothie and headed for the parking lot.

Emmanuel joined her as soon as she was out of sight of the juice bar. "You left her crying into her spinach smoothie."

"Kale," Pippa corrected, smothering a laugh. "She had kale and wheat berry, and I lost track after that. Her post-workout remedy is as much a mystery as the real killer."

He smiled as he held open her car door. "Did you get a lead?"

"Don't know yet. The names she mentioned didn't sound familiar."

"We'll figure it out."

She sat down behind the steering wheel and played with her keys. "Good thing we brought two cars," she said, zipping up her hoodie. She wasn't sure she'd stopped sweating yet. "That was one intense workout."

He grinned. "You're adorable when you pedal. Drink up. I'll follow you home."

Home. She smiled to herself through the entire drive. The man had a gift for making her heart feel lighter even when she was up against an insurmountable task. At first she'd thought his easy manner was a strategy as a detective. Now she knew it was just his way. These days, with everyone who recognized her shooting daggers at her or calling her names, it helped to know she had one person not named Colton or Wentworth on her side.

She turned into the driveway and pulled up at her assigned space behind her building and gawked at the mess that greeted her. Someone had dumped enough trash and kitchen scraps to fill her space, making it impossible for her to park. She drove on around to a guest space and walked back to take pictures and call it in.

Her legs were shaking, with anger rather than muscle overload now. Using her phone, she took several pictures. The odor alone made her post-spin-class-self smell like a daisy in a spring breeze. Just in case she thought this could be a coincidence, there was a sign in the center:

Leave the real trash in jail or else.

Or else what? Her condo had been invaded, twice, and now apparently the security was up to snuff, because her harasser had taken an easier shot at her today. Except it couldn't have been too easy to stage this without being spotted by someone. Still taking risks, still urging her to drop the Wentworth case.

She sent the pictures to Kiely for lack of a better immediate solution. What could be done? "I'm not stopping," she shouted, just in case the person who'd done this was watching and could hear her.

Emmanuel was striding over, having parked out front on the street as he normally did.

Seeing him, something deep inside snapped, and suddenly angry tears blurred her vision. She blinked furiously. She would *not* give her tormentor the satisfaction of knowing how much he'd upset her.

Lifting her chin and squaring her shoulders, she called building maintenance. This was just another roadblock in her way, nothing that would keep her from achieving her goal of proving Anna's innocence.

EMMANUEL BROKE INTO a jog when he saw Pippa standing in front of the space where her car should be. The smell hit him before the full scene struck home. Another threat, executed while she was away from home. Joe or one of his many connections had been watching her closely.

How closely was what worried him.

He caught her just as she charged forward as if she was going to shred that nasty sign with her bare hands. "Leave it. Let me call it in."

"Don't," she snapped. She twisted out of his grasp, but she didn't try to wade back into the mess.

"Why not? It's vandalism."

She swallowed, then her chin came up. "Because I'm done."

"Done with Wentworth?"

"No." She shot him a look that told him he should know her better than that. "I'm done playing games. We both know there won't be any helpful evidence in that pile of trash."

"We do not know that," he said, calmly.

She arched an eyebrow and folded her arms over her chest, daring him to come up with a better explanation.

"Fine." He took a good look, analyzing the scene. It was a common plastic kitchen trash bag split along a seam. Based on the astounding lack of evidence found at the other instances of harassment, she was right. They wouldn't find so much as a single fingerprint or helpful fiber. More confirmation of his theory that it was someone in the department working to keep Wentworth behind bars. "There's a chance someone got sloppy."

She rolled her eyes.

"Either way, you can't stay here anymore," he said, braced for an outburst.

"I will *not* be chased from my home," she snapped, her voice low.

He was about to suggest a compromise when her phone rang. "Kiely," she said to him as she answered. "Hi. I'm fine, stop worrying." A pause as she listened. "No." Another pause. "Yes." She glared at him. "My sister wants to talk with you."

"Hi, Kiely," he said, taking the phone as Pippa stalked back to her car.

"She didn't call the police?"

"Technically, I *am* the police," he reminded her, moving around the scene. "There aren't any obvious tracks, but I planned to take pictures before anything else happens. My thought was to shove this all into another bag and have the lab take a look anyway."

"Agreed." Kiely sighed. "I'll call Sadie to swing by. I know why Pippa doesn't want to bother anyone in the department, but if the perp made a mistake, it could be the break we all need."

"Exactly my thought," Emmanuel said. "I'll take care of it."

"Great. Thanks, Detective. And the next time we have a Colton family dinner or CI meeting, Griffin wants you to join us."

Not about to give an answer without clearing it with Pippa, he wasn't sure what to say. "Thanks."

Kiely chuckled and wished him luck before she ended the call.

"Here." Emmanuel walked over to Pippa's car and returned her phone.

"She's insisting you do something to investigate isn't she?"

"Yes."

She muttered an oath in French, her preference.

"I know you're tired of all of this, so why take a

chance that this time a critical error was made?" He could see her resistance to his logic, but he knew she'd come around. He held out his hand. "Come on, we'll go get a trash bag together."

She put her hand in his and they headed upstairs. It felt good to walk with her like this, as a team. As a couple.

"Building maintenance has extra bags," she said. "We can go in the back."

"All right." That would give him some time to think how they could best make a move that led to a resolution rather than more questions.

Chapter Twelve

The next morning Pippa was working at home again, too antsy for the office. The first payment to Capital X was officially overdue. She was trying to fit what Leigh had told her yesterday into the context of her notes from the official case file. Granted, her concentration was shot, knowing any minute now Capital X enforcers were likely to descend on the woman pretending to be Alison Carrington a few blocks away.

However her brother and the GRPD had coordinated the plan, Pippa couldn't get her mind off the risk to the undercover officer who had volunteered for this and the others who hoped to drop a net around the enforcers so they could unravel the operation.

Unlike Anna, Pippa had always valued the people who served the police department. It started with the example of her parents and the ways her siblings served the local police department and military justice, in the case of her other sister, Vikki. Spending this time with Emmanuel, falling for him, drove home the bigger risks of the people who chose to serve and protect the community. Pippa ran into the *proverbial* fire when necessary, but aside from these recent days, the direct physical danger was minimal. Would the woman work-ing undercover be able to avoid serious injury?

Considering all the bones Capital X broke in the name of business, she wondered if they had a kickback arrangement with local orthopedic specialists. Not that she expected doctors to be that corrupt, but referrals were a thing in every industry now.

Another totally irrelevant thought that had no bear-ing on what she needed to accomplish today.

She had to focus on the things only she could do. Kiely would give her the play-by-play if Capital X made a move on the Alison Carrington alias. Pushing away from her desk, she went to the kitchen to prepare a cup of tea.

Maybe the soothing brew would settle her racing thoughts. Leaving the tea on the counter to steep, she returned to her desk and the pictures of the scene when Hicks's body had been found.

Every time she studied this file, she did it knowing Anna was innocent. But a jury convicted her on this same evidence. Why? They had to have thought the in-formation backed Emmanuel's testimony.

The prosecutor presented a compelling case in court. A blood trail, the blackmail motive, even Anna's brooch at the scene. In the jury's shoes, with Anna's snobby reputation, that had probably been enough.

Anna had insisted on owning unique, often one-of-a-kind items, down to the smallest personal accessory. For years she'd seen it as a crime if someone else was spotted wearing the same outfit or jewelry design.

Like so many things, in Anna's view, David Hicks was technically disposable. Mr. Wentworth had put up with his wife's infidelity for years, most likely in an attempt to keep things stable for Elizabeth. Somehow staying married was less costly for the Wentworths than divorce. Factor in the negative publicity of a scandal affecting their charitable endeavors, and an objective person could find more motive for them to stay together.

Pippa knew marriages were tricky. By design the most intimate of partnerships, yet so often the most flawed. Maybe her view was skewed because of what had happened between her parents, but outsiders rarely got the full picture of another couple.

She turned the pictures of the crime scene around, studying them from all angles as Emmanuel would have done that day. The jewelry under the body bothered her almost as much as the idea of Anna doing the messy work of murder.

How long had the body been there before the coroner turned it over and found that brooch?

She checked the report and could only guess that Joe McRath might have had time to walk the house, find the brooch and plant it.

Anna was in a rarefied class all her own, but she wasn't stupid. Caught up in the moment or not, she wouldn't leave a piece like this behind. Her mind did not operate that way. Pippa closed her eyes and imagined Anna overlooking the moment when a prized piece went missing.

It just wasn't possible. Elizabeth's mother wasn't the kind of woman to ignore that kind of sparkle. According to the time of death, it had been a sunny day. The sunlight would've caught in those stones, and based on the location of the body, if the brooch had fallen to the grass, Anna would have noticed.

If Emmanuel hadn't planted the brooch—and she

knew he had not—it had to be McRath. The reports gave no indication of any other police officers entering the private suites in the Wentworth mansion until after the coroner cleared the body for transport. That was enough to get someone's attention, possibly enough attention to reopen the case.

Before she blurted it all out to a judge, or hinted at it in the media, she'd like to know why an honorable, decorated cop like Joe snapped. Whether or not McRath killed Hicks—and for the life of her she couldn't figure out why he would—only McRath had the opportunity to stage the scene so completely for his partner on that day, Emmanuel.

Would evidence tampering be enough to free Anna?

Could she prove it? Even Emmanuel, a seasoned detective, had not realized the murder scene was staged. And she would do anything to avoid the embarrassment of having him admit he'd been fooled. Her goal here was to free an innocent woman, Anna, not tarnish Emmanuel's reputation. With their recent personal involvement, if he changed his mind now about what he had seen then, his motives would be suspect. A detective working with a lawyer to free a convicted killer? She didn't want to think about the severe fallout that would rain down on him.

There had to be a way for her to draw out Joe.

EMMANUEL WALKED INTO the coffee shop near the "Alison Carrington" apartment and placed his order. Though it seemed normal, there was nothing relaxed about this particular morning. Everyone was braced for an unprovoked attack. While he waited for his order, his thoughts wandered back to that first day when Pippa had brought coffee to him in his car.

He hadn't been at his best in that moment, having just learned of Ingrid's death by RevitaYou. She'd shown tremendous compassion and unforgettable hospitality. He might have started falling in love with her right then.

Coffee in hand, he left the shop and strolled on down the block. To anyone watching, he was another man distracted by his phone, although he was alert to any danger or disturbance. He knew where the GRPD spotters were located. He knew where Kiely and Riley were hiding.

Emmanuel's only role here was as extra support.

The female officer playing the part of Alison took a seat at an outdoor table with her coffee and a small takeout. Working undercover wasn't nearly as easy as it seemed on television. It could be equal parts boring and extreme. In this instance, Emmanuel was strung up tight as a bow.

Set on silent, his phone lit up with an incoming call from Griffin. "What are you doing out here this morning?" his friend asked.

"You can't expect me to sit this one out," he replied.

"I can expect you to keep an eye on my sister like we agreed," Griffin said. "She's not here, is she?"

"She's working from home. I just checked in with her."

"Why doesn't that make me feel better?"

Emmanuel assumed it was because Griffin had plenty of experience with the daring nature of his sisters. "If I wasn't out here, she would be," he said instead.

"What's going on with you two?" Griffin asked.

He'd known this conversation would happen, but the

timing couldn't be worse. He walked along, circling the block. "I'm keeping an eye on her."

"Pretty close eye."

"Seriously? You just accused me of not being close enough."

Griffin might have laughed. "Stop before I need brain bleach. She's an adult. I'll shut up while we're working."

"Thanks for that." Anything to put an end to this uncomfortable chat.

"Just don't hurt her," Griffin snapped. "Pippa claims to be invincible, but she isn't."

Emmanuel wisely kept his mouth shut. His insights into Pippa were his own and likely wouldn't gel with her brother's perception. Not once had he believed her invincible. Too daring, maybe. And that was only because he'd fallen for her.

Which was ironic because her bold courage and determination had been the first things he'd found irresistible. Relationships were ridiculous. He didn't care for the way his feelings twisted him up when he needed to concentrate.

Before he could muster a suitable reply, he noticed the enforcers approaching their target. Neither man looked familiar to Emmanuel, but that didn't mean much. He ended the call, holding his position and watching the scene unfold.

The two men walked right up to her, almost as if they'd been watching. The smaller of the two men pulled out a chair and sat down. He had deep-set eyes, a shaved head, and a swagger and build that implied he had plenty of fighting experience. The larger man stood there looking intimidating, his big hands clasped loosely in front of him. They didn't seem to care that they were drawing attention from other patrons of the coffee shop.

Then the big man reached for the woman playing Alison, yanking her up and out of her seat. She twisted out of his grasp and started to run, per the plan. Her job, once confirming the men were enforcers from Capital X, was to lead them to a less public area down the block for the takedown.

She didn't make it that far.

The bald man was too quick, catching her around the waist and pinning her to his side so she couldn't escape. The bulky man hemmed her in and they started to walk away.

Another customer stood up and blocked their path, offering her assistance. He was knocked aside by the bald man.

Other customers erupted, and both enforcers were suddenly more concerned with getting away from an angry mob than breaking bones for missed payments.

Hopes of a quiet takedown were dashed. Everyone in the area leaped into the chase, police and citizens alike. Cell phones were recording it all for later analysis on social media.

Emmanuel joined the chase when the bigger man ran across traffic to his side of the street. He called out, identifying himself and ordering the man to stop. He pulled his weapon but didn't dare fire with so many civilians between him and his target.

He saw the man peel off down an alley and shared that with another uniformed team in pursuit. When he caught up with them, they were calling in the report that they'd lost the larger enforcer.

"Do we have anything?" Emmanuel asked. "A name, a dropped wallet or phone?"

"None of the above," the officers replied.

"All right. Ask around for any security footage. We might get lucky with facial recognition. I'll get back and help smooth things over," he said. When he reached the coffee shop, he discovered customers and police had the bald man in custody. Police and customers alike were celebrating the cooperative effort to stop a bad guy.

Pleased, Emmanuel headed back to the station. He wouldn't be involved in questioning, which was probably for the best, considering all the other things he should be sorting out regarding Joe and the Hicks murder.

He hadn't found anything on Joe that his lieutenant would take seriously, and he was running out of places to look for useful proof. Ever since responding to the first break-in call at her condo, it felt like two steps forward, one back, and then a brick wall at every turn.

Just like in the Wentworth case, the department was under serious pressure to make progress to resolve the threat of the poisonous RevitaYou vitamins and find the people behind its development. Riley Colton had pulled serious strings for this cooperative investigation into the deadly product and the loan operation that had bilked hopeful investors.

Joining a few others in the observation room, Emmanuel got chills watching the henchman stonewall Lieutenant McKellar and Detective Gomez. They wanted the name of the devious person at the top of the Capital X food chain, profiting from deception and death, but the bald man refused to cooperate. The brute in the interrogation room provided only his name, Gunther Johnson, as answer to every question.

McKellar, using a card from the man's wallet, finally got him to admit he'd gone to the coffee shop on behalf of Capital X, but he refused to say who'd sent him. A few minutes more of McKellar threatening far more serious charges and Johnson shared more.

"Look, I'm just an enforcer," he insisted. "I bust a few bones for good pay. Really good pay. Targets are a whole lot easier than organized fights. No crime in that."

Detective Gomez shared a look with McKellar. "Beating up people actually *is* a crime, Mr. Johnson."

"Well, so is missing a scheduled payment." Johnson shifted in his chair. "You can't get money for nothing."

Gomez stared at him and McKellar asked, "What do you know about the payments?"

"Nothing. I go out and encourage people to make their payments on time. You may not like what I do, but it's honest work."

This guy was priceless. Either this guy just didn't get it or, more likely, didn't care.

"Who pays you?" McKellar asked.

Johnson shrugged. "I do my job and cash shows up. Not like they withhold for benefits and retirement."

"So you just work broken bone to broken bone," Gomez said. "No retainer?"

Johnson puffed up with pride. "Trust me, it's steady pay. Plenty of people think they can blow off their debts. Capital X doesn't tolerate it."

"How many fingers have you broken this week?" asked McKellar. "This month?"

"Hell, I don't keep track. I go where I'm told, do

what's needed. Most of the time after we visit someone, they pay their debt and everybody's happy."

"I imagine the people with medical bills aren't happy," Lopez said.

Johnson snorted. "They can always get another loan."

McKellar didn't bother hiding his disgust. "And you don't know anyone at Capital X by name other than your fellow enforcer."

"That's right."

"What happens if you go out, break a few bones and the customer still doesn't pay up?" Gomez asked. "Your boss come after you?"

"Course not. You think I'm trash, but I got value. I broke some fingers on a skinny kid with big dreams. He went underground without paying up. I'm actually getting a bonus to look for that Brody Higgins when I'm not on other jobs."

Emmanuel rocked back on his heels. Pippa and her siblings would be thrilled by that admission. Delighted that the police had the man who'd broken up their foster brother. He sent her a quick text update.

Johnson didn't seem to realize what he just confessed. Gomez kept him talking about some other less pleasant meetings. But he wouldn't budge about knowing anyone by name at Capital X.

"Even if I knew names, I'm no snitch," Johnson said. "If I'm out here breaking bones for missed payments, what do you think they'd do to me if I talked?" He sat back in the chair, lifting his wrists so that the cuffs banged against the tabletop. "You caught me trying to rough up someone. Big deal. That lady gave her word and reneged on the deal. That's all I'm saying. I want my lawyer."

Emmanuel started back to his desk when he was waved down by Officer Simmons. "Detective Iglesias, I have a caller on the RevitaYou tip line I think you need to hear."

"Lead the way." Emmanuel followed him across the bullpen.

"The caller claims to have spotted the Toxic Scientist," Simmons explained.

Emmanuel's instincts prickled as he picked up the phone. "This is Detective Iglesias, how may I help you?"

"Yes. The police wanted us watching for that man who poisoned the vitamins. I'm looking at him right now. The Toxic Scientist," the caller said in an overexcited rush, referring to the media's nickname for Landon Street, the scientist who came up with the RevitaYou formula. "You should hurry if you want to catch him."

"Where are you?" Emmanuel asked.

"I'm at the Grateful Bread."

That bakery was only two blocks from the station. Emmanuel wrote out the name, and Simmons started organizing personnel to respond.

"Well, I'm across the street," the caller said. "But I'm looking right at him. He's wearing a light blue baseball cap and dark sunglasses, but it's definitely the Toxic Scientist."

"Your name?" Emmanuel thought the caller was female, but it was hard to be sure. The line went dead. "Hello? Hello?" He looked at Simmons and shared the description. "Let's move," Emmanuel said. "I want two officers with me on foot and roll backup from all directions to cut him off."

"We're ready."

Emmanuel and the others hurried out of the station toward the bakery. It would be a red-letter day if they managed to nab both a Capital X enforcer and Landon Street, scientific genius behind the deadly RevitaYou vitamins.

This was a huge break. With everyone searching, Emmanuel couldn't believe Street was still in Grand Rapids. What kind of fool would stick around when everyone was looking for the man behind that lethal compound?

Emmanuel approached the bakery as casually as possible. He even checked his phone as if this was a normal sugar run. It wasn't unheard of for the officers to make frequent runs down here, so their arrival shouldn't surprise anyone. Again, that made it an odd place for Street to show up after going completely off the grid.

They systematically combed the area, and no one spotted him. He was in the wind again. Damn it. No one matching the description was inside or outside the bakery. They fanned out to cover more area, but still nothing. While the others searched, Emmanuel went inside to question the staff, speaking first to the slip of a girl at the register and then her manager.

The cashier remembered waiting on a man wearing a light blue hat. "It was weird," she said. "His glasses were super dark, but he wouldn't take them off." She shrugged. "People are funny. I thought maybe he was blind."

"All right," Emmanuel said, amused. "Do you remember what he ordered?"

The cashier recited the order of a tall black coffee and a bear claw.

"Cash or credit card?"

"Cash," she said with a big smile. "He tipped two dollars."

Emmanuel showed her a picture of Street. "Was this him?"

She squinted at the photo on his phone. "Maybe?"

The manager invited Emmanuel to the back room to check the security cameras. The grainy video feed wasn't much help. The man who might have been Street kept his head down and his sunglasses on, just as the cashier said.

He did, however, take his coffee and bear claw to one of the tables outside where other cameras might have caught him after he left the bakery.

Emmanuel thanked the manager, placed an order for two dozen doughnuts and checked in with the teams searching while it was filled. The caller had said they were across the street when they spotted the Toxic Scientist. He walked that way, keeping in mind where Street had been sitting when the tipster called in. He imagined a man in a hat and sunglasses at this distance wouldn't be very distinctive. Whoever had called in the tip must have known Street to make such a confident identification. Resigned, he called the searching teams back and went to pick up the doughnuts for the station.

He walked in, an instant hero just for delivering the sugar rush.

While Emmanuel refilled his coffee, Joe McRath came in and, with a big smile, chose an apple fritter. "Thanks, Iglesias."

"No problem," he said, managing not to choke on the words.

With Joe around, Emmanuel immersed himself in

the Landon Street file, writing up the tip and the response, even though it had failed. While he worked, another name caught his attention. Flynn Cruz-Street was a half brother stationed at the US Army base nearby. He wondered if the brother had made the ID and urged another customer or passerby to call it in.

He could see that. It was a way to help without quite turning on family. Everyone wanted to ask Street what he knew about RevitaYou and why he kept working on a flawed product.

When he thought of sharing this news with Pippa, he realized she hadn't replied to his earlier text about Johnson. As much as he wanted to talk, reaching out again was more about the temptation than the work on his desk.

She'd been cool this morning, determined this would be the day she found a pertinent clue. He admired her determination to exonerate Anna, and he could relate to that single-minded focus. What he didn't understand was her suddenly pushing him away. She needed his help, and honestly he needed to help her. But she'd dug in her heels, insisting he had done enough.

That kind of talk made him wary. She was a woman used to going her own way, and frankly he didn't like the chances she was willing to take for her cause of the moment.

Striving for discipline and logic, he picked up the phone and called another of the Colton sisters. Victoria Colton was a paralegal in the JAG office on the same base as Flynn. It would be easier for her to follow up with the half brother about Street's possible location and reason for visiting a bakery right under the GRPD's nose.

PIPPA WASN'T MAKING any progress on her discreet inquiries about how much evidence was needed to trip a review of the case.

Taking a break, she noticed a text alert from Emmanuel. She read through his brief message that they had the Capital X enforcer who had broken Brody's fingers in custody. She breathed a sigh of relief that something was starting to break in their favor. She sent him a quick reply to thank him.

It was temping to keep the conversation going, but she needed to get back on task and she wanted to keep her work and his as separate as possible.

Her phone rang and she cringed at Elizabeth's number on the caller ID. If she hadn't had it memorized before, she certainly would now. Pippa understood Elizabeth's concern. No matter what Elizabeth said, Anna refused to stop taking RevitaYou. The increasing instances of illness and death didn't matter to Anna.

"Hello, Elizabeth. How are things today?"

"You have to do something," Elizabeth wailed. "She was awful today. I think she's getting sick. Tell me you've made progress."

She knew her friend was looking for hope. "I'm working every angle as fast as I can," she said. It was the same thing she'd said on every call yesterday and the day before.

"Pippa, I know I'm being unreasonable and asking too much. These deaths…" Her voice broke. "I know Mom won't quit taking this junk until she's out of prison. Please don't let her die in there."

She was doing all she could and failing her best friend. She didn't know how to help either one of them. The brooch was the key; she knew it. She just had to tie

McRath to putting it there and everything would unravel in Anna's favor.

"This is a nightmare," Elizabeth said, not for the first time.

Desperate to calm her friend, Pippa looked at the case spread out before her on the desk. "I'm planning another interview," she said, deciding on the fly. Confronting McRath directly was her only option. "Before you get your hopes up, it might not even happen. If I can work it out—"

"You can, Pippa. You can do anything."

No pressure. "Thanks for the vote of confidence," she said. "I need you to be realistic. If, and this is a big if, I can get the interview, it may turn everything around for your mom."

"Anything that moves the needle. Please," Elizabeth begged. "It would be a tragedy for her to die in prison just because she's too vain to be a normal prisoner."

Pippa heard the humor in her friend's voice, but she couldn't quite muster a laugh. If Anna died in prison, the case would slip away. No one would pursue the truth. And none of that would compare to the loss Elizabeth and Ed would bear.

She shook off the worst-case scenario. Anna was still alive and mostly well. Pippa would find a way to see the right person locked up behind bars for the Hicks murder. Wrapping up the call with Elizabeth, she turned back to the photos on her desk.

The brooch was the key. Who would've seen McRath in the mansion? She made a list of household staff, wondering if any of them would speak to her or if they were happier without Anna's demands day in and day out.

She went to send Emmanuel a text message, asking

for a few minutes of his time, and noticed he'd texted her about having one enforcer in custody. Good news on any front buoyed her spirits.

His reply to her request for a meeting came back so quickly that she wondered if he'd been watching for any contact from her.

They met at a food truck famous for its creative tacos and burritos near the station, and it was all she could do not to hold his hand or give him a kiss. But that kind of display would be noticed this close to the police station. For the first time, she regretted that they couldn't be seen as a couple in public. Not while she was leading the charge to overturn a conviction he'd investigated.

At the window, they ordered, but when he tried to pay, the woman wouldn't take his money. He argued, but it was clear he wouldn't win without holding up the line behind them.

"I can't stand it when she does that," Emmanuel said when they'd found a spot to sit down with their food.

"Why won't she take your money?" Pippa asked.

An older woman with weathered skin and bright dark eyes brought out paper baskets overflowing with tacos for her, a burrito for Emmanuel and crisp tortilla chips to share. She beamed at Emmanuel, and her gaze slid meaningfully toward Pippa. "Introduce me to your friend," she said with a gleam in her eye.

Emmanuel did the honors. "Pippa Colton, this is Maria Alvarez. Maria, Pippa is an attorney and a friend."

"A pleasure to meet you, Pippa," Maria said. The older woman squeezed Pippa's hands between hers. "We do not take his money because he saved us."

"Years ago, Maria," he said, exasperated. "You can't feed me forever."

"I can and I will," she countered. "You're a good boy." She patted his cheek before she returned to the truck.

She waited, but he dug into his burrito, his mouth too full to talk. "Come on, you know you want to tell me about it," she pressed.

"I really don't. Just eat."

That was no hardship. "This is amazing," she said. She knew he'd share the story eventually. She could see it in the way his eyes crinkled.

"It's not a big deal," he said when he dipped a chip into homemade salsa. "One of my easier cases."

"How easy?"

"They were robbed and the truck was vandalized. I solved the case, and they stayed in business. Of course if they keep feeding me for free, how long it stays that way is up for debate. But the food is so good I can't stay away."

Pippa laughed. "So the culprit must've been someone in the family?"

"You are smart." He nodded. "One of her grandsons got caught up in the wrong crowd and tried to make it look random."

"What gave him away?" she asked.

"Part of the vandalism was graffiti, and the kid's a pretty good artist," he explained.

"You recognized his work."

Emmanuel nodded. "We ended up charging the kid who slashed the tire, and another who stole a set of expensive knives. But they both got probation, along with the grandson. All three of them put in the elbow grease to get the truck back up and going. Last I heard, the kid who was so fascinated with the knives is in cooking school and doing well."

She couldn't suppress her smile. "You really are a talented detective and a good cop."

"Don't tell me you just figured that out?" he asked, his grin full of pride. "None of the discipline was my idea. I would have thrown the book at the two rowdy friends. Maria, though, she's all about second chances."

They finished eating, chatting about kids and neighborhoods and memories, but that only kept Elizabeth at the front of her mind.

"Pippa, you didn't come by for tacos." Emmanuel crumpled his napkin and dropped it into his empty basket.

She hated to ruin such a nice break. What she had in mind was sure to take the smile off his handsome face. "Elizabeth called again," she began. His smile disappeared just as predicted. "I need to make tangible progress for Anna."

"I understand that," he said.

"You do?"

"I may not like the woman, but she shouldn't be doing the time if she isn't the killer."

They were well past ifs in Pippa's opinion. It was pointless to drag this out when they were both busy, and she wasn't here to ask permission. "I'm going to set up a meeting with Sergeant McRath."

He paled. "You what?" He shook his head. "No way."

"I'm not dumb enough to accuse him of murder," she said defensively, keeping her voice too low to be overheard.

"Well, do share your plan." Emmanuel folded his arms over his chest.

"I'll approach him as the lead detective and ask if he'll help me review the initial persons of interest in the case."

"Uh-huh." His nostrils flared. "You take that route and you're playing with fire. He'll see through that so fast. It's too dangerous."

"To reiterate, I won't accuse him of anything."

"He won't see it that way." Emmanuel tucked in close to her. "If he is responsible for any wrongdoing then or more recently, he'll be on the defensive. It's too dangerous," he said again.

"Need I remind you we have a lead on Capital X only because I was willing to do the dangerous thing?"

"Yeah, and that's working out so well."

She bristled. She didn't expect him to roll over and cooperate, but she also didn't expect this much resistance.

"How many times can you do the dangerous thing without consequences?" he demanded. "You're an attorney. Stay in your lane."

She wanted to yell at him, but it would draw too much attention. "Fine. I'll stay in my lane. As an attorney, tenacious comes with the territory. And risk, as well." She had to stop; she was too close to making a scene that would wreck everything. "When I set up the meeting, I'll let you know."

He cut her off with a shake of his head. "There is no chance I'm letting you do this alone. Not after the attacks and harassment."

"Stay in your lane," she suggested.

He rolled his eyes and shifted to block her view. All she could see was him. "You *are* my lane."

Though her heart broke into a happy dance, she

folded her arms and stared him down. This was about her case.

"I can't talk you out of it?" he asked.

She shook her head.

"Will you wait long enough for me to arrange backup?"

She'd learned to read his expressions, and though he tried to hide it, she felt like she had an inside track now. "If I don't wait, what happens?"

He blanched again, and then color slowly crept into his face. He was angry, and it surprised her that she mattered so much. They were friends, on some level, and lovers. For now. Thinking beyond the present moment was foolish. She couldn't let blurry thoughts of a future push her off course now.

"I'll have you followed," he vowed. "If necessary, I'll take personal time and follow you myself," he said.

His deliberate tone unnerved her. Thrilled her. "As long as I'm not blamed for the crime spree that follows if you are off duty trailing me."

"Then we're going to go talk with Lieutenant McKellar and do this the right way."

"What do you mean?"

"We're both convinced McRath is guilty."

"Hold on," she said. "I'm convinced he railroaded Anna. It would be nice to know why. Nicer if he'd come clean."

Emmanuel snorted. "Because that's what all good criminals do."

Now she did smack him lightly in the shoulder, but it counted and it made her point. "I won't accuse him of murder without proof. The Hicks case went that way once already."

"Fair enough. Give me a second."

AFTER SENDING A text to his lieutenant as fair warning, Emmanuel led her into the station. "Let me do the talking," he said at McKellar's office door.

"By all means," she agreed. "Though this might go better if I had something to show my reasoning."

She had a point, but he wasn't taking chances. There was no way he was letting her put herself out there as a target. Although she didn't agree with his assessment, that was exactly what she was proposing.

It was one thing to use a fake ID and a laptop that couldn't easily be traced to her. A meeting with McRath was akin to being front and center on a shooting range. Especially if he was the man who'd trashed her condo and tried to strangle her. A detective like McRath would chew her up and spit her out before he admitted any wrongdoing.

Why couldn't she see what that kind of risk did to him? Why couldn't he tell her?

Probably because telling her now wouldn't make any difference on this particular issue. When Pippa made up her mind, he didn't think anything could knock her off track.

The lieutenant glowered as Emmanuel ushered Pippa into the office. Fortunately Joe had left for the day, so that was one hurdle they could avoid for the moment. Emmanuel started the introductions, but McKellar cut him off.

"I know who she is," he barked. "You have five minutes, out of courtesy to your sister, Sadie."

"Thank you."

She started to speak, but Emmanuel spoke over her. "We have reason to believe Anna Wentworth is innocent."

McKellar gave a derisive snort. "Well, allow me to clear my schedule. I'm not in the mood for Mystery Theater right now."

"You said five minutes," Emmanuel reminded him.

"Use it wisely," McKellar warned.

Emmanuel quickly reminded him about the missing evidence box and informed him it was still gone. He listed the trouble Pippa had endured from the red tape at the prison to the garbage in her parking space. "In every instance, McRath had means and access."

"Any proof? Eye witness, surveillance, anything?" He didn't give them a chance to answer. "Even if you're right, what do you want me to do? Other than free your client," he said with a glare for Pippa.

"Not you, sir. Me," she said. "I would like to set up a meeting with McRath to discuss the case."

"To accuse him of what?"

"I suspect he tampered with evidence, particularly the brooch found under the body," she said. "But I have no intention of making any accusations. My approach would be as an attorney convinced my client is innocent and interviewing the lead detective simply to gain insight and information."

"Back it up," McKellar said, wagging a finger. "The brooch?"

"Yes, sir. Based on my review of the case files, Sergeant McRath is the only person at the scene who went into the house, particularly Anna's suite. He is the only person who had time to remove the item and plant it under the body."

"Good grief, you believe that." McKellar rubbed his temples. "If you approach a decorated detective, he'll see it as a personal attack, an attempt to undo his hard work."

"Detective Iglesias has warned me of the same thing."

"You haven't given me a reason to agree to this interview."

"Lieutenant, I've known Anna Wentworth for most of my life. As a friend of the family, I can give you a host of reasons why she didn't kill Hicks, but the most compelling is her passion for her jewelry. There is no way she would've left that piece behind."

"And you?" McKellar turned on him. "Why are you suddenly so cooperative with the enemy of your hard work?"

He winced at the choice of words, but answered quickly. "If an innocent woman is in jail because I misread the scene, that's a mistake that needs to be rectified." He took a deep breath. "I have documentation of Joe's presence in the evidence room between Pippa's review of the Wentworth case and the day I discovered the case was missing. In addition, I suspect Joe was the man who attacked Pippa in her bed a few nights ago."

McKellar swore. "I was told there wasn't any conclusive evidence of the intruder's identity."

"I've trained with him for too many years not to know how he moves in a fight," Emmanuel said. He hated to implicate a partner and friend. A mentor he'd admired and learned from. "I wanted to come to you with more, especially a motive, but Pippa is concerned that Anna is at risk in prison."

The lieutenant swore again.

"My primary goal is to wrangle a confession that he tampered with evidence," Pippa said. "That should help me overturn the conviction."

"And if he does, I'm up against, it and the entire department will be overrun as we review every case he ever handled."

"I'm not minimizing what this could do," she said. "But an innocent woman is in prison for a crime she did not commit. Love or hate Anna Wentworth, she's not a killer."

McKellar rocked back in his chair. It didn't escape Emmanuel's notice that they had been granted an extra five minutes. "How is Wentworth at risk?"

"She's managed to start taking RevitaYou," Emmanuel said.

"How in the hell?" McKellar waved his hand. "Never mind. Prison reform isn't my priority today. You," he pinned Pippa with a hard look. "You cannot do this without backup."

"Yes, sir."

Emmanuel was a little jealous that she acquiesced to the lieutenant so easily.

"On top of that," McKellar continued. "I'll lead the backup team. If one of my detectives confesses to any kind of crime, I want to hear it firsthand. You'll wear a wire, provided by my technicians. Go set your meeting," he said.

"And if he chooses somewhere private," Emmanuel asked.

"Then he's a fool," the lieutenant replied. "He'll want

somewhere public if we're lucky. Somewhere remote if we're really lucky."

Seeing she was about to ask more questions, Emmanuel stood. "Thank you for your time, Lieutenant." He let Pippa add her thanks, and then he hustled her out of the office and straight out of the building. His heart was pounding. "Success," he said at her ear.

She stopped at the bottom of the steps. "You expected him to shoot me down."

He sighed; there was no easy way to do this, not with her. "No. I expected him to do the right thing."

"And he did," she said.

"Looks that way." He wanted to kiss her more than he wanted his next breath. "You need to get home." Wanting her to get there safely, he walked her to her car. "Sorry if I got a little tense about this."

"I understand." She flipped her car keys around her finger. "We can't leave an innocent woman in prison."

"No, we can't." He shoved his hand into his pocket, for fear that he would handcuff her and hide her away until he could get McRath on his terms. "I just want you safe."

"I don't want you taking chances either," she said. "But this is necessary."

She was right—they had exhausted all other options. "Together we'll get through it."

"I like the sound of that," she said.

He wished he didn't care so much. His life was simpler before she'd turned him inside out. Now she was rooted deep in his soul. It was uncomfortable. He always thought falling in love was supposed to be a beautiful, nurturing thing. He should just tell her. He would, when he knew how to give her the words without her believing it was a way to manipulate her.

He didn't want the truest feelings he'd ever had to be mixed up in a case he'd already botched. "Drive safe," he said. "I won't be far behind you."

She smiled, giving his hand a warm squeeze. In the past he might have appreciated her reluctance to confirm their physical relationship. Now that discretion cast a glaring light, making everything between them feel all wrong.

"I want to kiss you," he said when she settled behind the wheel of her car.

"I want that too." A sassy grin transformed her face from serious attorney to sexy girlfriend. "I'll keep you posted."

He knew she would. Pippa was a woman of her word.

"How does Italian sound for dinner?" she asked.

"Sounds great. I'll pick it up when I'm done here."

"Oh." She toyed with her keys again. "I thought I would cook."

"Seriously? Can't wait." That gave him something wonderful to look forward to. If she wanted to cook for him, chances were good she wasn't about to dump him for being overprotective. "Let me bring dessert."

"éclairs?"

"We'll see."

Returning to his desk wasn't easy when he wanted to follow her and shield her from every threat, seen or unseen. That wasn't how things got done in his world. She was strong and smart, and he trusted her even if he didn't trust her enemies.

Throwing himself into the last few things on his to-do list, he picked up the phone to return a call from

FBI agent Cooper Winston. "Give me some good news," he said when Winston answered. "Have you heard anything more on Wes Matthews?"

Brody had told them that Matthews had been the banker taking cash transfers from the RevitaYou investors. But the man had seemingly disappeared into thin air, like the Toxic Scientist, and all law enforcement agencies were trying to track him down.

"No such luck," Winston said. "I was letting you know he hasn't turned up in or around Grand Rapids. For that matter, he hasn't been spotted anywhere in Michigan. We did get a couple of reported sightings in the Caribbean. I have local law enforcement down there checking out those tips."

"Offshore banking must be good work if you can get it," Emmanuel said.

"No kidding," Winston agreed. "Don't worry. We're not letting this one fall through the cracks."

"Then we're all on the same page." Emmanuel updated his case notes after the call. He figured it would take a real team effort to reel in all of the moving pieces in the sprawling RevitaYou scam.

Finally he was leaving the station, and he sent a text to Pippa to let her know. He got a quick reply, which put a smile on his face. He stopped at the restaurant and picked up the tiramisu he'd ordered to round out the Italian meal she had planned to make. And after dinner, he could hardly wait to stay over again.

That served his purposes on two levels, loving her and protecting her.

He was only a few blocks from her condo when his cell phone rang, and the connection in his car announced the district attorney's phone number. Would this day never end? He answered with the hands-free option. "Detective Iglesias."

"You at a point where you can talk?" the DA asked.

"It's just you and me on this end."

"I just got the word that Gunther Johnson is willing to make a deal."

"No kidding?" That was phenomenal news. And a huge break for the case. "What's he demanding?" Emmanuel asked.

"He'll give a sworn statement about the name of the Capital X kingpin in exchange for a new identity and specific privileges that include a personal television and a down pillow."

Emmanuel was impressed. He'd underestimated Johnson. "He's thought it through. A new name means no one can call him a snitch in prison. That's one way to stay alive."

"Can't fault his logic," the DA agreed. "I guarantee, when this information gets out, it will set Grand Rapids on its ear."

Emmanuel couldn't wait to hear, but he couldn't ask. If the district attorney wasn't sharing details, it was because he didn't have it in writing yet. "Thanks for the call." He couldn't wait to tell Pippa that there was good news and positive momentum on the Capital X case.

Parking in front of her building, it was second nature to look around, scanning the area for any threat. So far all clear, which made him wonder if she'd set the meeting yet. At her door, he entered his code and walked in, announcing himself.

The rich scent of tomato sauce and spicy sausage brought his appetite to the fore.

Pippa came out of the kitchen and slipped into his

arms, greeting him with a kiss that set his blood humming. It reminded him of his parents returning to each other at the end of a day and, in that one moment, forgetting everything but each other.

"I could get used to this," he teased, his free hand gliding over her waist.

"Careful." She smiled. "Dinner on the table every night when you walk in isn't something you can count on from me."

"Well, to be fair, having me home at the same time every night isn't something you should count on either." But he wanted to come home to her, whatever time, and walk into the heat of her kisses and the quiet peace of a place they shared.

He really should tell her how he felt.

Instead, he settled in to enjoy the wonder of a normal night with an amazing woman. If she got a confession out of Joe, she might not need Emmanuel around for protection anymore. As much as he wanted to close this case, to get the right person behind bars for the death of Hicks, he felt a twinge deep in his chest. What if the closed case meant the end of his time with Pippa?

Chapter Thirteen

Joe couldn't get close to her. He'd kept his ear to the ground, but so far no opportunities had materialized for him to take out Pippa Colton and put this case to bed for good.

Not like when he'd been trailing Hicks.

Greed had made that slimeball easy picking. Or maybe it was a matter of focus. Admittedly, Joe had tunnel vision after the jerk dumped his little girl, breaking her heart, for a new moneybags lover.

A career on the force had taught him some cases resonated and when it came to family, they all pushed the envelope once in a while to see justice done. In his mind, if you took the right action, discreetly, the world was a better place. Wasn't that the true goal?

The rumors at the GRPD were enough to convince him that Colton had sunk her teeth into something that could wreck everything. She wasn't letting go. Far as he could tell, she hadn't connected him to the gun or how Hicks had arrived at the Wentworth rose garden, but he figured at this point it was better to act first and wonder no more.

She'd visited with Leigh. Thankfully, his daughter was an excellent witness and provided him with a clear rundown of the conversation. She'd described Colton as friendly. Said she'd left disappointed after Leigh couldn't point her to anyone who might've hassled Hicks while he and Leigh had been dating.

He still didn't see what Leigh had found so endearing about that loser, but his baby girl had been in love, certain they were going to live happily ever after and build a franchise of fitness centers for the young and beautiful.

Instead, Hicks shifted his attention to other women, women with more money to spend on him, and left Joe's daughter wondering what she'd done wrong.

ON THE EVENING of Pippa's meeting with McRath, Emmanuel struggled to contain himself as they wired her so they could listen in. A war over her safety raged inside him. Revealing his concerns would only make matters worse, so he locked it down. She needed him to be confident in her and in the plan.

The rest of the backup team was already taking their positions, hours ahead of the expected meeting time. Emmanuel kept swallowing the advice he wanted to give. She knew what she was doing, and she knew the Wentworth case as well as he did.

Fortunately Lieutenant McKellar took the lead, reviewing the location and all possible approaches with her. He even insisted on reviewing two escape routes, all factors she would have resisted if Emmanuel had tried to make suggestions.

"Heritage Park is a favorite of mine, Lieutenant. I know it inside and out," she assured him. "I'll be fine."

"Joe knows it too," the lieutenant reminded her. "He

chose it for a reason. If he is dirty, he will be on his guard and ready to do anything to save his ass."

To Emmanuel's relief, she was taking the advice well. They did a sound check and then let her head out in her personal vehicle when they had confirmation everyone was in place.

He and the lieutenant would be the last ones to reach the park. That made Emmanuel more nervous, but there was no way McRath would make a premature move on Pippa. She was too well-known in the community, her family too connected to take that kind of chance.

"If this goes sideways," he said to McKellar once they were alone, "I'll never forgive myself. Or you."

"Iglesias, if you're not good with this, you have to stay behind. I'm not risking two officers today."

"I'm good," Emmanuel lied. If McRath touched a hair on her head, he wouldn't hesitate to intervene and protect her.

"Thank you for meeting with me tonight," Pippa said when McRath finally joined her at the designated place within the park. "I do appreciate your time."

The older man grunted. "I admit these conversations aren't my favorite. Why are you even looking twice at Wentworth? She's a nightmare. Always has been."

"She has a daughter, Elizabeth, who's my friend," Pippa replied. After hours of debate, she thought appealing to him as a father was her best strategy.

"Stirring the pot for friendship?" he asked, incredulous. "Better uses of your time."

She'd known this wouldn't be easy, or straightforward. "I don't think so. Although my friend is hurting." She paused. "Hypothetically, without the overwhelming evidence against Mrs. Wentworth, who did you like for the crime?"

McRath shook his head, the light teasing his graying hair. "You lawyers play with hypotheticals. I play with reality. All of the evidence pointed to Mrs. Wentworth. She did the crime, and now she's doing the time."

"I just can't agree with you."

His lip curled in caustic judgement. "You know the prison system is full of innocent people, right?" He shook his head, gazing out over the park. "I got better things to do than cater to your feelings for a friend."

If she could find the right angle to open him up, he'd have plenty of time to contemplate his hypotheticals in prison. "I guess I just find it all too convenient," she began, trying another tack. "Hicks had run through several women. I know there has to be someone else involved, someone else who wanted him dead."

"Really?" His gaze narrowed, and she smothered the urge to run. She'd seen those mean eyes through the holes of a ski mask not too long ago. "Like who?"

"Well, that's why I'm here. Several women were angry with him and felt cheated. Do you think the killer might've been a different woman?" McGrath was a problem solver. He might well be a murderer, too, but that was just a bad way to solve a problem.

When he didn't respond, she rambled on. "I noticed you questioned Elizabeth. She normally tells me everything, but I can't help wondering if she was involved with Hicks?"

"All I learned about Hicks is that he charmed women into costly mistakes." McRath pushed to his feet, and even in the fading light she could tell she'd hit a hot button. "I am sick and tired of your kind digging into closed cases. My partner and I did good work, and you are wasting my time. Stealing that girl's money. All you damn attorneys want is a sound bite. A way to move up the political ladder. You make the job impossible for those of us out here taking calls and talking to witnesses and putting criminals behind bars to keep the city safe.

"The Wentworth case is done. *Over.* The bitch is in jail where she belongs."

Pippa didn't know what she'd expected, but it wasn't this vitriol and sheer hatred. "Detective McRath, I don't mean any disrespect. I only want justice. I know you don't want an innocent woman wasting away in jail. And she is innocent. I'm sure of it."

"That woman is *not* innocent," he barked. "She was sleeping around on her husband and barely knew the names of her staff. They worked with her every day, and she didn't bother to *learn their names.* Do you have any idea how many times she called the police with false complaints? Murderer or not, prison will do that woman and this city a world of good."

Were they catching all of this? "Joe, you can't mean that."

McRath pulled a gun, and it was all she could do not to scream. Only knowing she'd hurt someone's ears kept her quiet.

"Oh, I mean it."

"What are you doing?"

"I respected your father," McRath said. "But you, not so much. I'm sick of the whole damn mess. I'm sick of the lies and the deals and the cheats like Wentworth. You think you've got me?"

"No, Joe," she said quietly. "I have no idea what you're talking about."

"Bull. Get up," he ordered.

"Why don't you sit down and we'll finish our conversation."

"I'm done with you and everyone like you. Get up!"

She stood, intending to edge away and put the bench between them. It wasn't much cover, but it might buy her a few seconds.

"This way." He gestured with the gun. "Run and I'll kill your lover instead. I can't believe Iglesias fell for you. What a sap."

She froze, locked in a nightmare of losing Emmanuel. Her hands were cold as ice and her knees wanted to buckle. She needed him in her life to lean on, to love. Needed to be there for him at the end of the day, as his safe haven. Her fears about her feelings for him paled against the prospect of a future without him. She couldn't let Joe steal the beautiful opportunity to share her life with him.

"Come on, girl." He waved the gun. "You're going to pay for not letting this rest." He pushed the gun into her stomach, walking her backward toward the trees.

"Joe." She sucked in a breath as he grabbed her, spun her around. She couldn't resist too much. If he saw the wire, or dislodged it and broke the connection, it was over, and her efforts would be for nothing. "Whatever's on your mind, the gun isn't necessary."

"It is. You'll pay the same way that lying cheat Hicks paid. I put a bullet in his black, shriveled heart." His hand was clammy and bruising on the back of her neck. "Hicks hurt my daughter. Stole her money and then tried to blackmail his wealthy lover. The world is better off without him. You didn't heed my warnings, so it's time to stop you too."

If he got her into those trees, it was over. She wasn't that much older than his daughter, and she tried one last appeal to his fatherly nature. "You don't have to do this, Joe. I'm not going to say anything. I'll leave it alone. I'll stop."

His laugh was bitter and sharp. "I can't trust you to keep quiet. There's only one solution."

He was going to kill her. She could see it stamped in the unyielding lines of his face. She wouldn't be his first kill, and if they didn't stop him now, she probably wouldn't be his last. Emmanuel and the lieutenant must be hearing every word. Where were they? Her head was spinning and her composure in tatters. That had to be enough of a confession. Enough to clear Anna.

"Joe, put down the gun," she said. "Think about this."

"I don't have to put down a gun to think. That's the difference between you and me. I can think on my feet. I can react in the blink of an eye and make a decision and know it's the right one. You lawyers have to analyze and look for precedents."

"Put the weapon down!" Emmanuel's shout ripped through the evening.

McRath swiveled to fire, and she shoved him hard, hoping to throw off his aim. Gunfire erupted all around her, along with shouts for McRath to stand down.

McGrath hid behind her, using her as a shield between himself and the officers closing in. One of the officers called her name, urging her to duck down out of the line of fire. She was blocking the only clear shot.

It was like a scene from a classic Western movie, but she wasn't about to faint or swoon. Dropping to all fours, she charged McGrath, knocking him out of his hiding place. He twisted around and aimed the gun at her, but the next shot flattened him.

Officers swarmed McRath, and she heard someone pronounce him dead as she was led back to the lighted path. Emmanuel rushed over, and her knees buckled. He caught her, holding her close. She wrapped her arms around his waist and simply held on.

His heart pounded under her ear, his hand smoothing over her hair. He was whole. Safe. McRath would never hurt him.

"Pippa, you scared the life out of me."

She'd scared the life out of herself. Nothing was guaranteed and she was done holding back. "I love you, Emmanuel." She tipped her head up to study his face. "I'm in love with you. I should've said so long before now."

He didn't answer right away, kissing her instead. His lips fluttered over her hair, her eyelids, her nose and mouth.

When he paused, his warm gaze melted away the last of the chilling encounter. "I love you too, Pippa. I didn't think I'd ever want to say those words again."

"It's a big step." And nothing in her life had ever felt quite so right.

"A good one," he agreed.

She wanted him to take her home, take her to bed and forget the rest of the world. Hard to do in the glare of the emergency lights. She'd come out here to wrest a confession out of McRath that they could use to save Anna and she wasn't sure if they'd succeeded.

"Emmanuel." She caught his face between her hands, his short whiskers rasping against her palms. "Did we get the confession?"

"Yes. You were brilliant." He kissed her again. "Now don't ever do anything this foolish again."

But it wasn't censure in his voice as much as affection. Respect. And yes, love.

"Never without backup," she promised. She understood his reactions. She'd experienced a sharp and desperate fear when McRath had fired in Emmanuel's direction. "Do you think it's enough to free Anna?"

"Absolutely," he replied. "The lieutenant will send the information up the line as soon as we get back to the station." He drew her back as an ambulance rolled up.

"Thank you," she said. There were more words, better suited to a private moment. This wasn't the right time for her personal declarations. They both had work to do. "I'll call Elizabeth," she said.

His thumb grazed the skin just above her collarbone. "Elizabeth can wait until after the ER," he said.

"I don't need the ER," she protested as paramedics approached her. But she couldn't stop trembling, even when Emmanuel was close.

"For me?" When she met his gaze, his eyes were warm and full of all that love and emotion she wanted to believe in. "Please."

She supposed she might be in shock. A violent killer had nearly added her to his body count. With a nod, she let him lead her to the paramedics and didn't protest as they loaded her for a trip to Grand Rapids Central.

EMMANUEL HAD TO follow protocol and handle the entire operation by the book. Man, he wanted to rush. Focused, he helped McKellar clean up the dead body at their feet. No way to keep this out of the papers; the department was going to take a hit.

The lieutenant pushed a hand through his hair and muttered an oath. "They'll reopen every single one of his cases."

"I know," Emmanuel said. "For what it's worth, I know I did my job the right way."

"Still going to be sticky."

Knowing his lieutenant was correct, Emmanuel kept quiet. There would be some uncomfortable days ahead, but they would get through it.

"Hell of a woman," McKellar said.

Emmanuel couldn't argue with that. And he couldn't wait to share the praise with her as soon as possible.

"Go on to the hospital," McKellar said. "That's where your head's at."

With a quick thank you, Emmanuel bolted from the scene. He called Riley on the way to the hospital and filled him in on the sting operation and what a hero Pippa was. It didn't surprise him that Pippa hadn't made that call yet. More than likely she was still on the phone with Elizabeth.

"She's okay," he assured her brother. "They sent her to the hospital just as a precaution."

"Then why do you sound panicked?" Riley asked.

"It's been a wild night," Emmanuel said. He wasn't about to tell her brother just how dicey things had been out here. He wasn't sure he could even discuss it coherently yet.

"Thanks for your help," Riley said. "I'll pass on the word, and we'll be over to the hospital right away."

"About that." Emmanuel hesitated to make the request, but Pippa deserved his courage. "She probably won't be happy if you all descend on her tonight."

"We're family."

"Right. I get it. I'm just saying." He wanted a few minutes to tell her everything he should've said before she was face-to-face with a killer. "You know Pippa," he said. "If everyone's there—"

"She'll get belligerent," Riley finished for him. "Yeah, we can keep our distance until tomorrow. Let me know if her situation changes."

"You know I will."

"Thanks. I really do owe you. Between this and the Capital X case, we're all on edge. It helps knowing you've been watching her."

More than watching, but those were words a brother wouldn't take well. He was done pretending this was temporary, or convenient or simply a favor for a friend. "I'm sure Pippa will fill you in about Wentworth's release. One more thing while I have you on the phone." He paused to gather his courage. "I want to marry your sister." Blurting it out might not have been the right approach, but he was pulling up to the hospital and running out of time. "I can't ask your father, so I'm asking you."

"Does she want to marry you?" Riley queried.

"That's the big question," he admitted on a half laugh. "I think so," he said. "It may take some time for her to come around."

"Must have been some night in the park," Riley said. "If you're looking for my blessing, you have it."

"And your silence?" Emmanuel asked. "I don't want her to feel rushed."

"Wow. You really do know her." Riley chuckled. "Good luck, man."

The difficult part over, Emmanuel jogged into the ER. Thanks to his rapport with the staff, they allowed him back to see Pippa. They had her hooked up to an EKG, and his heart skipped.

"What's all this?" he asked, trying for casual and missing by a mile.

She shook her head. "They tell me it's a precaution. My vitals were a little ragged. It's been a rough night."

He was doubly glad now that he'd warned her family to stay away. He caught her hand in both of his, stroking some warmth and color back into her soft skin. "I called Riley and told him you were fine. That there was no reason to storm the hospital."

That earned a chuckle, and he felt like a knight in shining armor.

"Thank you," she said, raising his hand to her lips. "You know I love them. I just don't need anyone hovering right now."

"You want me to go?" The last thing he wanted was to cling so tightly that he smothered her and drove her away. "Tell me what you need."

"I expected you to go to the station," she began, her voice as shy as he'd ever heard it.

"That's all under control."

"I wanted to call Elizabeth and then…"

He felt as if his whole life hung in the balance of that one pause.

"Then if it's not too much trouble, I… I want you to hold me. All night." She looked down at their joined hands. "I sleep better when you hold me."

"Done," he said, touching his lips to her forehead. He knew what that soft-spoken request cost her. Pippa wasn't a woman given to asking for help. She coveted her independence, and he was honored and floored that she had turned to him.

Holding her all night might be enough to convince him she was fine after all.

Chapter Fourteen

Pippa was so thankful. Emmanuel had held her all night long that first night and in all the nights that followed. As much as the condo had been hers, it felt more like home when he was there. Her safe haven, a little personal space carved out of a large boisterous family and a demanding career, was better with him in it.

Having shared space with someone from the womb, those were thoughts she'd never anticipated. Naturally the Capital X investigation was ongoing, though her role was momentarily diminished. Her brothers and sisters had checked in after her encounter with McRath. They knew better than to scold her, though it was clear to her that they wanted to.

Although Emmanuel and the lieutenant offered, Pippa never listened to the tape of McRath's confession. It wasn't a moment she wanted to relive.

She'd spoken with Elizabeth every day until at last the system scheduled Anna's release.

Pippa and Elizabeth waited outside the gate. Restless, Elizabeth couldn't stop wringing her hands. "She vowed to be a kinder person," she said.

Pippa tried not to roll her eyes, but she had to avoid making eye contact with Emmanuel. "I'm sure she means it." She touched her friend's shoulder. "I hope she can break those old patterns. You deserve the best mom she can be."

Elizabeth gave her a big hug. "Thank you for believing me. Thank you for helping her."

An alarm sounded, and a light flashed over the door where Anna was expected to exit. Flanked by two prison guards, she walked out into the sunlight, wearing the same suit she'd worn in court when the guilty verdict had been read. She looked like a slightly softer, faded version of the woman she'd been before this ordeal.

Pippa stood back as Anna and Elizabeth were reunited, her hand seeking Emmanuel's comforting touch. She'd been wary that he wanted to be here, but he had just as much right, and frankly she still needed the support.

Once Anna released her daughter, her eyes locked onto Emmanuel. This would be the test. Would she revert to that arrogant, pushy, entitled woman?

"Detective Iglesias? I didn't expect to see you. Is there a problem?" she asked with a delicate tremor in her voice.

Emmanuel didn't move, but Pippa felt the tension humming through his body. "I wanted to be here to apologize personally. You can expect an official apology from the Grand Rapids Police Department, and I'm sure your attorney is working on reparations."

Pippa almost chuckled.

"Elizabeth tells me you were instrumental in uncovering the truth," Anna said. "Thank you."

Pippa exchanged a dumbfounded look with Elizabeth. Maybe Anna really could make this improvement permanent. As mother and daughter drove off, she turned to Emmanuel and caught him grinning.

"You thought I was going to read her the riot act," he said.

"Maybe a little," she admitted. "You didn't even ask for an apology for your mom."

"I thought about it, but what's the point? She's been through an ordeal very few people can imagine. And honestly she owes my mom the apology, not me."

"Maybe that will happen. Someday."

"Whatever she does, I'm the real winner," he said, opening the car door for her.

"How so?"

He shut the door and rounded the car to the driver's side. When he got in, he leaned over and caught her chin in his hand, giving her a heated kiss. "Without Wentworth or McRath, I wouldn't be here with you right now."

"Making out in front of a prison," she said, smiling against his lips. "So romantic."

On a soft laugh he started the car and pulled away. "I'll show you some romance," he promised.

"I'll hold you to it."

She was particularly fond of cozy dinners and waking up in his arms. This man had changed her. Although they were both still working demanding hours, she had a reason to take time for herself. For him.

A woman couldn't work 24-7 and call it a balanced life. Wherever they went from here, she would be better for her time with him. The trouble was she didn't want to let go and fall into old habits. If Anna could change, maybe she could too.

It was time to tell him she loved him.

EMMANUEL DROVE BACK to Grand Rapids, enjoying the randomness of their conversation now that the Wentworth case was over and done.

The trees were vibrant with changing color, and he didn't miss the correlation between the changing seasons outside and the changes Pippa had made inside him.

He had a ring in his pocket and a plan in mind as he turned back to Heritage Park.

"What are we doing here?" she asked.

For a split second he doubted his decision. Maybe this wasn't the best place, but she'd mentioned it was one of her favorite places in the city. She'd reclaimed the condo after McRath's destruction. Now they could reclaim this place too.

"I thought we could take a walk. Stretch our legs after the drive." He took her hand. "You said this was your favorite place in Grand Rapids."

Her gaze narrowed as she studied the landscape through the windshield.

"It's a beautiful day," he prompted. Reaching over, he gave her hand a squeeze. "If I made a mistake, we can go."

"No." She took a deep breath. "It's like riding a bike, right? When you fall, you need to get right back on."

"Something like that," he allowed. The ring in his pocket felt like a lead weight and a helium balloon all at once. It was as if the diamond wanted to be out, and all things weighing on his heart were tiptoeing around the facts.

With her hand in his they walked on a path well away from where she had confronted McRath. "You're a true hero," he began. "I want you to be able to enjoy this park again."

"I will. One difficult night can't erase all of the good memories." She gave him a smile, then turned her attention to the trees. "I've always loved the changing leaves."

"Me too," he said. "It's nicer sharing these changes with you." He had to stop dawdling and just say what was on his heart. "Pippa, I love you."

She stopped in the middle of the path. "What?"

He felt a thousand times better sharing the words. "I'm in love with you." He found a bench and sat down, drawing her next to him. Holding her hand, he continued, "My parents set a high bar in the way they cared for each other and for us. As far back as I can remember, I've thought I want a piece of that. That stability and trust. That beautiful partnership that exists between lovers.

"I've always wanted that and never found it. I gave up on it," he confessed. "I threw myself into my work, thinking that would be enough. It was. Until you."

"Emmanuel," she whispered as a tear rolled down her cheek.

His heart took flight, that she would trust him with her tears. "I love the way you focus, that glint in your eye when you're mad, how you drop everything and run when your family needs you. I want to be your family. I want to be the person who drops everything for you."

"But I don't want that for you," she said.

His heart stuttered, and he was glad he was sitting down.

"I love you too much for that." She kissed him. "Yes, you heard me. I love you too. But I don't need rescuing." Her gaze drifted across the park. "At least not very often."

"On those rare occasions when you do, I want to be the person you call."

"Oh, Emmanuel." She kissed him again. "I don't know when I fell. I think I fall a little more every day. Thank you."

Thank you? This wasn't going at all as he had hoped. They'd veered way off the script he had in his head. He fished into his pocket and pulled out the ring. Her eyes went wide and her lips parted.

"Pippa, I'm butchering this, obviously. Please make me the happiest man and say you will be my partner, my lover, my wife. I don't want you to change who you are, and I'm hoping you will apply all of that amazing courage to our future. I can't guarantee the road will be smooth—"

"Yes!" she exclaimed.

"Yes? Really?" He felt like a kid rather than the man she needed.

She held out her hand, her fingers shaking with excitement.

The ring looked perfect on her slender finger, and the autumn light made the diamond glow. But it was her kiss that told him everything he needed to know about happiness and hope in their future.

Together.

* * * * *

COMING SOON!

LET'S TALK
Romance

For exclusive extracts, competitions
and special offers, find us online:

facebook.com/millsandboon

@MillsandBoon

@MillsandBoonUK

Get in touch on 01413 063232

For all the latest titles coming soon, visit
millsandboon.co.uk/nextmonth

MILLS & BOON

THE HEART OF ROMANCE

A ROMANCE FOR EVERY KIND OF READER

MODERN

Prepare to be swept off your feet by sophisticated, sexy and seductive heroes, in some of the world's most glamourous and romantic locations, where power and passion collide.
8 stories per month.

HISTORICAL

Escape with historical heroes from time gone by. Whether your passion is for wicked Regency Rakes, muscled Vikings or rugged Highlanders, awaken the romance of the past.
6 stories per month.

MEDICAL

Set your pulse racing with dedicated, delectable doctors in the high-pressure world of medicine, where emotions run high and passion, comfort and love are the best medicine.
6 stories per month.

True Love

Celebrate true love with tender stories of heartfelt romance, from the rush of falling in love to the joy a new baby can bring, and a focus on the emotional heart of a relationship.
8 stories per month.

Desire

Indulge in secrets and scandal, intense drama and plenty of sizzling hot action with powerful and passionate heroes who have it all: wealth, status, good looks…everything but the right woman.
6 stories per month.

HEROES

Experience all the excitement of a gripping thriller, with an intense romance at its heart. Resourceful, true-to-life women and strong, fearless men face danger and desire - a killer combination!
8 stories per month.

DARE

Sensual love stories featuring smart, sassy heroines you'd want as a best friend, and compelling intense heroes who are worthy of them.
4 stories per month.

To see which titles are coming soon, please visit

millsandboon.co.uk/nextmonth

JOIN US ON SOCIAL MEDIA!

Stay up to date with our latest releases, author news and gossip, special offers and discounts, and all the behind-the-scenes action from Mills & Boon...

 millsandboon

 millsandboonuk

 millsandboon

It might just be true love...

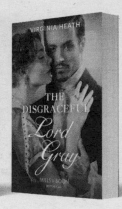

MILLS & BOON
MODERN
Power and Passion

Prepare to be swept off your feet by sophisticated, sexy and seductive heroes, in some of the world's most glamourous and romantic locations, where power and passion collide.

MILLS & BOON
True Love
Romance from the Heart

Celebrate true love with tender stories of
heartfelt romance, from the rush of falling
in love to the joy a new baby can bring,
and a focus on the emotional
heart of a relationship.